"Go away,"

Maria said desperately.

Sam winced inwardly. He didn't want to put her through this, but he had no other option. "I'm afraid I can't. We're going to be working together, remember?"

Maria shivered. For the first time, the impact of her decision hit her. He had estimated six days. Six days of looking for the missing child. Six days and numerous nights in Sam Mathers's company. No. She couldn't do it. She was meant to live alone, to be alone, to remain alone. Isolated. Unfeeling. Uncaring.

What had she done? Dread burned its way low in her stomach. Here she was, staring at a man who made her feel things she shouldn't feel and agreeing to search for a child she knew couldn't be found—at least, not alive.

She turned away from him. She didn't want this. She didn't want him.

But she had no choice.

Dear Reader,

Welcome to another month of fine reading from Silhouette Intimate Moments. And what better way to start off the month than with an American Hero title from Marilyn Pappano, a book that's also the beginning of a new miniseries, Southern Knights. Hero Michael Bennett and his friends Remy and Smith are all dedicated to upholding the law—and to loving the right lady. And in *Michael's Gift*, she turns out to be the one woman he wishes she wasn't. To know more, you'll just have to read this terrific story.

The month continues with *Snow Bride*, the newest from bestselling writer Dallas Schulze. Then it's on to *Wild Horses, Wild Men*, from Ann Williams; *Waking Nightmare*, from highly regarded newcomer Alicia Scott; *Breaking the Rules*, Ruth Wind's Intimate Moments debut; and *Hear No Evil*, a suspenseful novel from brand-new author Susan Drake. I think you'll enjoy each and every one of these books—and that you'll be looking for more equally exciting reading next month and in the months to come. So look no further than Silhouette Intimate Moments, where, each and every month, we're proud to bring you writers we consider among the finest in the genre today.

Enjoy!

Leslie J. Wainger
Senior Editor and Editorial Coordinator

Please address questions and book requests to:
Silhouette Reader Service
U.S.: 3010 Walden Ave., P.O. Box 1325, Buffalo, NY 14269
Canadian: P.O. Box 609, Fort Erie, Ont. L2A 5X3

WAKING NIGHTMARE

Alicia Scott

Silhouette®
INTIMATE™ MOMENTS®
Published by Silhouette Books
America's Publisher of Contemporary Romance

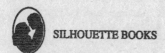 SILHOUETTE BOOKS

ISBN 0-373-07586-3

WAKING NIGHTMARE

ALICIA SCOTT

is thrilled that her dream of being published has finally come true. Born in Hawaii but a resident of Oregon, she recently graduated from college and is now working for a management consulting firm.

She has a deep appreciation for different peoples and cultures. And while reading and writing romances is one of her favorite hobbies, she also enjoys traveling and just talking to people—so much so that in her junior year of high school she entered a contest for impromptu speaking and won eighth in the nation!

Lucky enough to have journeyed to exotic locales such as Venezuela, Ecuador and Mexico, she intends on using them all in future books. Alicia brings her natural enthusiasm for life to her stories and believes that the power of love can conquer *anything*, as long as one's faith is strong enough.

To the Ruf family of Quito, Ecuador,
whose warm generosity and open hospitality
helped make this book possible.
I wish you the best always.

Prologue

The dark seeped into the hills, night falling fast and thick through the rolling fields and plunging valleys. The long day ended, and the farmers returned to clay cabins, slipping into bed and sleeping the deep, dreamless sleep of physical exhaustion.

Except for the woman.

Her light burned late into the night, until her eyelids drooped and her head nodded. Then, and only then, did she at last turn out the light and slip quietly into the deep mat of her bed. The woven blankets embraced her, and sleep rushed forth.

But even then, María Chenney Pegauchi couldn't escape the dream....

Darkness. Howling wind. Booming thunder. The windows of the little house in San Diego shook with the unexpected impact of the storm. Inside, María sat beside the small, huddled shape of her five-year-old son. Daniel's black eyes were wide with fright, but he was still trying to be brave. It was something new, since he'd turned five. He was a big boy now, he'd informed her one day, and big boys were brave.

But when another crack of lightning whipped across the sky, seeming to leap into the bedroom with them, Daniel abandoned all pretenses and buried himself against his mother with a small yelp.

Reaching down, she stroked his head in comfort. It really was a wicked storm, quite unexpected for this time of year. Thunder boomed once more, and she felt Daniel tremble against her.

"It's okay, Daniel," she whispered softly. "It's just a storm."

Lightning flashed, but it was a little farther away this time. Even then, she could feel his fear.

"I know," she said suddenly, wanting to keep his mind off the storm. "How about I read you a story?"

He nodded hesitantly, his eyes still dark with fright. She smiled at him, soothing him with her own calm as she reached into the bookshelf that was over the bed, finding his favorite story. Tucking him firmly beside her, she wrapped one arm around him and began to read.

In the beginning she made sure her voice was captivating, holding his attention. But as she read on, and she saw his head begin to droop, felt the full weight of his little body beginning to sag against her own, she softened her voice. Her words trailing away, she bent over as far as she could and inhaled the sweet scent of baby shampoo and tin cars. His eyes were closed. As quietly as possible, she shut the book, placing it on the floor next to the bed. It took a few minutes more to ease off the bed and pull the covers up around Daniel's neck. With a few more pats and pulls, she looked down at him with a tender smile. He looked so sweet this time of night. Her own little miracle, her own sleeping angel.

"Sweet dreams, Daniel," she whispered and bent down to kiss his cheek.

He whimpered a little, eyes struggling to open.

"Monsters," he whispered, still hearing the faint remnants of rumbling thunder. "Mamíta, there's monsters."

"Where?" she whispered. "I'll take care of them."

"The bed," he murmured. "They're under the bed."

Nodding sagely, she bent down and peered under the bed. "No monsters here," she informed him firmly. "They're all gone."

"What if they come back, Mamíta?"

"Shh," she whispered and kissed his forehead. "If they come back, you just call for me. I'll take care of the monsters for you, I promise. Now sleep, Daniel. Sweet dreams."

He nodded, sleep finally winning. She lingered one last moment at the doorway, not quite able to pull away. There were times she marveled at having him in her life. Times when she wondered, after all the loneliness and heartache, how she'd ever been so blessed. But he was hers, all right. The only good thing to come out of a two-year catastrophe with a shallow, coke-snorting husband. But that was all behind her now. Now it was just she and Daniel. And he was her slice of heaven.

Softly, she turned out the light and slipped out of the room. The last of the thunder rolled in the distance. The storm had passed. Soon, the new day would dawn.

Morning now. Sunlight streaming through sliding glass doors. Orange juice glasses clicking on the kitchen table. Birds singing in the distance.

Daniel was laughing his high-pitched little-boy laugh as he tried to pour milk on his cereal. But in his exuberance, he kept dumping too much and the milk sloshed out the other side. He looked at his mess, and then at her, his dark eyes gleaming so impishly she didn't have the heart to scold.

"Clean it up, Daniel," she tried to say firmly, but found herself smiling instead at his earnest attempts as she handed him a sponge. His uncoordinated hands seemed to merely rearrange the milk, not mop it up. Scrubbing harder, he bumped against the cereal box and added a small avalanche of little Os to the disaster. He looked at the new mess for a minute, clearly perplexed. Then, with a five-year-old's shrug, he sat down, anyway, and began to eat the cereal—dry—off the tabletop. Shaking her head, María went over to the table herself and wiped up the spilled milk with a few efficient strokes. That done, she ruffled his hair with her hand.

"Hey, big boy," she teased. "When are you going to learn how to wipe up milk?"

"Big boys don't wipe up milk," he informed her promptly.

She cocked her eyebrow at that. "And how do you figure this?" she quizzed.

"Mommys wipe up milk," he told her confidently. She shook her head in mock dismay, ruffling his hair once more.

They were soon done with breakfast and, as was their custom, they set out on their morning walk. Daniel's little hand was tucked tight and safe in her own, his quick little steps trudging along next to her own graceful strides.

It was a beautiful morning. A beautiful child. Her own adorable child.

Then, suddenly, they were no longer on the sidewalk in the suburbs. Now there were cobblestones under their feet, and a fierce sun was blazing hot overhead. She had her easel in one hand, Daniel held the other.

The bazaar, she recognized vaguely. Yes, suddenly they were in a Mexican bazaar. She was supposed to paint. Paint a picture.

Automatically she started setting up her canvas, but her head was beginning to pound, and she could feel the sweat already beading on her brow. The birds were gone. The morning was no longer pleasant. Instead, she could hear a deep, oppressive silence. And the sun, the sun was blazing mercilessly on her. But there was nothing she could do about it, about any of it. Things would unfold without her being able to control them. She couldn't help herself. She must sit and paint. *She must paint.*

Her heart pounded loudly in her ears, and she could taste her own fear. But why? What was going to happen? Why was she—

She looked around. Then she looked again. And again.

Daniel?

Where was Daniel?

She couldn't see him, saw only the blazing white-hot heat of the sun. Sweat began to pour down her brow in earnest, and her heart was thudding out a frantic beat. She couldn't see him. Daniel. *Dear God, where was Daniel?* The easel crashed to the ground as she rose, but she ignored it. She had to find Daniel. She had to find her son.

Suddenly there were people, way too many people, crowding all around her, blocking her way. She could smell the deep stench of sweat and unfamiliar bodies. All of them were milling and jostling, holding her back. And the sun was still so strong, blinding her eyes. She couldn't see and she had to be able to see. Where was Daniel? All these people, there were far too many people. She had to get forward, she had to *move.*

"Daniel!"

She had to find him. Urgency pumped through her even as ice seemed to flow through her veins.

Now she was walking, looking, running, searching. The sun blazed above her, blinding. Where was her baby, her child, her *hijíto? She had to find her son.*

"*Mamíta...*"

It was faint, far off, a delicate whisper of the wind. But she heard it, and tried hard to surge forward through the mass of people. Something was wrong, *very* wrong. Why wouldn't the people let her through? Didn't they realize she had to get to her son? And the sun... It hurt her eyes; she couldn't see, she *had* to see.

Suddenly she broke through the crowd. She was running, running desperately forward until once again she heard his voice, the five-year-old's wail coming to her on the wind.

"Daniel?"

"Daniel!"

There he was, just up ahead. His arms reached out to her, but he was being carried away. A monster. A monster had her Daniel.

"*No!*" she cried, feeling the scream vibrate in her throat as she ran faster.

Faster and faster, and faster still, she ran, her legs slapping against the long cotton tangle of her peasant skirt. Her heart pounded against her chest, the sweat raced down her cheek.

But the monster seemed to go even faster. She couldn't keep up with it. She was trying, trying so hard, running with all the fear and desperation in a mother's heart. But it just wasn't enough.

It just wasn't enough.

"*Daniel!*"

"*Mommy!*"

The monster turned, zigzagging and weaving through all the little stands that added to the crowded conditions of the bazaar. Even as she steadily fell behind, she still tried to follow, knocking down stands, scattering goods across the open-air market. She could still see Daniel, just up ahead, his little arms reaching out to her.

And then he was gone, the monster spiriting him around a sharp corner. The monster was smarter, she realized dully in her frantic mind. It knew where to go, where to turn. And it was faster, much, much faster.

But still she tried. She couldn't give up. She had to reach Daniel. Oh, God, her baby—

Far away now, she heard his five-year-old scream. And she ran, but she couldn't find him. He was nowhere to be found. Nowhere.

"Daniel!" she cried out frantically. The air in her lungs burned and she knew she couldn't keep the pace much longer.

Then she heard his high-pitched scream.

"It's the monster. It's the monster. But, Mamíta, you promised to save me! You promised, you prom—"

"Daniel!"

And then there was only the silence.

Chapter 1

Sam Mathers was ticked off.

As he sat behind his massive mahogany desk, his fingers furiously rearranged the knot of his one-hundred-percent-silk burgundy tie, while his dark leather loafers tapped out an impatient beat. He had dressed carefully today, wanting to be ready for the occasion. But his gray Pierre Cardin suit was fast becoming wrinkled as he was constantly getting up, pacing his office, then sitting back down. Conservative, the carefully cut wool gave him a sleek, professional edge, even if the lines couldn't completely downplay the powerful ripples of his upper body. His hair was carefully tamed into a proper *GQ* look, but his unrelenting jaw shattered the thin veneer of urbanity, marking him as a man more comfortable with direct action than smooth words. To complete the picture, he possessed a pair of riveting blue eyes that were currently turning a dark indigo with frustration.

If there was one thing he couldn't stand, it was wasting time. Time was one of the world's most precious commodities. It was the one thing that couldn't be bought and couldn't be sold. You could race against it—you probably would more than once in your life—and you might even win sometimes, but, more often than not you would lose. His eyes darkened a fraction more.

He didn't like losing, knew all too well just how much losing could cost a man.

In all honesty, he wasn't in a great hurry at this moment. Things were rather slow at his New York detective agency. He was between cases and could take a minute to relax if he chose. But time was still time, and there were better things to do with a half hour than sit and wait for his two o'clock appointment when it was now well past two-thirty.

His fingertips drummed restlessly on the blotter pad. Grudgingly, Sam had to admit that, had it been anyone else, he would have simply gotten up and left. But the secretary who had called and scheduled the appointment yesterday hadn't been calling for just anyone. She'd been calling for Russell O'Conner.

Russell O'Conner was ninety if he was a day, though he refused to commit to an actual birth date. And according to what Sam had dug up in his preliminary check, O'Conner had made quite the fortune bootlegging during prohibition and now entertained himself with any eccentric idea he could dream up. He also shunned the public eye with near paranoid intensity.

Sam frowned, and his hand came up for a moment to once again worry his tie. There was always the possibility that the call had been some kind of prank, but the odds of anyone else using O'Conner's name weren't that great. Due to his low profile, the southern recluse wouldn't exactly inspire impersonators.

No, Sam felt it was safe to assume that the appointment was indeed genuine, and *that* left him tense with both anticipation and puzzlement.

What in the world could a man like O'Conner want with him?

It was true that Sam's detective agency had worked with the upper echelons of society before. His specialty happened to be children, and more than one rich parent faced with a missing child and a ransom note had come knocking on his door. Yet, as far as he knew, O'Conner didn't have any children.

And though Sam's record was a good one, the best, it wasn't perfect, he reminded himself harshly. A small muscle jumped near his cheek in bitter remembrance. Had he been just a minute sooner, sixty damn seconds earlier...

He reined in the memory sharply, then glanced impatiently at his watch. It was 2:42. Well, O'Conner certainly didn't hold tight with punctuality. Sam swore once more under his breath, and his fingers resumed their drumming.

What would an eccentric old billionaire want with him?

The man could be some sort of philanthropist. God knows he had the money for it. Perhaps he was working on a project that involved children in some way. Maybe famine in a Third World country or child abuse in the States? Not that it mattered to Sam anyway. He'd worked everything from local ransom cases to international deals for UNICEF. He'd worked for people who made thousands of dollars a year in just the interest on their investments, and he'd worked for people who couldn't even afford the long distance call to his office. For the rich, he charged five hundred dollars a day plus expenses simply because he knew they could afford it. For the poor, he worked for free. Because it wasn't money that mattered to him.

Once it had, once when he'd been an ignorant child watching his mother walk out on his father because she just couldn't take the hard lot of poverty anymore. Then he'd done nothing but dream of making money, of making it big. Not because he had wanted her back, but because he'd wanted to show her up.

But he'd learned a thing or two since then. He'd learned just how hypocritical and snobbish rich people could be. He'd learned about clubs where you couldn't join if you didn't earn the right kind of money. He'd learned about people who measured your worth based on your clothes and your car. And he had nothing but contempt for such people. No, he would take one hardworking Abe Mathers over one thousand fickle Sarah Mathers any day. In Sam's mind rich people were weak, and Sarah Mathers had simply been a bitch.

As the years had gone by, however, Sam had been forced to "bench" his feelings. The rich might be snobs, but they were also powerful. Too often, they called the shots. And Sam had learned the hard way that it didn't matter if you liked the rules, just as long as you mastered the game.

So he had. He kept two Pierre Cardin suits for people like Russell O'Conner, and developed a veneer of civility. But his face was hard and his hands were calloused, and he was damn proud of both. He'd mastered the game, all right. Just like he'd always known he could.

The buzzer of the intercom abruptly penetrated his thoughts.

"Russell O'Conner's here," intoned the secretary.

"Send him in," Sam grunted in response. His hands fiddled with his tie one last time, and then he rose behind the desk to face the door. So the mystery man had come at last.

Russell O'Conner certainly looked his years when he hobbled through the door with the help of a cane and a younger looking man. He was hunched over slightly, a frail figure in a tan suit and a too-wide red tie. Above the starched collar of his shirt, his face looked like a shrunken mask, the skin wrinkled and leathery from too much sun. A sparse covering of gray hairs littered his crown, but when the old man looked up, it wasn't the wrinkles Sam noticed anymore. Instead, he saw only the sharp intensity of O'Conner's keen brown eyes.

"Afternoon," O'Conner barked, his voice old and rusty. Balancing himself with one hand on his associate's arm, he stuck out his other hand in greeting. "Pleasure to meet you. This here's my great-nephew and assistant, Conrad." O'Conner gestured to the younger man, who, with his conservative gray suit and red tie, did indeed look like a thirty-year-old version of O'Conner.

Sam's impatience was fast giving way to curiosity now, and he accepted the offered hand with a polite nod. He was surprised to find O'Conner's grip tight and sure. Releasing it, he also shook Conrad's hand briefly.

"Now, then," O'Conner said, easing down into a leather chair while Conrad took the other. "Down to business. I'm a busy man, you know. Very, very busy."

It was on the tip of Sam's tongue to point out that *he* was the one who had been kept waiting for nearly an hour, but he managed to refrain. There was no sense in critiquing the obvious. They were both here now and were ready to get down to business. He took his own seat behind the desk, steepling his hands before him. He didn't say anything, waiting for O'Conner to make the first move. In a matter of seconds, the man had taken a file from Conrad and tossed it onto Sam's desk.

"There you go. It's all in there."

Sam raised an eyebrow, but silently took the file. Inside he found a map, a number of newspaper clippings in Spanish and two letters addressed to one Russell O'Conner. He set aside the newspaper clippings for now and let his eyes skim down the letters and then the map. An incredibly proficient reader, Sam digested the preliminary information in a matter of minutes.

"These are legitimate?" he asked tersely, indicating the letters, which had been sent from someone named Mark Leah.

"Legitimate?" O'Conner quizzed in his raspy voice. "Why, I've known the Leah family for more than thirty years. They are fine and upstanding folks, and Mark is no different. He received a degree in agriculture and then went down to Ecuador to help teach new farming techniques to the Indians. That's when he started hearing the stories of disappearing children. He did some investigating, and as you can see from the letters, he's put a few things together."

Sam merely nodded, keeping his expression impassive and his eyes neutral. He wasn't a man to give away his thoughts, nor did he believe in rushing into things. "So," he said dispassionately, "this Mark identified a total of ten missing children over a twelve-month span of time. For all you know, the children could have just run away, or gotten lost. I really don't see how this concerns me."

O'Conner frowned, his brown eyes stern. "Read the newspaper articles. Those aren't isolated instances of discontented children. No, it's far worse than that!"

But Sam still didn't return his attention to the articles. Instead, he shrugged his strong shoulders nonchalantly, even as his blue eyes remained sharply alert. "It sounds like a matter for the Ecuadoran police," he said casually. "Perhaps you should take the matter up with them."

In spite of appearances to the contrary, Sam's adrenaline was pumping. He was truly interested. Missing children, allegations of kidnapping. This was right up his alley. After all these years, however, he'd learned that only a fool rushed ahead. No, the smart man remained calm, learning all the details, absorbing all the information. And then, only then, did he act. Sam would hear O'Conner out, but only after the smallest of niggling doubts had been answered would he make a decision.

"These are the Indians," O'Conner was snapping, clearly impatient with Sam's persistent skepticism. "They live in the hills on their farms and in their villages. They don't have phones or sewers or TVs, and they don't go to the police with their problems. Now, of course, the village leader, he hears about it. Probably got together a few of the boys and conducted a search. But that's it. Whoever the little one is is gone, and they're sad, but there are other mouths to feed. End of story. Except now, of course. Now you're going to do something about it!"

O'Conner spoke the last words with the confident arrogance of a man used to getting his way. Sam chose to ignore the statement altogether, continuing to play the devil's advocate.

"Motive?" he queried. "Any particular reason why someone would want these children? Child labor, voodoo rituals? Why?"

O'Conner shook his head. "You're not listening. It's much worse than all that. Much, much worse. Come now, Mr. Mathers. I'm a wealthy and busy man. The Leah family may have been close friends of mine for years, but that doesn't mean I'd start a wild-goose chase based merely on the words of their son. No, Mark was on to something. You look at the newspaper articles, and you'll see."

This time, Sam relented. It was obvious O'Conner believed intensely that there was some serious problem, so he would humor the old man. Sam's Spanish was rusty and not exactly equal to the task as he picked up the first article. It had been years since his navy days, and he hadn't used it much since. But he remembered enough to grasp general concepts while he slowly plowed his way through the clippings. Even then, he could only doubt his translation.

"Organ donors?" he asked incredulously, all pretense of indifference dropping away.

"Yes," O'Conner rasped, nodding his ancient head emphatically. "They kidnap these children and carve them up like Thanksgiving turkeys for rich kids in the States. If your child needs a liver and you've got the money, it's not a problem."

Sam shook his head. He'd heard a lot of things in his time, seen some things that were worse. But this? It was too cold, too calculating to contemplate, let alone accept. Kidnapping innocent children and then murdering them for their organs...

"Look," he said. "How seriously can you take these newspapers? There may be some allegations here and there, but for all you know it's simply local rumor."

O'Conner waved away Sam's challenge. "But the children *are* disappearing. Not too many at a time, just one here, one there. It's not until you add it all together that it forms a real picture. And the farmers don't have the communication networks for that kind of thing. They stick to their own land and their own communities. No, it takes someone like Mark, someone traveling from community to community and asking around to put it all together. Ten children, Sam. In these rural areas, ten kids are a big deal—this isn't New York. Something's going on down there, and it needs to be taken care of."

Sam frowned, glancing from Mark Leah's letter to the newspaper articles. Things were rarely that simple, rarely that black and white.

"Why don't you have this Mark guy look into it," he ventured carefully out loud. "He's already down there and interested."

O'Conner shook his wrinkled head. "No. Mark has a good heart, but he doesn't have the training for this sort of thing. He helps plant crops and irrigate fields. He really doesn't have the time to start looking into this, and even if he did, he wouldn't know where to start. A problem this serious needs serious attention."

Once again Sam digested the news, but still doubt remained. Surely someone would notice if something this outrageous were happening. You couldn't just kidnap and kill children without raising suspicion along the way. And the idea alone was almost too horrific to be credible. How could a rational, civilized individual even begin to consider the cold-blooded murder of children for body parts? No, he thought to himself. It was probably just some myth created to reinforce anti-American sentiment in South America. But then again, if there was a shred of accuracy to the reports... He could only shake his head.

"I don't know," he said at last. "It sounds very far-fetched."

O'Conner grunted, but didn't seem surprised. "I can understand you being cautious," the older man said. "It's not a bad thing. In fact, I anticipated that you might need a bit of convincing. So I had a few of my assistants do some research into the matter. Conrad, get out the map."

There was a bit of rustling, and then Conrad produced a rather beat-up looking map marked with several pinpoints.

"See here—" O'Conner indicated with a bony finger "—these marks along the border, from Florida to Texas, these are where unidentified children's bodies were discovered. The local police put them down mostly as migrants' kids, probably even illegal aliens. Of course, the parents couldn't come forward to identify the bodies, because they'd be sent back to their country for not having green cards. I suspect there're actually a good many more of these cases, but these marks represent bodies that were badly decomposed, burned or generally missing a few things."

Sam looked up sharply. " 'Missing a few things'?"

"Body parts," O'Conner clarified abruptly. "Organs. Now, you look here," he continued, pointing to a line of marks on the map. "There's a good fifteen marks along the border of possible victims. That's *fifteen*."

"What about the FBI?" Sam asked. "Surely they'd look into something like this."

O'Conner shook his head. "Too spread out. Look here, it's just one or two over a very large area. Like I said, the local police do a bit of investigating and then simply close the files. Some of them get chalked up to possible satanic cults, especially on the Texas-Mexico border, where it's been a real problem. Most of them fall through the cracks of an overworked station. That's why we need a man like you. Someone to really dig into things, see what's going on. And consider this, Sam. Mark identified ten children vanishing in a twelve-month span of time. Of the fifteen marks, eight of them have appeared in the last year."

Sam's mind raced over the possibilities. "You haven't proved any clear connection yet," he said at last. "There's a big gap between children missing in Ecuador and unidentified bodies in the States. For all you know, they really *are* migrants' children."

O'Conner's sharp eyes narrowed shrewdly. "But I *have* made the connection. See this mark here, this one in Florida? This body was tied down with weights, but the strings got worn through and it floated unexpectedly in a storm. It appeared last week, and according to the coroner, it's badly mangled and both the kidneys are gone. Now the police are still looking into it, talking to area workers, you know. But I don't think they'll find anything. No, my man looked into it and he says the child is definitely an Otavaleño Indian, from Ecuador. And Mark verified that a child vanished from the hills exactly four weeks ago. The body discovered is the right age and size. It *could* be just a coincidence. It could be. Or, it could be the same child. But either way, you've got to find out, Sam Mathers, because Mark says another child disappeared six days ago. Now, surely, you see the need."

In spite of himself, Sam nodded, his eyes returning to the colored pinheads on the map. Yes, he was beginning to see Russell O'Conner's point, all right. While Sam wasn't one hundred percent positive that the most recently missing Ecuadoran child was the same as the body discovered in Florida, there was that possibility. And if the possibility was true...

"Now—" O'Conner pounced, not waiting for Sam's reply "—time is what's important. Judging by this first case, the children are killed within two and a half weeks of being kidnapped. Mark knows for sure a child disappeared a week ago, but there may be others he hasn't heard about, in different areas. You'll have to find out. And fast. You've got to move fast." O'Conner stopped long enough to take a deep breath, then nodded at his assistant. "Give him the ticket, Conrad."

After a moment's search through his briefcase, Conrad unquestioningly withdrew the aforementioned ticket. He placed it at the corner of Sam's blotter, and after a moment's hesitation, Sam picked it up.

He eyed it warily. "A round trip ticket to Ecuador?" he asked. "Return flight open?"

"Leaves eight tomorrow morning," O'Conner said curtly. "Be prepared."

Sam bristled at the tone, his eyes darkening. He felt like he was being railroaded, swamped with information without being given a moment to say yes or no. And while O'Conner's hypothesis was truly horrible, it wasn't necessarily true. No, Sam wanted to do some digging of his own first. And he wanted more than just a scant moment to rationally consider everything that had just been thrown his way. "I haven't even accepted the case," he pointed out, keeping his voice curt.

O'Conner merely snorted, clearly not regarding that as a major issue. He waited expectantly. Sam returned the shrewd old man's gaze levelly with his own uncompromising stare.

"Why me?" Sam asked finally.

"You're the best," O'Conner said immediately. "And I want the best."

"Seven hundred dollars a day, plus expenses," Sam said, suddenly wanting to see just how far O'Conner would go.

But the older man shook his head. "Five hundred is your standard rate," he said cannily, "and I won't pay a dime more. Of course, all expenses will be paid. Just keep the receipts and send Conrad the tab."

"I'll think about it," Sam said shortly. "You'll have an an swer by six o'clock tonight."

O'Conner's eyes narrowed, and he appeared to be weighin the answer. After a moment, he grunted to himself and turne to Conrad.

"Write him a retainer," he snapped. "If he doesn't take th case, you can always cancel the check."

"There is one more thing," the old man said, turning bac to Sam with a calculating look in his eyes. "There's a woma involved. Perhaps you've heard of her. María Chenney Pegau chi. For a year or two, she was Mrs. Waller, but mostly she goe by Ms. Chenney to the American press."

Sam's eyes narrowed. He recognized the name, all right. " thought she disappeared two years ago," he said warily.

O'Conner looked almost sly for a moment. "Young man, n one can 'disappear.' Especially from me."

Sam bristled immediately at the arrogance of the last state ment, but firmly kept his temper under control. So Russel O'Conner was a supremely overconfident old coot. The ma was a self-made billionaire, after all.

Keeping his tone even, Sam asked, "What does a rich 'in hiding' artist have to do with all this?"

O'Conner looked at him innocently. "You're the private de tective," he prodded. "Don't you remember the story? Fiv years wasn't that long ago."

Just as Sam was about to lose his patience, and demand straight answer from the elderly manipulator, a memory flashe across his mind.

"Her child was kidnapped in Mexico," he said slowly, th case coming back to him. "If I recall correctly, the remains o her son were recovered in Texas, just over the border. Cops fi nally ruled it a cult kidnapping. I believe they thought som black magic or devil worshipers took him."

"His heart was missing, cut right out. It could have bee them cult groupies like they said or..."

"You think he was a victim of these 'organ pirates,'" Sa finished for him, a chill creeping over him.

O'Conner nodded in approval. "But it doesn't matter wha I think. What's important here is what *Ms. Chenney* thinks and it just so happens that she never believed the police re ports. Not one bit. She's a sharp young woman, too, sharp a a tack. Ought to be," he said, smiling suddenly and revealing

teeth yellowed and stained with a lifetime of coffee and to-
bacco. "After all, she's my goddaughter. And as it happens,
she's currently residing in Otavalo, Ecuador."

Sam's mouth tightened. *Goddaughter?* O'Conner honestly
wanted him to work with some goddaughter? His jaw clenched
and he squared his shoulders. He'd better set the man straight,
here and now. Sam Mathers worked alone. Always had, always would.

"She's irrelevant," Sam began firmly, but O'Conner cut him
off.

"She can help you," the old man said. "She knows the language, she knows the people. Hell, her mother was an Indian.
She could get you around much faster than if you were on your
own."

But Sam shook his head sharply. "I work alone," he stated
coldly.

"You can speak Quechua, then?" O'Connor inquired with
feigned innocence.

"Quechua?" Sam quizzed darkly.

"What'd you think?" the old man cracked with glee. "That
the Indians spoke Spanish? Maybe some do, but by and large
they've got their own language, their own ways. They're de-
scendants of the Incas, a very proud people. Certainly not the
type to simply answer some strange gringo's questions. Why,
as far as they know, it's the gringos who are stealing their children. No, you'd have to have an in. Someone who's one of
them, someone who knows their language and their ways. Yes,
you definitely need María, no doubt about it. Besides, she's
done this thing before. When her own child was taken, she
searched high and low for him. It really was a damn shame.
Such a beautiful child. But, all that aside, she knows the people and she knows the situation. You'll need her, all right."

There was a moment of silence as Sam pondered the situation. The case interested him, it interested him a great deal. But
the woman. It was unacceptable. He worked alone, he *liked*
working alone, and he certainly didn't want to break that habit
now with a woman. There was no way it would work. He narrowed his eyes thoughtfully. It was time to see just how serious
O'Conner was about this "goddaughter."

"Then I will have to decline the case," Sam stated firmly. He
kept his gaze level. "It's that simple."

Whatever reaction he'd been expecting from O'Conner, the one he got wasn't it. Before his eyes, the old man's wrinkled face broke into a wide, confident smile.

"Oh, you'll take the case all right," the old man rasped surely. "Because I did my homework. I know all about you, Sam. I know about your temper, I know about your stubborn streak. I know all about the cases you've won. And I know about the cases you've lost. Tell me, young man, does the McCall girl still keep you awake at night? Do you still wake up seeing her small little body dead on the warehouse floor? Yes, I thought as much. Because you're a good man. You are. You do what's right.

"So you take your two hours before six to decide. You read the articles, do your preliminary investigating. You'll see I'm right. Something's going on down in those hills of Ecuador. Something that's making a lot of bad people rich, and hurting a lot of innocent kids. You'll see I'm right. And then you'll go. You'll even work with María simply because she's the best one to help you, and you take your work seriously. You'll go, all right. Because that's the kind of man you are. You do the right thing."

Sam's face had darkened at the words, his eyes reaching a dangerous shade of blue as he listened to the arrogant, eccentric old man lay out his life. For a moment he was tempted to refuse just because he *did* have a huge stubborn streak that rebelled at such treatment. But even as O'Conner's analysis angered him, in a far corner of his mind he was impressed by it, too. The old billionaire certainly had done his homework. Sam *was* the type of man who did the right thing. And if there were even the remotest chance that this black market of children's organs existed, then it was time someone did something about it. There was no man better for that job than himself. He *did* take his work seriously.

And, late at night, he did still dream of little Laura McCall's lifeless body. One minute too late....

"Six-thirty," he said at last, when he trusted himself to speak. "I'll call you by six-thirty."

O'Conner was shrewd enough not to argue the extra half hour. He nodded curtly.

"I look forward to hearing from you," the man said. Then, with another brief nod and a firm handshake, the billionaire and his assistant were gone.

Sam didn't waste any time watching the departure. He was busy taking off his jacket and rolling up his sleeves. His eyes passed over the check at the corner of his desk, but he didn't pick it up. Not yet.

He had only two and a half hours, and there was plenty of work to be done.

Traditionally Sam was a man who believed in thorough research. Leave no stone unturned, that was his personal motto. But he was also a man who knew the meaning of speed and how to cut corners. His own intellect and rapid reading skills helped in that area—though calling in three assistants from their previous assignments helped, too.

In two hours he had compiled an amazing assortment of information. He'd learned that Latin America was indeed alive with the so-called "baby parts" stories. According to reputable newspapers within Latin America, Indian children were being kidnapped and killed, their organs sold to rich American parents for their own children. Both the Mexican and U.S. governments had denied such stories, pointing out that not one had been adequately substantiated.

The official policy line of the United States, in fact, was that such stories were merely a part of the Yankee imperialism mythology. And it was true, many of the stories—there was a particularly disturbing one Sam came across about a man getting on a Mexican bus and spilling a suitcase filled with organs—were not only gruesome, but were medically impossible. Even the most advanced of preservation techniques couldn't keep a heart good for more than twelve hours, a liver for more than thirty hours, and kidneys for more than forty-eight.

Yet Sam had also run across an estimate of the current waiting list for organs. It was well over twenty thousand people and increasing each year as medical science made new discoveries. While more and more diseases and chronic disorders were believed to be treatable by means of an organ transplant, thus increasing the demand for them, the supply of available organs was woefully inadequate. Which meant that the waiting list was growing constantly. It didn't take a genius to figure out that, where demand greatly exceeded supply, some people would eventually find a way to fill that demand—in exchange for a huge profit. Already there had been cases of the poor willingly selling their second kidney—which the body could function without—in return for thousands of dollars, regardless of the fact that such procedures were illegal.

Which further suggested, Sam noted grimly, that out there somewhere were doctors willing to overlook the law, though there was a big difference between a person willingly selling their organ and trafficking in murdered children. Still, there was a black market for living children, where wealthier couples that wanted a child so badly they were willing to pay lots of money and ask few questions, got what they wanted. Sam could see the same premise working for wealthy parents whose child was dying before their eyes. They'd no doubt be willing to pay whatever the doctor asked, not asking any questions. Not wanting to know, just wanting to save the life of their son or daughter.

Finally, the fact that so many countries had laws prohibiting the trafficking of children's organs made the whole thing seem more probable to Sam. It seemed to him that laws were rarely passed unless the chance of someone actually doing the unwanted activity had been deemed a possibility.

All in all, he found that he couldn't rule out "black market organs" as a possibility. And it was a possibility that made him sick. And furious. And determined. Besides, the fact remained that these children were gone. He still wasn't so sure about all the correlations O'Conner's man had worked out— they seemed to be based more on assumption than hard facts— but he was willing to accept Mark Leah's reports of Indian children being kidnapped wasn't a fabrication. One possibility was that they'd been killed for some illegal market, and one more child had disappeared just a week ago. Someone needed to find him. Someone like Sam Mathers.

All his life, Sam had known he was different. By some twist of genetics and fate, he'd been born stronger, bigger, faster, harder than most. Back in the dust of Alabama he'd worked the fields on nothing but sips of water and pieces of bread long after other boys had collapsed and fainted under the strain.

But Sam had made another realization early on, as well. He'd grown up in poverty, watching his father work himself to death, witnessing his mother's abandonment and observing his sickly younger brother's slow decline. Sam had buried the young Joshua when he'd been just twelve, and he'd laid their father down beside him on his seventeenth birthday. Life, as Sam

Mathers saw it, was hard, cruel, and it was the weak, the innocent, that suffered. In short, life was unfair, and Sam Mathers was strong enough, smart enough and arrogant enough to decide to do something about it. The day he'd decided this had been the day he joined the navy.

There his brute strength and keen mind had kept him ahead of the rest, and he'd practically flown up the ranks. In the navy, however, he had seen the kinds of sights that only confirmed his original beliefs. He had seen the children of El Salvador, crying for their parents as missiles fired through their villages. He had seen other children, all over the globe, growing up in the brutal, biting grasp of poverty. He had watched, he had grown hard, and he had grown determined.

Someone had to watch out for the children. Someone had to try and protect them in a world that so often exploited their very helplessness. And in the last ten years, Sam had done a good job. Not a perfect job, but a good job. O'Conner had been right on the mark. He took his work seriously.

And Sam Mathers did do the right thing. In fact, there was only one thing that stopped him from picking up the phone and giving his agreement right now.

The woman.

Sam hadn't been lying when he'd said he worked alone. He had a few assistants, but they followed *his* orders. He had certainly never tried to work *with* someone, and he wasn't about to start with a woman. Yet, as he turned the matter around in his mind, he couldn't come up with a better idea. He *didn't* speak the Indian dialect. He *didn't* know the culture. He *didn't* know the people.

He could hire a guide, some sort of translator, he supposed. But if you had to pay someone, then their only obligation to you began and ended with the cash. And you never knew just how seriously they took that obligation. No, paid help simply wasn't trustworthy, and Sam couldn't afford to take the risk.

Once again, it was a matter of time. Each day that went by, the chance of the most recently kidnapped child being killed increased. At most, he figured he had ten days—if the pattern held. But then again, the sophisticated equipment and training required for the kinds of transplant operations involved would demand the ''donor'' be brought to the States for the procedure. The child was probably kept for a day or two to confirm matching blood types. All of which cut down the remaining

available time in Ecuador to eight days, six to be safe. Six days.
Or another child might die.

But how helpful could María Chenney Pegauchi really be?
He knew her type, all right. Rich, spoiled. Expecting the world
to serve her, only concerned with her own needs. Sure, she'd
had it harder than most, losing her son like that. But one tragedy didn't change a lifetime of upbringing. She was probably
vain, self-centered and impossible.

Like Sarah Mathers.

Sam sighed and rubbed his temples. The pictures kept swirling in his mind, and he couldn't seem to get rid of them tonight. Sarah walking out that door even as Joshua cried in his
thin little-boy's voice for her to stay. Trying to run, trying to
catch up with her, but his short legs not being able to do it. The
bitch hadn't even looked back to see her youngest son crying in
the dust.

Joshua, years later, his blue eyes solemn now, his face
pinched with continuous pain. Getting thinner as the days went
past, his face flaming with the fever. For days and nights Sam
and Abe had worked with the boy, bathing his brow, forcing
gruel down his throat. None of it had worked. He had never
complained, never cried. His eyes had been too old, too de-
void of hope, for one so young. And then one morning, he'd
died.

Sam had never hated Sarah as much as he'd hated her that
morning. He'd fed that hatred, let it rage through his muscles
as he took a pickax to the dry, unrelenting ground and dug his
brother's grave.

So many years ago, practically a lifetime. And still he remembered the bitter taste of the dust as he hacked at the
ground, the deep sting of unshed tears in his eyes.

And he still remembered what he had vowed in the long,
harsh afternoon as he'd hacked through drought-stricken dirt:
he'd vowed never to make the mistakes of his father and
brother. They had let Sarah Mathers get to them. They had
loved her, and she had played them like fools. No, the world
was a harsh arena where only the strong survived. Sentiments
like love made people weak. It had bled the gentle Abe dry, and
it had lowered Joshua into an early grave.

Once more, he could see it all in his mind. Sarah and Joshua.
One so selfish, the other so brave. One so harsh, the other so
fragile. And, for a moment, the memories of the bitter taste of

the dust, the strain of the pickax, hacking over and over again, overwhelmed him.

But when he at last drew his hand through his hair and pulled himself away from his thoughts, he knew the decision had already been made.

Those children needed him. And so he would go to the little rich heiress. And as God was his witness, if she didn't cooperate and help him find those kids, she would rue the day she'd ever heard the name Sam Mathers.

Chapter 2

The dark rolled into the hills.

The woman didn't notice at first, her attention focused absolutely on the canvas in front of her. And when she did notice, it wasn't the blackening sky nor the distant peal of thunder she noticed, it was the *feel*. The feeling of building intensity, the feeling of barely restrained power, the feeling of the darkness pouring in.

Hunched over her canvas, the woman shivered.

And deep within her, the feeling grew.

She wasn't a woman of many feelings. At least she tried hard not to be. Because deep in her heart, María Chenney Pegauchi knew how much it hurt to feel. She knew of pain so deep that it could bring you to your knees. She knew of terror so horrifying, all you could do was hope to awaken, even as you realized that you were not dreaming.

She knew the price of caring.

So now she worked hard not to remember such things, and she worked hard not to feel. Sometimes, she even succeeded.

But now the storm was rolling in, the thunder pealing, the lightning flashing, the wind howling through the mountains. The air in the small log cabin crackled with the electricity in the air, the flames hissing in the fireplace as a few stray raindrops managed to hurl themselves down the chimney.

And deep within her, the emptiness grew.

She wanted to curse at the emptiness, to call up the rage that was the one emotion she allowed herself, the emotion that had saved her from cracking completely so many years ago. But the rage wouldn't come, only the emptiness. That growing hollow pit in her stomach that reminded her of how far she'd come and how little she'd gained.

She threw down her paintbrush and the storm roared its approval, but still the emptiness grew. Her hand crept, unbidden, to her stomach.

A person could only run so far, she knew. A person could hide for so long, telling herself it was for the better. But running wasn't finding, and hiding wasn't living. She knew. Oh God, how she knew.

"Don't think about it," she whispered to herself. "You're doing fine."

The wind, however, howled its displeasure at the words, and the thunder boomed its disagreement, too. And the still air crackled, causing shivers to dance up her neck.

She had come to these mountains just two years ago, but she had been running for three years before that. She'd jetted across Europe, Asia and finally Australia, running from her own failures, only to have the press find her over and over again. When you were a world-renowned painter worth several hundred million dollars, it wasn't exactly easy to disappear.

But eventually she had remembered this land, the hills of Otavalo, which had sheltered her people for centuries since the time of the Incas. Her mother had sworn off this heritage, abandoning the hills and the people that were her roots, but María had remembered them from a brief visit when she was just a little girl. She'd remembered the vivid blue of the sky, the swaying green of the fertile fields, the slow, easy pace of living that had remained the same for centuries. So she'd come back here, to a land so remote that there were no televisions, no telephones, not even running water. The Otavaleño Indians enjoyed the simpler ways of life, and she had embraced them, too.

In the beginning, it had been hard. Her back had ached from the endless hours of trying to plow her own fields. Her delicate artist's hands had cracked and bled from the blisters. But over the months that had followed, she'd learned. She'd filled her days with harsh, physical labor, attempting to exhaust herself into dreamless slumbers. And while the nightmares still found her at times, her hands had toughened, her muscles had hardened and her face had darkened with the sun. Best of all, the press had never managed to find her.

She had a life now, she told herself fiercely, but the feeling within grew none the less, the emptiness mushrooming. Her days started at sunrise, and by the time she had tended her own fields, fed her own livestock and cooked her own meals, the sun had set. Her nights started then, nights when she moved from her mud house to this little log cabin where she tried—again and again—to make the magic flow. Only to fail, night after night after night.

The storm ripped through the mountains again, the thunder booming so close the cabin shook with the vibration. She put her hands over her ears to block out the noise, but she couldn't keep the emptiness at bay.

And underneath the emptiness lay the pain. She wouldn't remember, she told herself desperately. She just wouldn't remember. But the storm always brought the memories, the flashing lightning always awakened the nightmares. Each night she tried to forget. Each night the dreams came, anyway. She'd run and run and run, but she would never escape her own failure....

"¡Mamita! Look what I found, look what I found!"

"Yes, Daniel. It's a beautiful stone. You can add it to your collection when we get home."

"Are you almost done? Can we go home now?"

"Almost, love. I just need to add a few finishing touches."

"This picture is pretty, Mamita. I'm gonna be a painter, too. Can I, can I?"

She laughed, ruffling the short, silky black hair so much like her own. The bright sun was blazing down, but both were used to the heat by now. They had been in this little Mexican town for weeks now, María compiling a small selection of daily scenes. She was just now putting the finishing touches on a portrait of the bustling open-air bazaar, and then she and Daniel could return to the little villa they'd been renting.

"I think you can do whatever you want," she told her impatient son now. *"But why don't you go play with the other boys for just a while longer, and I'll get ready."*

"Okay. But I want ice cream."

"Ice cream? Who would want ice cream?"

"I do, I do, I do," he chanted happily. *"Lots and lots of ice cream."*

She laughed again, giving in as he turned and raced back to the group of boys playing with marbles. He was so young, and so strong. And she loved him with all her heart. Humming softly now, she returned to the canvas, completing what had to be done. Daniel was right, it was *"pretty."* Perhaps her best work ever. So she was happy. Her work had gone well, and she had a wonderful, adorable son.

Then she turned, trying to pick out his black, silky head from all the others at the Mexican bazaar. And she looked...and she looked...and she looked....

And then she was running, faster and faster. Pushing and shoving her way through the hordes of mingling, milling people. The blazing sun, the stench of sweat, the wet trails of her frantic tears.

Running, running, running...

The monster...

"Daniel? Daniel!"

Thunder boomed yet again, pulling her abruptly out of the reverie. Her pulse was racing, and her hands sweating.

"Damn." She cursed without compunction. There was only the storm to hear her, and the pain was back, the emptiness that tore savagely at her control. She could cry if she wanted to. After all, there was only the cabin and the storm, no one at all to care. But she didn't.

And maybe that was the problem. Maybe, after all these miles, all the tears, she wanted to have someone to care. Someone who would offer a shoulder to lean on, just once. Someone to kiss her hair and tell her it would all be better soon. Because it had been five years since Daniel's murder, and it hadn't gotten any better. It hadn't gotten any better at all.

But there wouldn't be anyone, she reminded herself fiercely. After all, there had never been anyone. Her parents had been too caught up in their jet-setting life to have time for a little girl.

And when she'd finally turned twenty, returning from the long line of Swiss boarding schools she'd attended, they had gone and gotten themselves killed in a stupid, senseless automobile accident. She'd almost fallen apart then, but she'd managed to pull it together. Back then she'd had her work, for her career was beginning to take off, her first New York showing just two months after her parents' funeral. A year later, she'd met Johnny.

He was an artist, too. And at the time, he'd seemed sensitive and caring. She'd been vulnerable, that was the only excuse she could think of now. She'd fallen for his soft blue eyes, the ones that had hid a calculating mind, and had married the man. One year later, she'd given birth to Daniel. And just one year after that, she'd written a check for one million dollars to the coke-snorting, two-timing addict. Basically, she'd paid him not just for a divorce, but to get out of her and Daniel's lives forever. He'd overdosed the following year, ending the matter once and for all.

She might have been lonely then, but it certainly hadn't seemed so at the time. She'd had Daniel, with his laughing black eyes and black hair. He was a miniature version of herself and by far her greatest achievement. Until he was five years old and waiting for her to finish her work. Until some unknown men had kidnapped him right out from under her nose, while she sat there, just a few feet away. Until the monsters had taken her son and killed him.

She'd started running then. Running from the pain, running from the terror, running from the bitter taste of her own failure. Running and running and running. But to what? The storm pealed outside, echoing her own doubts. She'd run so far, done so much, survived so much, bled so much. Still she had nothing.

And on nights like tonight, she just couldn't keep the emptiness at bay. On nights like tonight, the wildness of the storm called to her, the rolling thunder pounding out her pain. She wanted . . . something . . . someone.

In the movies, came the stray thought, a man would be out in that storm. A man with eyes so dark and a soul so strong he could take on even nature. The man would knock on her door, sweep her into his arms and with blazing kisses claim her as his own.

And, came the bitter thought, she would throw him back out into the raging night, for there was no other choice for a woman like herself. She was beyond the point where any man could make a difference. Even if one dared, she would hate him all the more.

No, she'd learned too well. She'd learned not to feel, she'd learned not to care. The only thing that had enabled her to survive before was the vow that she would never again go through such pain. All her life she'd tried to care. And again and again she'd borne the pain of loss. She would not go through it again.

The thought brought her strength, and she raised her fist to the storm, feeling the rage that had escaped her earlier flood back through her veins. She was strong, she was tough. She could survive anything, anyone, anywhere.

"I did it," she told the storm fiercely, and the glass shook with the force of the thunder's reply. "I survived! And I won't go back. I won't ever make the same mistakes again!"

But her defiance only seemed to madden the storm, and with a shrill cry, the wind whipped over the tiny cabin. The glass of the bay window shook, and the flames in the fireplace sputtered. But she stood her ground, remaining in front of the window.

She had one instant of warning, one flashing premonition of what such power could do to such fragile glass. She had time to take two steps back when the limb from the tree came crashing down, crashing through the glass as she instinctively threw her arms up for protection.

She felt the slivers of glass as they drove into the tender brown skin of her arms. Felt the sting of the rain as it plastered her long black hair. She opened her ebony eyes, bare to the storm, and, deep inside, the emptiness bloomed.

Daniel. *I'm so sorry, so sorry.*

Once more, she tried to push back the memories.

But even then, she still felt the pain.

Sam had been traveling since eight in the morning, and his mood was fast progressing from bad to worse. When he'd decided to take the case just the night before, he'd known that it would involve a lot of sleepless nights and hard work. That didn't bother him. He'd trained his body long ago to need little and to settle for even less. No, what was burning into his gut slowly but surely was frustration.

He'd been struggling up this damn mountain in a tin can of a rental car for near forever, and now the fan belt had broken, and he was still hopelessly unaware of his destination. What kind of a private detective traveled three thousand miles only to become lost within a five-mile radius of his destination?

Damn it, that woman had to be around here somewhere, he even had a map to testify to it. O'Conner's sources had tracked her to one of the hills outside of Otavalo. The area was incredibly rural, and Sam had already yielded the right of way on the narrow road to sheep on several occasions. In parts such as these, there were no such luxuries as addresses, let alone street names. But for crying out loud, O'Conner's goddaughter had to be here somewhere. This was the only road he'd seen thus far, and it hadn't branched off at any point. It just kept climbing, up and up and up.

Well, there was only one other option, and that was to keep going. Stopping the car altogether and with another muttered stream of curses, he grabbed a few basic supplies, slammed the door shut and set out on foot.

The hill rose steeply, and the air ran thin. He'd made it only fifty feet before his lungs started to burn. Far from disliking the sensation, the physical exertion went a long way toward tempering his frustration. He trudged on.

He and his three assistants had been up all night compiling even more information relevant to the case. They'd poured over mountains of reports, and after several hours of reading and rereading, Sam had settled upon their strategy. Time was of the essence, so he'd given each assistant their own angle to cover and orders to move—ASAP. Phil had joined Sam on the first leg of the flight to Miami, where Sam had connected for a flight to Ecuador. In Miami, Phil had departed to start gathering information on the most recently discovered unidentified body.

Chris was working on the different organ banks, acquiring more information on who donated, how the organ was tracked, as well as putting together portfolios on doctors who specialized in such procedures. He was also tracking records of children who had received organ transplants in the area around the time of death of the discovered body. Finally, Steven was in charge of tracing the life history of one female painter, María

Chenney Pegauchi. Sam had specifically ordered a focus on the events of five years ago, when her son had disappeared. If he had to work with the woman, he wanted to know everything about her. He didn't like surprises.

With his assistants pursuing those angles, he was left with the direct action. He had six days to find a child who had been kidnapped almost one week ago. The trail would be very cold by now, the clues almost impossible to find. He didn't have much time.

Not much time at all. So far, he was working on complete overdrive. His plane had touched down after dark, but the rental agency had still been open, so he'd gotten a car and hit the road immediately. Apparently there had been a big storm the night before, and as he'd gotten closer to the hills, the bumpy roads had been strewn with fallen branches and debris. It had meant a bit of careful driving, but it hadn't stopped him.

He wanted to meet this María Chenney Pegauchi tonight, get the ground rules covered, and then set out again at first light, he thought as he trudged up the hill. Of course, now they'd have to take her car, but that shouldn't cost them any more time.

If only he knew what to say to her. This whole aspect of the case still disgusted Sam. He walked faster just thinking about it. He didn't want to work with some damn princess. She'd probably expect him to cater to her every need. Well, he'd set her straight from the start. This wasn't any weekend tour. This was business, and it was going to be hard and brutal and she'd better just get used to it. The first time she so much as complained, he'd give her something to complain about.

Sam grimaced, breathing a little harder from the altitude. Fine, he would set her straight, but first he had to find her. You'd think there wouldn't be too many mansions out in an area this rural. You'd think that even one would stand out like a sore thumb. But he'd been driving higher and higher up the hill for nearly an hour even before stopping, and had been on foot a half hour more since. For God's sake, the glowing night dial on his watch indicated it was nearly midnight, and the top of the hill was almost upon him. Where the hell could she be?

His lungs were straining by now with the exertion, but he didn't slow down. Instead, with a grim set to his lips, he bent his head and kept climbing. A moment or two later he saw the lights.

Civilization at last, he thought with relief. Perhaps they could help him find the elusive Ms. Chenney. It took him another fifteen minutes to reach the yard of the house, as it was completely dark now and he had to pick his way carefully.

The dwelling looked small and rustic. By the dim light given off through the windows, he could make out the rough texture of mud walls and the slight overhang of thatching that served as the roof. Halfway across the yard, his head ran into something low and hard, sparking a long, muttered stream of curses. His hands were just making out the shape of drying corn on the cob that had been strung across the yard when the door opened.

"*¿Quién es?*" came a woman's soft voice.

"*Buenas noches,*" Sam replied in his rusty Spanish, his mind already struggling to find the appropriate words that would find him Chenney.

"You are American," the woman's voice interrupted flatly in English. "Are you lost?"

The light shining from the doorway obscured her form, leaving her to seem just a voice in the shadows. But her English was perfect, without a trace of an accent. Sam felt the tightening in his gut, the prickling of his hairs standing to attention on the back of his neck. How many women could there be in these hills that spoke English?

"I'm looking for a friend," he began carefully, for having found his prey he didn't want to alert her to the fact she'd been tracked down. "Perhaps you can help me."

"A friend?" Her voice was openly suspicious.

"I've come all the way from New York to find her," Sam continued slowly. "It's very important."

"And who is this friend?" the woman questioned skeptically.

He paused for a moment, weighing his options. He decided to plunge forward.

"María Chenney Pegauchi."

He watched the outline of her body go rigid against the light and felt the tension suddenly leap from her. Inwardly he smiled. It was to his advantage that she wasn't good at acting.

"You must be mistaken," María said stiffly as the first tendrils of fear clutched her stomach. It had been two years. She'd thought that the press had forgotten about her, that they'd finally given up and moved on to more interesting game. But now this man was here, this huge, shadowed man standing in her front yard. A thin sheen of sweat broke out on her brow and she clenched her hands at her side. "I know María," she continued thinly, "and she wouldn't associate with a man like you."

Before the last word had faded into the night, Sam felt the first punch of irrational rage slam into his gut. A man like him? What the hell was wrong with a man like him? Dirt under the fingernails? Honest sweat on his chest? Muscles trained by hard work instead of imported machinery? The little snob. Abruptly, he reminded himself that she couldn't possibly have seen any of those things in the dark. Still, he'd had a long, hard day, and his temper was overly active.

"Well, maybe she needs to spend more time with *a man like me*," he drawled out, trying to keep his biting tone in check.

"Who *are* you?" María demanded, this time from the doorway. Her heart was pounding in her chest, her pulse racing as she moved forward a bit. Maybe this was just a bad dream, maybe she could just close her eyes and this horrid man and all the implications of his presence on her doorstep would be gone. It didn't work. She'd closed her eyes briefly but when she opened them, the man was still there, features obscured by the night. His body was large and powerful, and just fifteen feet away. "What do you want?" she asked, controlling a shiver. The words were broken, the fear ill-hidden as her hands clenched once more at her sides. "Why are you here?"

Sam heard the fear in her voice and it effectively banked his anger. For the first time he realized how he must look to her, a shadowed stranger of such size and strength appearing suddenly in the night. He took a deep breath and attempted to start over.

"My name is Sam Mathers and I'm a detective from New York," he said evenly. "I've come here to locate a missing child. He's Indian, too, and . . ." The words really stuck here. "I—would like your help."

"You are not from the press?" María quizzed suspiciously.

He shook his head in the dark. "No."

"Identification?" she demanded.

He nodded in the dark, bringing out his wallet to flash her his private detective license.

She studied the card from the doorway, barely able to make out the name in the dim light. Sam Mathers. Private Detective. Suspicion died hard, though, and the years had bred wariness. She honestly didn't know whether to believe him or not. In the end she decided it didn't matter. Either way she just wanted the man to leave, and the sooner, the better.

"I don't believe I can help you, Mr. Mathers," she said coolly, glancing away from the ID. "So if you would, please be on your way—"

"Perhaps you didn't hear me the first time," he cut in sharply as he put back his wallet. "Look, a young boy's disappeared from around here recently, and there could be others. I've come to help. But I'm not Indian, so I don't understand the culture and I don't understand the language. All I'm asking is for your assistance, a few days of your time, nothing more."

She went rigid in the doorway. No, she hadn't really been paying attention the first time, but now the words hit her hard. A young child? Kidnapped? Her stomach rolled and a wave of nausea overwhelmed her. She felt like she was in the midst of some horrible, horrible dream and she just couldn't wake up. She didn't want to know this, she thought vaguely. She didn't want to think of such things. She wanted to go back to her life of nothingness, back to her garden and her chickens and her mud cabin. Back to her ignorance.

"I can't help you," she said again, but the words were broken when she wanted them to be firm.

"No, Ms. Chenney," Sam said coldly. "You *can* help me, it's just that you *won't*. Don't the lives of children mean anything to you?"

"Stop it," she bit out harshly, retreating a step in the doorway. "Just stop it." Her hands came up as if to ward off his very presence. "You have no right to be here, you know," she whispered from the shadowed entryway. "No right to simply pop into my life and demand my help on some wild-goose chase. These are the mountains, for God's sake. Bad things don't happen here," she insisted more firmly. "They just don't."

"Well, they just did," he contradicted flatly. "Now, are you going to do something about it or not?"

All at once a myriad of pictures flashed through her mind. Daniel playing marbles in the midst of a busy and colorful market. Daniel looking at her with his trusting little-boy eyes. Daniel laughing as she teased him about ice cream.

Daniel...lying blue and lifeless on the cold metal slab in the morgue.

She shook her head, but still she could feel the memories pressing at her temples, blinding her with pain. She couldn't bear this. She just couldn't bear it.

"Go away," she said desperately to the strange man who had brought such terrible memories. "Please, just *go away.*"

"What's the matter, Ms. Chenney?" Sam drawled out, his anger and frustration temporarily blinding him to the underlying pain in her words. All he could see at the moment was the rich little heiress, refusing to get involved. The princess, refusing to dirty her hands. He needed her help, damn it. A child, maybe more, was out there in the night, all alone, needing rescue. And there wasn't much time, he couldn't afford to be late again, he couldn't afford to fail another child, lose another life. Abruptly, visions of Laura McCall flashed across his mind. The pale pink of her jumper sprawled on the dusty floor of an abandoned warehouse— He stopped the memory in time, but not before he felt the anger, at himself for his own failings, at this woman who was threatening his chances of preventing another death, of redeeming himself.

"Did I interrupt your little vacation?" he found himself retorting caustically. "How rude of me. I don't know how I'll ever live with myself." Then, his control snapping, he said abruptly, "Why don't we both just cut the crap here." He took a determined step forward. "I don't know why you dislike me, Ms. Chenney, and, frankly, I don't care. All I care about is that child out there. Whether you like it or not, he needs your help right now. So why don't you just start dealing with it so we can get to helping him. And while I'd love to give you a little time to work it into your *social* calendar, I figure that come six or seven days from now, that child might be dead. I'd sure hate to have that on my conscience, Ms. Chenney, even if you can live with it on yours."

The biting sarcasm of his words penetrated her haze and rallied her rage. "That's such a nice little speech, Mr. Mathers," she retaliated, refusing to retreat this time. She stood straight and proud in the doorway, hands clenching into fists at her sides. "Such a great man you must be. Why, you're not just a detective, you're a judge and juror, as well. Well, listen to me for one moment of your precious time. You haven't the right to be here. You haven't the right to stand in judgment of my life and tell me what my conscience can or cannot stand. You may be a detective, Mr. Mathers, but you're not a psychic. You don't know one damn thing about me.''

He had to laugh at that. "Honey," he said, drawing out his words with relish, "I know lots about you. I know you were born in Los Angeles on August 4, 1963. I know you were sent off to Madame DuChante's boarding school in Switzerland, in 1974. I know you graduated in June and your parents died in July. Then of course you married Jonathan C. Waller, gave birth to a son and divorced your husband, all in the space of two years. And I know what happened to Daniel on August 3, 1989. I know about you all right, Ms. Chenney, maybe too much.''

She was too stricken to speak, his cold description of her life chipping away at her control, leaving her bare and vulnerable. He'd recited her life's story as if it were a meaningless passage in some book, and yet she knew nothing about him. Except that she hated him right now, hated him in a way she'd never hated another person before. Was it just ten minutes ago that she'd been all alone in her cabin, shut up tight in her isolation? And now, all of a sudden, this man was here, and her world was crashing around her as if it were a million shards of glass. She could hear a faint buzzing in her ears and for one desperate moment, she thought she might collapse right in the doorway.

But then with grim determination, she pulled herself together. She'd come a long way. She wouldn't let herself be overwhelmed by some stranger. Not after all this time. She wouldn't.

"Congratulations," she told him, keeping her head high against the pain that was blossoming within her. "You know how to read hospital certificates and newspaper articles. Really, even a rookie journalist can accomplish that. But you're still wrong, Mr. Mathers. You know the facts of my life, you know the events. But you don't know *me*, Mr. Mathers. You still don't know *me*.''

He should stop now, he told himself. He was taking this much too personally, not acting cool or logical at all. But he couldn't help himself. Here she was, trying to turn him away, just as he'd known she would. Yes, just like some selfish little princess, incapable of thinking about others.

Just like Sarah Mathers all over again.

"Oh, I know you, sweetheart," he found himself adding sarcastically. "I know all about your type—all silk and satin and manicures and Mercedes-Benz's. You grew up with a mansion of servants at your beck and call. Every want met, every need fulfilled. Never had to think of anyone else, did you, María? Just basked in the glory of your birthright."

The words were harsh, his own anger hotter than it should have been. It carried him forward until the light from the doorway swept across his face in a maze of planes and shadows. She gasped at the first sight of him, but he was too caught up in his own anger to hear.

He took another step forward.

María backed away unconsciously, feeling the intensity that swept before him like a physical onslaught. But she couldn't keep her eyes from his face, from the rumpled mane of thick blond hair, from the stubborn cut of his square chin that was now revealed to her. He had a hard face, strong and blunt and unapologetically male. And it wasn't just his face. This close she could see the broad cut of his shoulders, the rippling movements of his muscles as they flexed impatiently under the thin cotton of his short-sleeved shirt. He was indeed a huge man, not too tall, maybe six feet, but broad and strong. Like a warrior, she thought dimly, her breath catching in her throat. If his physical presence wasn't intimidating enough, the night wind suddenly picked up again and whipped around her, bringing with it the scent of Sam Mathers. No heavy cologne, no carefully selected spices. Just the clean smell of soap mixing and blending with the richer scent of light sweat.

Unbidden, another feeling rose inside María, and this time it wasn't fear that made her tremble, it wasn't foreboding that opened her mouth in a silent gasp. It was a feeling much darker, one she refused to acknowledge even as it clutched and pulled at her stomach.

It should be storming out, she thought dazedly. Thunder should be rolling, lightning flashing. Yes, it was only fitting for the arrival of such a stranger.

Abruptly she pushed the thought away. She felt disoriented, as if she were watching her life spiral out of control. Why had he come? Didn't he understand that she couldn't help him? She just couldn't. Taking another deep breath, she pulled herself together, forcing herself to meet the blazing heat of his eyes.

There was fury in the blue depths, but it only served to fuel her own anger all the higher.

"As you can see, Mr. Mathers," she replied haughtily, "there aren't any Mercedes-Benz's here."

"Did you get tired of the luxury?" he shot back ruthlessly. "Tired of the spas, the villas, the resorts? It was very clever, María. Jetting around with the rich elite of Europe, Asia and Australia, only to vanish in the hills of Ecuador. What? Did you decide to play peasant instead?"

Her gasp was audible this time, her outrage unmistakable.

"How dare you?" she said fiercely. "How dare you barge into my life like this with your absurd assumptions and your gross generalizations—"

"Are they?" he interrupted, covering the last of the distance between them with powerful steps until he was mere inches away. "Tell me, María, if you aren't selfish, if you *aren't* spoiled, then how can you turn your back on a child who needs your help?"

"You don't know anything," she reiterated coldly, turning her face away from his piercing scrutiny. Sam watched her narrowly, despite himself feeling something clench tightly in his gut. Her looking away from him had revealed one side of her face fully to the light. The slim ray swept sharply across her delicate features, highlighting the fullness of her lips, the high curve of her cheekbone, the elegant line of her nose. It was her eyes, however, that momentarily froze Sam's sharp retort. They were tilted exotically, and were framed by eyelashes so thick and lush it was all Sam could do to keep from reaching up and rubbing his finger over their silky sheen.

God, she was beautiful.

But he had no sooner thought it, than it made him even angrier.

"So you keep telling me," he answered, coming back to her denial. "But so far, you aren't proving me wrong, either. What is it, María? What is it that keeps you from helping? I've already told you, in six days, a child could turn up dead. Now, I might be able to find some other, friendlier, native Ecuadoran to help me, but that would waste a damn costly part of those six days. I can't afford that to happen. So it's up to you, María. You *have* to help me."

"No," she said, but the word came out as barely a whisper.

"Yes," Sam corrected her, feeling her hesitation and moving quickly to capitalize on it. "Come on, princess, help me out."

"Don't call me that," she said, but there wasn't much heat left in her voice. She felt tired all of a sudden. Tired and worn. Just this morning she'd been harvesting her corn, feeling the muscles of her back work, watching the quick dexterity of her hands. Maybe, for just one moment, she had been content; she'd once more managed her fields all by herself. But now this man was here, talking about monsters that she thought she'd managed to leave behind. She didn't want to help. She didn't want to know about this child, or any others. She didn't think she could bear to go through it all again. The hope, the caring, the crushing pain when inevitable failure occurred . . .

But Sam Mathers was still in front of her, waiting for a reply. Why had he come? Why had he come and spoiled the only peace she'd been able to find? She wanted to rail at him, she wanted to weep. He had come and told her about the monsters and now there was no going back. Her peace was gone. Even if she didn't help him she would always know that some poor child was out there, alone and helpless. That other children, too, could be taken. It was like some large mystic circle and she just couldn't escape its grasp. She kept running, and fate kept finding her again. What could she do?

"I can't help you," she whispered softly, her gaze sweeping up to meet his own intense scrutiny. "Can't you see that? If you followed my life so closely, then surely you know everything I did last time. The hired detectives, the police, the FBI, the offered rewards. All the fame and the fortune I had was useless in the end. It didn't do any good at all, Mr. Mathers. They still killed my baby. There was nothing I could do."

For a moment, there was silence. Abruptly, Sam felt his anger draining away. No, he didn't know all the details yet. He didn't know everything she'd done to try to save Daniel. He only knew the results. Her son had been murdered.

The remorse hit him sudden and hard. In the back of his mind, he recognized that she had been right; he'd played both judge and juror. What right did he have to barge into this woman's life, dredging up her past pain, berating her for not getting involved? In this light, she certainly didn't look like any haughty princess now, coldly refusing help. Instead, with the light slanting across her face, she looked vulnerable and alone in the harsh night. Her eyes seemed to glow in the shadows, her cheeks were pale, her shoulders slightly slumped.

She looked like what she was—a woman in pain. There was a moment, a long hard moment, when he had to consciously ball his hands at his sides to keep from reaching out. It would be so easy to draw her into his arms, to press the slight weight of her delicate head upon his shoulder. Inside he swore at himself, at this infernal need to comfort. She was a grown woman, she could take care of herself. Besides, he'd learned long ago that not all pain was meant to be comforted. And it was too easy to mistake need. Too easy to turn into someone like his father, a man who had died trying to soothe the rancid soul of a woman who hadn't been worth it.

Besides, Sam couldn't afford to comfort María. Instinctively, he knew that it would most likely hurt her a lot more if he did before all was said and done. A point that was made all the sharper by the knowledge that, even if he'd wanted to, he couldn't just turn around and walk away. He had a job to do. He needed to find this child. Daniel had died five years ago. Nothing in the world could bring him back, or ease his mother's pain. But if Sam didn't find a way to get María's cooperation, another child would die, another mother sentenced to grief.

"This time it will be different," he said, his voice softer.

"You can't promise that," María said quietly in the night. "You can't promise me we'll actually find the child. You simply don't know."

"We have to try," he insisted stubbornly. "To know and not do anything is worse."

She shook her head. "Hoping is worse. Wanting is worse. *Caring* is worse. No, Mr. Mathers," she said suddenly, the words firmer this time. "I can't help you. I just can't."

"You have to," he returned intensely. "For God's sake, are you really so willing to sentence that child's mother to what you went through? Think about your son, Ms. Chenney. Remember what it felt like. Do you really want another woman to go through all that?"

They were the wrong words to say, and he realized it immediately. Her head shot up, her shoulders went back, and her eyes were suddenly ablaze with the dark fires of a deep rage.

"Don't you tell me about my son, Mr. Mathers," María bit out. "I know all about my son. I was there, damn you. I was there when he was taken, and I was there to identify the body later. So don't you preach to me about things you know nothing about. It wasn't your son who died. You weren't the one that stayed up each night hoping that this night they would find him, that this night he would come home to you. You weren't the one who tried every avenue, every possible way to get your son back. And you weren't the one to bury him later, all alone with nothing but your tears and the knowledge of your own failure. No, don't talk to me about pain, Mr. Mathers. And don't you ever imply that I want another woman to go through what I went through. I know all about that pain, and I wouldn't wish it on my worst enemy. But that's exactly my point. I won't go through it again, either. Never again.''

Her chest was heaving, her eyes flashing. The words were raw, and they effectively silenced any argument he might have had.

"Go away," she told him, repeating her earlier plea in a stronger voice. "Just get the hell out of my life and don't come back."

Part of him believed everything she'd said. Part of him was almost tempted to leave. Had she been a cold heiress, it would have been easy for him, he would simply have bullied her into cooperation. Had she been the spoiled princess, his role would have been simple, his anger simple. But she wasn't cold or spoiled, she was a woman full of pain and anger. And he'd brought that on, he had forced the issue. Yet it was already too late to walk away. He'd hurt her, and he was sorry. But he needed to help that child even more. If he had to terrorize her into it, he would. Five years was too long for one woman to be in hiding, anyway. Sooner or later, she was going to have to deal with the real world, and it might as well be now when she could do some good.

He chose his words carefully.

"All right," he said levelly. "I apologize for my comment. I know you wouldn't wish your experiences on anyone. But that doesn't change the fact that there is another child missing. As I see it, you now have two choices. You can shut that door in my face and curl back up in your cozy bed, or you can help. And I think you know as well as I do that it's already too late to shut the door. You go back to your bed now, and you'll be lying there all night, thinking of that child. Wondering. Fearing. Hating. You wanted your isolation, but it's already gone.

So really, you might as well take the next option. Help me, María, and we'll find this child. This time, you'll win."

His words were compelling, wrapping themselves around her slowly, almost seductively. Part of her understood. Part of her did know that it was indeed too late. The monsters had followed her, and even if she shut the door, in the dark of the night she would still know they were there. And, more than anything in the world, she found she wanted to win. For once, she wanted to know that one child had survived, that one child had finally made it.

But she still couldn't find the words that would seal her fate. She still couldn't say yes. Because of the fear. Because, deep in her soul, she knew they could never win. She'd tried so hard with Daniel, using every resource a world-famous, multimillionaire artist had at her disposal. And it hadn't done any good. She hadn't been able to protect her own child.

Her baby...

She turned away, unable to face the night anymore.

"I can't," she whispered finally.

"You can," he told her firmly.

"No."

"Yes."

"Please, just go away."

"I have no other place to go."

There was silence. "You don't have a car?" she asked, surprise breaking through the lethargy that seemed to have overcome her.

"It broke down a ways back."

More silence. She seemed to falter in the doorway. "I need some time to think," she managed to say, overwhelmed at the discovery that Sam couldn't just disappear from whence he'd come.

"I don't have much time," he told her evenly. "I need to get started first thing in the morning."

She seized upon that, welcoming the out.

"The morning, then," she said. "Give me until morning." She'd be stronger then. Surely she could handle him in the morning.

He hesitated, wanting to secure her agreement now. But the strain was obvious on her face. To push her much further would be like Russian roulette; he'd either get her agreement or break her completely. He didn't want that.

"All right," he said finally. "I'll camp here for the night."

She looked unhappy, but relented. She would feel better if he was far away, but it seemed there was nothing that could be done about that now. It was only for the night. In the morning, she decided with near desperation, she would get rid of him, once and for all.

She nodded. "Agreed."

He nodded back. And in both of their minds, they thought the same thing.

It would all be taken care of in the morning.

Chapter 3

"Wait here," she told Sam, "I'll bring you some blankets." With that, she turned, retreating back into the house.

He obeyed only for a minute. Then, as her back disappeared from view, he stepped inside the tiny hut, his eyes looking around intently. He was a private investigator, after all, and he'd learned long ago that you didn't collect information by waiting for invitations. He wanted to know more about this rich princess who lived in a mud cabin, and since she wasn't exactly volunteering details...

Whatever he'd been expecting in regards to her living quarters, this wasn't it. Not only was the house a far cry from a mansion, but he'd seen shacks that offered more comforts. For all intents and purposes, María Chenney Pegauchi was living the life of an Indian.

The cabin seemed to consist of one primary room, with a doorway that led into a small offshoot of a room on the right. In the center of the main room was a ringed fire, and judging from the black soot that coated the walls, there wasn't a chimney to go with it. To one side was a wooden table, and at the moment it was piled with ceramic bowls. All made by hand, he noticed, and a nice job of it, too. Hanging overhead was an assortment of cooking utensils. A light touch revealed them to be made from tin with wooden handles. There was a huge cooking pot for stew and smaller pots and pans, as well.

More curiously, while he found an assortment of spices drying on one wall, there was no food anywhere he could see. So either María didn't eat, or there was another place for storage. And, considering she was a famous painter, he thought it odd there was absolutely no sign of oils or canvases. Letting his curiosity lead him, he passed through the open doorway into the next room. This was apparently the bedroom, and it contained a rough wooden dresser against one wall, while a stack of straw mats were piled with woven blankets against the other. Standing in the middle of the room with a few more blankets was one very furious-looking Señora Pegauchi.

"I told you to wait outside," she snapped angrily as she watched his huge form fill the doorway.

"I wanted to see your house," he said simply.

But the mildness of his tone only enraged her further. It was bad enough he'd come to the hills, bad enough he'd awoken her pain, but now he was standing inside her house, her last sanctuary, her last retreat. She drew herself up, donning easily the cold, haughty ways of her past.

"Really?" she bit out cuttingly. "Well, do tell, Mr. Mathers. Does my house pass inspection? Or would you like to go to the Hilton now?"

"It's very interesting," Sam said, taking in her flushed cheeks and flashing eyes. This was how he'd imagined her, he realized. Cold and sterile and every inch the rich bitch. There was no vulnerability here, no more shadows in her eyes. Now she looked every inch the type of woman he'd anticipated. And she was one of the most impressive sights he'd ever seen. He forced himself to look away, once more taking in the pile of straw mats that served as her mattress.

"This is certainly a long way from your usual haunts," he commented nonchalantly. "Tell me, princess, how long do you plan on living like this?"

"Forever," she said coldly. "Forever and ever if I have to look forward to men like you who won't leave me alone."

He shook his head. "I don't believe you," he said easily, watching her reaction closely. "Sooner or later you'll miss your spas, your manicures, your designer men. A woman like you doesn't live like this permanently."

She didn't back down, he had to give her credit for that. If anything, she seemed to straighten even higher, her chin sticking out, proud and arrogant, before him.

"Oh," she shot back with a finely arched brow. "And what would you know about a woman like me?"

He couldn't help it. What had started out as an experiment began to take on a life of its own. In the beginning, he'd only wanted to see how she would react to his probings. Now, however, he was captured by those very reactions—the flush of her cheeks, the fire in her eyes, the angry heaving of her breasts. She was beguiling as the anguished mother, he realized, but enrapturing as the femme fatale.

He couldn't quite help himself. His hand came out to pick up slowly a long strand of her black hair. It flowed like silk between his fingers, and he watched it slide through them like black fire.

"I know," he whispered softly as his eyes found and held her own, "that a woman like you is accustomed to certain ways, certain manners. I bet you've never had a man ignore you when you wanted his attention. I bet you've never had a stranger appear on your doorstep and walk right into your house and play with your hair. Am I wrong, María? Tell me."

She wanted to, but she couldn't seem to manage the words right now. His eyes were hot, gazing into hers, dark with a kind of intensity that sent a shiver through her and made her want to lean a little closer even as she knew she should pull away. He filled the small expanse of the room so completely, her senses seemed to overflow with the sight and smell of him. What about touch? a voice in her mind whispered. What would it be like to just reach out and touch?

She jerked back as if scalded by the mere thought. She didn't like Sam Mathers, she reminded herself fiercely. But she couldn't seem to tear her eyes away from him, either.

"What do you want?" she demanded at last, calling upon anger to get her through this latest difficulty. "If you can't bully me into accommodating you, then maybe you'll seduce me to agree instead? It won't work," she told him defiantly, but the words alone were making her pulse race. "I don't like you."

His eyes narrowed at her words, his feet moving forward on their own. He noted the defiant tilt of her chin, but saw it tremble at his approach. Her eyes burned with emotion, drawing him closer even as her words sought to send him away.

God, she was a beautiful woman.

A true princess.

The last thought drew him up abruptly. Yes, she was a princess, a woman whose life was a far cry from his own. She might be living in a hut now, but that didn't change a lifetime of mansions, villas and resorts. He would do best not to forget that.

Like ice in his veins, the thought chilled him, bringing him out of the spell she'd put on him. Silently he berated himself. Where was the logic and reason that was the mainstay of his profession? Where was the control? In that instant, he felt only a contempt for himself. He'd come here to save the life of a child, not to make a fool of himself over a woman.

Not to make the same mistake as his father.

He stepped back, noting with grim amusement that she watched him through suspicious eyes.

"The blankets, please," he said in clipped tones. "It's already very late and we need to get an early start in the morning."

She watched him a minute longer, bewildered by his sudden withdrawal and surprised by the sharp pang of loss making its way through her. She tightened her spine against it.

Taking a fortifying breath, she matched his clipped tones with cool words of her own. "Here are two mats and three blankets. A small fire should keep the wild animals at bay. Now get out of my house."

He didn't argue. But he couldn't resist one last lingering look at the shapely contours of her body, taking in the slope of her breasts and the curve of her hips. Her eyes flashed fire at him the whole time, her head held high even as her cheeks flushed a deep red. He gave her a slanted look, his eyes dark indigo.

"Sleep tight, princess," he said. "While you still can."

He was gone before she could reply, which was just as well because she couldn't think of a good retort, anyway. Her heart was beating much too fast, her pulse racing away.

She commanded her feet to the doorway, locking the front door for the first time in two years. But her mind remembered all too well just how Sam Mathers looked, his chest so strong, his shoulders so broad. If he wanted to get in, she knew with certainty that the door would not stop him.

She shuddered. How could one man's eyes be so blue?

She crawled back into bed. But it was a long time before she slept.

The sound of someone sobbing woke María up. She lay there for a moment in the pitch-black darkness, trying to collect herself, though by now she operated more on habit than with thought. And she really didn't need to think too hard to figure out that the crying was her own.

For as long as she could remember, she'd never cried in the daylight. Not when she'd fallen and broken her arm when she was seven. Not when her mother had sent her off to boarding school at twelve. Not when she'd attended the funeral of her parents, nor when she'd divorced her husband. Not even that horrible day when she'd looked up from her canvas and Daniel had been gone.

No, she never cried during the day, when the sun was out, when others might see her tears. Only at night, when the darkness was soft as velvet, when she was fast asleep. Then she would awaken to find her cheeks wet, her throat dry, and a lump so big in her chest that at times she feared she'd never be able to breathe again . . . and wished she *would* die.

But things had been getting better of late. Last night she'd been upset, but storms had a tendency to do that to her. Something about all that electricity in the air, all that turmoil, affected her. But other than the storm, it had been almost three months since the last time. Until tonight.

It was Sam's fault. He'd come, disturbing old wounds, without any consideration for the damage he might do. Him and his missing children. What did he want from her? Didn't he realize that she hadn't been able to save her own son?

Two years ago, she'd come here for peace. She'd been running from the guilt for years before that, trying to drown herself in the overindulgent opulence of exotic resorts and exclusive spas. She'd tried parties, she'd tried champagne, she'd tried gambling. She had tried just about anything to ease the emptiness inside. And she'd thought, each time, that maybe in this place, maybe with this fresh start, the loneliness wouldn't be so bad. The emptiness would diminish and she would be able to forget her loss, be able to paint again. The magic would return to her fingertips, and at least she would have her art back.

Then, one day, she'd looked around at all the designer clothes, sparkling jewels and sun-drenched skin that continually surrounded her and wanted to scream out loud, "Don't you realize how fake this all is? Don't you realize how much we own and how little we really have? Don't you?"

It was at that instant that she'd realized she just couldn't take it anymore. For the sake of her sanity, for the sake of the little self-respect she still had, she had to get away and start over again.

So she'd come here to the land of her childhood. It was an ancient land, unchanging, constant, basic. There were no diamonds here. No champagne. Just hard work and deep sweat. Just the constant cycle of planting and harvesting. Here, she wasn't María Chenney Pegauchi the famous painter, nor the rich heiress. Nor was she the tragic mother. She was just a farmer, part of the land, part of the cycle that went back to time immemorial.

Here she found what little solace she could, probably all she would ever have. No, it hadn't been easy, but she'd made it. She had even brought in a full crop of corn all by herself for the second time, and this harvest was even better than the one before. No, life wasn't perfect here. But maybe it was a little better.

Until now.

And now she was crying in her sleep. And the feeling was back, the feeling of hollow emptiness, the feeling of deep yearning she wasn't ready to recognize. Sam had come, and in coming he had only proved what she'd already known. She truly was alone now.

And the child, a little voice whispered within her, *he's alone now, too. Alone with the monsters . . .*

The thought made her gut wrench, and abruptly she felt the thick burn of tears in her throat. Was he crying for his mother even now, waiting for her to come and save him, as mothers were prone to promise they would late at night, when shadows inspired five-year-old fears?

What could she do? she argued with herself. Last time, she had tried everything, and it had failed. *She* had failed.

It's better to at least try, than to know and do nothing.

But the pain . . . Oh, God, the pain. Standing in the cold morgue, seeing her child, her *baby,* lying on the steel blue slab, she'd thought she would shatter that day, shatter into a million brittle pieces. A mother should outlive her child. A mother should hold and comfort her baby, soothe his scratches, bandage his knee and send him out into the bright, sunny world.

A mother shouldn't have to identify her child at the morgue. A mother shouldn't know that after all those times of kissing his wounds and promising to make it better, she hadn't protected her child, after all.

A mother should not have to bury her own baby.

Her eyes burned, and she could still feel the tears stuck in her eyes, but they wouldn't flow. And over and over it ran in her mind. All the memories, all the pictures. Daniel laughing and throwing his arms around her. Daniel crying and running to her for comfort. Daniel sleeping and cuddling up in her arms.

Daniel was gone. She knew he was gone, she had identified the body and attended the tiny funeral all alone. Daniel's grandparents were already dead, his father, as well. It had been just María and a handful of friends, watching the tiny, doll-like coffin sink into the ground.

She couldn't bear it, she couldn't go through it all again.

But the other child was still out there, all alone, crying for his mother, crying for someone to help him. Like Daniel must have cried.

She was going to do it, she realized in a flash. Sam had come and destroyed her peace. Now there was no going back.

The only question was, would she survive this? Could she go through it again?

She had no answers to that one. None at all. Absently, she began to stir the fire, setting a pot of water on to boil. It was already almost dawn, the sun just beginning its rise over the snowy peak of the Cayambe. She would have to pull herself together. There were probably preparations to be made.

Her stomach rolled at the thought, her head pounding. She leaned against the shaky tripod that supported the pot. God, why had Sam revealed so much? She just wanted to escape, she wanted to get away from all the bad in the world.

But it had found her once again, that evil she couldn't seem to destroy and couldn't seem to leave behind.

Another child . . . Another innocent child.

She couldn't bear the pain.

Somebody knocked on the door.

For a moment she was startled, her head jerking up. It was still so early, even the farmers would still be asleep. There was, of course, only one other person who would be up. Sam Mathers.

It had to be him.

María stared at the door for a long while with wide eyes. The knocking came again. Then, moving almost as if in a dream, the long white folds of her nightgown whispering against her legs, she rose and approached the door.

Rap, rap. Rap, rap.

The wood was warm beneath her hand as she touched the door.

Rap, rap. Rap, rap.

It vibrated, sending tingling waves up her arm. Half-mesmerized, she watched her hand as it slowly moved to find the cool metal of the latch. Her hand drew it back.

Rap, ra—

The door fell open, and Sam's hand dropped to his side.

"Is it morning so soon?" she asked softly.

But Sam didn't answer. Instead, for the second time in a space of just hours, he felt himself slam-dunked by the completely unexpected.

He'd thought he'd seen her clearly last night, but now she was right in front of him, wearing only a thin white nightgown and basking in the warm glow of a predawn fire.

And God, she was more than just beautiful. She was stunning.

Her hair was down, a long black curtain that gleamed in the firelight. It curved around her throat, falling to brush over the warmth of her breast. He could see the outline of the breast clearly through the white folds of her nightgown, as well as the indent of her waist, the long, lean tapering of her legs.

He couldn't swallow, but slowly and surely he managed to drag his eyes back up her form. And found himself face-to-face with the darkest black eyes he'd ever seen. They were shiny now, huge and luminescent with what? Pain? Anger? Desire? He didn't know. Her lips were trembling, slightly parted to reveal an even line of tiny white teeth. Her tongue crept out and licked them nervously as he watched in fascination. And then his eyes came to her cheeks, the delicate slant of her cheekbones still clearly damp with a long, thin track of newly shed tears.

Without another thought, his hand came up and very gently, for surely hands as huge as his would bruise such tender skin, his right thumb carefully brushed the dampness away.

She recoiled instantly.

"Don't." But the word was barely spoken as her eyes remained fixed on his face.

In the early-morning shadows, he was even more commanding than she'd remembered. The broad shoulders, powerful biceps and firm stance were nothing short of fascinating. His blue eyes were set in a hard, square face. There was nothing polished or refined about him, she concluded. No carefully tailored clothes or padded suits, either. No drowning cologne or overgelled hair. Just a man, clear and simple, without apology or guile. Oh, no, this man was nothing like her ex-husband. She had found only fear and despair with Johnny Waller. He'd used her body, leaving her cold and ashamed. She didn't think her pulse had ever raced for him. She didn't remember ever noticing his eyes or wanting to run her hands through his hair. She'd never looked at him and felt this deep yearning twist right in the heart of her stomach.

Nervously she licked her lips, looking away. She wanted to run. There was no way she was going to be able to do this. No way she was going to be able to be around this man and stay sane. Oh, why wouldn't he just go away, out of her life, out of her house, out of her dreams.

"Did you sleep okay?" Sam attempted to say from the doorway, his sudden interruption jerking her back from the turmoil.

She struggled for an easy reply. "As well as can be expected. And yourself?"

He merely nodded, watching her with sharp eyes. There were shadows under her eyes to go with the tear tracks on her cheeks. It appeared that Ms. Chenney Pegauchi wasn't as cold as he wanted to believe. Apparently, she'd had a rather long night. Once again he felt the uncomfortable pangs of remorse. He didn't want to hurt her, but truly there was no help for it. Dawn was breaking and it was time to get to work. The child needed Sam and Sam needed María. Simply put, she would have to help him.

"Have you given my proposition any more thought?" he asked carefully.

A great deal too much, she thought. Outwardly, she just nodded.

"And?" he prodded.

Once more she looked away, her eyes searching the room for some kind of answer. The blackened walls offered none. She'd come here looking for sanctuary. It was gone now. Somehow, some way, she'd have to find the strength to deal with that.

"Do you really think you can save this child?" she asked finally.

"Yes."

She looked at him with knowing black eyes. "I don't believe you," she said flatly.

"I'll save him," Sam replied just as levelly. "So are you in?"

"I don't want to go through it again," she told him honestly. "I don't know that I can take it a second time. Can you understand that?"

He nodded. "Yes, but it will be different this time," he told her quietly. "This time, it will all work out."

She smiled bitterly.

"That's what they said last time. 'We'll find him, ma'am. Don't worry, ma'am. He's out there somewhere, ma'am.' I believed them, the investigators, the police, the FBI agents. Right up to the time I identified the body at the morgue, I believed them. You can't imagine it, Mr. Mathers," she said abruptly. "You can't imagine the horror of losing your own son. You can't know what it's like to do everything and *still* fail. You just can't imagine."

He shook his head at that. "You'd be surprised," he said softly, more to himself than her.

She didn't hear, anyway, she was too lost in the memories she just couldn't seem to escape. Daniel. The other missing child. Daniel.

But there was another missing boy out there somewhere. Was he crying for his mommy, was he waiting for the nightmare to end? She closed her eyes against the pain. *Running wasn't finding, hiding wasn't living.*

She'd promised herself she'd never go through pain like that again. She liked her nothing life. Undisturbed save for the nights when especially strong storms blew through the mountains. Save for nights when the thunder rolled and her soul yearned for something more.

She wanted to hide. She wanted to reach out. She wanted to remain dispassionate. But it was too late. She already cared.

"I don't like you," she said finally in the early dawn. "I don't like you for coming here and I don't like you for putting me through this. But by God, you had better live up to your billing, Mr. Mathers. You had better be the best damn investigator there is. Because that child needs you, and I don't think I could survive a second failure."

"Then you're in," he affirmed softly.

Slowly, she nodded her head.

He felt a small ripple of triumph flash through him, but didn't dwell on it. He'd secured her agreement. That was good. But it was also just the first of many hurdles to come. The clock was still ticking, the race was on. He wasn't a fool, the journey would be a hard one. It would be especially difficult for her, he imagined, after everything she'd been through. And it would be difficult for himself, as well, he decided, spending so much time with her. Abruptly he clamped down on the thought. So she was a beautiful woman. It didn't have to mean anything. He was a man on a mission, and not some young, rutting fool.

It was the child that mattered.

"Then," he said curtly, "we need to get ready to go, because it's six-thirty now, and we've got a lot of ground to cover. This isn't any joyride, princess. I'll warn you now, I'm going to push you like you've never been pushed before. I want to visit the site where the child was taken. I want to interview all possible witnesses—family and friends—and I want to do it all this afternoon. We've only got a few days, so you'd better be prepared to move fast. A lot of the time you'll be sleeping on the ground and eating while you walk. I'll expect you to pull your own weight. I don't have the time or tolerance for any less. You understand?"

She smiled wanly, some of her spirit beginning to return now that the decision had finally been made. "You make a hell of a partner, Sam Mathers. Sweet-talk me anymore and I'll quit right now."

"Just so long as you understand."

"Oh, I understand all right. Don't worry, this 'rich heiress' won't be causing you any trouble. I can take care of myself."

He had his doubts about both those comments, but he kept them to himself. The important part was that he had her agreement. The second day was dawning, and the search was on.

Chapter 4

Having secured María's agreement, Sam's first order of business was to take a quick bath. Exploration revealed, however, only one cold mountain stream for the task. It would at least keep him from lingering, he thought with gritted teeth. Pulling his clothes off, he set the travel bar of soap he'd brought with him on the bank, and then grimly plunged in.

His teeth were already beginning to chatter as he picked up the soap and began lathering up, his back to the path that had led him to the stream. His concentration was focused on shutting out the water's freezing temperature and thus he didn't hear the footsteps coming from behind him.

María froze on the bank of the stream, her own bar of soap firmly in hand as her wide eyes registered the distinctly naked man in her stream.

He was now dunking his head deep into the stream, throwing it back and causing water droplets to fly out like crystal rainbows in the early-morning sun. His back glistened with moisture that beaded and sluiced across rippling muscles. She could see the clear definition of his pectorals, and just beneath the waving water, the taut outline of his buttocks.

Her mouth went dry, her eyes opening wider with the shock. In her stomach, she felt a deep, unwanted stirring. He was magnificent. Basic. Hard. Uncompromisingly, unapologetically, male. Very, very male.

And then he turned around.

He just looked at her for a moment, recognizing even at this distance the slight erratic movement of her chest, the glazed look of her eyes. His own reaction was a brief, primitive surge of male pride. She, the princess, she wanted *him*.

His body reacted instantly, and her round eyes couldn't keep from registering the change.

It was much too hot, she thought weakly, trying hard to swallow but not quite able to manage. From the front, he was even more incredible. She'd never seen such muscles. They weren't overdeveloped, but sharply defined, from the bulge of his biceps to the rippling washboard of his stomach—

This shouldn't be affecting her, she tried telling herself rationally as she stood mesmerized on the bank. She'd seen plenty of naked male models as an art student. Not to mention the fact that she'd been married for two years. She'd even been a mother, for God's sake. But still, she couldn't quite tear her eyes away. Couldn't quite run even when the last logical command of her mind ordered her to do so.

Suddenly, crazily, she had the urge to step forward—just three or four steps would do it—and run one long finger down his glistening chest. How would those water droplets taste on her tongue?

As if knowing, Sam stepped forward, as if heading out of the stream.

The fear reared hard, panic flooding through her in a surge of desperate adrenaline. She wasn't supposed to be doing this. She wasn't supposed to be feeling such things. Not her.

"No," she ground out. He stopped instantly.

"Princess," Sam growled darkly from the stream, his own desire sparked hot by the low burn of her eyes, "if you really mean that, then I suggest you stop looking at me like some gourmet meal. Or I may just choose to ignore your words and follow your eyes, instead."

She managed to take a step back this time.

"What are you doing here?" she demanded breathlessly.

"What the hell does it look like? I'm trying to take a bath."
He could still see the flush of her cheeks, still see the way the sharp intake of her breath pulled her blouse tight across her

chest. And the look in her eyes... No man should have to withstand such things.

"You should have told me," she said sharply, her confusion giving way to anger. "If you'd really wanted privacy, you should have said something."

"And," he retaliated sharply in frustrated desire, "if *you'd* really wanted to give me some privacy, you would've turned around and left after seeing me here."

"I...I was going to," she stammered out.

"Well, sweetheart," he drawled slowly, "I don't see anyone stopping you now."

She flushed darkly, feeling the mortification and outrage flood through her all at once. She tried to speak, but there were no words to defend herself. He was right. She should have just walked away. Why hadn't she? Why hadn't she listened to the sanity that had gotten her through all these years? What in the world was she doing ogling some man who was nothing but trouble and probably a great deal worse?

"Go away," she managed at last, her voice barely a whisper.

Sam gave her a twisted smile from the stream. "You seem to be saying that a lot," he replied evenly, not quite willing to let the matter drop. "But I'm afraid I can't oblige you. We're working together now, remember?"

From the embankment, María made a small strangled sound. For the first time the impact of her decision hit her. Six days. He had estimated six days. Six days looking for the child. Six days in Sam's company. Which meant being together day and *night*. No. No, no, no. She couldn't do it. She wasn't cut out for this. She was meant to live alone, to be alone, to remain alone. Isolated. Unfeeling. Uncaring.

What had she done?

Too late now, the voice whispered. *You already agreed. Six days. Six nights.*

She swallowed heavily, and once more felt dread burn low in her stomach. Such a fool. She'd promised herself never again. She'd promised herself a future of safe isolation. And now here she was, staring at a naked man who made her feel things she shouldn't feel and agreeing to help find a child she knew couldn't be found—at least not in time.

She turned around, willing the yearning to stop twisting her insides. She *didn't* want this. She didn't want *him*.

Clutching her soap tightly, she strove for sanity. She kept her back safely to him and asked, "Shouldn't we be leaving soon? I thought you were in a hurry."

Behind her in the stream, Sam's desire was fast dissipating under the impact of the cold water. Actually, he shouldn't have reacted to her at all. It wasn't as if women hadn't gazed upon him before with blatant eyes. But it had been different seeing it in *her* eyes. Eyes so dark. Eyes that were normally so damn controlled. For a minute, just a minute, he'd broken the control of the heiress.

Not that it meant anything, he acknowledged to himself. This was business. Strictly business. And it wasn't going to be easy business to be so close to such a beautiful woman day and night. Especially if she looked at him like that again.

Even the thought caused a faint stirring, and his jaw muscles clenched tightly to keep control. He would *not* let her get to him.

Finding his voice, he ground out, "The sooner we get going, the better."

He started sloshing his way to the bank.

At the first sound of his approaching steps, María didn't wait any longer. This time she did listen to the sane part of her mind, and fled.

Sam returned to the house just ten minutes later, finding María already busy puttering around in the kitchen.

"Are you hungry?" she asked stiffly as he walked in. She'd settled for a sponge bath, using her well water, but it seemed the brisk sponging still hadn't managed to cool the fire in her cheeks. The image of his naked chest was too raw in her mind, and she was careful to keep her eyes averted. Unfortunately, judging by his slanted look, he was only too aware of her thoughts.

"Yes," he responded easily, pulling out a wooden chair from the table. Swinging a leg over it, he settled down casually. "Can I do anything to help?" he asked.

She shook her head. "It's not much—" she dished up something from her black kettle into a wooden bowl "—but it'll have to do."

"It looks good," he offered as he accepted the bowl. However, it also didn't look like anything he was familiar with. He picked up a fork, then, on second thought, he exchanged the fork for a spoon. "What is it?" he asked as he finally settled on a utensil.

"Choclo," she informed him curtly, dishing up her own bowl while still avoiding his eyes. "It's just corn in a cream sauce."

He tried it, chewing thoughtfully for a minute. It was fairly simple, but he liked it. He complimented her on it, but she was still busy ignoring him even as as she sat down.

"So," she said between spoonfuls, "what *is* your great plan?"

"I want to start at the site of the kidnapping," he replied briskly, glad to get to the matter at hand. "I'd like to interview the family, go over the scene. I'm hoping that I might be able to pick up the trail, or at least gather a few clues. It's been a week, so that could make matters more difficult, but we have to start somewhere. That's where you come in," he added, looking across the table. "I understand most of the Indians here speak Quechua, so I'll need you to translate. I'm proficient in Spanish, at least, so there's a chance I can pick up some of it. But it would probably be best if you asked the questions, since you can speak their language and you're also one of them. Before we get to the site, I'll go over the kind of information I'm interesting in getting."

María swallowed, looking down at her corn and feeling her appetite disappear. She was supposed to ask questions. Ask anguished mothers, anguished questions. She set her fork down for good, and stared at the wall.

"When was the child taken?" she forced herself to ask.

"Seven days ago."

"Where?" It was barely a whisper now.

Sam didn't answer. Instead he pulled a map out of his back pocket, cleared a spot on the table and spread it out.

"Where the red dot is," Sam told her, indicating with his fingertip.

She looked away from the wall, studying the map instead for a long moment. "But that's just the other side of the hill."

"Is it?" he said nonchalantly. Beside him at the table, her face had gone several shades paler, and her eyes were beginning to look drawn. Once again he was reminded of just how raw her wounds still were. And once again, he was confronted with the other side of the haughty princess—the beaten mother. Suddenly he felt distinctly uneasy about this. Perhaps she'd been right the night before, perhaps he really should just leave her in peace. What right did he have to put her through this?

Abruptly, he remembered how she'd looked this morning, answering the door in her white cotton nightgown, her eyes shadowed, the tear tracks still fresh on her cheeks. Just for a minute, he'd wanted to reach out and gently trace the curve of her cheek. Just for a minute, he'd wanted to guide her head to his strong shoulder, for the look in her eyes had clearly indicated that, already, she had suffered too much.

He'd wanted to hold her. He'd wanted to stroke her hair. He'd wanted . . .

The intensity of his emotions startled him, and he curled his hand into a fist on the table. He wasn't a sentimental man, and he certainly wasn't one to get drawn in so easily. No, he'd learned the lessons of his father too well. Abe Mathers had let himself be taken in. He had bared his soul to the frail hope of love . . . and had let Sarah Mathers walk all over him. No way would the son follow in his father's footsteps.

"There are other dots," María was saying, pointing to the map. "What are they?"

Keeping the image of his father before him, he slowly relaxed his hand and managed to reply, "The other kids."

Her face paled another shade. He could see the faint motion of her throat as she tried to swallow. "And?" she asked thickly. "What happened to them?"

He didn't want to say the words, but she had a right to know what she was up against. The sooner she understood the odds, the sooner she could help him beat them. That child out there needed them. He had to remember that.

"We have reason to believe those kids are already dead," he said evenly. "One of them turned up in Florida just a few days ago." Once more he paused, then he decided to just get it all out at once. "She was missing a few organs," he finished.

Her reaction wasn't quite what he'd expected. She didn't pale further, she didn't faint. Instead her face went abruptly blank, almost like a television that had just been snapped off. And in the black depths of her eyes he could find neither anger nor fear. He found only an intense emptiness that worried him far more.

"That's why you came here, isn't it?" she asked. "Because they really are just like Daniel."

"That's part of it," he admitted carefully.

She gave him the cool, dispassionate stare he was beginning to recognize as her defense against the horror she'd faced, was about to face again. "It won't be any different this time, no matter what you claim," she said. "I told you. I tried everything before. Cops, private investigators. Even the FBI. *And none of it worked.* They killed my son, and now they'll kill this child, too."

The near-prophetic certainty of her words was frightening. But he was a fighting kind of man, and he fought her words now, as he intended to fight the odds against him in the search.

"No," he told her firmly. "This time it *will* be different. *This* time, you and I are going to make sure it is." And he believed those words, because he *had* to believe. Because he had to win this time, if only because he'd lost before. The familiar picture of Laura McCall in her little pink jumpsuit rose unbidden in his mind. She'd been found lying on the cold warehouse floor. The price of failure, the penalty for tardiness. He'd been too late, and it haunted him still. Though Laura had been his only failure, it was one too many. He would not allow it to happen again.

"Then you're a fool," María said abruptly, interrupting his thoughts as she suddenly got up from the table. "And I'm a bigger fool for even listening to you."

"We'll be bigger fools yet if we don't get going," he said evenly. "There isn't much time."

"And just how do you plan on getting around?" she quizzed with an arched brow. "I thought your car was broken."

"We'll have to take your car," he said, "given the condition of mine."

"Sure," she replied flippantly as she took the kettle down from its supports. "Would you like to take the Porsche or the Mercedes?"

"The Mercedes?" he said hesitantly.

She gave him a twisted smile. "Why certainly, sir. It's parked behind the mansion, by the servants' quarters."

He looked at her for a moment. Somehow, he should have guessed this was coming. Certainly none of her living conditions had held up to expectations.

"Surely you have transportation of some kind?" he asked, feeling the first hint of impending doom.

She nodded. "Yes, they're called my feet. Look, you have two as well."

He swore softly under his breath. He honestly hadn't antic-ipated this at all. "How about a bus? Is there one we can catch?"

"Only at the bottom of the hill," she said. "That would en-tail a good three hours' walk just to reach the bottom, then another hour to ride around to the other side of the hill. Once there, of course, we'd have to walk back *up* the hill." She paused, then abruptly the sarcasm drained out of her. "Actu-ally," she found herself saying, "from here, it's probably much faster just to walk over the top of the mountain."

He sighed, but nodded grimly. Once again he was being de-layed, and, once again, he couldn't afford the time.

Sixty seconds, Sam. If you'd just been sixty seconds sooner...

He forced the niggling whisper away, focusing his mind on the matters at hand.

"How long would that take?" he asked.

"Three hours. It would be hard, though. The mountain is very steep and the altitude here is incredibly high. Are you sure you're ready for that kind of trip?"

He raised an eyebrow. "Sweetheart," he drawled smoothly, "it's not *my* stamina I'm worried about."

She flushed and tilted her head, looking every inch the prin-cess. "I can take care of myself," she said haughtily. "I've been doing so for a long time now."

But as soon as the words were out, she felt the emptiness in-side her. *She was supposed to ask questions.* How? How could she ask the same questions she'd been asked all those years ago, knowing of the pain they caused? And worse, knowing how easy it was to raise false hopes, because you wanted to believe, *had* to believe that somehow it would all work out. And when it didn't...

And when it didn't— God, what had she done?

But there was no backing out. The man before her might as well be the devil, and she the poor innocent that had blindly sold her soul.

She turned away, no longer able to look at him. Mechani-cally, she retrieved her bowl and began to clean it.

Sam, having seen the look that entered her eyes, gave her a few last moments to compose herself. He turned his attention to folding back the map, knowing that all too soon she was simply going to have to deal with it. The clock was ticking, and they couldn't afford any more delays.

"All right, then," he said finally, tucking the map into the back pocket of his jeans. "It's time to go."

Her head remained high, but her cheeks were still pale. Right now, right this minute. So this was it. There was a moment of panic. She wasn't ready for this yet, she thought frantically. She wasn't ready to start absorbing the implications of a missing child just three hours from her own home. She wasn't ready to start questioning other mothers and feeling their anguish. She didn't want to go through it all again.

But already Sam was moving, looking at her with expectant eyes. She could only nod. This was it.

She kept herself busy after that. As long as she just kept *doing*, then she didn't have to think, didn't have to remember. Hadn't she learned that a long time ago? But it only took her and Sam fifteen minutes to finish putting the house to order and pack the necessary supplies. They didn't take much—there were miles to hike where their own body weight would be burden enough.

And then they were ready. For better or for worse, it had begun.

And already, she felt the pain.

They walked for nearly an hour before taking their first break. Despite being in excellent condition, both of them were breathing heavily.

"Next time—" María was gasping, as she bent and hung her head down by her knees "—next time we take the Mercedes."

Sam nodded easily, recovering his own breath. But he couldn't resist giving her a curious stare. "Why didn't you keep it?" he asked bluntly.

For a minute it looked as if she was going to frost over, or demand to know how *he'd* known that she'd owned one. But then she just shrugged. "It didn't go with the neighborhood."

"Well, you wouldn't have to worry about anyone stealing the hubcaps," he pointed out noncommittally.

"Actually, theft is one of the biggest problems here."

"So much for moving to the countryside to avoid all that."

She gave him a piercing look as she straightened up. "You seem to make a lot of generalizations, Sam Mathers. For your information, theft is fairly common around here. Some people even think there's a serious problem with lying, but I think it's more a matter of different perspectives. Not everything is what it may seem. This land is different. And the people, we are different, too."

"We?" he quizzed skeptically, taking in for the first time her deep purple skirt and white peasant blouse. "Do you really consider yourself to be one of the Indians? You may dress it, you may even try to live it. But face it, María, your entire life was spent in private jets and mansions. What do you really have in common with the people here?"

"I am one of them," she said proudly, her chin coming up squarely. "We share the same heritage, the same roots. My life was once different. But it isn't anymore. Wait until we meet the family. You'll understand then. I'm not the outsider here. You are."

Sam merely shook his head. "You can take the boy from the city," he quoted, "but you can't take the city out of the boy. You are who you are, María. Rich, spoiled, part of the elite. Simply changing your clothes doesn't change that."

Her black eyes flared, the anger biting in. "Are you always this charming?"

He shook his head. "I just call 'em as I see 'em," he told her.

"Well, perhaps you should try looking in other places."

For a moment, he had to forcefully hold back the sharp retort that jumped to his lips. "Look in other places?" His mind was suddenly filled with the picture of his mother. Sarah Mathers, walking out the door in the dusty Alabama twilight, her youngest son pleading for her to stay with plaintive cries, her husband simply watching with his sad, worn-out brown eyes. Then she was gone, never looking back, never coming back.

He pushed the picture away. It was the past, and it was over. Only the lesson remained.

"Come on," he said abruptly, "it's time to get going again."

It took them another two and a half hours to reach the small farm. It opened up in front of them unexpectedly as they broke through the pine forest. Sam could see the inevitable small field of corn arranged in careful rows, laid out on the mountainside. There was a gray mud house like María's, but its thatched roof was falling down, and he could see holes where the hard clay had broken off and not yet been replaced. There was another, smaller, hut that probably served as some type of shed, but the wooden door was swinging open on broken hinges. Not far off, a few lean pigs were tied to stakes by ropes leading from their necks.

It was a desolate picture, Sam thought, especially amid the lush fertility and brilliant colors of the land. It also brought back memories of another run-down shack in a dusty land and during a bitter time that was best forgotten. He closed his eyes for a moment to close off the memory, but when he opened his eyes again, the bleakness remained in their blue depths.

Suddenly his attention was diverted by a movement to his left. There was a young child just five feet away. Wearing a dark brown poncho with a gray felt hat, he blended right in with the dark backdrop of the forest. They all stared at one another for a long minute. But just as María was going to reach out a hand, the child bolted. He soon returned with a small woman, who gave Sam looks that were a combination of suspicion and fear. Except for the dark green skirt she wore with the white peasant blouse, she was dressed exactly like María. Her long black hair was braided down her back and tied with a brightly colored thong. She also had a good dozen strands of gold plastic beads around her neck. She turned immediately to María, speaking a few low but rapid words in Quechua.

María responded with a smooth flow of musical words, gesturing to herself, then Sam, and then to the woman. From the smattering of Spanish that was included, Sam could gather that María was introducing them to the woman. For the most part, though, the conversation took place in the Indian dialect.

Wanting to help ease the woman's fears, he took a small step forward as he introduced himself personally in Spanish. Upon stepping forward, however, he immediately became aware of the size difference. The woman was positively tiny, probably not an inch over four-eleven. María was significantly taller, but her slender build made it a great deal less threatening than Sam's own huge bulk. He felt like some giant trespassing through Lilliput, and began to understand one of the reasons for the woman's fear. He moved back then and concentrated instead on trying to make his two hundred pound frame seem small. It didn't exactly work, but at least the woman directed something at him in Spanish. Unfortunately, her thick accent made it hard for him to understand her.

"I want to help," he tried again in Spanish, "I want to help you find your child."

The woman glanced at María then, and María nodded her encouragement. Finally, the woman consented with a small nod. Beside her, the little boy watched with solemn black eyes.

"Ask her who saw the boy last, when and where," Sam instructed María softly.

More rapid words flowed, then María turned back, reciting the answers. "He went to sleep with the rest of his brothers and sisters last Wednesday. He got up before the rest, did a few chores, and that is the last they know."

Sam frowned. "Was he armed, with a knife, tool, anything?" he asked the woman directly in Spanish. She replied, but he couldn't understand all the words so María translated it for him.

"He had a small knife he sometimes carried, but that was found next to the bed. Nothing else is missing."

"What was he wearing?"

"She isn't sure," María said after a bit. "But over the top was a brown poncho, and his gray hat, boots, white pants and shirt are now gone. The garb is very typical, Sam. He was probably wearing the same as the child with her now. White pants, white shirt, gray hat, brown poncho if it's cold. Any male child would be wearing close to the same."

Sam sighed softly. So much for a distinctive description.

"And from where did he disappear?" he asked finally. "Do they know the spot?"

"No."

"Any favorite places he liked to go off to? Hobbies or friends?"

"She says her son liked to play in the fields," María said at last. "And there is a stream near here."

There was a longer exchange. Sam found out that the boy was nine years old, helped his father tend the farm, and that there were three other boys he liked to do things with, all of whom were accounted for. The boy also had six brothers and sisters. As the oldest, he had the most chores around the farm. He would often get up early to begin his duties.

But he didn't come in for breakfast that day, the woman told them. And he didn't come in for lunch. So she had sent her youngest to call for him. Maybe he'd fallen asleep under the trees. Maybe he'd forgotten the time. Her youngest had called and called, but the boy had not come.

Then it was night, the dark falling. Again the youngest son had called. Again her firstborn had not answered. She'd sent the child out again in the morning. And now every morning and every evening he went to call for his brother.

Perhaps the child was just lost, the mother ended hopefully. When he heard his brother's call, he would come. Perhaps even now, he was on his way home.

María could only nod. She no longer trusted herself to speak. She knew what it was like to build such false hopes. She knew what it was like to stay awake late into the night, trying to convince yourself that maybe he *was* just lost. That maybe even now, he was on his way back.

Unable to stand it anymore, she turned away and concentrated on staring at the pines through the thick blur of her gaze. Why had she done this to herself? Why had she forced herself to go through it all again?

Behind her she could hear Sam thank the woman in his rusty but competent Spanish. He promised the woman he would keep her informed if they learned anything. And finally, right before leaving, he turned to the mother one last time.

"God bless," he told her in Spanish. The woman nodded, and her eyes grew bright. Whether she was a Christian or not, María didn't know. Many of the Indians had been converted by various missionaries who had passed through, so it was possible. But she thought it rather odd, sweet, even, that Sam should do what he'd just done. But then she stiffened. It was best she didn't think about Sam *or* what they were doing. She didn't want to think about any of it. She just wanted to go back home.

There were no such luxuries. Instead, Sam took her to the three neighboring farms to question the friends of the boy. By the third interview, she was beginning to learn. If she just didn't look at the person too much . . . If she could just keep them as abstracts in her mind, as if she were talking to a radio or something, then it wasn't so bad. Then it was possible to keep the words steady, and her face dispassionate. Then it was possible not to hurt so much.

The three friends had little to add, except that they said the boy never talked about going to the city. He'd liked the farm, and the only place he'd talked of wanting to see was the San

Pablo lake on the other side of the hill. He'd heard it was even bigger than the river where they liked to go and play.

It meant little to María, but Sam asked for directions, and after thanking the three children, he headed straight down to the river. It was just fifteen minutes from the farm.

By now it was getting late and María was edgy and tense from the strain of the day. The mother's eyes had looked so sad and worn. Her mouth had trembled, and by the end of the questions she'd seemed to gain years. María understood those eyes. She understood the strain and she understood the kind of despair that aged a woman so suddenly. She understood all too well.

"What are we doing here?" she demanded to know once they arrived in the darkening forest around the river.

"We're looking for where Pedro disappeared," Sam said calmly.

"Don't call him that!" María said sharply.

Sam gave her a level look. "Why, does his name bother you?"

Instead of answering him, she merely replied, "It's just not necessary." With effort, she controlled the hysteria building within. "He's gone, his name isn't important."

"But it is for you, isn't it, María?" Sam asked with laserlike intensity. "Once he has a name, he becomes real, a living, breathing child. He's no longer just an abstract mission, he's a child who desperately needs us."

"Yes. I know," María said, and in spite of her efforts at control, her voice cracked. She looked down to find her hands fisted tightly at her sides. "Believe me, I know."

Sam watched her for a moment longer. Her face was truly pale in the fading light, and once more he felt the guilt gnaw at him. This really was hard for her; he imagined it must be like going through her own son's kidnapping all over again. Damn it. He should have left her behind—

He cut himself off. There was no going back. He needed her translating abilities, and there wasn't time to find anyone else. That was the way of it. Besides, he thought, trying hard to convince himself he was right, it had been five long years. Sooner or later she had to move back into the world.

"I don't know why you're looking for him here," María said. "It's just a river."

"Exactly," Sam said, turning his attention back to the river's bank. "You can't kidnap a child in the middle of an open field. Someone would notice. Especially a nine-year-old boy who would kick and scream and definitely put up a fight. But here, in a secluded, darkened forest..."

"But he was doing his chores," María pointed out. Her voice was beginning to get more unsteady, and she was having trouble swallowing as the picture he painted stood out starkly in her mind.

"True," Sam agreed with a nod. "But if you were a nine-year-old boy and you had finished a chore or two, where would you go to relax, have a little fun before the real work began? You could skip a few rocks, maybe climb a tree or take a quick dip..."

He didn't seem to be talking to her anymore, but more to himself as he slowly worked his way down to the very edge of the riverbank. María shivered. She could see it all. Nine-year-old Pedro walking down to the river. Perhaps he'd already skipped a stone or two, perhaps he'd just been looking for another when the men had come.

Come and snatched him. Just like Daniel.

For a minute she was overwhelmed. The feeling of near-hysteria built and built, clogging her throat, dimming her eyes....

The sky had been so clear that day when the call had come. She'd picked up the phone, not really expecting anything, for it had been a full week without any news at all. Already, Daniel had been gone a total of four weeks and three days. But the man on the other end had wanted her to describe Daniel for him. What had he been wearing that day? Any birthmarks?

By now she was used to the questions, as she had been asked them all before. Dutifully, she had answered. And when she'd finished, there had been a long pause, too long. The man had tried to clear his throat, but the words had been stuck. And then the feeling had come, the deep, ominous feeling of foreboding that had built within her with horrifying rapidity.

The day had been hot, much too hot. She'd had to open the windows on the Mercedes. The leather seat had stuck to her legs on the drive down, and she remembered wishing that she had worn pants instead of shorts. On the radio, they had played old fifties songs, the kind Daniel had liked but would have someday outgrown the way kids did. And the sun had been shining even as she had parked the car. It had been such a beautiful day.

Her tennis shoes had squeaked on the tiled floor of the building. It hadn't looked too bad on the outside. Tall, lots of windows, rather clinical-looking. But she'd had to take the elevator down. And the air-conditioning had been on too strong, it had made her shiver. Then the doors had opened, and the smell had hit her.

But even then, it hadn't seemed real. She wasn't the sort of person that had to go to morgues, wasn't the sort of person that went to identify bodies. Of course a mistake had been made. She would rectify it, and they would all move on.

And then they had rolled out the slab. Then she had seen . . .

"María!" a voice intruded loudly. "María! For God's sake, snap out of it!"

With a jerk her eyes snapped into focus, and the building was gone, as was the smell. She was back at the river, the water rushing by, the air pure and sweet with dusk. Sam abruptly released her shoulders.

"Are you all right?" he asked sternly.

"Of course," she said, but her voice was much too high, the hysteria still hovering on the edge. She felt the urge to reach out, to touch his hand, his shoulder, to prove to herself once and for all that he was truly real, that that day was truly over.

But she didn't because she was afraid that if she moved, she would shatter.

Sam was still there, staring at her with unfathomable blue eyes. His own pulse rate was still high, racing with the shock of turning around to see her staring at the river with eyes so filled with horror it had taken his breath away. He'd called her name, but she'd only shaken her head, too lost in some awful scene he couldn't begin to imagine. Even now her black eyes were still muddy with the past, rimmed by the shock. He was torn between shaking her again or simply pulling her close.

Shaking her seemed far safer.

She stopped him with a wave of her hand. "It'll pass," she said softly. "It always does."

Sam could only nod, standing inches away. "Daniel?" he asked simply.

"Yes," she whispered.

"Is it still that hard?" he asked.

"How can it ever be easy?"

"It's been five years," he pointed out softly.

She shook her head. "He was my son, my only son. I don't care if it was ten or twenty or even thirty years ago. He's still my son. He will always be my son."

Sam nodded. "I understand that. But sooner or later, you've got to let him go, María. Sooner or later, you've got to get on with your life."

She turned away from him. "How would you know?" she told him dully. "Do you have a son?"

"No," he said evenly, "but I know what it's like to lose someone close to you. Come on, María, we all lose someone we love sooner or later. The trick is not letting it ruin your life, too. The trick is doing something about it."

She scoffed lightly into the falling dusk. "What?" she said. "You want me to be like you? Jetting around like the Lone Ranger, butting into other people's problems, other people's pain, without any regard for how they might feel?"

His lips thinned at her words, for they were closer to the truth than he would've liked. "At least it changes some things," he replied evenly.

"Oh, yes," she agreed grandly. "It changes some things, all right. It means I can't sleep through the nights anymore. It means I've got to go through the whole damn experience all over again. The hoping, the caring, the waiting, the praying. The pain. *All over again.* Thanks a million."

"It won't be like that this time," he insisted stubbornly. "This time, it's going to end differently. It has to."

"Yeah," said María, but the sarcasm was draining out of her words to be replaced by exhaustion. "That's what you say. But that doesn't make it so."

For a long moment there was a pause, and then, without even knowing he was doing it, Sam walked closer to María and turned her to face him. His hand came up and gently tilted her chin until her eyes met his.

"Believe *me,*" he told her softly, intensely. "Believe *I* can do it."

"Don't you get it yet?" she asked sadly. "That's exactly what I'm telling you. I can't believe. I just can't."

"Then there's no pain for you to worry about," he said abruptly and his hand dropped back down to his side as he turned away, "because, princess, you're already dead."

He walked away from her then, leaving her standing in the middle of the riverbank, alone and silent. She didn't call him back, didn't try to argue his words. Instead she just stood there, feeling the emptiness grow and burgeon inside of her until it was all-encompassing.

She stood on the riverbank as the muddy waters flowed by, stood on the riverbank where Pedro had vanished, stood on the riverbank as Pedro and Daniel seemed to merge and tangle into one boy, lost, wanting his mother.

But she'd already failed Daniel. She'd brought him into the world, nurtured him, loved him...and then failed him all in the span of just five years. She'd promised him she would take care of him, promised he would be safe forever. She had lied.

Now Pedro was gone, another little boy swallowed up by the monsters that weren't just hiding under the bed or in the closet. And she couldn't just kiss the boy's forehead, soothe his brow and the monsters would go away.

This time they were real.

She'd tried to fight them before, she'd tried to fight them with her fame, with her fortune, with her overwhelming love of her precious child. But they had won, and in doing so, they had destroyed her.

Slowly, she began walking again. She didn't know how else to fill the void.

Chapter 5

Night had fallen completely by the time Sam called off their search. Without a flashlight to see by, there was little more they could do. So far the day had not been too productive. If the riverbank was indeed the spot where Pedro had been kidnapped, then the trail must already be too cold, for he couldn't find any traces of evidence. He'd hoped for a few clues. Perhaps footprints to tell him how many people were involved. Or maybe tire tracks, fabric pieces, anything to start giving him a grip on just who was doing it and how. Instead, he'd found nothing.

Now, hindered by the rapidly approaching night, Sam turned his attentions to finding them a place to sleep for the night. María's footsteps were dragging from the lengthy walking stint, though she hadn't complained. In spite of himself, he was impressed.

"Well," he said at last as he turned to her, "we might as well find a place to stay. In the morning, I'd like to finish going down the hill so we can catch a bus and cover real ground. Can you think of any place we might be able to stay between here and the bottom?"

She shook her head, too tired for words.

"Do you want to walk back over the top of the hill to your place and then catch a bus from there?"

Three more hours of walking. Again, she shook her head.

He nodded. "Well then, it looks like we might as well camp here."

He spread his arms expansively to include the small clearing in the pine forest where they were currently standing. To one side ran a thin river, adequate to get water for boiling. It was a fair site, all things considered, María decided, and frankly, she desperately needed the rest. The day had been far more grueling than she'd imagined after all these years of solitude. Already images of the tormented mother and the lost little boy were again swirling around in her mind. She wanted to shut them out once and for all. She wanted to return to the peace of her ignorance, return to her sheltered existence.

But there was no going back anymore. And the future continued to scare her. What if they didn't find the boy? What if the monsters won once more? What if—

Unconsciously her hands came up and rubbed her temples. Five feet away, Sam watched the gesture, his face grim in the night.

She was suffering, he could see the strain all over her face. And it tore at him. He wanted the haughty heiress back. He wanted the sharp, icy woman of before. He couldn't stand to see her like this, especially since he knew that he was responsible. She'd been right from the start. He hadn't really known what he was asking from her when he'd bullied her into joining. He'd thought of only his mission.

But it was an important mission, he reminded himself stubbornly. Yes, it was, would, be hard for her, but neither of them had much choice.

None of which quite stopped the guilt, however, as he began to gather wood for the fire. Guilt which was compounded all the more when, without one word of complaint, she began clearing an area for their camp.

No, she wasn't what he'd been expecting at all.

Working together, it only took them twenty minutes to establish a camp. María built a circle of small stones for the fire, while he collected the wood. Then as he arranged the fire, she gathered up two piles of leaves to spread their blankets over for sleeping. She also drew water into a small clay pot she'd brought and boiled it for coffee.

Finally, Sam found a larger log and pulled it up for them to sit on. All the work done, they found themselves forced to face each other once more.

"There's a little food left," María said finally. "A bit of jerky, some bread, I think. You can have it if you'd like."

Sam frowned. Frankly, in her current drawn state she looked like she needed the food far more than him. Besides being pale, traces of dust now streaked her cheeks from all the walking. And long tendrils of her hair had escaped from the confines of her braid to curl around her face. She definitely looked like she could use a good hearty meal, not to mention a good night's rest. Besides, Sam concluded inwardly, he'd taught himself long ago to do without much food or rest.

"It's okay," he told her, indicating the food. "You can have it."

Far from being grateful, she stiffened beside him. Oh, no, she didn't want to accept any special treatment from this man. She liked it far better when she could view him as some arrogant, insensitive clod, crashing through her life. Hating him was the only consolation she had in this whole mission. Besides, she understood anger. It was safe, far safer than the other things that sometimes tightened her stomach.

"That's not necessary," she replied evenly. "You can have the food."

He looked at her sharply in the night. Funny, most women he knew would have gratefully accepted it. Instead, she looked as if he'd insulted her. Treading carefully now, for he really didn't want to upset her any more than she already was, he tried to reach a compromise.

"How about we split it?"

With a curt nod, she concurred. The food truly was a pitiful amount, however, when she drew it out of the backpack. It had been a long time since she'd been around a man, and in all honesty, María had underestimated just how much a man could eat when she'd done the packing. Now, looking at the handful of jerky and bread, then at Sam's solid frame, she knew the whole amount would never be enough to sustain him, let alone half. Then, when she tried to take a bite of her share, the bread seemed like ashes in her mouth, and the jerky like lead. Finally, she handed it all to him, and settled for sipping the coffee.

Beside her, Sam watched with a worried frown on his face. He stuck to his share of the food, wanting her to eat her part. She really needed to keep up her strength. Tomorrow was going to be another long day.

As if sensing his thoughts, María asked finally, "What do we do tomorrow?" Her eyes were focused on the flickering flames of the small campfire.

Sam was quiet for a moment, contemplating the matter himself.

"There are the families of the other missing children," he said at last. "One is not too far away. I'd like to talk to them."

She gave a twisted smile in the night.

"Why?" she challenged softly. "What can they really tell you? They'll be just like the mother today, worried, heartsick. But they're not detectives. Children aren't even kept on tight leashes here—where can they possibly wander off to? They won't know anything. And you'll just rub raw wounds and raise false hopes by showing up at their homes."

He saw her point, but he shook his head, anyway. "They don't have to know a lot, María. Just something here or there. A person they maybe remember seeing in the area. Something out of the ordinary that day. Any little detail like that can provide a lead."

"I don't like it," she whispered.

He was silent, what could he say? She'd be better in the morning, he told himself. A night to sleep on it would do her good. She'd come around. In the meantime, he sought to change the subject.

"We should try to get some transportation. Walking around on foot is too time-consuming, and buses are too unreliable. Also, I need a phone."

For the first time that evening she showed a spark of life. She tilted her head to give him a sideways look. "Why do you need a phone?" she challenged.

Actually, he needed to check in with his assistants, not to mention Russell O'Conner. But he had no intention of telling her that. Confidentiality was the mainstay of his profession, especially considering the fact that O'Conner had told him specifically not to mention his name. Instead, Sam simply shrugged his broad shoulders.

"Just need to make a few calls, that's all."

She wanted to argue, she discovered suddenly. Yes, she wanted to prod and push until he finally exploded into a full-scale rage. She wanted the anger, for surely it was better than the dead hollowness that weighted her down now. She wondered if he could understand something like that. Understand that anger was the only emotion she truly understood anymore. It was sharp, cleansing, in its own way. Certainly it was better than pain. And definitely it was better than the fear.

She knew he wouldn't understand that. He thought she was afraid of the families, of the questions. And she was. But did he know how afraid she also was of him?

Did he have any idea how he looked right now, in the flickering light of the fire? Did he know how it rippled across the hard angles of his face, the curving muscles of his arm? Did he know how it made her stomach tighten and curl in ways it wasn't supposed to do anymore?

But she wasn't a woman who felt such things, she reminded herself flatly. As her husband had assured her many times, she had the sexuality of a peanut. No, she definitely couldn't be feeling these things, thinking these things. Especially not for a man like Sam Mathers, who seemed to view her with nothing but disdain.

But the words didn't stop her stomach from tightening again.

And it didn't stop the fear, either. He was too alive, she thought vaguely. Larger than life, sitting beside her in the cooling night. In short, he was everything she wanted to escape from.

Vitality. Energy. Passion.

"I want to know who you're calling," she challenged out loud.

He looked at her, seeing with surprise the sudden color that now highlighted her cheeks. Her eyes were no longer dead, but burning with some kind of intense fire. Her breath was shorter, too, he could see her chest rise and fall in small, waiting gasps.

His body reacted instantly, and with an urgency that caught him completely off guard. How did she do it? Go from a drawn, worn woman to a fiery Amazon in ten seconds or less? And would he ever learn how to deal with either of them?

Oh, yes. Yes, he wanted to learn to deal with this one right now. He wanted to reach out and drag her across the log until she landed hard against his chest. He wanted to bury his hands in the thick plait of her braid, freeing the silky strands until they enveloped them both in a thick, black mystery. And he wanted to tilt her head back and claim her lips—hard. He wanted to silence her, claim her, brand her all in one hot kiss. Until she forgot the past and the future and phone calls and questions. Until she thought of only him, and all that latent passion he saw in her eyes burned only for him.

He wanted . . .

He swore inwardly, violently, his fists clenched abruptly at his sides, because for a minute he feared he might actually do it. Might actually reach across and fulfill every blazing thought burning through his mind.

And maybe she saw it all in his eyes, for suddenly her cheeks flushed even brighter. But unlike him, her hands weren't clenched into fists. Instead, her head was held high, and deep in the burning embers of her eyes he could see the challenge. And the waiting.

She was waiting to see what he would do.

He tore his gaze away, focusing abruptly on the thick dark green of the pine forest at night, dragging in huge gulps of cold night air to clear his senses.

He would not be a part of the madness. This was business. He knew all too well what a woman could do to a man if he wasn't careful. Control was the key. You could never give up control. He'd learned that well enough from his mother, and he wouldn't be forgetting it now.

"The phone calls are none of your business," he answered finally, his eyes still averted but his tone neutral enough.

María, however, was still wired. "I thought we were partners," she pointed out sharply.

"We are," he agreed easily. "But some information must remain confidential to fulfill the needs of my client."

"And who is your client?"

"That, of course, is part of the confidential information."

The answer did not make her happy. He could tell the minute he risked turning his head to see her eyes. She looked positively livid. Then abruptly, she stood.

"Fine," she said stiffly, though her eyes were far from submissive. "I'm going to bed now."

With that she turned and walked smartly away.

"Are those two blankets all there is?" he called out to her.

"They were all that would fit into the backpack," she returned over her shoulder. Already she had reached the first pile of leaves and was pulling up the blanket.

He frowned from where he was sitting on the log. The night was chilly, hammering home just how high up they were. He took in her short-sleeved blouse with a critical eye. No, one blanket certainly wasn't going to cut it.

"We'll have to sleep together," he said abruptly.

She stilled over the pile of leaves, her eyes growing wide. Almost immediately a dozen impressions of him assaulted her mind. The flickering shadows of the fire dancing over his muscled biceps. The rainbow sparkle of a cold mountain stream sluicing across his broad chest. Such a strong, powerful man. How would he feel, wrapped around her? Probably like sleeping with a fire itself, a strong molten fire of steel. And what would it be like to wake up, curled in such an embrace? How would it feel . . .

Her mouth went dry, and her breathing was much too fast.

She furiously shook her head. Turning around she stated adamantly, "I will not sleep with you." Then she brought up her chin for good measure.

He gave her a sardonic look from the firelight. "I'm not talking torrid passion here," he informed her curtly. "But the night's damn cold and we need to be practical. Two bodies together will stay warmer than two bodies apart."

She still shook her head stubbornly. Oh, no, she wasn't going to succumb that easily. She needed her distance. The families were hard enough to bear. She couldn't give in to this man as well. She wanted her isolation back. She wanted her nice, sterile existence. Mustering her strength, she drew her spine rigid.

"I . . . will . . . be . . . fine," she reiterated, each word slicing neatly out.

It was on the tip of his tongue to argue, but then he relented. Let the stubborn woman have her way. She'd see his point soon enough. He shrugged indifferently. "If that's what you want," he told her.

She nodded curtly. "Good night, Mr. Mathers."

"Good night, María."

As he'd suspected the air continued to cool. And just a half hour later, he passed by her pile on the way to his own to see her shivering beneath the thin spread. His lips thinned and he sighed heavily. The princess wasn't going to like it, but she didn't have a choice anymore as far as he was concerned. Smiling grimly, he picked up his blanket and walked back to María's side.

"Move over," he said curtly.

"I most certainly will not," she objected. Even lying flat on her back, she managed to give him a withering glance.

"Don't be a fool," he said impatiently. "It's damn near freezing out here and body heat's about all we have."

"I will not sleep with you," she insisted.

"Don't flatter yourself," he snapped back, her stubbornness getting to him. "I'm giving you ten seconds to move over or I'll pick you up and do it myself. One, two..."

She glared at him mutinously. Pride demanded that she argue, but the chattering of her teeth would hardly make it convincing. She didn't want him next to her, but she truly was freezing.

"Eight, nine..."

With one last glare, she moved reluctantly over. He ignored her look, lying down on the right and throwing the blanket over them both.

At first she tried to keep herself completely to the left, not touching him at all, but with a growl, he rolled over, wrapped one powerful arm around her and pulled her abruptly against his hard length.

"I believe you're missing the point," he grumbled in her ear. "Now go to sleep."

But for María, that was easier said than done. It seemed only a matter of minutes before his breathing slowed to the rhythmic sound of sleep, but she stayed awake and rigid for a long time after that.

It had been ages since she'd slept with a man. Ages since she'd felt the hard warmth of a man's body burning through the thin layers of her clothes. Johnny had certainly never held her like this. He'd been one to do his thing and roll back over to sleep within minutes afterward. In the beginning she'd minded. After a month of silently enduring his panting and pawing, she'd been grateful.

She'd been a virgin when she'd married Johnny, and after the horrid experiences he'd given her, she didn't plan on ever suffering through the act again. Johnny must have been right that she had no sex drive, because she certainly didn't miss it. At least it had given her Daniel. For that, she would have gone through anything.

Yet lying here against this man was completely different. She'd been afraid of that. His body possessed a toned ruggedness, a rippling strength. Frankly—and she tried to tell herself this was just the artist in her—his body was beautiful. But lying against him, she wasn't thinking of models or painting. No, instead she was feeling the corded muscles, the burning strength. She was feeling the heavy brand of his arm wrapped tight against her stomach. And, once again, the strange yearning in her stomach was growing.

Lying in the dark, freezing night, the stars clear overhead, the trees swaying with the faint wind, she bit down on her lower lip and willed the yearning to go away. But even then, it was nearly an hour before she slept.

A light sleeper, Sam jerked awake at the first sound, but it took him a fraction of an instant longer to orient himself. Then it took a minute more to realize that the sounds were coming from the woman next to him.

The princess was crying.

For a moment he felt the usual torn confusion. Tears made him suspicious; he'd watched Sarah Mathers use them all too often to get her way. Tears called up compassion, for he'd seen others mourn in genuine pain. But what about this woman, the one curled so softly in his arms?

He didn't know. Then he realized she was still sleeping. Lightly, he shook her shoulder.

"Wake up, María," he whispered gruffly. "Come on, sweetheart, wake up."

But she only burrowed herself closer against him, unconsciously seeking the warmth of his frame, the strength of his arms. Without thinking, his hand came up and gently stroked her hair. He could feel the trembling of her slender build against his body, feel the force of her anguish. It tightened his mouth into a harsh line, and he felt a sudden overwhelming need to protect her.

Surely she was too small, too slight, to deal with such pain. How could such graceful shoulders carry such a heavy burden? He absorbed it all into his own powerful frame, comfort-

ing her with the rhythmic stroking of her hair as he gently tried
to wake her up.

"María," he said, a little louder this time. "Come on, María.
It's only a dream. Wake up."

Gradually the sound penetrated, and her eyes fluttered open.
The tears gave the black depths a vulnerable, opalescent glow
in the dim firelight.

"Are you okay?" he asked softly, temporarily mesmerized
by her eyes.

It was then she became aware of her position, huddled deep
into his arms, the tears still streaming down her face. She acted
on instinct, pushing herself back, hastily wiping away the tears.

For a moment, he felt a sudden sensation of loss at her rapid
departure. He shook his head against it.

"Sure," she was saying rapidly, sniffling loudly. "I'm okay.
Really."

But her eyes didn't look okay. They looked dark with pain
and a deep loss that tore at him. By nature he was a sucker for
people in pain. And even now, as he told himself this could all
be some feminine ruse, a part of him still wanted to reach out
and dry her tears. He steeled himself against the pull. Control,
Sam. Always stay in control.

But he hated to see her like this. *This* was all his fault. He'd
dragged her down into all of this. He'd made her come along.

Then again, he did know one way to jump-start her. Anger.
The little princess liked to fight.

"Bad dreams, princess?" he drawled out loud in his most
sardonic voice. "I imagine sleeping on the dirt isn't exactly your
style."

The tactic seemed to work for her spine stiffened immediately. Her chin came up and the tears dried quickly.

"Of course," she snapped back, matching his sarcasm. "I
never sleep in the dirt and I certainly never sleep with men like
you."

In spite of the fact that he was the one to start the exchange,
he couldn't quite control his own reaction. The words cut, and
they cut deep. Once more she was the heiress, and he the common laborer. All of a sudden, the words were leaping out on
their own. "Well now, princess, you weren't complaining about
sleeping with me a few minutes ago. Why, you were fairly curl-
ing up against me and purring like a cat. Then, of course, I
seem to recall a certain lady watching me bathe by the river-

bank. And I'll tell you, your eyes weren't complaining then, either."

She gasped, sputtering for words. The dream was forgotten, the emptiness in her stomach gone. All she could feel was the anger. By God, she would show him. "The only reason you're beside me now is because you insisted upon it," she retorted sharply. "Not to mention that *you* are the one who barged into *my* life. How dare you even suggest that I might want you here. I don't!"

"I don't know," he drawled back as her eyes flashed darkly just inches away. "You sound too defensive to me, and you know what they say about women and protesting."

"Enough!" she roared, struggling now to untangle herself from the blankets so she could leap to her feet. "You are the most overbearing, insensitive, inconsiderate, rude man I have ever had the displeasure to meet! I do not like you!"

His hand whipped out to grab her wrists, halting her rise from the leaf bed. Eyes a steely blue, they were just inches from hers. His voice dropped down to a dangerous whisper. "I already told you, sweetheart, it doesn't matter if you like me at all. And it doesn't matter if I am a rude, overbearing man, because we're not in any mansion, princess. And this certainly isn't any cocktail party. All that matters is that I'm the best damn private eye there is. At least you'd better hope so, or your sleep won't be getting any better after this."

His retort silenced her abruptly, her eyes growing wide once more with the shock. She turned away. Still, he noted with pleasure that she didn't wilt this time. Instead, her face settled, her shoulders squaring with a grim composure that was somehow as hard to watch as the horror that had shone from her eyes earlier that evening.

"I haven't slept well for five years," she said softly. "Do you have any idea just how long five years can be?"

The simplicity of the words shook him. They weren't words of pity, nor even words of pain. They hung on the air between them as a bare statement. It cut him far deeper than mere sobs would have done. Abruptly his anger was gone, and he felt vaguely ashamed at how he'd let his own tactics get out of hand. He'd thought to fight her pain with anger, but how could you undo five years of damage?

"I know," he found himself saying. He let go of her wrists, allowing her to relax once more in the makeshift bed. She remained apart, the cool night air slivering between them.

"Did you ever have a child?"

He shook his head.

"There's nothing quite like it," she told him, her voice still quiet and sure. "There are no words to describe the feeling of your own son wrapping his arms around your neck and smiling, calling you Mommy. The trust given by one's child is so absolute, the love so pure, that it staggers one. And if you should ever fail that child . . . Well, it's just too much to bear."

She smiled wryly, just inches away. "But then again, I guess that must be hard for you to understand."

He nodded, though in truth he did understand. He understood far more than she realized. Joshua had been his brother, not his son, but it had been Sam who had taken care of him, getting him food, trying to get him medication. Sarah Mathers had been too enraptured with herself and her plans to make it big to bother with the petty details of raising children. And when she'd walked out on them all, it had been Sam who'd held Joshua, trying to console the broken child. Just as years later, it had been Sam who had dug the grave.

Yes, he knew how it felt to fail. Joshua, little Laura McCall. He knew all too well. And once again it was disconcerting to realize all that he had in common with this woman. He'd thought to keep her away from him. He'd thought she would be just another rich bitch, like so many others he'd met. Instead, she wasn't quite like any woman he'd known. He wasn't sure whether he should be suspicious or relieved.

Who was she, really?

His sharp detective's gaze scanned her once more, searching for the slightest sign of subterfuge or falsehood. But all he could see was the clear depths of black eyes. They were still slightly shiny from the tears, still slightly soft from the pain, but mostly they were clear and true in the night.

Beguiling eyes.

All at once he was painfully aware of just how close she was to him. And how she'd felt, soft and warm, in his arms in that one waking moment before consciousness struck them both. She was such a beautiful woman, delicate and strong and curved in all the right places.

Unconsciously, he reached down and drew the covers up over her. And when he smoothed the blanket back up to her neck, it seemed almost accidental that his fingers should linger on the delicate slope of her shoulders.

From there they found their own way to the curve of her cheek, lightly stroking the silky skin. Her eyes grew darker, but she didn't pull away. Instead, her lips trembled just a few inches away, and his thumb found them, too.

Soft, like rose petals against his callused fingers. Full. Lush. Made to be kissed, to be crushed, to be tasted. He found himself leaning slightly closer, and her breath accelerated slightly to come out in tiny gasps.

She was hypnotized by his eyes, unable to pull away, just watching, waiting. Closer, he came, and her eyes watched with half fear and half anticipation while her stomach clenched once more in its relentless ache. *Yes,* whispered a small part of her. *Oh, yes.* But the rest of her was rigid with dread. She'd never liked this before. Closer. Just one more—

The night wind swept up, snapping them both with its chilling bite, clearing the desire suddenly from Sam's gaze. He blinked his eyes like a man recovering from a spell. He'd really been about to kiss her, his mind registered in shock. He had really been about to kiss the princess.

And she'd been about to let him.

Once more he felt a surge of primitive satisfaction even as he pulled abruptly away. He couldn't kiss her. He couldn't get involved. It would distract him at a time when he couldn't afford distractions. Never give up control for a woman, Sam. Never give up control, he reminded himself intensely.

María watched him pull back, and felt the sharp tug of disappointment. For a moment, she couldn't meet his eyes. He must know that she wanted him to kiss her. And yet he hadn't. He'd pulled away.

She truly was a fool. Rolling over, she gave him her back. It was as much contact as she could bear.

"Go to sleep," Sam told her gruffly when he could finally speak. "Tomorrow is going to be a long day."

She didn't argue. She just nodded her head and sank back down into their forest bed, her body rigid and uncomfortably aware next to his. The emptiness ripped through her. Why had he pulled back?

I don't go for your kind.

Johnny had been right. She wasn't pleasing to a man, or at least not enough to influence the great Sam Mathers. Unexpectedly, tears burned her eyes once more. She squeezed her eyes shut, willing them away. This is what she'd wanted, she told herself. To be left alone, to live alone.

Wasn't it?

The night had no answers, and the exhaustion was too deep. With a small sigh, she gave in to the seductive pull of slumber. Things were always better in the morning. Or so she'd told herself for five years. Five, long, lonely years.

Minutes later, she was asleep.

Sam watched her a bit longer, not quite able to take his eyes from the tempting curve of her hips and buttocks just inches away from him. The heat in his loins was almost unbearable.

"Rutting bastard," he muttered to himself.

This time, he was the one who found sleep a long time in coming.

María was up with the sun, untangling herself from Sam's arms before she had to think about the night before. She didn't want to remember her tears. She didn't want to remember the feel of his arms. She didn't want to remember that instant when she'd known he was going to kiss her. And she certainly didn't want to remember the moment he pulled back, dismissing her once and for all.

No, she told herself. All she wanted in the world was to simply find the missing children and get back to her life before any permanent damage was done.

She was a woman who knew her limits. People were definitely one of them. Her parents had been virtual strangers, she'd been an outsider in her class, and God knows she'd come out of her shell only to marry one of the lowest life-forms on the face of the earth. Then there had been Daniel, and she'd blown that, too.

The only thing in this world she understood well was solitude. Solitude and her paintings. Of course, in the last five years there hadn't been any paintings to speak of. She'd tried, oh, she'd definitely tried. But the magic had left with Daniel. Now, there was only the emptiness.

By the time Sam first stirred she'd already thrown wood on the fire and was boiling more water for coffee. There was still her part of the jerky left from last night, since Sam had refrained from eating it. Other than that, there was no more food. They would have to either return to her cabin or get supplies from the town soon.

When Sam sat down on the log, she handed him his cup without meeting his eyes. He seemed equally intent on avoiding hers, and thus they drank without exchanging a word.

The silence was only broken when María started to fold up the blankets. "We have to get some supplies soon."

Sam nodded. "I have some of the money, the sucres, if you can find us a place."

"If you still plan on continuing to the bottom of the hill, we can stop in Otavalo there."

He agreed with a small nod. "I need a phone, too."

She paused for just a moment, waiting to see if he would tell her more than he had last night. But he remained silent and after a moment she gave up. "Well, good luck with finding a phone," she told him sourly.

"Surely there has to be one somewhere."

"Look, Mr. Mathers," she said impatiently, "you're in the hills of Otavalo. There doesn't *have* to be anything."

"We'll find one," Sam insisted. "And you can stop calling me Mr. Mathers. After I've slept with a woman once, I let her call me Sam."

She bristled instantly. "I happen to like 'Mr. Mathers,'" she said stiffly. "Is there something wrong with that?"

He shrugged casually, enjoying her defensiveness. "Nothing. I just prefer to go by Sam, that's all."

"Sam sounds like a name you'd give a pet dog," she informed him.

He scowled at that, some of his good humor abruptly disappearing. He'd wondered how she would be in the morning, wondered how she would react by the light of day. Now he knew. Any trace of the woman he'd seen last night was gone. This was the princess before him now, the rich, haughty heiress. Unfortunately, when she stood this close, her hair loose down her back and her eyes flashing black fire, his body had a hard time telling the difference. "If your disposition isn't sweet during the evening," he growled out in response, shifting slightly away, "and it certainly isn't sweet during the day, just when are you in good humor?"

"Never. I've found that people appreciate the consistency."

"You know what I think," he said, driven now by sheer perversity, "I think you insult me deliberately. I even think you do it just because you're afraid that I'm too likable. I think you'd insult me less if I truly was as insultable as you want to believe. Now, why should that be?"

"Of all the convoluted thin—"

But she didn't get any further. Out of the blue he took a step forward, easily crossing the distance between them. And before she had a moment to think, a moment to react, his large hands pulled her in and his mouth found hers. Hard.

At first she was perfectly rigid with shock and outrage. There was a brief instant of struggle, but he absorbed her attempts at pushing and kicking easily. And then, somewhere between the outrage and the shock, came the true registration of his mouth upon hers.

It was softer now, gentle, even, coaxing as he gave in to the persistent urgings of his own desire and lightly traced the outline of her mouth with his tongue. There was a part of her mind that dimly recognized she should do something, but it was overwhelmed by the onslaught of new sensations.

Johnny had certainly never kissed like this.

The tongue came back, a bit more demanding this time, and she slowly yielded, relaxing against his hard frame, tilting her head back for a better angle. In response, his hand came up and gently tangled itself in the long black mane of her hair.

It felt so wonderful, she thought dimly. So soft and slow and gentle and exciting. She wanted it to go on and on and on. Without thinking she parted her lips, welcoming him further.

He did not hesitate, bringing her closer against him as the urgency hit him. He could feel the soft swell of her breasts pressed against his chest, the silky curtain of her hair falling luxuriously down his arms. The curve of her hips rubbed tantalizingly close to his own. With a low growl, one hand found the rounded form of her buttocks and pulled her closer.

And suddenly the soft and slow was gone. It was urgent now, urgent and hot and demanding. Wild and exciting, and she felt it all the way down to the pit of her stomach, where it shivered and rolled through her.

Dimly, she heard the sound of somebody moaning.

It penetrated her consciousness, and in that instant, two realizations hit. First, she was being kissed by a man she was supposed to dislike, and second, the person moaning was herself. Without another thought, she jerked herself out of his arms. Caught unaware, he didn't stop her.

For a long moment, no one said anything. They just stood there, breathing hard as María felt her cheeks flush a deep, dark red.

"I'll be damned," Sam muttered, more to himself than anyone.

"Why did you do that?" María demanded, gasping. "That was totally uncalled for!"

But Sam shook his head, starting to regain his own defenses. "Quite the opposite," he told her. "I believe that was the best way I've found yet to shut you up."

She opened her mouth to argue, but the flashing gleam in his eye clearly told her what the consequences would be and she didn't know if she could handle that twice in one day. Eyeing him warily, she backed up and cautiously picked up the backpack.

"I think we should be going now."

He nodded curtly, snapping himself out of the rest of his daze. He'd acted on instinct, but the results were more than he'd planned. Much more. Now he followed her lead in retreating. "Yes," he agreed curtly, getting back to the relative security of the matter at hand. "How far to the bus stop?"

"A few miles downhill, I think."

"Then we're off."

They made good time going down the hill, though neither spoke and both were careful to keep a solid distance between themselves. María shot him quick glances whenever she thought he wasn't looking. Her mind was still reeling from the impact of the kiss, and the myriad reactions that were nearly overwhelming.

Last night she'd been wrapped up fully against his rippling form, and he'd pulled back rather than kiss her. This morning, she'd been angry, and he'd kissed her so hard her lips still tingled. Not to mention other parts of her anatomy. She didn't understand it. She didn't understand her own reactions, for frankly, she'd never cared much for kissing. And she certainly didn't understand his reactions.

He'd made it all too clear what he felt for her. Not much of it was good. And there was also the fact that she wasn't exactly the kind of woman to inspire passion or recklessness in a man.

Why had he done it?

And would he do it again?

The thought made her flush furiously once more, and she sneaked another look under the cover of her eyelashes to make sure he wasn't watching her. So far, his attention appeared to be a million miles away. It was safer that way.

Her fingers crept up on their own and lightly ran across her bruised and swollen lips. She'd definitely liked the kiss, she had to admit. It had been slow, giving as well as taking. Nothing at all like Johnny's. Whatever else she held against Sam Mathers, she'd have to admit it, he was a good kisser. And herself? Was he, even right now, wondering what had possessed him to kiss a cold and frigid woman? She didn't know much about kissing, as he'd probably discovered. He was probably thinking of what a disappointing experience it had been.

That was okay, she promised herself stiffly, and her head came up. She wasn't a woman of emotion anymore, she wanted her solitude, needed it. And for a woman like that, there was certainly no room for a man like Sam Mathers. This would all be over soon, one way or the other. And then she could go home to her piles of unfinished canvas and her corn and her chickens. She could go home to the emptiness.

Sam himself was less than happy as they trudged down the hill. His blue eyes stormed almost black with a mixture of frustration and confusion. He never should have kissed her, but he wanted to do it a helluva lot more. He shouldn't get mixed up with some rich lady, but she obviously wasn't going to tell him no. Her tongue could be sharp as an ice pick, but her body was soft as silk. She probably just saw him as some minor diversion, but God, her kiss had been powerful . . . and hungry.

Don't do it again, he commanded himself sharply. God, what would it feel like to hold those soft breasts in his hands, cupping, shaping and pinching until she moaned for more. Until she was dizzy and desperate with desire for *him*, Sam Mathers. For him.

Don't do it, he told himself.

Tonight, maybe tonight . . .

An hour later they were both crammed into a rickety bus piled high with luggage and produce and at least a few dozen chickens. They each had barely enough room to stand, and judging by the way the bus tilted every time they went around a corner, Sam was certain they were going to die before ever reaching the second child's house.

In his blue jeans and polo shirt, he was receiving a fair amount of looks from the other Indians. María, who blended right in with her dark coloring and traditional garb, seemed oblivious to all the attention. After a bit, she fell into conversation with the man next to her, and Sam was left alone with his thoughts.

He had to figure out how many people were involved, how they were kidnapping the children. Force, bribery? Where were they keeping the children, and how in the hell were they getting them out of the country?

"Sam," María said sharply, jerking him from his deep concentration. "Señor Alva here says that a boy disappeared nearby not long ago. But this was a little different. The boy, perfectly healthy, vanished suddenly, then stumbled home one week later. He says demons kidnapped him."

"The boy's alive?" Sam asked curtly.

"Yes. And think fast because we're approaching the stop by that area right now."

"Then we'll get off," he told her firmly.

She nodded, her face growing pale. More questions, more prying. At least this boy had beaten the monsters.

It took them a bit of asking around and another two hours to locate the house. The afternoon was just beginning, and the *señor* was out in the fields, leaving the *señora* and her four youngest kids at home. It was Juan, the eight-year-old, who had been taken.

The family was distrustful at first, and Juan, in particular, cringed away from Sam's unfamiliar countenance. It took several minutes of cajoling on María's part to gain the *señora*'s permission to talk to Juan, then several minutes more to convince the boy to talk.

But María soothed him with soft words and a light touch of her hand. She had a musical voice and clear black eyes. Watching her reach out to the boy, Sam was half-convinced she could hypnotize any man. Her smile was so breathtakingly sweet as she tried to calm Juan's fears.

She'd certainly never smiled like that for him.

The fact hit him like a sharp pang, and abruptly he forced it away. He was spending entirely too much time thinking about this one woman. She may look sweet, but bitter experience had taught him well enough that could all be a show. He would do better to remember that, and keep his mind on business.

These children needed him.

With some concentration, Sam could pick up bits of the conversation, even though it took place primarily in Quechua.

Right now the boy was talking about simple things. He liked to work with his hands. He had visited a cousin in the city once, and the cousin was a *zapatero*—a shoe repairman. Maybe some day he would do the same.

The information wasn't necessary, but it helped relax both the child and María. It also gave Sam time to observe the boy. His face was calm, his hands animated. He had clear eyes, and he didn't look to his mother for guidance. From all appearances, he was telling the truth.

But now, after a gesture from Sam, María's questions became more specific.

Remember that day, Juan? What were you doing? Who came?

Juan shrank back now, looking uncertain and more than a little scared. With low tones, María once more soothed him, her hand reaching out to his in support.

He had been out by himself, Juan confided finally, wandering through a small forest of eucalyptus trees, when suddenly he'd been grabbed from behind. There were loud angry voices. Three different ones he thought—but two spoke a strange gibberish he didn't understand.

They had thrown a canvas bag over him and made him walk for a long, long time downhill. Then he was shoved into a vehicle. It was cold and hard and reeked of gasoline. He didn't know how long they drove to the place, he had dozed off.

He could still hear talking, but gradually it had faded away. He was tired and scared, but he had managed to move enough to wiggle out of the canvas. Then he'd crept out of the back of the truck, climbing over the sides. The demons were gone, so he'd started to run.

And he ran and ran and ran. For two days he ran. Then he was back home, away from the demons.

Sometimes he had dreams. Sometimes they came back. And sometimes, after storms, after the dreams, he would wake up shivering and covered with sweat.

"*Gracias,* Juan," María said when they were finished. The boy was shaking slightly, his eyes freshly stark with the remembered fear. Sam could see it reflected in María's own eyes. The memories were hard for her. But still, she remained calm and composed in front of the child. Her hand once more squeezed Juan's hand. "*Nosotros vamos a ayudarte,*" she said in a clear voice. "*Yo te lo prometo.*" We will help you. I promise.

After everything she had said to him, Sam was surprised at her words. And he was even more surprised by the surge of pride that rushed through him watching her. He'd been worried about her yesterday, more worried than he liked. But she was doing better now, especially talking to this scared boy.

And for the first time, he could see how she must have been as a mother. So capable and gentle and patient. It was a far cry from the woman he had met at the hut, suspicious, cold, withdrawn. Those men had done that to her when they'd stolen her child.

It was in that minute that he discovered he hated those men with an intensity that was staggering. The muscle in his jaw leapt and his fists clenched at his sides. But then, with conscious effort, he forced himself to relax once more.

Squatting down, he addressed Juan directly with a few words of Spanish. The boy was clearly more uncomfortable around such a large white man, but with María's steady presence beside him, he answered Sam's few questions. And when Sam uttered a few words in English, the boy confirmed that, yes, that was how the demons spoke. Sam nodded and thanked the child once more.

The boy's eyes were still clear and guileless. And the fear was definitely real. Sam believed him, and the information provided was very interesting. *Very* interesting.

Juan's mother, with her worn face and capable hands that wove for her family's living, offered them food then. As it would be rude to refuse, they accepted, although both were conscious of just how little food the family probably had in the small hut.

As they sat down at the tiny table, María offered a few low instructions to Sam. "I don't know what she will serve," María informed him. "But whatever it is, eat it." Sam nodded, having traveled enough in the navy to be familiar with this etiquette by now.

In Spanish Sam thanked the woman for her generosity, and she understood him enough to smile and nod back.

Soon, after what could have been only a half hour or so, she fed them a soup that appeared to be made from potatoes, and then some type of meat that looked very unfamiliar. But Sam just smiled, nodded and resolutely took a bite.

"What is it?" he asked María when the woman had turned around.

"I'll tell you later," she promised him.

"Does that mean I'm better off not knowing now?"

"Something like that."

It wasn't the best thing he'd ever eaten, but it wasn't too bad, either. It was also very humbling, for he realized he was probably eating a week's worth of food for the woman's family. No stranger to poverty, the gesture touched him deeply. When he was finally able to purchase supplies, he would be sure the woman received anonymous compensation.

Finally all was said and done, the goodbyes and smiles exchanged, and Sam and María headed back down the hillside. Dusk was beginning to fall, turning the hill a deep green and rose. The air was cool but clear, and once again the pure beauty of the land struck him.

Alone once more, they were both suddenly self-conscious. It was funny, but watching María with the child had made him forget all about her upbringing. When she'd tried to tell him that she fit in here, in these mountains, she hadn't been as far off track as he'd assumed. In many ways, she did belong.

Or, an uncomfortable voice spoke up, *perhaps she just knows how to act. After all, she knows you're watching. Perhaps she just acts like that when you're around.*

He frowned as he walked, feeling the uncertainty once more. Sarah Mathers had certainly been good at acting. All shrew and shrill one minute, then all soft and cajoling the next, as soon as she found something she wanted.

And this woman?

He didn't know. She didn't fit the stereotype as well as he would like. But perhaps she wasn't so different, either. That was the thing about women, you never could tell.

Not that it mattered. He didn't have anything in common with a rich heiress, anyway. He just needed her temporarily as a guide and a translator. Once that was done with, they'd both go their separate ways.

No strings attached. That was how Sam Mathers liked things.

That resolved, he struck up a neutral conversation.

"So what did I just eat?" he asked.

"Oh," María began, and beside him he saw the corners of her mouth twitch suspiciously, "the soup was typical enough, but the meal is an Otavaleño specialty. It's called *cuyes*. Basically, it's—uh—a type of rodent."

"Rodent?" he found himself echoing. In spite of himself, his face paled slightly and he could feel his stomach roil. "Like, as in a rat?"

"Not exactly. I don't know an English equivalent for them. I guess they'd look more like guinea pigs to you. Something along those lines."

"Oh." A guinea pig? He supposed he'd eaten worse in his time, but somehow that thought wasn't comforting. "Well," he said finally with a diplomatic shrug, "I guess I am glad you didn't tell me during the meal."

"No problem. What now? Where do we go from here?"

He thought about it for a moment. "Supplies first, then we decide."

"The city, then," she said.

He nodded. "To Otavalo."

Chapter 6

It was dusk by the time they reached the small town of Otavalo. With its cobbled streets and clay buildings, it reminded Sam of some little scene from a western movie. It was an attractive town, and for its diminutive size, it carried all the sights and smells of a much larger city. Even now at dusk the streets were filled with the brightly colored skirts of Indian women packing up their wares while the air was filled with the earthy aromas of roasting meat, squawking chickens and raw wool. Children ran wild through the narrow alleyways, trying to jump up on truck tailgates for a short ride to the next block.

There was much to see, and a part of Sam was truly intrigued. But the practical, controlled side of him said this was no time for sightseeing. There was too much work to be done.

Juan's testimony had been extremely helpful, and Sam wanted some time to mull it over. If only the child had seen more. Without even a glimpse of the men, nor even an idea of the boundaries or landmarks where he had been taken, Juan had been unable to give them the kind of specific information Sam sought. But at least it was a starting point. What all could actually be gleaned from it remained to be seen. Also, Sam still needed a phone to check in with his men, not to mention with his client. Hopefully one of his assistants would have learned something. Two days were almost over, and the clock was still ticking.

After a small discussion, María recommended a nearby hotel where they could get a bite to eat, beds to sleep in, and, most important, phone lines to the States.

The Hotel Otavalo was definitely designed for tourists. And if the modern decor and new carpets didn't give that fact away, the bill certainly did. Still, for U.S. standards, it wasn't too bad. According to María, the real shock would be the phone bill. Twenty-four dollars for every three minutes.

With Russell O'Conner picking up the tab, Sam wasn't really concerned about the expense. No, at the moment his real concern was his stomach. Besides the recent rodent fare, neither of them had gotten much to eat all day.

They both headed straight for the restaurant. It was there for the first time that Sam noticed all the stares María was receiving. All day long it had been Sam, with his burnished blond hair and blue eyes, who had stood out. But in this hotel, it was María, with her traditional Indian garb, that drew the shuttered looks and speculative whispers. He frowned, but María seemed unaware.

After a small perusal of the menu, Sam decided on a nice thick steak, while María ordered the trout almandine. She also had ceviche, an Ecuadoran specialty made up of shrimp in a Tabasco-lemon sauce and served with popcorn. It took a bit of persuasion, but eventually Sam tried a bite. It was very good, and he was pleasantly impressed after his last meal of barbecued rodents. For dessert he had *mora* pie, not unlike blackberry, and then sat back, feeling full for the first time in days.

"If you keep eating like that we'll have to buy new supplies every day," María told him dryly. She was currently savoring the last bite of her own *mora* pie, and although she'd never admit it to him, the meal was the best she'd eaten in a very long time.

"First thing tomorrow," said Sam, then he yawned, large and contentedly. "We'll buy the supplies then."

"Where to next?"

"I don't know," he said slowly and took a sip of strong, black coffee. His eyes narrowed slightly as his concentration kicked in. "From what Juan said, I would assume that there were three men. Two men he didn't understand, so they're obviously foreigners. The third, however, was an Indian. Probably the guide, I would say. So we're dealing with three men who are actually grabbing the kids. They put Juan in a truck and drove a distance that took him two days to cover by foot. Unfortunately, we don't know if that was the final location or not. It could just as easily have been a small break. But they're driving somewhere. Obviously Otavalo isn't the main camp. Where, then?''

"So,'' María added, "we're looking for a place where it would be easy to hide Indian kids and three men, two of whom are foreign. Say a place with lots of people, both Indian *and* foreign. But that doesn't narrow it down much. Tourism is a major industry here. Any of the large cities, Quito or Guayaquil, and even some of the smaller cities like Otavalo, would qualify.''

Sam tossed it around in his head a bit. "Just how easy is it to get kids out of the country here?'' he asked after a moment.

"Now? It's tough. Before, you could adopt. You could also take your child outside of the country without your spouse's consent. But then the rumors of killing children for their organs began. The government contended that people were using adoption agencies as covers for the children they were exporting and killing. And in cases of divorce or separation, one parent would take the child and simply disappear. So now it's much harder. You can no longer adopt an Ecuadoran child. And it takes the signatures of both parents for a child to leave the country.''

Sam frowned. "But if the government is that aware of the problem, why isn't it doing more about such children as Juan?''

María shook her head. "Sam, you're still thinking like an American. Everything falls under laws and government in the States. But this is Otavalo. This is a city of Indians who are directly descended from the Incas hundreds of years ago. Many things are done now as they've been done since then. For these people, something such as a federal government is an abstract, irrelevant to their daily lives. Remember, there are no such things as phone lines or sewer systems in these hills. Nothing to link the people to some higher body. Most of the Indians here couldn't even tell you who is president. And when they have problems, they don't go to some abstract organization such as the state police or officials. They work within their own communities, with their own leaders. Now, in the major cities like

Quito, it may be very different. But the hills here are for farm-ing and crafts, and that is what the people do.''

"In other words," Sam finished for her, "this is the perfect place to kidnap a child without state officials ever knowing.''

She nodded, saying, "Now you're understanding.''

"But again," Sam insisted, returning to the original issue, "how would you get a child out of the country?''

María shrugged. "Like most things in this country, for enough money, it can be done.''

"But someone must be paid off, some government official bought.''

"Sure. Just take your pick.''

"Let's assume for a minute that the other half of the opera-tion is in the United States.'' Sam didn't say anything further on that, but he was thinking of the child's body found in the marshes of Florida. Not to mention the fact that the delicate procedure and high-tech equipment necessary for organ trans-plants limited them to advanced countries. "There are flights from both Quito and Guayaquil to Florida, correct?'' he con-tinued.

María nodded, the strain beginning to show around her eyes again. *The other half of the operation.* It was too hideous to even contemplate. She pushed the thoughts away.

"So, once more," Sam thought out loud, "we're looking at a major city. Now, Quito's not that far from here, an hour or so by car, right? But Guayaquil... That really requires a plane, correct?''

María nodded, already reaching his conclusion. "Then we go to Quito.''

He nodded, then another thought struck him abruptly. Quito was the capital of Ecuador, and there the main language wasn't the Indian dialect anymore but Spanish. While a bit rusty, he could manage Spanish on his own. Therefore, María's trans-lation skills were no longer necessary. Still, Sam found himself thinking fiercely, he could use a good guide. She would know officials, places. And the clock was racing too fast. Anything that would save time was critical.

But what if she reached the same conclusion? What if, even now, she was realizing her purpose for being on this venture no longer existed? What then? Instinctively he knew that she would try to pull out. She would want to go back to her corn and chickens. But he couldn't let her do that, he decided vehemently. No, she was just going to have to continue to help him whether she liked it or not. He wasn't going to let her back out and become selfish now. No, it was for the children. He needed her help to find the children, and he wasn't letting her go until it was all over.

Period.

But what about the danger? These people killed children for money. If they got on to the fact two people were on their heels, well, one or two more murders probably wouldn't bother them much. As far as Sam was concerned, that was part of his job and he was more than willing to take the risk to find the children. But María? Did he really have the right to risk her life, too? Not to mention the pain he'd already put her through. Her wounds still seemed so fresh, painfully close to the surface. He didn't like the pain he saw in her eyes. He didn't like to find her crying in her sleep. It made him feel like a first-class heel. Maybe, maybe for her sake, he should just let her go.

Abruptly, the thought made him furious. Damn it, he was Sam Mathers. A cool, controlled, logical man. The best in the business, and he'd gotten there by not letting such frivolous emotions get in his way. One woman's feelings should be irrelevant. It was the children who mattered. María could fend for herself, but they couldn't. And by God, he had pledged to help find them. Since when did he let himself get all soft-hearted and maudlin? Especially over a woman. He'd told himself from the start she wouldn't get to him. It was about time he stuck to that. She was simply part of this case, and he would utilize her in any way possible to help find those kids.

End of story.

Unbeknownst to him, his eyes had grown a hard, sapphire blue while the muscle next to his jaw clenched tightly. Across the table, María watched his whole face turn grim and wondered at the thoughts racing through his head. Was he angry with her now? What had she done? And then, with sudden clarity, it came to her, too. If the next stop was Quito, then Sam wouldn't need her anymore. She was just a translator after all, but most of the Indians in Quito understood and spoke Spanish, since it was the primary language there. Sam could get by on his own. She could go home.

For one desperate minute, she did just want to run. Run back to the corn and the chickens and forget everything. But she'd been running for five years now. Running and running and running. And still she'd never forgotten. Still, in the middle of the night, the nightmares found her, and the tears coursed down her face. She'd lived without emotion. She'd lived with only emptiness. And still, she'd never forgotten. Daniel, her baby, the life she'd carried in her own body and fed with her own milk. Daniel, whom she'd loved more than her own life. Daniel, whom she'd failed.

There was no going back anymore. Home had once been her salvation, its isolation her peace. But Sam had destroyed that simply by appearing on her doorstep. How could she go home now and worry about chickens and corn when she knew there were children out there, kidnapped, held by the monsters, crying for their mothers?

She hadn't wanted to care. She'd wanted to stay in the tight little bubble she'd built for herself. But it was too late now. Knowledge had a way of penetrating even the thickest of defenses, and now there was no consolation to be found. No, for better or for worse, she was a part of this. Until they found those kids, there would be no peace for her. And God, let them find them still alive. Otherwise there would be no end to the pain.

She couldn't bear to go through it all again. But she couldn't bear just to go home, either.

Sam Mathers was stuck with her now. Let him deal with it.

That resolved, she attempted to sip her coffee casually while she awaited Sam's dismissal. Still he said nothing. Finally, she took a deep breath and broached the subject on her own.

"About tomorrow..." she prodded quietly.

"Yes, tomorrow," Sam repeated evenly, keeping his eyes cool. "We have to leave early," he said abruptly. "Right after gathering some supplies. Say, food, clothing, blankets. Can we take a bus?"

She was silent for a moment. So he wasn't going to bring it up, he wasn't going to ask her to leave. The relief was stronger than it should have been. She took another sip of coffee and squared her shoulders.

"We could catch a bus," she told him, "but it would be slow."

There was a small pause. *We?* Then she was still with him. She wasn't going to back out. And he wouldn't give her another chance. Returning to the matter at hand, he shook his head. "What about renting a car?" he asked.

"Don't worry about it," she said abruptly. "I can find us a car."

"Where?" he prodded suspiciously. "Do you keep a Mercedes stashed in town?"

"I don't own a Mercedes anymore," she repeated flatly. He still looked unconvinced, though, and suddenly, she found the words drawn from her. She hadn't told anyone, but now, for some odd reason she didn't care to explore, she wanted this man to know. Maybe because, sometimes, his blue eyes darkened with worry when he looked at her. Maybe because even now she could remember what it was like to wake up, and find his strong arms around her. For whatever reason, the words came out on their own.

"I don't have any of the money anymore," she said softly. "At least, not directly."

Across the table, Sam's hand froze on its way to the coffee cup. According to his research, she'd been worth almost a hundred million dollars at the time of Daniel's kidnapping. While her three-year flight around the globe had no doubt eaten away a portion of it, it was hard to run through that kind of money. The interest alone could probably feed a small city for a year.

"How did you manage that?" he asked finally.

María just shrugged. "Gifts, donations, loans. I bought four paintings—two van Goghs, a Monet and a Renoir—and gave them to a gallery in Daniel's name. That took care of quite a bit. It's not that hard, you know. It's only money."

Spoken like someone who'd had it all her life, Sam thought instantly. Spoken like someone who'd never needed it. Someone who'd always had food, houses, medical care. Someone who was rich. There was a fleeting moment of bitterness, but it quickly passed. That had been a long time ago. Another lifetime. Still, to have that kind of money and to simply give it away...

"Why?" He had to ask.

Again, she shrugged, attempting to look casual, but the long day and tight strain were catching up with her. She shouldn't say anymore. She'd wanted to remain isolated, remember? But once again, the words were drawn from her. There was a part of her that, after all these years, needed to talk. And there was a part of her that, after all these miles, wanted Sam to know.

"Money's only value is what it can get for you," she told him. "And it can't get me what I want anymore, so there isn't any point in having it."

He already knew the answer to this last question, but he heard himself say the words, anyway. "And just what is it you want?"

"I want my son back, Sam. I want Daniel."

There was silence after that. A small contact had been made, and neither knew what else to say. Instead they finished their coffees, Sam paid the bill and they departed the restaurant. He gave her the key to her adjoining room in the hall, then both disappeared into separate doorways.

Sam refused to delve too deeply into the sudden urge to follow María into her room. It had been a long day. María looked beat, and he had phone calls to make.

He had to wait an hour before the phone operator called him back with an open line to the States. There was a one-hour time difference, so he didn't even try the office.

He got ahold of Stevens first, who he'd placed in charge of tracking down more information on María. Unfortunately, the man had little to report.

"I've got clippings and clippings on her mother and father," Stevens said over the line. "But to tell you the truth, the daughter kept a low profile. I can hardly find anything on her at all. There's lots on her paintings, her ability to capture the spirit of her subjects, the vivid colors, etcetera, etcetera. New York critiques, that kind of thing. I have one small announcement of her wedding, and then a paragraph stating her divorce. You know, for a painter of such incredible stature, she kept almost completely out of the limelight. I can't even find much on her ex-husband or his death."

"And the kidnapping of her son?"

"Only superficial articles. One says he disappeared. One talks about how she was offering a million-dollar reward for his return. That didn't run until the child had been gone two weeks. According to the coroner later, the kid was probably already dead by then. Then there's just one last concluding article, saying the child was most likely killed by a cult. That's about it. Tomorrow I'm going to try and access the police records. Hopefully I can get details there."

"Sounds good," Sam told him. "Keep me informed on what you learn. I want to know if you find any connections at all with what happened five years ago to what's happening today.''

"I will," Stevens promised.

After a last few words, they hung up, and Sam attempted to call Chris, his assistant in charge of investigating the different organs banks. Chris wasn't in, though, so Sam moved on to Phil. Give him another day, Phil said. He was scheduled to talk to a Florida police detective in the morning and might learn more about the discovered body then. An unidentified corpse, it was still sitting in the morgue after the brief autopsy. He might even, he'd said, get a chance to examine it himself, though he wasn't looking forward to it. Sam merely grunted, indicating that wasn't an issue in his mind. On the other end of the phone, Phil sighed upon hearing it. He'd already expected that. He'd learned a long time ago that Sam Mathers operated in the realm of doing whatever it took to get the job done; likes and dislikes were irrelevant. With a promise to keep looking into things, Phil finally hung up.

Ten minutes later Sam concluded the conversations. With a sigh, he realized that the most important phone conversation was fast approaching. It was time to call O'Conner. Maybe he'd get lucky. Maybe the eccentric would be out.

No such luck. Not only was O'Conner in, but he wasn't happy.

"What took you so long to call?" O'Conner's sharp voice cracked over the line. "I expected to hear from you days ago."

Sam took a deep breath and gave a brief synopsis of the events. "We interviewed the family of one of the missing kids, plus we talked to a child who was kidnapped and managed to escape. Based on what we've learned, we're heading to Quito tomorrow. Right now, I'm looking for two Americans and one Indian, who seem to be doing the actual kidnapping. As it requires several forms to remove a child from Ecuador, we're hoping to uncover the rest of the operation by tracing the paper trail. Government officials have to give permission, or have to be *paid* to give permission, so someone must know something. We just have to find out who. Any questions?"

"How's María?" O'Conner asked abruptly.

"Fine," Sam said noncommittally. "Her translating has been very helpful."

At the other end of the phone there was silence, then a small grunt.

"How many days has it been?" the older man demanded.

"You walked into my office three days ago."

"Well, what are you waiting for?" he snapped back. "Time to get moving again. I want this child found."

Sam didn't even try to argue. He simply said goodbye and hung up. Russell O'Conner certainly had his own way of doing things, Sam thought as he stretched out tiredly in the chair. Oh well, it wasn't his job to like it. He just needed to find the child.

Abruptly, he found himself thinking of María. What must it have been like for her to find her son suddenly gone? And worse, what had it been like to never be able to find him? To try so hard, and then fail. He wondered how many times she must have run through it in her mind. Did she wish, even now, that she had offered the million-dollar reward sooner? Did she still wonder, even after all these years, if maybe she'd done just one thing different, that it would all have worked out?

Probably. It was hard to let go of past mistakes. Hard to reconcile that your own judgments could make the difference between life and death. Even after a year, he could still see Laura McCall in his mind. And he would always wonder about those sixty seconds.

Glancing up, he saw the clock already read midnight. He grimaced as he stretched once more. These last few days had been incredibly long and strenuous, with literally hours upon hours of walking up steep hills. What he needed now was a nice long shower and a good night's rest.

At least he got the shower.

He'd barely emerged from the bathroom, towel wrapped around his waist, when a loud sound crashed in the distance. In two steps he was reaching for his pants and his small traveling bag, which contained a gun. Then, with a sudden jolt, he realized it was only thunder. A storm must be moving in. He walked over to the window and pulled back the curtains. Sure enough, the normally clear sky had turned black with teeming clouds and not far off, a bolt of lightning lit up the sky. It looked to be a doozy of a night.

On the heels of that thought came the completely unwarranted, completely unwanted, concern. Would María mind the storm? He could remember all too clearly the night before when he'd woken up to find her crying in his arms. He recalled the softness of her body, curled up tight against his. And the depths of her black eyes, shiny with tears, opalescent with grief. Perhaps he should check on her, make sure she was settled for the evening.

Not giving himself any more time to think about it, he pulled on his jeans, zipping them but not bothering with the button. Then he walked to the dividing door between their rooms and opened it up.

She wasn't in the bed.

He found her standing at the windows instead, the curtains drawn all the way back to reveal a full wall of storming clouds and streaking lightning. Like himself she must have showered, for her hair hung long and wet down her back. But she'd gone a step further and washed her clothes; they now hung damp and dripping across the chairs and table. In their place she was wearing a long white sheet, which was wrapped tightly under her arms and fell down to pool at her feet. The white contrasted vividly with her almond skin and black, black hair.

He found he could no longer breathe.

And then she turned, the third flash of lightning catching her eyes. Deep in their depths, he saw the swirling maze of deep, dark emotions. Rage. Grief. Desire.

"It's a storm," she said softly. She'd been standing here for the last ten minutes, listening to the thunder, watching the lightning. Such violence, such passion. It had a way of drawing her in, of pulling at the emptiness inside. Once she had been capable of such intensity, too. Once she'd been the passionate artist. Now, there was only emptiness.

Except when storms came. Except when the black, churning depths called to her. She could feel it in her blood, she could hear the pounding tempo in her own heartbeat. To feel, to experience, to live. She'd promised herself never again, but still she couldn't pull away.

To live. To feel. To be.

All these years, with only the emptiness.

And now here was this man. Through the mist of her own roiling emotions she could see the deepening blue of his eyes. He was beautiful. He stood just twenty feet from her, the tight rippling muscles of his stomach, chest and arms bared to her. A long drop of water fell from his short hair and rolled slowly down his chest. She watched its trail with dark eyes, and wanted to reach out and wipe it away.

"It's a storm," she repeated, and this time the words were barely a whisper. It was like the dream, she thought dimly. There was a storm, and then the stranger was there. The man who would claim her as her own. The man that would make the yearning, burning emptiness go away. To feel. To live...

Her lips parted unconsciously, a light flush on her cheeks. Her fingers crept up, unconsciously tracing the full curve of her lips as her eyes darkened further with the memory of his kiss. Hard, soft, demanding, wanting. She shivered, somehow possessed from within by the storm-swept madness from without.

Still Sam didn't move. He just stood there, looking at this exotic beauty who had suddenly unfolded and blossomed before his very eyes. Gone was the frosty, biting woman he'd known such a short time ago. In her place was the most ravishing creature he had ever seen.

The thunder boomed again, shaking the glass with its force. He didn't wait any longer. The sane half of his brain tried to tell him no, tried to tell him that it was probably just the storm, probably just all the emotions in her eyes. But when she'd touched her lips... He just couldn't take it anymore. In three long strides he was there, pulling her close as his mouth hungrily claimed hers.

She moaned, yielding instantly, her head already slanting back.

It was burning and hot, the hottest sensation she'd ever felt. There was no room for doubts amid this heat. No room for the uncertainty and ignorance she still held after two years of marriage. The storm ripped through the night, and the desire ripped through her blood, leaving her without thought, only instinct and madness.

She was caught up in the spell, mesmerized by the storm, seduced by her own longings. And he was the stranger she'd waited years to find.

She was soft in his arms, soft and silky and everything a man dreamed of. If her responses were a little slow now, in the heat of the moment, he didn't notice. He only knew that some deep part of him had been waiting for this. Some deep part of him had been wanting this. And now he could wait no more.

With one powerful surge of his muscles, he swept her up in his arms and carried her to the bed. Her arms clung to his neck, her face buried itself in the crook of his shoulder.

There was no place for logic here. No place for the logic that had dictated his life, no place for the logic that clearly told him not to get involved.

There was only the storm, the teeming clouds, the pounding thunder, the brilliant lightning. It lit up the room, then abruptly enclosed them in darkness, sealing them in, together, alone in the heart of the night.

This stormy night, the outer world had ceased to exist.

His hair was damp against her fingertips, damp and silky as she urgently ran her hands through it. Drops of cold water splattered and landed on her arm, her shoulder. His warm mouth found them and slowly kissed them away.

She wanted him, wanted him with the building yearning of a lifetime, wanted him with the power of the storm. Greedily her hands pulled him closer, finding the burning warmth of his lips with her own.

He could feel her urgency, feel the longing in the kiss. But with long, stroking caresses he tried to soothe her. She was much too beautiful, much too silky and soft and curvy to be taken quickly. But the urgency was catching. In spite of his years of experience, in spite of the careful straining for control, he felt it slip out of his grasp, swirling away with the thundering rain and the booming night.

Roughly he kissed her lips now, finding her mouth open and hungry for his own. He tasted her, drinking in the rich flavor of coffee and passion. And from her mouth he found the tender curve of her earlobe. He bit down gently, and she surged against him. Already her hands were running down the length of his back. Already dipping and gliding around the top of his jeans. With a groan, he peeled the denim down and out of their way. In a matter of seconds, he'd done the same with her sheet.

It was an electric feeling, the touch of skin against skin, the softness of her against the muscled hardness of him. Her hands faltered, momentarily unsure, but then his hand found the curve of her breast, and with a startled gasp, she was lost once more in the desire.

His touch wasn't gentle anymore. It was hard and demanding, fierce and urgent, and she matched it with her own wildness as she felt the sensation build deep within her stomach, the burning.

His lips found the tender nub of her breast, biting it lightly, then soothing the mock pain away with slow, delicious licking.

Her fingers clung to him, pulling him closer, arching her back to accommodate him.

His hand drifted lower, caressing the long, delicate curves of her body. Over her hips, down the gentle roundness of her thigh, playing lightly with her knee. Then it drifted back up, caressing the tangled nest of black curls, seeking and then finding the heat within.

She surged wildly at the first probing touch of his fingers, her breath gasping out as electric currents shot through her blood to settle, low and throbbing, in her stomach. It was a wonderful sensation, an unbearable sensation. She wanted . . .

She didn't know. The fire was new, the heat was new. He touched her in ways Johnny never had, made her feel things Johnny had never made her feel. She just wanted it to go on and on and on. But then it got too hot, the sensations too wild. Her teeth found the muscled curve of his shoulder and sank in deep with frustration.

He groaned in response, parting her legs and surging forth all in one heart-stopping movement.

There was a moment of pain, a moment when she gasped hard and bit down once more with the strain of the stretching. It had been so long, so very long. And then it passed, and he filled her completely. The pain was gone, and newer, different sensations took its place.

It was incredible, he thought, like sinking into liquid velvet. For one desperate moment he thought he was going to lose control completely, and gritted his teeth against the ecstasy. But then there was no need as her nails scraped down his back and with a long, shuddering gasp, she convulsed around him. Her eyes were wide and brilliant with the shock, deep and opalescent with passion. With another low groan, he surged into her one last time, joining her.

Afterward, he lay on top of her and her ears were filled with the powerful thunder of his pounding heart. Neither spoke. They simply lay there as the rain pattered against the window in its now-soft lullaby. The storm, like the passion, had moved on.

After a few moments, he gently untangled himself and settled down beside her. After another moment, his hand came out and, without a word, he pulled her against him. She didn't protest.

Weary now, too tired for the thoughts that crowded their minds, both drifted off to sleep.

As was her nature, María woke first, with the rising of the sun. There was a moment of confusion. Her back was burning from the heat of the body curled against her own, and a thickly muscled arm lay heavily around her waist. Then, with a sharp jolt, it came to her, and her eyes flew open.

She'd slept with Sam Mathers.

For an instant she felt pure mortification. What must he think of her now, with her fumbling inadequacies and almost total ignorance of intimate matters? Not to mention how wild she'd been. God, had she really bitten him?

Her cheeks flushed a fiery red, and she felt the despair sink in. She'd promised herself never again. She'd promised herself a lifetime of isolation, of control. And now look what she'd done. One raw moment of overwhelming emotion, of the thundering storm, and she'd given it all up.

It mustn't happen again, she told herself. Never again. She wasn't a woman of passion, she was a woman of emptiness. And she liked it that way, she told herself fiercely. She would not go through the pain of caring. Not again, never again.

Cautious now, she carefully tried to disentangle herself from his sleeping form. He stirred, mumbling softly in his sleep, and she instantly froze. But after a long, breathless moment, he unconsciously pulled the covers higher and appeared to drop back into deep slumber. With a low sigh, she pulled herself free and hastily scrambled for her still-damp clothes as she fled to the bathroom.

The moment the door clicked shut, his eyes opened, wide and alert. But he didn't move, he simply lay there, listening to the sound of running water, straining his ears for more.

Considering her passion the night before, she'd certainly been in a hurry to get away from him now. With a sigh, he abruptly rolled over, tucking his hands under his head as he stared at the ceiling with bleak blue eyes.

He truly was three times the fool. What had he done? He'd told himself he wouldn't let the woman get to him. He'd told himself he would stay in control, focus on work. Yet practically the first time she looked at him with passion in her dark eyes he'd virtually attacked her.

Even now she was probably feeling regret. She'd been vulnerable last night. Yes, passion had been in her eyes, but there had also been anger and pain. He should have walked away. He should have left her in peace.

What the hell had he done?

All his life he had been so controlled. All his life he had worked fiercely, diligently toward his goals. And now he was behaving like some hormone-ridden teenager with a woman he was supposed to be *working* with. Damn it, he should have run in the other direction the moment he opened her door and saw the state she was in.

But even then, he could still feel the exquisite pleasure-pain of her nails raking down his back. Such passion. Never in his life had he felt anything like it. Never in his life had he let go of so much of his own control. He'd lost himself in her last night, lost himself in her dark gaze and soft skin.

He shook his head. Sam Mathers was not the kind of man who lost control. And certainly not over a woman. It was the storm, he consoled himself. After the pressure of the last few days, it had affected them both.

But it wouldn't happen again. Sam Mathers never made the same mistake twice.

Purposefully now, he rolled over and in one fluid motion was on his feet and walking out the door.

If it hadn't been for the rumpled sheets, it might have looked like nothing had ever happened.

But unfortunately, when María finally emerged from her long, scalding shower, these were the first things that she saw. The bed seemed to glare at her, the discarded sheet an open taunt. So he'd left already, without a word. She couldn't blame him for that. Just exactly what was there to say?

Suddenly, she felt completely lost. Her friends knew about things like this, even her parents had probably handled them without any bother. But she, herself, María Chenney Pegauchi, didn't even know where to begin. She'd never had a fling before. No, instead she'd saved herself for some low-life scum that had used and abused her.

So much for being a woman of the world.

Maybe it was better this way. Maybe she should take his hint and quietly slip from the hotel before anyone knew. She knew this area, she spoke the language. Private detective or not, she could hide from him if she chose. Maybe she could find another mountain, maybe another cabin tucked in a beautiful, peaceful paradise. Maybe this time the monsters wouldn't follow her.

And then what? Two more years of gardening and sewing and weaving and walking? Two more years of staring at blank canvases and wishing the magic would return? Two more years of waking up in the middle of the night with tears on her cheeks and an emptiness so big inside it hurt? Two more years of nothing?

So what was there? She couldn't go back, she couldn't go forward. She could only stand here in the middle of this room in her damp blouse and skirt and wish she'd never met Sam Mathers. And wish even more that it was the truth.

Damn.

She never should have slept with him. When the storm came, she should have bolted the door. What business had he had, anyway, traipsing into her room with a bare chest? What business had he had kissing her like that, holding her like that, touching her like that? What business did he have acting like he cared?

She would have cried, but it was daylight now, the time for tears over. One thing stood out, though. *She* had no business getting involved with a man like Sam Mathers. She knew her limits, knew what she was and wasn't capable of. She'd come to Otavalo seeking peace and isolation after the agony of her life. She'd found it in the emptiness, found it in the curve of the hills and the rhythm of the plow. She wouldn't give it up now. Not for anyone. Not even for Sam Mathers.

She was perfectly composed an hour later when the door finally opened. Her hair had been smoothed back, her clothes pressed and dried the best she could. They were the only clothes she'd brought, since the backpack hadn't been big enough to hold many supplies. Besides, originally they had been going only to the other side of the mountains. She hadn't anticipated the trip being this long. A call to the maid last night had at least produced a small traveling-size toothbrush and toothpaste. That helped her feel a little more composed.

Sam had gone through similar preparations. After a long stinging shower, he had found a maid to wash and dry his clothes immediately, as well as produce a comb for his use. Now he felt once more together and in control.

He didn't waste any time.

"About last night," he began.

"Forget about it," she interrupted coldly.

"Exactly," he rushed on. "It never happened."

She nodded stiffly, her back becoming even more rigid in the fight for distance. It was exactly as she'd thought. He couldn't wait to dismiss her. And beneath the ice, deep beneath the steel she'd shrouded herself in, she felt the first stinging slivers of pain.

As for Sam, he felt at once confused and angry. She seemed to dismiss him rather easily, as if what they'd shared had been absolutely nothing. Strangely enough, the fact that it fit in perfectly with his own mindset didn't make him feel all that good. In fact, he was feeling pretty lousy right about now. Abruptly, he stopped the train of thought. He didn't want to think about it. It was over now. Better to end things now before they got out of hand. Logic told him so.

"Fine," he said curtly. "We need to leave. I want to be in Quito by eight."

She nodded just as curtly, her eyes cloaked and distant. "It will take me a half hour to get transportation. I'll leave now."

"I'll go with you."

"It's not necessary."

"Look, it's not like I have much else to do."

"Buy the supplies," she returned coolly. "It would be more efficient, and I thought you were in a hurry."

"Fine," he growled.

"Fine," she agreed. There was a definite gulf between them now. A huge, yawning chasm neither quite knew how to fill. After a moment's hesitation, she gave up trying and simply walked out the door.

Still, her hands were shaking from the effort at control by the time she hit the streets.

He didn't care.

She shouldn't be surprised, she knew. She shouldn't be shocked. She'd known that he wouldn't. Yet still it hurt. Damn it, she'd made love with him. The first man she'd ever let touch her besides Johnny. And it had meant nothing. *"Forget about it." "Exactly."* Right.

It was the storm, she told herself savagely. She hadn't been herself. But she was in control now. She would keep her guard up, her resolve steady.

But damn that man. Damn him for coming into her life when she wanted to be left alone. Damn him for touching her the way he had. Damn him for making her feel when she was no longer supposed to be a woman of feelings. Damn him for being the stranger in the storm, for being so strong and attractive. For having such blue eyes and gentle kisses. Damn him for being a sight better lover than her husband had ever been. Damn Sam Mathers for being everything that she might have wanted, everything that she'd once hoped to find.

But not now, she knew. Now she was a woman meant to live alone. She was happy that way, she assured herself. Someday the painting would come back to her, someday she would sit at the blank canvas and the pictures would flow again. And then her life would be complete. That was all she needed, all she wanted.

She was sure of it.

So, none of this could ever be allowed to happen again. She wouldn't allow herself to be taken in by his touch, she wouldn't give herself to someone who obviously didn't care.

No, it would not happen again, she assured herself as she walked rapidly. Never again.

But for some reason, that thought did not make her happy.

Chapter 7

He found her just an hour later, parked in front of the hotel. He'd actually walked by her three times by then, for the vehicle certainly wasn't what he'd expected. He still had a sneaking suspicion about a stashed Mercedes or at least another small yellow Ecuadoran sardine can. Never would he have imagined the gigantic, twisted and rusting hulk of an ancient truck. And she sat in it pretty nonchalantly for a woman who'd probably never driven anything less than German imports.

She had her elbow out the window, the ruffled sleeve of her white peasant blouse rippling in the wind. Somewhere along the way she'd picked up a gray hat and now had it pulled low around her eyes as she leaned back in the bumpy seat with its stuffing and springs spilling out everywhere.

"Where in the world did you get that?" he asked incredulously.

"Miguel's," she said calmly, as if it was the most natural thing in the world. "One of his children got lost once and stumbled upon my farm. I took the boy home, and Miguel has been grateful ever since. He just needs it back by the end of the week, and there are a few supplies I'll pick up for him while we're in Quito."

Sam nodded and the conversation stalled. Neither quite met the other's eyes, both half-surprised that the other hadn't run off. It was going to be a long morning.

Finally, struggling to find anything to fill the awkward void, Sam gestured to a huge pile sitting on the corner. "I think I got everything," he said. "Maybe you should take a look."

That he was asking for her input seemed like a small peace offering, and María relented enough to climb down from the huge truck. Her emotions still felt raw and bruised from the morning. She was careful to keep plenty of distance between them, and she avoided all eye contact. She was too afraid of the pity or contempt she might find there.

"What is all this?" she managed to ask in a level voice.

Sam shrugged. "Food, blankets, clothes. That sort of stuff."

And he could have gotten a great deal more. It appeared that the town was really one huge open-air market. Walking around earlier this morning, he'd found streets lined with independent vendors, hawking their wares. Everything from basic clothes and food, to some of the most beautiful handicrafts he'd ever seen. If memory served correctly, María's own mother had left Otavalo for New York on the merit of her incredible pottery art. After everything he'd seen today, Sam could believe it. The skills in weaving, carving and sculpting were magnificent.

"Clothes?" María was asking.

Once more he shrugged casually. "You didn't really pack any when we left your place, and I didn't think you'd want to continue wearing the same ones for the next week. I just got a few more blouses, skirts. You know." He couldn't quite seem to stop shrugging. His pulse was still racing, and it was beginning to anger him. He didn't want to feel this awkward or self-conscious around her. He didn't even know why he'd bought the stupid clothes. It was just, well, she needed them. Besides, he figured he must owe her something for the way he had barged into her life, for the things he was putting her through. Or so he told himself.

But when had he ever noticed things like clothes before? Once more the uncertainty of it all hit him hard. In truth, he'd never bought another woman clothes, never even gave thought to such things. And now, all of a sudden, he'd found himself before some small, wizened Indian woman, picking out skirts, wondering what colors María might like.

She was beginning to affect him all right, and he didn't like it. He wanted his aloofness back, he wanted his cold mantle of arrogance. She was just a woman, for God's sake. A rich heiress playing peasant with an Alabama-born detective. The only thing she could possibly feel for him was hatred for interfering in her life.

"The clothes are fine," he heard her say. In spite of himself, his posture relaxed slightly.

"Fine," he echoed gruffly.

"Apples, dried beef, oranges, bottled water, bread, cheese, bananas. Really, that should be plenty of food. Quito's a major city, you know. They have supermarkets there."

"Just covering the bases," he replied stiffly.

She nodded, her eyes finding a nice safe spot on the sidewalk to focus on. "Let's load up, then, and we'll be off."

He agreed by picking up the bushel of bananas and swinging them into the back of the pickup. The clothes and blankets soon followed, as well as most of the food. He just kept out a few oranges, along with the bread and the cheese, for breakfast.

María headed back over to the driver's side, grateful Sam didn't try to stop her. At least he wasn't one of those males who had to drive when a woman was present. It really would be much faster and practical with her at the wheel. She, after all, knew the way, something he must have already thought out.

"I'll pay you back for the clothes," María said as they climbed into the truck. "When we return, I'll give you some money."

"It isn't a problem. Don't worry about it."

"I said I'll pay you back," she said, sharply this time. She didn't want to accept something that personal from him. Not after this morning. No, she wanted as much distance between them as possible. Maybe that would save her sanity. Think of their time together as business, just business, and she'd be fine. They would find the kids, then go their merry ways—alone. That would be good.

"Are you ready now?" she asked finally, but she didn't really wait for an answer. Instead, she simply turned the key and coaxed the ancient motor to roaring life. A plume of black smoke belched out the back, and Sam eyed the truck with fresh suspicion.

"Are you sure this will get us there?" he asked dryly.

"Absolutely not," she informed him and stepped on the gas.

For the first twenty miles they bounced their way along in complete silence. Sam spent his time watching the lush rolling hills pass by until soon they were driving down granite canyons covered with red dust and dry weeds. It was an amazing land to him. Beautiful in its fertility and striking in its desolation. Amazing.

"Are you really from New York?" María asked suddenly, interrupting the silence. "You don't talk like you're from New York."

"I've lived in New York for the last ten years," Sam conceded.

"And before that?"

He shrugged. "I traveled a lot."

"Where?" María persisted. For the past twenty miles she'd been trying to think of anything but the man beside her, and she'd been failing miserably. Curiosity, she tried to tell herself. She'd been with him for days now and still she knew nothing about him. Of course, maybe it would be better if she didn't know. Maybe it would make him more of a stranger, unneeded and unwanted. Maybe it would make it easier to walk away in the end.

But the need to know him, to understand him, was too strong. It was consuming, urgent, desperate. By some twist of fate her life had become meshed with his. He took up her time, her energy, her emotions. He made her angry, he made her feel. He'd touched her intimately, and yet even after all these things, she knew almost nothing about him. Maybe if she could boil him down, see how he ticked, the attraction would go away. Maybe then she could have peace.

He was still silent across from her. "Does it matter?" he asked at last.

"I don't know," María said. "But it seems only fair that I have some information about you. After all, you've learned everything about me."

"Not everything," he said.

She glanced at him sharply. "What do you mean?"

He paused for a moment, then looked at her with his penetrating blue eyes. "I haven't learned why a world-famous painter has no sign of oils or canvases in her house."

Her eyes returned to the road, her face not giving anything away. "And I," she replied evenly, "haven't yet learned why a man from New York should speak with a slight southern accent."

That gave him pause, and his intense eyes turned away to once more focus on the barren canyons.

"Sandy," he said at last. "I was born in a small town called Sandy. In Alabama."

"How old were you when you left?" she prodded.

His jaw muscle clenched and unclenched. He picked up the cheese from the dashboard and concentrated on cutting a piece with his pocket knife. Too old, that's how old he'd been when he'd left. A damn sight too old.

"Eighteen," he said out loud.

"What? You ran away to the big city?" He didn't answer and she continued, anyway. "Guess there can't be too much demand for private investigators in a small town. Did you go straight to New York?"

"I joined the navy."

That intrigued her. "And that's where you learned private-investigator-type stuff?"

"You could say that."

"And your Spanish, is that where you learned Spanish?"

He nodded and took a huge bite of cheese and bread.

"So," María persisted, undaunted, "then you moved to New York."

He just nodded.

"How did you become a detective? Is there a special school or anything?"

He was silent for a moment longer, then he gave in with a sigh. He'd already told her this much, he might as well just finish out the story. It wasn't as if it was anything exciting.

"I ran errands for a one-man detective agency," he told her. "Eventually, the detective decided that, given my size, having me along as a bit of muscle might come in handy. So he started training me. I picked up some more stuff on my own. Eventually I saved enough to open my own small business. Things grew from there."

"Do you like it?"

"I wouldn't be doing it otherwise."

Her voice grew somber, her hands gripping the wheel tighter than necessary. "Do you always find the people?" she asked softly.

"No," he said. "Not always."

"I hired a private detective when Daniel disappeared," María volunteered suddenly. "A friend of a friend recommended him. I suppose he did all right, all things considered. He came up with a lead or two. But he didn't find Daniel," she said quietly. Abruptly she shook her head, forcing her attention back to the winding ways of the road.

"It must have been hard," Sam said, watching her face. "It must have been very, very hard."

She gave a small, bitter laugh. "There is nothing worse in this world."

"Is that why you ran away?"

"Ran away?" she asked. "Ran away from what? The good life? Trust me, it wasn't so good. And you have to admit, it isn't so bad here."

She was right. The land here possessed a simple beauty he found very appealing after ten years of New York. The air was wonderful to breathe, snow-capped mountains beckoned on the horizon. It was an untouched, unspoiled land. The kind where dreams could still happen and wishes could come true. If you believed in fairy tales, that is.

"I've been wondering," María said abruptly. "I can see how you could get children out of this country, with a bit of bribery. But I'm not so sure how you'd get them *into* the States."

"I've been thinking about the same thing," said Sam. "But that's got to be it. Really, it's the only way the operation could work. It takes time to match up blood types, and organs are only good outside of the body for a minimal amount of time. Four to twelve hours, depending on the organ."

She winced slightly in the seat, her face paling. Once more she could see Daniel's body lying on that cold slab. But worse than the picture was the knowledge that they hadn't just kidnapped and killed him instantly. Instead they'd kept him alive for weeks, weeks in which he must have cried for her. Weeks in which he must have thought in his blind five-year-old trust that she would come and save him from the monsters, just as she'd promised him all those nights when she'd tucked him into bed, kissed his sweet brow and gently turned out the lights.

But she'd never come. The monsters had won that round and destroyed them both.

Across the seat Sam saw the color drain from her face while her hands tightened into a death grip on the wheel. All too easily he could imagine what she was thinking. A part of him tried to say it was for her own good, sooner or later she had to come to terms with the past. The other part of him wanted to kick himself for being such an insensitive lout. He wasn't sure which side had won until he saw his own hand reach across the seat and lightly brush her shoulder.

"We'll find them this time," he said by way of consolation. "We will."

She didn't look at him. She didn't want him to see the pain in her eyes, she didn't want him to see her stripped and helpless. She didn't want him to see the eyes of a woman who had failed her child.

"We're almost to Quito now," she said finally, changing the topic altogether. "Where do you want to go from here?"

He let her change the subject. It was going nowhere, and, logically speaking, it shouldn't matter to him one way or another what she felt or thought. She was just along for the ride, that was all.

So he turned his attention back to what to do next. "I want to speak to someone in the equivalent of a child's welfare office," he said. "Someone who would handle the forms, paperwork, etcetera, of children exiting the country."

"You'll need an appointment."

"Well, it's too late for that. We'll just have to find some other way of convincing them." Abruptly he turned and looked at her sharply. "You're a famous Ecuadoran, surely your name must carry some weight."

She stiffened noticeably in the seat beside him. "I don't exactly qualify as famous anymore," she said frostily. "If you'll recall, I haven't had a showing of my work in five years."

He did recall. After all, she'd never answered *his* earlier question about the lack of painting materials in her cabin.

"Did you give it up completely?" he asked.

"No," she said, but she sounded defensive. "It's just, well, I don't have anything I think is worth showing right now." *Like anything completed,* an inner voice mocked. But she didn't say anything out loud. She didn't want to talk about it. It hurt not to be able to paint. All her life it had been her outlet, and then all of a sudden, it had fled with Daniel. And she couldn't bear for its absence to be as permanent as his. So she kept trying in the little log cabin above her hut, determined that, this time, she would make the magic flow. This time.

Yeah, right.

"Simply showing up at a government office won't work," she reiterated flatly, returning to the relative safety of the previous topic. "You'll have to think of a better plan."

Beside her, Sam simply shrugged. "It'll work out," he told her easily. And she supposed for him it probably did seem easy. After all, this was what he did for a living. If only she could be so sure.

It took them an hour to find the right office for the government agency. After all, María spent very little time in Quito, and as the capital of Ecuador, it was a good-sized city. With its cement structures, seeping gas fumes and milling population, it was also a far cry from the quiet beauty of Otavalo.

María had been right, the receptionist didn't recognize her name and was much less than cooperative. She gave María's Indian garb a disdainful look, but was openly surprised by the quality of her Spanish. In a culture where dress and language often indicated social status, María was definitely incongruous. She dressed as if belonging to the lower class, but spoke the perfect Castilian Spanish of the upper class. With the secretary, however, it seemed to be the clothes that dominated. Or perhaps just the fact that María was female. Because the moment Sam started talking, the secretary was all ears.

To his credit, María acknowledged later, Sam didn't flirt. He didn't have to. His blue eyes and excellent physique were more than enough to enrapture the besotted woman, and she hung on to every word of his rusty Spanish. Standing behind Sam, María settled for quiet fuming. At least it didn't last too long. After a few exchanged pleasantries, Sam produced a ten dollar bill and the receptionist—no doubt trying to make a good impression—disappeared through the closed doors.

It took her nearly fifteen minutes to reappear, and then she was followed by a middle-aged man in a sharp gray business suit.

"Hello, hello," the man said with a thick accent. "My name is Augustine Pero. How can I help you?"

Sam rose, accepting the man's hand and introducing himself and María. After a brief exchange of polite chitchat, they retired to the man's office. Pero indicated two chairs in front of his desk for them to take. While they sat, he situated himself in his own seat, looking at them both with open expectation.

"I would like to know how to get a child out of the country," Sam started right away.

"I see," the man said gravely. "Is this yours, and your companion's?"

It took a moment for Sam to understand, and then he realized that Señor Pero thought he and María were lovers. Not only lovers, but that they had a child together. For a moment he almost refuted it, then he stopped himself. Asking questions about their own "child" would arouse much less suspicion. So, with a stern look at María to silence her, he nodded smoothly.

"Yes," he said. "My *wife* and I have a three-year-old boy we'd like to take with us. I'm an American, and María is, naturally, Ecuadoran. Would there be any problems?"

"Of course not," Señor Pero replied easily. "If you both just sign the necessary forms, there will be absolutely no difficulty."

Sam nodded, fixing a pleased smile on his face. "See, love," he remarked with feigned relief to María, whose eyes had opened wide, "I told you it would be simple." He laughed a little self-consciously, looking at Pero, as he reached over and took María's hand, saying, "She does worry so."

Under the sudden tight squeeze of Sam's hand, María managed a faint smile. What in the world was he doing?

"Now, then," Sam continued, "if we sign the forms now, is that fine for all times?".

"All times?" Pero asked politely.

"Well, I'm away on business a lot, which has made it very hard for us, you understand. So I decided, well, the boy's getting old enough to travel, so why not bring him along on occasion? Generally, I like to go on ahead, and then have my wife and son join me, get some work done first, you know. But I imagine it will be a good three or four times a year. If we just sign these forms now, will that take care of everything?"

"I'm afraid not," Pero informed him calmly. "If you and your wife were traveling together, it would not be a problem. But if just one of you leaves with the child, I will need both signatures each time it happens."

Sam nodded, feeling María's discomfort in the tightness of her grip. What Pero was saying was nothing new; María had told him the same. What Sam really wanted to find out, now that he'd identified the right official, was just how "flexible" a man like Pero could be.

Sam looked troubled. "That might not always be possible," he said slowly, "especially if I'm away for a while. And really it would be a shame if my wife and son couldn't visit my parents from time to time without me. Surely there are other arrangements that could be made."

The words were openly insinuating, and Señor Pero frowned. "I do not know what you mean."

"We are very wealthy," Sam said casually.

Across from him, Pero's eyes narrowed and then intensified suspiciously. He glanced over Sam sharply and gave a slower perusal to María, who was clearly avoiding his gaze. She'd never tried to pull off anything like this in her life and she was openly uncomfortable. *Married?* Her and Sam? And with a child, no less? It was beyond comprehension.

Señor Pero still frowned, but he seemed to have reached a conclusion. "The people in my department are of the best quality," he informed them both haughtily. "I do not believe you will find any evidence of corruption here."

Right, thought Sam. Like the secretary who had gotten them an instant appointment for ten bucks. His eyes swept over the government man one more time. Mr. Pero was wearing a very expensive suit. It looked like English tailoring. Surely that had to have cost a little bit of money. About how much would a job like his pay, anyway? Enough to cover that kind of wardrobe?

"My apologies," Sam said abruptly. "We didn't mean to imply anything improper at all. Of course you run a fine office here. And what an important job it is, too, protecting all those children from perhaps being illegally kidnapped and spirited out of the country. You can be proud of yourself."

There was just the faintest tone of sarcasm there, and by the slight darkening of his eyes, it was apparent that Señor Pero caught it. Sam inwardly winced, forcing himself to sound more sincere.

"Thank you for your time in answering our questions. We do so greatly appreciate it. Don't we, dear?"

María's head jerked up. "Of course," she intoned automatically. "Thank you very much."

Her heart was beating fast and she could practically feel her face flush with the lie. How had she gotten dragged into all this?

Sam was standing now, extending his right hand while his left hand was pulling María to her feet. It was all she could do to follow suit.

Pero took Sam's hand, but his eyes were still suspicious, examining the couple carefully. With another nod, Sam turned and ushered María out the door, one hand resting protectively on her back as they exited. They'd barely made it outside when she was whirling around, brushing his hand away.

"Why did you lie to him?" she bit out furiously.

"Because," Sam said very calmly, "if he is the man we're seeking, I don't want him to know yet that we've tracked the operation to here. I just wanted a chance to meet the man, feel him out a bit. What did you think of his 'You'll find no evidence of corruption here' speech?"

"He's a sorry excuse for a liar," María snapped back.

"My thoughts exactly," Sam said, walking down the street. "I think we need to do some more checking."

"What are you going to do?" she asked after a moment, her voice cooling down.

"I'm not completely sure yet," Sam said. "Which of these parking spaces do you think is his?"

"Whose?"

"Pero's, of course."

"What does his parking space have to do with anything?"

He gave her a cool look. "Would you just help me find it?"

She frowned for another moment, but then turned away to examine the parking lot.

"Over there," she said after a minute. "Those spots say reserved for employees. If his suit is anything to go by, I'd say the Mercedes is his."

"Yes, his suit," Sam mused thoughtfully. "How much does a suit like that cost down here, anyway?"

"It was an extremely well-tailored suit," María said, confirming his earlier observation. "Probably close to a thousand dollars."

"Don't you think that's a pretty expensive suit for a man of his position?" Sam asked as he peered into the car's windows.

María simply shrugged. "His family could very well have money, you know. It's not that uncommon here. Money has a way of staying among its own kind—money marries money, money works for money. That kind of thing."

Sam nodded. "Keep a look out for me, will you?"

She looked at him sharply. "Just what are you planning to do?"

"I'm going to break into his car, of course. Hmm. With this alarm it could be a little tricky. Get ready to run."

"Oh, God," María muttered, and began to quickly look around. She couldn't believe this. They were both going to wind up in jail. She was certain of it. But at least the parking lot was fairly obscured from view. No windows from the office building overlooked it, and there was only light traffic passing by the open side. Mercedes were fairly common cars among the upper class here. Hopefully anybody driving by wouldn't notice anything unusual about an American trying to get into his Mercedes. Of course, they might question a man trying to wiggle underneath one.

"*What are you doing?*" she whispered frantically when Sam's shoulders disappeared under the car.

"Disconnecting the alarm," came the muffled reply.

There was a bit of squirming, then the small click of a wire being cut. Sam reemerged holding his pocket knife triumphantly.

"What did you do?" María asked, unable to keep the fascination out of her voice.

"I clipped the wire connecting the alarm with the speakers. In short, the alarm still works, but when it's tripped, there's nothing hooked up to amplify the noise. Really, whoever installed the speakers should have buried the wires so they'd be inaccessible. Fortunately for us, people rarely think of those things. Now, keep looking, it'll just be a minute more."

He turned away from her, and with quick, deft movements, forced open the lock. Then in one smooth action he had the door open and was quickly checking over the inside. He sat down on the driver's seat and went through the glove compartment. He was careful to note the order of the contents as he went. True to his words, within minutes he was done.

"Let's go."

"What did you find?" María asked as he closed the glove compartment and then shut the car door. He took off walking and she ran a few steps to catch up with him.

He didn't answer her directly. "Let's go to the bank."

"Sam," she said sharply. "Sam, damn it, tell me what's going on."

"I know his bank account number," he said simply. "He left his checkbook in the glove compartment, really a stupid thing to do. At any rate, now you're going to get his bank statement for me."

"I am?" María asked incredulously.

Sam nodded calmly, his mind already running through the best scenario to achieve his goal. "Yes, it would have to be you. I wouldn't make a good Mrs. Augustine Pero."

"Neither could I," she replied firmly. "Look, I'm a painter. Not an actress. This is your line of work, not mine."

Sam stopped long enough to give her a level glare. "You can do whatever you put your mind to, María. Look, you're the one who keeps telling me we'll never find these kids. And I'm telling you now that we can. But we're going to need your co-operation to do it. So let's go."

She could only stare at him, the panic beginning to rise up in her throat. He was serious about this. He honestly thought she could simply walk into a bank and pass herself off as someone else. Didn't he understand that she wasn't that kind of person? She was a painter, an observer. Not a participant. And she'd never done one wild, rebellious, improper thing in her whole life. She couldn't do this. She just couldn't.

"Sam," she tried again, but he cut her off with a sharp movement of his hand.

"You can give me all the excuses you want," he told her flatly, becoming impatient now. The clock, after all, was racing. "I don't care. They won't change my mind. This will be relatively simple, and I'll even tell you what to say. It will all be over and done with before you know it."

"What if I'm arrested?" she protested weakly.

"Don't worry. I'll be sure to post your bail."

"I don't think you can post bail here."

"Then I'll break you out."

And that was the end of that. Within a very short time, María found herself at the Bank of Pinchincha, introducing herself as Mrs. Augustine Pero.

Chapter 8

They did have to make one stop before going to the bank. María's traditional garb marked her as a Native Ecuadoran, as well as a member of the lower class. Such a woman could not be the wife of a man like Señor Pero, which created the need for more suitable attire.

After a brief search in a bright modern mall, María selected a fairly simple silk dress. With a basic square neckline, it came down to a belted waist and fell to just above her knees in clean, tailored lines. The deep purple color brought shiny highlights to her glossy black hair and brightened her eyes. With nylons and matching pumps, she'd gone from being an Otavaleño Indian to a woman who probably did own two van Goghs, a Monet and a Renoir.

She was self-conscious when she stepped out of the dressing room. The silk felt strange and exotic against her skin after so many years of cotton and hand-spun wool. She had to resist the temptation to run her hand down the smooth fabric over and over again in wonder. It felt luxurious and sinful. It felt like something a woman playing private detective might wear.

She was feeling slightly decadent and slightly anxious when Sam turned around. He glanced casually at first, then his eyes came back and lingered. The dress draped familiarly down her body, caressing her soft curves, flirting with her long slender legs. His jaw clenched in the effort not to reach out and follow the lines of the fragile fabric with his own callused hands.

He'd known she had a wonderful body. He'd felt it pressed against him in slumber, he'd had it writhing against him in passion. He'd touched it, tasted it, worshiped it. And looking at her now, he wanted to do it all over again.

But who knew what this woman would do? This woman here, this woman draped in silk, was every inch the rich heiress, every inch the royal princess. Any minute now he expected to see her arch one eyebrow and shoot him that cold frigid look that women like Sarah Mathers had mastered so well.

Oh, she was beautiful in silk. But for a sharp instant, he felt a panging loss for the woman in cotton. For that woman, he'd felt an affinity.

But not this woman. This was the heiress that would most likely return to her villas and spas the minute the case ended. This was the kind of woman he avoided, and the kind of woman whose life was light years apart from his own.

He turned away.

"That ought to do just fine," he said, trying to keep his voice even.

María looked at him in surprise, sensing his displeasure and feeling the disappointment hit her hard. Her hands fell away from the silk, and her shoulders slumped ever so slightly. Funny, she had been without this kind of clothes for so long, and had never missed it. On the farm, her skirts were more than adequate for any hour of the day or night and she liked the simplicity. But the skirts were also voluminous and shapeless—anything but sexy. Not that there had been a need for sexy outfits, given her life of solitude. When she'd looked in the mirror, however, and had seen the old María in a beautiful, elegant dress, her first thought had been of Sam. What would he think? Would he like the way the silk clung, would he like the bare curve of her calf?

And maybe, a small voice whispered, maybe she'd wanted him to like it, to like her.

Who had she been fooling? She wasn't any seductress. She wasn't an actress. She was just a painter, and these days she wasn't any good at that, either. She just needed this to end so she could finally go home, where she belonged. With slow steps, she returned to the dressing room.

The minute she turned, however, Sam found his eyes drawn back to her, like the moth to the flame. Hungrily they took in the sight of her swaying hips and curved thighs. Desire seized him, fierce and tight in his gut, a brilliant flame in his eyes.

This woman definitely wasn't like the first María he had found. No, this woman was by far more dangerous.

They drove to the bank in silence, Sam at the wheel and María staring out the window with a sense of impending doom. All too soon they were there. All too soon Sam was repeating their simple plan and looking at her with expectant eyes. She climbed out of the truck slowly and began the one-block trek to the bank.

She looked back once, half hoping he would call it off at the last moment. Instead, he nodded reassuringly at her. Taking a deep breath, she continued walking.

Such things were easy for him, she knew. Barging into people's lives, crashing rental cars, breaking into Mercedes. Working outside the rules seemed simple to him, nothing to worry about.

But she couldn't say the same for herself. All her life she had followed the rules. When she'd had a 9:00 p.m. curfew, she'd been home by 8:30, and those were the days her parents weren't home until 4:00 a.m. themselves. When the rules said shower before getting into the pool, she diligently took hers, regardless of how cold the water was and of all the other people who simply walked straight through. Even her career choice had been one that was perfectly acceptable to her class and family. After all, wealthy young daughters of rich established parents were not supposed to have real jobs. And painting did sound so...cultured. That she'd been successful at it was hardly essential or necessary.

So she'd followed the rules, played things straight. And it had gotten her nowhere. Which was why she'd come to Ecuador, the closest thing to defiance she'd ever done, although nobody knew she was here. Except Sam, of course. The rest of her peers and the media probably figured she was in some exotic medieval castle somewhere.

So what in the world was she doing now, running across the country with a man she barely knew? And what was she doing standing in line at a bank about to claim she was somebody else's wife?

This must be someone else's life.

"Your account number please?" the teller asked in perfect Spanish.

María started looking nervous, then blushed guiltily because of it. With a small little laugh, she managed to spit out the requested numbers. "I would like to make a deposit," she added. She and Sam had agreed that that was the best approach. Banks were very scrupulous about who could make withdrawals, but anyone could deposit money. No signature, nor ID required.

"And your name?"

"Ma . . . Señora Augustine Pero."

The woman smiled politely, then looked back at the ancient computer screen.

"I'm sorry," she said after a minute. "But I don't see a Señora Pero listed here."

María blushed again. "We are newlyweds," she managed to say, just as she and Sam had rehearsed. Her own nervousness added credibility to the words. "Perhaps Augustine forgot. It has only been one week."

The woman beamed back at her. "Congratulations. Señor Pero didn't even tell us! Well, just one moment."

The woman looked back down, and quickly, so the teller wouldn't see her shaking hands, María slid the money forward. It was a small amount really, about ten dollars worth of sucres. A trivial payment for the information they hoped to gain from this venture. And from there things seemed to go smoothly. They took her money and gave her a receipt, and she managed to look blankly at it just as she and Sam had discussed. She questioned the total, telling them it could not possibly be right. Why her parents had deposited a huge sum as a wedding present. There was a flurry of concern, a statement was printed and they went over it carefully. Finally, saying that she would talk to her parents about it, María slid the statement into her purse. Could she have one from the month before as well, just to make sure? They produced it, she slid that into her purse as well.

Then, with another polite nod and some small closing words, she waved a quick goodbye. It was then she became aware of the teller's frowning gaze. Maria followed that gaze, straight to her ringless left hand.

Time seemed to stand still as María slowly looked down at her bare finger. Of course. A ring. How silly of her.

Smiling blankly she looked back up. "It's being sized," she said brightly and then not waiting one more moment, she turned and fled.

Sam was waiting for her in the truck as she ran breathlessly back out. It took a long moment for her to jump her way back up without tearing her skirt, but then she was sliding into the seat, her eyes glowing, her hands shaking.

"I did it, I did it, I did it," she told him excitedly. "I honestly did it."

He smiled calmly back at her. "Was there ever any doubt?"

Her laughter came in one long breathless rush that sent tingles down deep into his stomach. "Oh, yes, there was," she told him lightly. "Oh, there certainly was."

He couldn't say anything, he could only look at her. At first, he had been shocked by the change in garb. She'd gone from looking downright exotic in her ethnic garb to looking incredibly elegant. But if he'd thought that change had taken his breath away, it was nothing compared to her now.

This was María excited and laughing. This was María with sparkling eyes, flushed cheeks and animated hands. Gone was the cool reserve of a haughty face. Gone were the haunting shadows around her eyes, that tight look of iron control. The lines of strain around her eyes and mouth seemed to have melted away, leaving radiant youth and healthy glow.

She looked younger somehow. Perhaps more innocent, flushed with the thrill of her first successful rebellion.

Sam saw for the first time the child she might have been once and the woman she might have become had the fates been a little kinder, the years a little less harsh.

He felt a tightness swell unbidden in his throat, and for a minute he was forced to turn away.

"Sam?" she asked softly across the way. "Sam, are you all right?"

"Of course," he snapped back. "I'm perfectly fine."

She didn't say anything, she just watched him. She wanted to touch him, she realized suddenly. She wanted to reach over and run her hand across the broad width of his muscled shoulders. She wanted to feel the heat of his skin through the tight cotton of his blue polo shirt. She wanted to whisper her fingertips through the golden molasses of his hair, and feel it slide over her skin. She wanted to touch his face, the roughness of his whiskers, the softness of his lips.

And she wanted him to grab her, to pull her fiercely into his arms and kiss her with all the breathless wonder he'd shown her before and she was still so unsure of.

She wanted to touch and be touched until her pulse raced and she swooned with the burning, yearning heat.

He made her feel, she thought fiercely. After all these years of emptiness and rage, he pushed her, challenged her. He made her fight, he made her run. He made her *live*.

Her hand reached out, only for a moment, and then she pulled it back, retreating to her side of the truck. Who was she fooling? she thought for the second time that day. He made her feel, yes, but she was no longer a woman of feeling. She was a woman of emptiness. To want anything more would only leave herself open to the pain.

He made her fight back, but that didn't mean she'd win. And a woman could only afford to lose so much.

Sam was the one who finally broke the silence.

"Do you know any good parks?" he asked as he pulled the truck out of the parking space.

She pulled herself together enough to consider the little she knew about the city. "I think there's one down by Amazonas Boulevard," she said after a bit. "Why?"

"Time to evaluate what we know and figure out our next step. Food wouldn't hurt, either."

And so, not ten minutes later, they were sprawled under a tree crunching on dried beef and fruit with masses of screaming children running around them. To the left an impromptu soccer game had taken on a life of its own, and periodically they could hear the screams and groans of the onlookers. Out of deference to her new dress, Sam had produced one of the blankets, but María still had to sit very demurely with her legs curled off to one side.

The position was a damn sight too sexy as far as Sam was concerned, so he was careful to keep a good twenty-four inches of space between them at all times. He was spending too much time in the company of an attractive female, he told himself. It was wearing his nerves.

After they finished eating, María pulled out the bank statements from her purse and they began going over them. There were three identical deposits that occurred in two-week intervals. Sam thought it was safe to consider they were the man's employee checks. But even then, María assured him, the amounts could not cover Señor Pero's apparent life-style.

"What about this?" Sam asked, pointing to a large deposit that had been made over two weeks ago. "This says what, five million sucres? How much is that?"

María leaned over closer to peer at the entry, her long black hair swinging forward to brush against his arm.

"Oh, about five thousand dollars," she figured. "That is a lot of money for Ecuador. You have to consider, you can have a steak dinner for four thousand sucres, or roughly, four dollars. At those prices, five million sucres can only last you a short while. Minimum wage itself is fifteen thousand sucres or fifteen dollars a week."

"*How* much?"

"Fifteen dollars a week," she repeated calmly. "Why do you think tourists like it so much here? With these prices, they're in heaven."

"So what can you do down here that would earn you five million sucres?"

María shrugged. "I don't know. Be high up in a major business. Perhaps have invested money in the States. Maybe it was a gift or loan."

"Perhaps it was a bribe."

María nodded. "It *is* possible. But, Sam, you can't convict a man on this much evidence."

"No," he agreed, "but look at the date, María. Look, six days ago one of the missing children floated up in Florida. The coroner estimated her time of death about six to seven days previous. Which would be right about the time Pero made his deposit."

María looked very pale, her black eyes huge with distress as she leaned back. "You think Pero received five thousand dollars for letting her out of the country," she whispered. "And then the kidnapper killed her."

Sam nodded grimly. "It's a definite possibility. I mean we could be on the wrong track, but there certainly are an awful lot of coincidences here."

"What do we do now?" she asked softly.

Sam frowned. "We still don't know enough. Like how many children do they take out of the country at one time? Just one child would be fairly expensive, but too many could be risky. Either way, they would need reservations and passports."

"Maybe we should start checking with the airlines," she suggested. "See what kind of 'family' reservations there are, how far ahead you'd have to plan to get seats."

"Exactly," he told her. "See, you are pretty good at this detective business."

Her cheeks flushed lightly at the unexpected praise. "No," she said with a shrug. "Sometimes it's just obvious."

"Everything is obvious," he told her, "once you find the right way to look at it."

Which was perhaps the problem. He was beginning to "detect" other ways of looking at her. Like taking in the long curves of her legs, the silky shine of her hair. Like watching the black depths of her eyes and the light color of her cheeks. Like following the sweet fullness of her lips, the startling white of her tiny teeth.

Before he'd seen her only as a spoiled heiress, someone without heart or compassion. Now he was beginning to see her more and more as a simple woman, one that was sometimes infuriating, sometimes spoiled, sometimes sad, sometimes happy.

Had it been only last night that he'd felt her in his arms? Had it been only last night that she'd been soft and pliant against him, wild and wonderful in his arms?

Looking at her now, he wanted her again.

She could tell the direction his thoughts had taken by the sudden darkening of his eyes. The brilliant blue turned deep and intense. His breathing quickened, his lips parted subtly. She should turn away, she thought, even as she leaned ever-so-slightly closer. She should flee, she knew, even as she moistened her lips.

She definitely shouldn't be doing this.

His lips found hers. The kiss was soft and sweet and slow and long. It was the suspension of time and reality, a stolen moment, a savored one. It was the meeting of his firm lips against the fullness of her own, the rasp of his whiskers against the smoothness of her cheeks. It was man meeting woman, deep and hungry and hinting of more, wanting more.

A child's laugh sounded in the buzzing distance. A crowd roared, the noise cutting through, penetrating the spell. Abruptly, María jerked back, already turning away.

"Don't," she told him. *"Don't."*

His breath was still ragged, his thoughts still befuddled.

"But I want to," he found himself saying. "And you want me to, as well."

She couldn't quite admit to it. "No," she said. "It happens, but I don't want it." These words were sharper, laced with a deep intensity that cleared the last of his fog.

Of course, how could he have forgotten? He was the man that had forced his way into her life. The man who had brought her pain. All for the sake of the case. And that was all he cared about, right? The case.

"You're right," he said abruptly. "I don't know what I was thinking."

"Consider it forgotten."

Yeah, he thought to himself. Forgotten, just like she'd forgotten last night. It didn't matter, he told himself fiercely. Only the children mattered. The rest was simply physical hunger, and he was a man who knew how to go hungry.

"Time to get back to work," he said shortly. "I think it would be best if we split up."

She nodded blankly, doing her best not to look at him. If she did, she knew he would see the desire in her eyes. She didn't want to feel this way. She didn't want to remember his kisses. She didn't want to long for more.

Let it go, she told herself sharply. Let it go!

"You can check with the airlines," Sam was continuing, "I plan on watching Mr. Augustine Pero for the rest of the evening. In fact, better yet—I'll drop you off at the airport to find out things there. Then, after a half hour's passed, I want you to call Pero's office. Tell him you're from the bank, and that there's a problem with his wife's deposit. Be sure to describe his 'wife.'"

"But then he'll know what we did," she protested. "Why do we want that?"

"Because," Sam explained. "I want him to put two and two together. I want him to think someone is hot on his trail. When the heat is on, I want to see where he'll go, who he'll call. Maybe in his panic, he can lead us to the bigger fish. You have to understand, María, we don't have much time here. Maybe three days at the most, before the children will be taken to the States. The chances of us finding them there are slim. No, we need to find them here, and that gives us limited time. We can't afford to wait, and watch, and observe. I want to force Augustine's hand, and force it now. Let's see what he does."

"And if he does nothing?"

Sam sighed. "Then we may have to start over, which is time we certainly can't afford. At any rate we'll never know until we try. One thing, though, I need something a little less noticeable than this huge truck. Got any people who owe you favors here?"

She shook her head. "You'll have to rent something this time."

"Well then, I can do that at the airport as well."

She nodded and together they picked up the remains of their picnic and prepared for another long afternoon.

Sam spent the time squashed into the little yellow rental car, waiting for Pero to materialize. He waited and waited. The time María was supposed to call came and went. And still he waited. Finally, a little after five, the secretary walked out, got into one of the cars, and drove off.

Sam waited five minutes more, then got out of his own car, stretched his cramped body and approached the building himself. Looking through the glass doors, he could see that the door of Pero's office was shut. Slowly and carefully, Sam edged open the outer door. There wasn't any bell to give him away and after a cautious entry, he was at the secretary's office. Rapidly he looked across the woman's desk, noting the day calendar. With deft movements, Sam skimmed over the entries, taking a few notes.

Sliding the file drawers open, he managed to reveal several Spanish rag mags and a long listing of files he quickly reviewed. Nodding to himself thoughtfully, he crept back out without a sound. Five minutes later he was pulling into the Hotel Oro Verde, where he and María had agreed to meet. She was already waiting.

"How did it go?" he asked with no preamble.

She looked miserable. "They wouldn't tell me anything," she told him. "I tried to make up a story like you would, but I'm not good enough. Unless I have a specific name to give them, they won't look up any reservation information. All I could manage to learn was that this time of year it's best to make reservations at least two weeks in advance."

He nodded. "At this point," he said slowly, "I'm assuming they do make the reservations in advance, perhaps as a kind of deadline for them to meet. They certainly wouldn't want to hide the kids for too long here. The chance of escaping or discovery is too high. If the last pattern holds true, it looks like they probably bring in new kids every few weeks or so. Since the last kids were brought in two weeks ago, we don't have much time left. But," he said with a sigh, "we just might learn more tomorrow. Pero's got an appointment from two o'clock on, but there was no name, no address, no phone number. We'll have to follow him."

María looked skeptical. "Really, the appointment could be for anything."

He nodded. "I know, but that's the way this job goes. It's a lot of legwork, with a few scattered breaks that lead you to the next long stretch of fieldwork. It's all we've got, María. I wish it was more. Time ticks by too damn fast."

The last words were more for himself than anyone else, but still María gave him a searching look. There was a grimness in his eyes, and perhaps a starkness there, too. He really did take his work seriously. It wasn't just a case or an assignment, she realized. He was worried about the missing child he'd been hired to find and any others who might be with him. He really wanted to find them. It touched her unexpectedly, stirring emotions that were best left untouched.

She shook her head slightly, trying to keep her mind on "professional" matters.

"This *is* very tedious," she agreed. "I thought it would be over quick and easy. We would find them or we wouldn't." Her brow furrowed. "I don't like the not knowing," she told him. "I don't like the waiting."

Yeah, Sam thought, his emotions still dark. Better for it to be over with quickly. Better to get him out of her life as fast as possible.

"I'm hungry," he said abruptly. "Let's eat, then I have a few more phone calls to make."

She nodded, and let him lead the way to the hotel's restaurant. The food there she found to be excellent, but the conversation was stilted and tense.

The night was drawing to a close. It was only nine, but they'd risen at five, and now both were growing tired. And the falling of the night brought new questions, new situations they hadn't yet learned how to handle. Her mind kept drifting to the previous night. Last night and the storm. Last night and his body stretching, laboring over hers.

Unconsciously she shivered, and the fork dropped nervelessly out of her hand. It landed with a clatter, jolting them both.

"I'm...I'm sorry," she managed to stutter, and then quickly bent over to pick it up. She straightened in time to catch the banked heat in his own eyes before he turned away. Swallowing heavily, she returned her attention to the dinner.

It was the storm, she told herself, last night was because of the storm. It will not happen again. But her food tasted like ashes on her tongue and her mouth was much too dry. She compensated by drinking more wine.

For Sam, the dinner was little better. He'd registered them in two rooms across from each other, eliminating the temptation of an adjoining doorway. She didn't want him in her life, and he was determined not to intrude again. It was a simple physical reaction he told himself. And like all such things, it could be controlled. Just mind over body, that was all it took. Mind over body.

But his mind went over her body too much. Now, sitting across him in the elegant simplicity of her deep purple dress, she looked more tantalizing than ever before. The dress dipped down and formed a deep V that tempted him with little glimpses every time she leaned forward a little. She leaned forward a lot.

Even the way she held the wineglass, graceful fingers wrapped so delicately around the fragile crystal. She had beautiful hands, with long finely shaped fingers. The nails were blunt he knew, remembering once more how they'd felt raking down his back in raw passion....

"I'm done," he said abruptly, pushing away the last of his unfinished food. "I think I'll return to my room now," he managed tightly. He had already charged the dinner to his room account.

She nodded, not trusting herself to speak. When he rose it pulled the cotton of his blue shirt tightly across his chest, accenting the muscles clearly. Suddenly, desperately, she longed to touch them.

Just run her fingers lightly down his chest, perhaps trace the rippling planes. To touch him, to feel the hard strength of him, the vitality. To feel so...so alive. That was it, wasn't it? At the end of it all, in all of her life, in all of her dreams, he and the way he made her feel, was the closest she'd ever come to really living.

She wouldn't do it, she told herself desperately. To touch him again, to feel again, would be pure madness. Hadn't she learned these things yet? Hadn't she learned that nothing would come of it? He would leave, the passion fading quickly. And she had nothing to bind him with. Nothing at all.

Averting her eyes, she took another sip of the white wine and let it slide coolly down her throat. He watched her for another instant, seeming to wait for something, some sign. But she didn't look back up, and minutes later, he was gone.

She waited five more minutes to give him time to get on the elevator and up to his room. Then, as soon as she thought it was safe, she grabbed her purse and fled from the restaurant to the safety of her own quarters.

Once he was safely entrenched in his room, Sam called the hotel operator and arranged to get a line going back out of the country. A half hour later he was checking in with his people in New York.

This time he got some good information. Phil had met with one of the Florida police detectives in the morning, and had learned that the child's body that had been discovered had contained traces of laudanum.

"She was probably drugged for the flight," Phil concluded. "You know, on a long flight like that there's nothing unusual about a child sleeping through it. They probably carried her through customs like you would any sleeping child. Hell, they probably looked like a family holding an exhausted child."

"And the markings?" Sam quizzed. "Were the incisions professional or not?"

"That's harder to tell," Phil confessed. "The water and fish had really done a number on the body, fraying the edges a great deal. The coroner's guess is that the incisions around the abdomen were done with a smooth instrument like a scalpel, but he can't be certain. Even then, lots of people own scalpels. There are no traces of prescription medications in her body, and if antiseptics had been used around the cut, there aren't any indications left. Frankly, the coroner is ruling it a slapstick job, performed by some deranged lunatic. He's not thinking doctors at all."

"But it could be," Sam prodded.

"Yes, it could be."

"All right, Phil. Good work. Now I want you to start checking hospitals in the area. We know from the time of death that the operation happened roughly two weeks ago. After all, a kidney's only good for twelve hours outside of the body so it had to be within twelve hours of her death. Due to the tricky nature of organ transplants, it must have happened in some hospital or clinic somewhere. Find out which children have received organ transplants lately. Try to trace the kidney through the organ bank that does the matching. Or, some may have come from immediate accident victims—trace this supposed 'accident.' Find out if it really happened. I know we're talking a lot of legwork here, Phil, but you've got to do it fast. Pull all-nighters in the county library if you have to. We're down to just three days. And then we may lose the next one."

On the other end of the phone, Phil nodded. It would be a lot of work, but he wouldn't complain. He, too, knew the story of little Laura McCall. After a few last words, the conversation ended.

Next, Sam got ahold of Stevens. The man had also made progress.

"All right," Stevens said the minute he picked up the phone. "I learned more about María and her connection with O'Conner."

"Go on."

"It seems that O'Conner really was a close friend of the family. In fact, he helped bring María's mother from Ecuador to set up her pottery galleries. Then, of course, María's mother met the wealthy father, and the rest is history. When María was born, O'Conner sent a beautiful china doll all dressed in silk with real pearls around her neck and in her ears. I learned that from the priest at the baptism, who was quite impressed. And it seems when María's son disappeared, O'Conner also used a great deal of his own wealth and contacts to try and find the boy. Unfortunately, he met with the same results María did."

Sam mused over the information. "Well that explains O'Conner's interest in the whole affair. It seems he's appointed himself guardian angel to the whole family. Do you know what he did to try and find Daniel? Private investigators he may have hired, perhaps the FBI?"

With a sigh, Stevens confessed that he really didn't know yet. All he had were statements from people talking about O'Conner's interest in the matter. But Stevens promised to keep checking.

"All right," Sam concluded. "See what you can dig up. See just how in-depth O'Conner's philanthropy runs. Remember, we're on a short time clock here. I'll call back in a day or so."

After that, Sam had no choice but to move on to his next, and last, call. When O'Conner first picked up the phone, Sam kept his voice casual. He informed the billionaire of the progress that had been made, and mentioned the bill that had been rung up thus far. O'Conner took most of it with sharp little grunts, then asked a few questions about his goddaughter.

"How is she?" O'Conner demanded to know.

"Doing well," Sam answered with a sigh. "She's even turning into a fairly decent detective."

"Sharp as a tack, isn't she?" the old man interrupted. "There's a woman with brains. Even when she was young, you could tell. Saw it all in her eyes, right? Dark black eyes. I remember now. Beautiful eyes."

"Anything else, sir?"

The other man was silent for a bit, then finally, O'Conner whipped out, "Get back to work now. By my calculations there isn't much time left. Sounds like you have a few leads, but then they're based on a lot of assumptions. Be careful, Mathers. We don't have time for fool's errands."

"I know," Sam replied firmly. "And if you don't mind, I think I'll get back to work now."

Sam set the phone down with a shake of his head. He still wasn't convinced the stubborn old man wasn't a lunatic, but then, he was a sharp lunatic at that.

The conversation, though, had unsettled him. O'Conner's words kept coming back, again and again, in his mind.

Beautiful eyes.

She did have beautiful eyes. *Very* beautiful eyes, the kind that could steal a man's soul. He tried to shake the thought from his head, but couldn't quite get it back out. He didn't know what to think of María anymore. In the beginning, it had been simple. In the beginning she'd seemed to represent everything he disliked most about females, and especially about rich females. She'd seemed cold, hard, haughty.

It had been easy to look at her, and see Sarah Mathers.

But then there'd be the times he could see the pain in her eyes. The pain of a mother, still grieving for her child. God knows he'd never seen that look in Sarah's eyes. Especially not on the day she'd walked out on her husband and two children.

There were times when just looking at María made his gut clench. Half of him thought he should just let her go—he'd caused her so much pain by bringing her along on this mission. Yet the rest of him rebelled at the mere thought of telling her to go home.

He needed her, he told himself. She was honestly helping bring the case together. She knew the area, and as a female could play roles he couldn't. It was very logical, he assured himself, to keep her with him. Very rational.

The child, the missing child, was what was important. María could help him find the child, and thus, he wanted her around.

But he didn't see the missing child when he looked at María's black eyes. And he certainly wasn't thinking about the case when he watched the curve of her legs as she walked.

Grimly, he shook his head.

He'd made it his whole life by being tough, by having control. He'd never fallen victim to the foolish notions of love or caring as others had. He knew better, he reminded himself sternly.

He'd seen what "love" could do to a man. He'd dug his brother's grave, and he'd buried his father, too.

No. His fascination with María had nothing to do with any of those things.

Sam Mathers was much too smart for that.

Forcefully, he returned his mind to the matters at hand. And as he laid down on the hard bed, the image sprang into his mind of another innocent child.

He'd been too late with Laura. One minute too late.

He wouldn't let that happen again.

Chapter 9

They were up bright and early again the next morning, eating bread and cheese for breakfast in Sam's room while he mapped out the plan of attack for the day. After a bit of debate, they decided on spending the morning trying to hunt down forgers. After all, someone had to be making the passports for the children to leave the country. Then, around twelve, they would go to Augustine Pero's office, wait for him to leave, and tail him to his appointment.

It seemed simple enough.

They spent the morning on foot. María had changed back to her traditional garb, wearing one of the new skirts and another white peasant blouse. As the morning was cool, Sam had donned a black leather jacket over his traditional polo shirt and faded jeans.

It was a long and tedious morning, giving María an insight to what the major part of Sam's job must be like. There was endless walking, endless questioning. The only things they didn't find endless were answers.

By the time it was twelve, both their moods had soured.

They wasted fifteen minutes arguing over how to best fit the contents of the large, borrowed truck into the trunk of the considerably smaller rental car. María kept insisting that the stuff would never fit, so they should move it up to the hotel rooms. Sam, however, saw no reason why the contents couldn't be *made* to fit, which he eventually proved with a combination of persistence and pure brute strength.

He then had the audacity to gloat over this small victory for hours, until María felt compelled to smack the smirk right off his face. In point of fact, she'd taken the step forward to do just that when her blazing eyes caught his triumphant gaze and suddenly they both found it much too hard to breathe.

He watched her for a moment, *daring* her to take that last step forward, to find his lips with her own. For a long, tense minute they both just stood there in the electric silence.

And then, abruptly, María turned away. She just couldn't do it. Instinctively she knew that to give in now, would be to lose herself forever. He was a dangerous man, and she was a woman who had already been burned.

After that, they stayed far away from each other, retreating into silence as they drove through the streets of Quito. Then they arrived at Pero's office.

The appointment wasn't until two, but Sam wanted to be early just in case. They had no way of knowing, after all, what time Pero would choose to leave, so two hours seemed like a safe time allowance. And since he was a man used to waiting by now, Sam made the best of it. Settling back against his seat, he turned off the car and pulled out some of the fruit, jerky and water they'd brought along and set about eating lunch. María helped herself to an orange.

"Who do you think he's meeting?" she asked Sam after a bit, surreptitiously licking orange juice off her hand. He was still tense from their earlier exchange, and now his eyes, seemingly of their own volition, watched her small pink tongue dart out and lick the tart juice. His stomach muscles automatically retracted, and he had to forcefully suppress himself from reaching over, grabbing her hand, and licking the rest of the juice off himself.

She was trying to kill him.

"Sam?" María prodded again, interrupting his tortured thoughts. She turned toward him impatiently, "Who do you think Pero's going to meet?"

Sam took a huge bite out of his cheese and bread, finding himself suddenly ravenous. "I don't know," he finally managed to say after swallowing. "But I'm hoping it's the man who's running this operation. Or at least whoever's in charge of things from this end. Then, again, for all I know, it could be a doctor's appointment.''

"But you don't think so?"

"No, I don't."

Silently she finished her orange and then cleaned her hands properly before speaking again. She'd wanted to ask this for quite some time. "Why are you involved in this?"

He was having a hard time focusing on her words, his eyes once more drawn to her hands, wondering if she might lick them again....

"What?" he said tightly.

"Why are you here? Why are you staying with this?"

He turned back to the bread, managing a small careless shrug. "I'm a private detective. This is what I do."

She shook her head. "Surely there's plenty of other cases you could make money on rather than running around the globe like this. You seem to be very good at it. I bet you have your choice of cases."

"Then this must be my choice."

"But why?"

"Why not?" he told her. But then his evasiveness gave way to a more intense reasoning. "Can you think of a case better than this? Can you think of anyone who needs a private detective more right now than this missing child? Can you think of any better case for me to be working on?"

"No," she agreed softly. "No, I can't."

They both drifted back into silence.

"I don't want to believe it," María said finally. "I don't want to believe those men are out there. I don't want to believe that they really make their living killing children for profit."

"Well, you'd better believe it, sweetheart, because it certainly seems to be happening."

"Do you think so?" she asked. "When Daniel died, I heard people talk. Down in Mexico, they said the gringos did it. The rich gringos who needed organs for their own children. I didn't believe them. But then when they found the body..."

She paused, knowing she should probably stop now before she gave too much away, but the rest kept pouring out. "The Texas police said it was probably connected with some cult on the border. In a way, it was easier to believe that. Some insane, satanic cult—that made sense to me, because only monsters, only insane people, could be capable of killing children. But then," she whispered, her eyes peering out to the horizon, "then there were other children found in other places. And the people talked, and I began to wonder. And then I knew what they'd done to my child."

Her voice cracked a little, her head lowering to gaze sightlessly at her fidgeting hands. Then abruptly, her head came back up and he found himself staring into the startling intensity of her shining black eyes.

"Do you understand yet?" she asked him fiercely. "Do you understand why I left? Do you know what it does to acknowledge that that kind of evil not only exists, but that it can happen to you, too? Suddenly, you're vulnerable. It's a hard world and you have no armor left. Because that's how we get through, you know. We pick up the paper, turn on the news, see all the atrocities and comfort ourselves with the thought, 'It can't, won't, happen to me.' And then, once it has . . . I couldn't take it anymore. Every paper, every news story, reminded me of Daniel. The world became such an awful, horrible, corrupt, evil place to live. So I left, Sam. I wanted nothing to do with such a place."

Her eyes were still fastened on his, waiting for his acknowledgment. Slowly, he found himself nodding. Yes, the world could be an awful place. That was why he'd become a private detective. Because he'd seen all the injustices and he couldn't stand to see any more. Still, he was a strong, hard man. In many ways, he'd been bred for the harshness of the world from day one. But this woman, all of her life, had led a soft, comfortable, pleasant life. Until one day. It must have destroyed her.

Suddenly, he felt anger rip through him like a sharp pain. Damn it, something that evil never should have happened to her. She should have been left alone with the love of her son, her work. Those men out there had killed more than the child, they had killed the mother, as well.

And what about Sam Mathers? that tiny voice whispered. Was he really any better? Dragging her through this merry-go-round, forcing her to relive painful memories? And what if they *didn't* find the kids? What if he led her to the same end? What if the clock raced on, and this time it wasn't Laura McCall's body but María's that was facedown in the dust?

The image was so strong he had to shake it from his mind. No, he wouldn't let that happen. He wouldn't fail like that again. That was where he and María Chenney Pegauchi were very different. She'd run from such a horrible world; he fought against it.

"Look," he found himself saying, "you still live in that world. You can't run from evil, María. It's here even in the hills you love so much. You can only fight it. And if you fight it long enough, hard enough, you'll win."

"How can you be sure?" she asked softly.

"I grew up watching a lot of John Wayne movies," he told her firmly, then relented enough to give her a small wink.

She responded with a faint, shy smile. "I think you're a closet idealist, Sam Mathers. An idealist in a cynic's body."

He grinned with feigned innocence. "Now, what's so cynical about this body?"

"Your eyes," she replied immediately. "They're the bluest, hardest eyes I've ever seen. And when you want to, you can pin a person down with them as if you were stabbing a helpless butterfly. And your mouth, too. It doesn't smile much, you know. You keep it in a grim, tight line as if you have the weight of the world upon your shoulders. Is that what it's like being John Wayne in this day and age? Does it keep the weight of the world on your shoulders?"

Her observations were a little too close to home, and he flinched away defensively. "Well now, princess," he drawled out, "someone's got to have the weight of the world on their shoulders, because God knows the rest of mankind is running like hell from the burden."

She winced, the barb striking home. "Maybe some of us don't have strong-enough shoulders," she whispered.

Involuntarily, his eyes fell upon hers, delicate and finely formed beneath the white cotton of her blouse. They were beautiful shoulders, gently curved, nicely sloped. And they did look fragile. The kind of shoulders a man should stroke gently, kiss softly. The kind of shoulders a man should protect.

But he wasn't that kind of man. No, she'd been right the first time. He was the cynic, demanding the same from her as he demanded from himself. She wasn't anything like him, though. She'd grown up in private boarding schools while he'd sweated through the fields of Alabama. She'd been raised on Swiss chocolates and French wine while he'd downed his grits and milk. He'd been born into hell and trained not just to survive, but to win. He only knew harshness, only understood bleakness. He kept himself distant and cold and told himself he liked it that way. But not this woman. No, she was soft and feminine, and filled with a gentle kind of grace you just didn't see much anymore. At first he'd thought she was all ice and steel, but then he'd seen the soft tremble of her shoulders, the tears in her eyes. She was a woman who had traveled a lot of miles, seen a lot of heartache. And she certainly deserved better than some cold, hard man like himself. They had begun their lives worlds apart, and the differences were with them still.

She was strong, though, he reminded himself after a moment. She might have trembled sometimes, but so far she hadn't complained. She'd done everything he'd asked. She'd talked of her fears. Once, she'd run away. But she wasn't running now.

No, this princess, with her delicate shoulders, was still by his side. He shook his head at the dichotomy, willing the conflicting pictures away. He searched his mind for a new subject, and pounced on the first nagging question that rose to mind.

"Why don't you paint anymore?" he asked abruptly, assuming the offensive now.

Her chin came up, and she looked immediately defensive. "I'm a painter," she told him, but the words were a little too loud. It made one wonder which of them she was trying to convince. "I . . . I just don't have anything that's ready for the market yet," she said by way of explanation. She couldn't bear to tell him the truth, to tell him of the half-filled canvases that mocked her every day. Once painting had been as natural as breathing, her outlet, her passion. But it had fled with Daniel, and the paralysis shamed her. World-renowned painter, and she couldn't even complete a tulip.

"I see," Sam said, his detective's instincts switching to high gear. "And where do you keep these masterpieces? There weren't any in your house."

But she simply clamped her lips shut and turned away. Oh, no, she was under no obligation to tell him anything. God knows he'd dragged out enough of her dirty laundry, enough of her private pain. This one, this one at least, she could keep to herself. Let him wonder about the absence of her paintings, let him be the one in the dark this time. He kept his secrets, she would keep hers. And then at least she'd have something left, some little hidden part of her still intact when the case ended and he returned to the States once and for all. Besides, revealing such a fundamental failure, revealing the barrenness of her soul, was something she did not want to do in front of someone as strong, as centered, as Sam.

"Just somewhere," she said, purposely making her tone light.

She expected him to become angry at her refusal, perhaps even sullen. She certainly wasn't prepared for kindness.

"María," Sam began softly, having watched the play of deep emotions dance across her face. He could see the pain there, and yes, the secrecy, too. The detective part of him wanted to push it further, but the man in him realized he'd already hurt her more than enough these last few days. On its own, his hand reached across the seat to gently touch her shoulder. "It's okay if you're not a painter anymore," he found himself telling her. "You started young, you know. Maybe it's time to move on to something else."

She looked down at his hand, so large and rough against her own delicate skin, and abruptly she felt the sting of tears behind her eyes. She could handle his anger. She could handle his silence. But she wasn't prepared for kindness. She had no defense against tenderness.

"I am a painter," she insisted.

But the weakness of the words belied her, and she turned away, unable to meet his gaze.

"Then I'm sure it will all work out," Sam said, and found that he truly meant the words. He was torn between the overwhelming need to take her into his arms, and the prevailing logic that told him such a thing could lead only to madness.

"It'll be okay," he said again, but the words weren't quite enough for either of them.

Because it wouldn't be okay, thought María. Because nothing had been okay since that horrible moment when she'd looked up from her canvas and found Daniel gone. She'd been running ever since. Running from the monsters that had taken her son, running from the pain. But here had come the monsters again, and now Sam had found her. And she knew, knew deep down inside, that she was going to be hurt all over again. She'd become too involved, with the case, with the man beside her. She should never have let him touch her, never succumbed to the storm. Never succumbed to the caring.

"Here he comes," she said suddenly, the opening of the office doors catching the corner of her eye. "It's Pero."

"Show time," whispered Sam, his eyes immediately turning to the man who was now walking down the sidewalk toward the parking lot. Within minutes Pero had opened the Mercedes' door, thrown his leather briefcase onto the passenger's seat and gotten in.

"Duck down," Sam said. Then, not waiting for her reaction, he grabbed her shoulder and pulled her down with him, flat against the seat. "He's pulling out now," he said by way of explanation as his eyes peered cautiously over the dashboard.

"Oh," said María blankly. Sam looked down at her to find her dark eyes just inches from his. They were larger than he remembered. Larger and deeper, swirling with undercurrents. And there was a definite sheen to them that he didn't quite understand.

"Are you okay?" he asked softly.

She could only nod, her eyes not leaving his. She was too close to him, she thought half-frantically. Much, much too close. She could smell the spicy scent of the hotel's soap, see the clear blue of his eyes, feel the warm whisper of his breath. The rippling muscles of his arms were curled around her waist, and she could feel the heat of his body just inches away. She wanted to kiss him—wanted it badly. Wanted to curl herself up in his arms and just for one moment forget about the evils of the world and lose herself in the wonders of his touch. She wanted to forget about canvases that refused to cooperate, about the pictures that would no longer flow from her brush. She wanted to forget the dreadful fear of those people out there, those people that had stolen her son, those people who were kidnapping children still. She wanted to forget the doubts of herself, her own abilities. She wanted to forget, for just one moment, her fear of caring.

She wanted to kiss him, wanted to lose herself in him. Wanted him to touch her, to make her feel like she'd never felt in her life. It would only be a fleeting moment, though. Just one moment, and then he would be gone, leaving her as the people she cared about always seemed to leave. In the end, she would be alone again, and the pain would be that much sharper for having cared. She wouldn't do that to herself, she promised vehemently.

She wouldn't go through the loss all over again.

"We have to follow him," she said out loud, but her eyes were still dark with longing. "He's getting away."

Sam frowned for a moment, still drawn to the undercurrents he saw in her eyes, still intrigued by the mystery of her thoughts. But she was shutting him out. Like she'd done earlier. *Remember, Sam, he told himself, she didn't want you in her life to begin with.* He sat up abruptly.

"You're right," he said coolly. "Let's go."

They followed Señor Pero for the next hour. Twice they thought they had lost him, only to stumble upon him again as they searched through the side streets. But luck must have been with them, for at just a little before two, Augustine turned up a long street that went up, up, up, to an elite neighborhood of beautiful houses. He took the third street, and rather than turning as well, Sam continued to drive straight. After fifty feet or so, Sam pulled momentarily over to the side of the road. They waited five minutes, then backed up and turned, one by one, onto the streets themselves. With a little searching, they found Pero's car parked in front of a huge white house, which was totally enclosed—as most houses were—by a white wall. For added security, there was even a guard posted in a little wooden booth out in front.

"What now?" María asked him. "There's no way that they'll let you in without an appointment."

She was right, of course. Sam hadn't thought about the level of security in this city. Unlike the United States, where it was common to walk up to most doors, here it seemed that everyone was surrounded by walls with main gates that only opened after you announced your presence through an intercom. Of course, Sam had worked with much more sophisticated systems than that. But such things took time, the right equipment and, at the very least, nightfall. He didn't have any of those things now.

"You're going to do it," he said after a bit. "You can get in."

María shook her head vehemently. "This is your cup of tea, remember?" she told him. "I sketch pictures, you break into people's homes."

"No. This can work," he assured her. "Now listen up. Earlier today, we saw all sorts of Indian women walking around with huge loads of oranges or sweaters or whatever on their backs to sell. You can do the same. Aren't there door-to-door salespeople in Quito?"

"Sometimes women will walk up and down crying that they have fruit to sell," María admitted. "But that doesn't mean the house needs any."

"Then it's a good thing we have lots of things in the trunk," Sam told her. "We can start with the oranges and work our way to the sweaters. Surely they've got to need something."

Her eyes were huge, and a part of her wanted to shake her head. Oh, no, she wasn't any good at this sort of thing. But Sam was already unloading oranges, and somehow, somehow, it seemed easier to just go along. She'd promised to help, hadn't she? And the missing child needed her. . . .

Sam was busy pulling out the last of the oranges from the car.

"Okay," he told her. "Time to load up."

Her black eyes still large and uncertain, she wordlessly obeyed.

"María," Sam said firmly upon seeing her face. "Look at me."

She didn't have a choice as he took her chin in his hand and gently tipped it up. "I'll be right out here," he told her reassuringly. "If anything goes wrong, I'll help you. Trust me, María. It will work."

She nodded, swallowing back the fear. She took a deep breath and exhaled slowly. Then she bent down and began to rub dirt on her arms and clothes. Sam added a few worn tears to the fabric, and then, after a long skeptical look, he took some ground coffee from their supplies and used it to stain her teeth. Ten minutes later she was bent over almost double with the weight of the fruit on her back. She looked older and dirtier now, a poor woman selling fruit.

Grimly, she swallowed one last time, tasting the bitter grounds, then headed down the street. Down the street to the house where the monsters lived.

Her voice cracked the first time she tried to cry out *"Naranjas, frutas, naranjas!"* But gradually, it grew in strength as she trudged down the street. *"Naranjas, frutas, naranjas!"*

Her first time through, there was no response. Resolutely, she turned around and trudged down the street once more. This time, she went straight up to the gates of the white house and rang the button. There was a brief, cackling noise, then a maid came on the line.

After a bit of persistent whining, she managed to gain the maid's agreement to at least look at the oranges. There was a small buzzing noise, and then the gate opened.

As another maid led her into the house, she worked on calming her frazzled nerves. In all honesty, she was doing fairly well in her role. Her uncertainty kept her head bowed and her eyes down. She spoke little and kept the phrases short and guttural. As her even teeth hardly fit the image, she kept her mouth shut and her lips pulled tight. When she talked, all anyone could see was short glimpses of stained teeth.

There was a bit of bartering when the cook decided to go ahead and buy some of the oranges. María made an honest attempt at getting the best price for the oranges that now weighed heavily on her back. But the cook was sharp as well, and it took them a good five minutes to reach an agreement.

It was then María realized the crux of the matter, something they should have thought about long before. As a lowly peasant, she'd been led straight to the kitchen, and her only contacts had been with the maid and then the cook. At this rate, she could hardly eavesdrop on some conversation in some room, with some man she'd never even met!

Perhaps she could ask to use the bathroom, but God knows they would watch her like a hawk. Frantically she searched her mind, only to come up blank as the maid took down the amount of oranges she'd purchased and handed María the money in exchange. In a matter of mere minutes they were hustling her toward the door, her opportunities fading fast.

Think, María, she commanded herself desperately. *Think, think.* What would Sam do in this situation?

It was then she saw the vase, and the answer came all too clearly.

It took just an awkward stumble, a small little trip at the edge of the Persian carpet, and she managed to swing her still-considerable load to the left. With a crash down came the thousand-dollar vase, shattering on the floor in a symphony of brilliant splintering.

"*Mi Díos*," breathed the maid, looking at María with eyes so huge they threatened to pop right out of her head. "*Mi Díos*," the maid said again, and seemed completely incapable of saying anything more.

She didn't have to. Like a bunch of ants scurrying toward a fallen cake, the other maids converged upon the entryway.

There was an uproar of shouting and finger-pointing as chaos descended. María gathered enough to understand that they all knew the master would be furious and all wanted to be sure that everyone else knew they didn't do it. Slowly, attention came back to María.

The largest maid, an old hulking woman, didn't waste any time. She stepped right forward, and before María could even react, smacked her hard across her face. María reeled back from the impact, tasting the blood from her cracked lip even as her mind struggled to register the event.

She hit me.

It seemed too impossible to take in.

She hit me, María tried again. Honestly hit me.

Forgetting herself, she raised her face, dark eyes open in shock and wonder. The hand raised again, and she cringed, waiting.

"*¡Pare!*" ordered a commanding voice from the stairs. "*¿Qué pasa aquí?*"

Immediately the hand dropped down and the maids scurried around with their excuses and finger-pointing. María stayed in her corner, dropping her head down until her eyes could peer cautiously out to watch the man who descended into the din.

He was older-looking, elegant in his own way, with a fit figure and graying temples. His skin was olive, his eyes dark. And he looked ominous the way he walked, like a man used to being obeyed rigidly and immediately. He didn't immediately look evil, she thought. In the right setting, under the right circumstances, he was probably quite charming. But now, heading down the stairs, there was a sternness in the way he held himself, a harshness in his black eyes that scared her.

He came forward, catching her chin in a hard grip before she had a chance to step back. With a cold and assessing glance he took her in. The disgust for her apparent status was evident in the slight flaring of his nostrils, the disdainful crinkle of his brow. He had taken her in, registered her and discarded her like an old newspaper. For a moment she felt a small spark of defiance. She wanted to spit in his face, strike down his hands. It must have shown in her eyes, for his grip tightened, cruelly crushing her tender skin as his eyes narrowed.

Sharply she humbled herself once more. Poor fruit vendors were not defiant, she reminded herself. They couldn't afford to be, and right now, neither could she.

Then, as abruptly as he had taken her chin, he dropped his hand, turning away to attack his maids with a rush of Spanish.

He did not consult María, nor address her with a single word. Instead he laid out her fate to the maids in clear ringing sentences that would not be disobeyed.

The Indian woman had broken his priceless vase and did not have the money to pay. So she would just have to work it off.

It was a harsh sentence, and María made a few faint protests about her husband and children needing her to be home even as she marveled at the success of her plan. As she'd anticipated, the man dismissed her protests with a callous sneer. Then he turned and walked back up the stairs.

So her plan had worked; she was still in the house. The only sticking point, of course, was how to leave when the time came. She would have to cross that bridge when she came to it.

One minute later she was standing in the bathroom, under the supervision of the hulking maid with the stinging hand, Señora Rita Cielo Guape. It wasn't so bad, María thought as she got down onto her knees to scrub the floor. She'd gotten what she'd hoped for. And in the short trip to the bathroom she'd managed to catch which room the man had disappeared back into. Now she just had to find something near there to clean, and hope she could overhear something.

Could that man be the ringleader? she wondered as, under the harsh scrutiny of the maid, she began to slowly scrub. It was possible. It was obvious he was an arrogant, calculating man. On the other hand, he was also very refined if one went by the quality of his suit and the decor of his home. His hand, when he'd touched her, had been the soft hand of a man unused to physical labor. It had also been cold. Briefly, she remembered his fingers tightening on her chin. Yes, he was a cruel man, as well.

It took her an hour to manage it. By then she was once more wired with budding panic. Pero could be leaving at any time. Perhaps she'd already missed anything of use. Perhaps all this had been for nothing.

Her hands were now a raw and angry red from the harsh detergents she'd used to scrub the floors. But at least she was done, and now she had a dust cloth instead. She worked her way up the stairs toward the closed doors. The other maids had become involved in their own tasks, not paying much attention. She hummed a little under her breath, nervously dusting her way up the stairs until she was right outside the door. She found a good spot and began to dust it diligently while she strained her ears for sound.

At first she heard nothing, then gradually her ears adjusted to the muffled noises. Slowly, in her mind, it became a conversation.

The higher voice was Pero's, she was almost sure. It was jumpy and nervous as it whirred rapidly through its panicked points. Then another voice cut sharply through, this voice much lower, icy in its control. Evidently the señor did not share Pero's concern.

She had to lean forward to hear his voice, and in her concentration, she forgot all about her guise of dusting. So she was totally unprepared for the sharp blow that suddenly landed on her ear, bringing her head solidly between the heavy hand and the unforgiving wall. Dazed, she looked up to find the hulking maid looking down at her with glowering eyes.

María didn't wait for the maid to strike again. She'd heard enough to pick up a few things. Now she let her self-preservation instinct guide her. She bolted. With one swift heave, she knocked back the startled maid and then ran for the stairs.

She heard the loud yelp behind her, heard the clickety-clack of running feet against the hardwood floors. She turned once to see the maids race frantically down the stairs behind her and heard sharp bellowing as the cold-eyed man opened the solid pine doors onto the commotion reigning below. But María didn't wait for the maids nor the man to catch up with her. Instead she grabbed the nearest thing she could find, a decorative china plate, and threw it at the scampering blue sea of maids. There was a sharp cry, as it landed on someone, but she didn't look back to see the who's or where's.

She flew out the glass doors, hurtling her way across the yard toward the front gates. There was a moment of panic as the gates refused to push open. Desperate, she tried pulling, only to have them remain stubbornly still. Then her mind cleared long enough to realize there must be a release button.

She heard the authoritative clop of dress shoes against cement, and in some deep part of her she knew it must be the man coming down the steps, coming toward her. Her frantic fingers found the cold metal of the button. She pushed, the loud buzz penetrating through the confusion as she at last swung the gate open and whisked through its wooden frame.

She didn't stop at the security guard's yell, her mind set on one thing, and one thing only. To get back to Sam and tell him what she'd heard.

A sound rang out behind her, sharp and clear, rushing through the air. She heard it before she felt the heat flare through her arm. It was a full second more before she realized it was a gunshot.

"Sam!" she screamed, her legs pumping fast. She burst over the small hill; the end of the street was only fifty feet away. Fifty feet . . . then forty . . . then thirty . . . then twenty . . .

"Sam!"

Another shot rang out and the adrenaline surged even stronger as she heard the whistle of the bullet rocketing past her ear. But then a louder sound penetrated the air. It was a car engine being revved into life. The car appeared as if by magic, the door opening as she raced across the street. It opened, welcomed and then started moving even as she slid into place. Dimly she remembered to slam the door shut behind her as they zipped down the hill.

"Are you all right?" Sam asked. He looked grim, his hands rigid and white on the wheel as he sent them hurtling around a corner much too fast for safety or sanity. But he didn't slow down. He'd lost ten years of his life when he'd heard the sound of gunshots. And ten more when he'd heard her scream. "Talk to me, María," he demanded urgently. "Are you all right?"

She found she could only nod, her heart still pounding too loud for words. It was a full two minutes before she could manage a complete breath.

"I did it, Sam," she managed to gasp then. "I really did it."

These words were different from when she'd returned from the bank. These words didn't have a surprised, wonder-filled edge. Instead they contained a fierce determination, a steely strength. Even more worried now, he managed to risk taking his eyes from the road long enough to glance at her face. When he did, he swore violently, slamming his fist so hard into the dashboard that she jumped.

Already he could see the bruising of her cheek, the blood drying at the corner of her mouth.

"Damn," Sam swore vehemently to himself. "How could I have ever been so stupid!"

But María didn't appear to have heard, her attention too caught up in the bruised swelling of her cheek. Tentatively, her fingers came up and traced the tender area. It hurt, but it wasn't an unbearable hurt. It was a tolerable kind, the type you could put ice on and it would go away in a day or two. No, this pain was much different from the soul-numbing, inner emptiness she'd been wrestling with all these years. That had been the pain of failure. This, she thought in a haze, hands touching her cheek, this was the pain of success.

"Sam," she said suddenly, her voice firm with conviction, "you were right, Sam. I am tired of running. I do want to fight back. I want those men. I want them to pay for everything they've done. You should have seen him, Sam. So cultured and civil-looking. Until you saw his eyes. They were sharp, but so cold, so lifeless. Like a man without a soul. He's an awful, awful man."

Sam nodded next to her. He'd already known that, though, he raged at himself. He'd already known that the type of people who did such things could only be cold and cruel. And yet, he'd sent an unprotected woman straight into the lion's den. Hadn't he caused her enough pain yet? Hadn't he done enough damage?

God, when he'd heard her scream . . . How could he be such a fool? He should have gone himself, no matter if he couldn't pass for an Indian. He should have done something, *anything* rather than endanger the life of this beautiful woman.

"It shouldn't have happened," he found himself saying tersely. "It should *not* have happened."

Sam looked at the rearview mirror. No one was following them, so he allowed himself to slow down, turning into a series of side streets and roads until God knew they'd probably lost even themselves. Then, only then, did he pull over to the side of the street, kill the motor and turn to her.

With shadowed eyes, he surveyed the damage. On her cheek a dark bruise was already beginning to swell and grow, marring the previous perfection of her face. Unable to help himself, his hand reached out and gently brushed her hair back, tenderly smoothing his thumb over the swollen area.

Then his eyes noticed the red stain seeping into her cotton sleeve, and his face darkened with rage. "What happened to your arm?" he asked tightly.

For the first time, María became aware of the dull throb radiating from her right shoulder. "Oh," she said weakly, "I think one of the bullets must have hit."

Sam's jaw muscle tightened convulsively. Just what the hell had he been thinking, anyway? Keeping his temper tightly in check, he managed to reach across her body to lightly probe the wound. There was no exit hole, but there was no small bullet lump either. After another minute's examination he realized the wound was just a graze. Still, it could have been much worse. One more inch here or there ...

How could he have been so careless?

This time he gave in to the urge, and reaching across the seat, he pulled her gently into his arms. She trembled slightly at first, and then released all the pent-up shock and fear in one long, shuddering breath.

"God, Sam," she whispered shakily, the impact of it all slamming home at once. "They were really trying to kill me."

He nodded, stroking her hair lightly, not sure where to touch, not sure how to undo all the damage his foolishness had wrought. *He* should have been the one to go in. *He* should have been the one to take the risk.

"It's okay now," he breathed finally, calming her with the deep tempo of his voice. "It's all over now."

He felt her relax that last bit, her full weight now slumping against his chest. Still, she was so light in his arms, so fragile. He wanted to just hold her, to comfort her, and perhaps even to comfort himself.

But he was still a man on a job, and time was ticking away at a frantic beat. He'd lived his life with too much control to abandon it now, even for someone like María.

"María," he asked gently, "do you remember hearing anything?"

She nodded against the warm security of his chest.

"Tell me, sweetheart," he prodded. "What did you hear?"

With a sigh, she pulled back from his arms, drawing her strength around herself once more. Time for business.

"Well," she began, "I gathered that Augustine Pero is very nervous. He wants to just sit on this next 'shipment.' But the other man said no, it was too risky to keep the children that long. He said they would move out by the end of this week. That's three days, Sam. *Three* days.''

Sam nodded. ''We'll have to move fast, then.''

She nodded, though it made her heart hurt. Sam saw her wince, and his jaw muscle twitched convulsively.

''Was it the man that hit you?'' he asked tightly, already wishing he could sink his fist into the bastard.

''No. It was his maid.'' There was another pause as she sank back against the seat a little deeper. ''I think if the man had hit me, it would have been worse. He looked very strong. He looked very cruel. Or maybe cruel isn't the word—he was just so cold, so very, very cold. I think if a starving puppy whined at him for food, he would simply kick it away and not think of it again. I didn't like him.''

''Did you catch his name?'' Sam asked. ''I didn't see any mailboxes.''

''Pero called him Santiago once. That's all I know.''

''Were any other names mentioned, any other people?''

''Not that I heard,'' she said. ''But I didn't have the opportunity to catch much.''

Sam nodded, laying his hand once more on her shoulder. ''You did well, María,'' he told her, trying to inject a light tone into the conversation as much for his sake as for hers. ''You can now officially call yourself an honorary detective.''

She smiled wryly, but then her face turned serious.

''I want to get them, Sam,'' she said earnestly. ''I want to get those men that talk about children as if they were a shipment. I want them to pay for what they've done.''

Sam nodded in complete understanding. After all, it was the same determination the drove him. Still, he felt it was only fair to caution her.

''I understand that, María,'' he said. ''But remember, the good guys don't always win. We're doing well, we're making the right moves. But that still doesn't guarantee that we'll win.''

She looked at him skeptically. ''I thought you were the one who always won.''

He was silent for a moment. It was tempting to just shrug off her comment. But then the image flashed of Laura . . .

The words seemed to come out on their own, a mere whisper. ''No, María, I don't always win.''

She looked at him long and hard, seeing the sudden shadows in his eyes. And suddenly it was very important for her to know. He knew all her failures, all her vulnerabilities save one. She wanted, *needed*, to know this about him.

"Tell me," she demanded urgently. "Tell me."

He sighed deeply in the seat next to her, his eyes seemingly lost on the horizon. He didn't want to go over it. It was something that had happened long ago and something that haunted his sleep still. The more you care, he thought bitterly, the harder it is to let go. The harder it is to forget.

And then he wondered how hard it was going to be to forget the beautiful María Chenney Pegauchi. How long would she haunt his dreams?

Chapter 10

"There was a case," Sam began slowly, "that occurred about seven years ago. If you were in the States at that time, you may have heard of it. It was very well publicized, especially the ending. A child was kidnapped and held for ransom—the child of a very wealthy couple."

"The McCalls," María breathed softly.

Sam nodded. "Exactly. Then you know what happened."

"Only that the child was killed," she said. "I don't remember the rest. Besides, I thought the police handled that case."

"Officially, yes. When Mrs. McCall received the first ransom note, she went ahead and discreetly contacted the police. Their detectives put together a special task force to deal with it. But the McCalls also decided to hire a private investigator. They hired me."

"Go on."

"It was a tough case," Sam said, his eyes narrowed. He'd gone over it a million times in his head, over and over again. Each time he saw all the things he could have done. Each time, the memory ended with the picture of the little girl on the warehouse floor, dead.

He shook his head slightly, trying to clear away the fog of the past. Taking a deep breath to keep his voice steady, he contined. "The kidnappers wanted an even million, and they gave the McCalls only twenty-four hours to gather it. As I'm sure you know, no matter how rich a person is, liquidating a million in cash in just twenty-four hours isn't easy. They couldn't do it. The cutoff was midnight, and at eleven o'clock, they only had $724,000. This, by the way, isn't atypical. In the majority of these cases, full payment isn't made. The McCalls were under orders by the police to simply drop off what they did have.

"I had a lead, something I'd been working on for the last ten hours. At 11:15, it was decided to give me the go-ahead. They would make the drop with the money while the police would take out the scene. I would continue trying to hunt down the location where the child was held. By the end of the meeting, there were thirty-four minutes left.

"At 11:47, I finally located the man my lead had supposedly seen with the girl earlier that day. By 11:51, I had 'persuaded' him to tell me where the girl was being held. It was an abandoned warehouse a good fifteen minutes away. There was one patrol officer a bit closer. I said I would meet him there. At twelve o'clock exactly—our watches had been synchronized with the kidnapper's as he had ordered—the detectives jumped on a man picking up the drop. At 12:01, they learned he was nothing more than an errand boy. At 12:02, I arrived at the warehouse as the cops were just pulling in. At 12:03, we burst through the doors. They had shot her through the head. She was already dead."

He fell silent, the last of the words trailing off flatly in the small confines of the car. And the words were flat, having been repeated night after night to himself. With each review they had become more and more dispassionate. The intense emotion faded, only the sense of failure remained.

"You did what you could," María offered, but this time she felt the inadequacy of the words.

He shook his head grimly. "No," he said shortly. "I could have been faster. I could have been more careful. In hindsight, there are a million things I could have done. But it doesn't make a difference anymore. Laura McCall is dead, hindsight won't bring her back."

"You still think about her, don't you," María said. "Even now, you think about her."

"Yes," Sam said softly, and he nodded his head slowly. "Like you think of Daniel. Like her parents still see her play-

ing on the swings, running through the house. We all still think
about them. No matter what happens to the person, the memories live forever.''

"What if the memories aren't enough?'' María asked.
"What if all you've ever wanted was having the person back?''

"María,'' Sam said gently as he turned to face her with level
eyes, "Daniel is dead. Like Laura McCall is dead. *They are
never coming back.*''

"I know,'' she whispered, turning away from his gaze to stare
at the dashboard. Her fingers fidgeted restlessly. "That's why
I think of Daniel so much. It's the only way I can keep him
alive. Just like you keep Laura McCall alive in your mind.''

"But I don't,'' he told her fiercely, his dark blue eyes snapping at her. "I don't picture that girl alive, María. In my mind,
I will always see her the way I saw her that night, dead in the
middle of an abandoned warehouse. And hopefully that image will be enough to keep several more children alive. I didn't
hide after her murder. I didn't give in to it. This world is filled
with injustice, María, and it's the children that suffer. Laura
McCall's death was senseless. Daniel's death was tragic. And
it's a bigger injustice still to simply let such things go. I've declared war on injustice, María. And every child I save is one
more I've snatched from it. In the end, I intend to win.''

The words were intense, ringing clear and true in the tiny
rental car. His eyes were equally passionate, a hard, determined blue. But there was something else there—a fierce anger and, shifting slightly beneath, an intense pain. She wouldn't
have thought someone could feel so strongly about somebody
else's child. Unless . . .

But Sam was already turning away from her, his blue eyes
switching to look straight ahead. In a matter of seconds, the
passion was gone, and he was once more the controlled man she
knew so well. And whatever had been in his eyes was now
locked under that control.

She shifted in the silence, her shoulder throbbing. Finally, she
spoke.

"You think I gave up, don't you?'' she asked quietly.

"Yes,'' he told her. "Yes, I do.''

"It's different,'' she argued. "You were hired to find that
girl. Your responsibilities came with a paycheck. Mine were
different. I was his mother, Sam. I was supposed to protect
him.'' Her voice broke slightly, and this time she was the one

who looked away. She forced out the last of the words in a voice filled with quiet heartbreak "Do you know how many times I promised to keep him safe, Sam? Do you know how many times he ran to me with his scrapes and scratches, trusting me to make them better? Yet in the end, I couldn't protect him at all. In the end, I was helpless, too. In the end, Sam, in the end . . . I failed him."

"In the end, you were human," he told her firmly, his tone relenting. "In the end, you did what you could. It's just that this world isn't perfect. Sometimes, the wrong people succeed, the right people lose. But you have to keep trying."

"That's easy for you to say," she answered shortly. "You failed a stranger. I failed the child I loved more than life itself."

Her eyes left the dashboard just long enough to meet his, and she was shocked by the sudden anger burning in his eyes.

"Do you think you're the first person to fail someone you love?" Sam bit out harshly. "Are you so naive that you really believe that? At least strangers took your child. Something sudden, something completely senseless. I watched my own brother die for two years. I watched his shoulders shake with a deadly cough, his cheeks burn with fever. I watched his eight-year-old body slowly waste away bit by bit until, in the end, he was grateful for the release.

"And I tried everything, María. I shot deer on the neighbor's farm even though they could arrest me if I was caught. I went without my own food so that he could have more. I worked harder, faster, longer, trying to earn enough money to buy more medication for him. But in the end, none of it was enough. He simply wasn't strong enough. He didn't have the will to live, he didn't have the spirit to fight. And my will and spirit weren't strong enough for us both. So I watched Joshua die bit by bit, and I buried his body when at last it was done. He was my *brother*, María. I would have given my life for his if I'd ever had the chance. Just like you would have given yours for Daniel's. So don't talk to me about failing someone you love. I know all about that myself. And it still isn't a good-enough excuse for hiding. If anything, you should fight harder now, because you know the price of losing."

There was a wealth of pain in the words which deepened his voice and turned it to gravel. His blue eyes were brilliant with the pain, bright with anger. The intensity of his feelings shocked her, humbled her, touched her. She was torn by the desire to look away in shame and reach out in comfort. In so many ways he was a harsh man, a demanding man. But listening to him now, she understood why. The need to touch him, just a small gesture of compassion, grew almost overwhelming. She had to clench her fists at her sides to resist.

Slowly, she managed to tilt her head up. "I'm not running anymore, Sam," she said steadily. "I'm learning how to fight now."

He looked at her, sitting just a few feet away, and his eyes fell on her bruised cheek and blood-caked wound.

"Yes," he said softly, the anger leaving him as he reached out a large hand to touch her cheek. "And now you have the battle scars to prove it."

She smiled at that and gave him a sideways glance. "Do these mean I'm no longer a princess?"

But abruptly his face froze, his control once more shuttering into place. He turned stiffly back to the steering wheel. "No," he said shortly. "You'll always be a princess to me."

Sitting beside him, María could feel the smile dying on her face. For one moment she had thought they'd actually connected. For one moment, he had confided in her, let her in. And now, without any warning or explanation, he was shutting her back out again. Hurt, and not wanting to show it, she looked down at her hands, balling them into fists on her lap.

They really were two different people. He was so hard, so grim, and his background so different. And yet sometimes, sometimes, she thought that maybe they weren't so far apart, after all. He made her feel things. He made her want things. Well, none of it mattered. His feelings for her were all too abundantly clear. She was just some princess.

Her head began throbbing again, and unconsciously, she rubbed her temple.

Sam watched the motion from the corner of his eye, and felt the frustration bloom once more in his gut. She looked so vulnerable, sitting there with her bruised cheek. He wanted to reach over and pull her into his arms once more. He wanted to feel her cheek against his shoulder, feel the soft sigh of her breath against his neck.

But he didn't move. He'd already told her too much, let her get too close. As her comment had reminded him, she was a princess. No matter what, they were two people with completely different upbringings and completely different lives. This match was temporary, a matter of business. When it ended, he would go back to New York and his agency. And María? He hoped that maybe she would get on with her life. She was certainly learning not to run anymore. Maybe she would return to Europe. Perhaps paint again.

Either way, they would both go their separate ways.

And that was the way he wanted it, right, Sam? the small voice taunted. He liked his isolation. He liked his control.

Right?

Wordlessly, he started the engine and began to drive. María let her head drop back against the seat as her shoulder began to seriously throb. She closed her eyes. Moments later, she was asleep.

Sam, however, remained intensely alert as he drove. Stubbornly, he shut all thoughts of the woman beside him out of his mind, turning instead to the matter of the missing child. Time was running out, the countdown drawing to a close, and frankly, he wasn't sure of the best way to pursue things from here.

One thought was to go to the local police with their suspicions. Then again, all they had *were* suspicions, no hard facts, no evidence. Sam was also concerned about handling the entire case in Ecuador. He was a foreigner and unfamiliar with the laws. If he did end up in a shoot-out or having to defend himself, there was no telling how it would look. And, judging by what María had said earlier, for a price, officials were more subjective here. If Santiago could afford to payroll Pero, perhaps he had a cop or two up his sleeve as well.

It all bore thinking about. On the other hand, Sam decided as he searched for a recognizable main street, letting the kidnappers get back to the States would be too risky. In Miami, they could just slip through the cracks, disappearing completely. No, it would be better to pursue things from this end.

Unbidden, a stark image rose to mind. Joshua, eyes feverishly bright, shoulders shaking with the force of his coughs. Wasting away before Sam's eyes. Living in some delirious world where he still called his mother's name.

But now things were different, Sam told himself as he finally found a recognizable street and turned onto it. This time, the child would survive. Because Sam was bigger, stronger and smarter than he had been in those long-ago days. And he'd learned from the mistakes of his brother and father.

The hard way.

Not wanting to wake María, Sam carefully shut the car door and went into the pharmacy himself to buy aspirin, antiseptics and bandages. He had a feeling things were going to get rougher before they were finished. Then he drove them both back to the hotel, rousing María so he could lead her through the lobby.

She was still groggy when they reached her room, and not giving it another thought, he took the key from her, unlocked the door and led her in. He left her on the bed to fetch a glass of water for the aspirin, then set about reexamining her right arm. The wound wasn't deep, and had already stopped bleeding on its own.

Trying to be as gentle as possible, he wet a washcloth with warm water and placed it over the wound to soften the clotted blood.

"It doesn't hurt too much," she told him groggily. "I think you were right and it is just a scratch."

"We'll see," he said tightly, the wound a harsh reminder of just how much danger he'd put her in. After a few more minutes of soaking, he removed the washcloth and judged the clotted blood to be loose enough to remove her blouse without tearing the wound open.

He reached down to pull off her shirt. Immediately she stiffened.

"What are you doing?" she asked warily.

He looked at her calmly.

"I'm going to have to check the wound, and the only way to do that is without the shirt."

"It's just a scratch," María said quickly. "I can take care of it."

He paused, the defensiveness of her words making him wary. For crying out loud, he'd already seen her without her shirt on. They had made love before, even if she had turned away from him so easily afterward. Grimly, he forced the thought away. It didn't matter what she felt for him personally, he told himself. If she wanted to shut him out, turn away again, well that just wasn't going to work this time. Damn it, she was wounded and he was going to take care of her—whether she liked it or not.

He pulled the shirt free of her waistband, ignoring her small gasp of shock. "Think of me as your doctor," he informed her curtly.

She would have liked to. However, she'd never slept with one of her doctors before.

Sam paused, trying to figure out the best way of pulling the buttonless shirt over her head without jostling her arm.

María repressed a shiver. He was leaning so close she could feel the heat from his breath. And she was agonizingly aware of his hands, resting right beneath her breasts.

She blushed furiously. "I can take care of it," she insisted again.

He glanced up angrily, intending another impatient retort. But then his eyes fell upon her flaming cheeks. She was embarrassed, genuinely, truly embarrassed. The discovery floored him. This woman had been married, hadn't she? She'd even given birth to a son. And yet she was still embarrassed to remove her blouse in front of a man when she obviously needed medical attention. His eyes narrowed. For crying out loud, what kind of louse had she been married to that she still had to overcome such an elemental thing as nudity?

Under the onslaught of his gaze, her cheeks only reddened further. Oh, she was very embarrassed right now. But how could she explain the situation to him? How could she tell him that, yes, she'd been married, but the few times her husband had seen her naked, he hadn't been that impressed. And while Sam might have seen her once before, that had been the night of the storm. She hadn't been herself then. This was much different. This was with all the lights on, all the awareness turned full blast.

But he kept staring at her, and she finally decided that to try and explain her discomfort would only further it. She gave in, averting her eyes long enough to gingerly pluck at her blouse with her one good hand. But she encountered the same problem Sam had: how to pull the blouse off over her head without inflicting serious pain.

After watching her silently for another long moment, Sam finally gave in.

"Here," he said firmly. "Let me do it."

With that, he gathered up two handfuls of the thin white material, and proceeded to rip the blouse in half. María gasped at the impact, but he ignored her. "I did buy more blouses, remember?" he told her.

She could only nod with huge eyes, this new turn of events beyond her immediate realm of comprehension.

In another moment he finished pulling the blouse away from the wound and off her completely. At one point his hand brushed her breast and she flinched noticeably. The jaw in his muscle clenched at the action, but he remained silent. And then the deed was done. The blouse was off and she was sitting there in her brilliantly colored skirt and her plain white bra. Self-consciously, her good arm came around to cover herself.

If Sam noticed, he didn't say anything. For all intents and purposes, his attention was focused on the wound.

It was indeed superficial. The skin had been torn considerably, and some white threads from her blouse had become ingrained in the wound. She had been very lucky, though, he thought. Had she swerved to the right at the sound of the shot, it very well could have done serious damage.

And it would have been all his fault.

His face darkened as he set himself to the task of cleaning the wound. He tried to be as gentle as he could, first brushing it with the warm, damp cloth, but he had a feeling he was still hurting her. The only gunshot wounds he'd ever tended had been on one of his men and on himself. That had been considerably easier, they were men. They were tough.

María, on the other hand, looked unbelievably fragile sitting on the edge of the bed. With her slender build, shadowed eyes and ashen features, she looked exceedingly vulnerable. The type of woman that was meant to be sheltered and protected.

And she had been, he reminded himself. Her entire upbringing had been in comforting wealth. No worry for her about how to pay the bills, how to make ends meet. No worry about dirt under the fingernails, and certainly no worry about things like gunshot wounds.

At least not until she'd met him.

And here she sat now, a woman whose life had been a virtual pastel painting, shot in the right shoulder. Yet there were no hysterics when he applied the stinging antiseptic. No crocodile tears, no complaints. She flinched at the first contact, and he knew it must hurt, but her jaw merely tightened, not a sound escaping.

She'd been right in Otavalo. She might have been a rich kid once, but she wasn't anymore. He'd called her a princess. He'd accused her of being self-centered, a coward. But she wasn't. And suddenly, he was the one who was afraid.

He'd had a lifetime of bitterness and betrayal to protect him from selfish women. Years of disdain to harden his heart against a princess. But against a woman of such quiet dignity? Against a woman who was truly afraid, but who would fight, anyway? Against a delicate, beautiful woman who was blushing even now as he gazed upon her sensible bra?

No, nothing in his life had ever prepared him for María Chenney Pegauchi. Nothing had ever prepared him for such fierce desire, such gentle wonder.

He felt his hands begin to tremble, and he realized he wanted to touch her as he'd never wanted to touch a woman before. He wanted to kiss away the fear and strain around her eyes. He wanted to soothe the throbbing pain of her wound with gentle caresses. He wanted to find her lips, so full and soft, until she moaned against him. Until her hands wrapped themselves around his strong neck. Until she lost all shyness and surrendered herself to him once again.

He wanted...

It must have shown in his eyes, because her black gaze suddenly darkened with her own longing. Breathing became much harder, her lips parting softly to drag in more air. They stared at each other for a long, heated moment.

Unconsciously, her hands came down from her chest until she was as unprotected and vulnerable as before.

And his eyes took it all in. The gentle swell of her breasts covered by nothing more than two serviceable but small triangles of fabric, the white of her bra a stunning contrast to the rich almond of her skin. As he looked, the nipples tightened in response to his gaze, hardening before his eyes until all he wanted in the world was to lean down and draw one of the tender buds inside his mouth.

He bent slightly closer, and María softly whimpered. The sound slammed into his gut, urging him closer. His tongue flickered out, finding the first nipple through the fabric, and she gasped in response.

He thought he might shatter with the force of his desire. His lips closed around the nipple firmly, and he sucked on it hard. Far off he heard her cry, felt her arch her back, giving herself over to him. The sense of triumph was brilliant, intoxicating, heady.

"Let me do this, sweetheart," he whispered against her left breast. "Let me taste you."

His fingers found the clasp of her bra and released it, pulling the fabric away from her breasts until they were wonderfully naked. Once again his tongue darted out. Once again his lips found and suckled her nipple.

The sensations were wonderful to her, like wildfire ripping through her blood. Her fingers buried themselves in the thick richness of his hair, tugging him closer, wanting more.

But the moment she tightened the fingers on her right hand, a different sensation ripped through her body. Pain, brilliant and fierce.

She couldn't stop the sharp gasp that escaped her lips, and Sam's reaction was instantaneous. He froze.

For a long moment neither of them moved. And then Sam slowly drew back, his breathing still harsh. His eyes, however, were stark in their self-condemnation.

"Forgive me," he breathed, and the self-loathing in his eyes made María's heart wrench. "I didn't mean to hurt you again. I'm so sorry."

Then, before she could protest, he was drawing back completely, finding the sheet on the bed to pull up over her trembling form. "Rest now, sweetheart," he whispered softly. "It's the best medicine for you."

She wanted to protest, but her own emotions had been thrown into complete turmoil. She'd wanted to keep this man distant from her, far away from her heart. But he had only to look at her with his deep blue eyes, and she wanted him. The feel of his lips on her breast... She was suppose to remain cold toward him, and yet he made her feel so alive....

Already, he was walking away.

For a moment, she almost called him back. For a moment, she almost gave in to the ache burning low in her stomach. But then, with supreme control, she turned the feelings away. She was a woman without emotions, right? A woman without feeling should feel nothing when a man walked away from her.

And thus she didn't say a word, not even when she heard the door click shut. She just sat there in rigid silence on the bed, even as she felt the tears burning her throat.

Then, slowly, she leaned back down against the pillows. She closed her eyes and let sleep take away the pain.

Five minutes later, Sam Mathers was back on the streets of Quito. For him, the night was only beginning.

María awoke with a start in the darkened room. With all the curtains drawn, she was momentarily disorientated by the pitch-dark blackness. But gradually her eyes adjusted and her senses kicked in. Her first thought was that her arm hurt like hell. Dimly, she remembered the events of yesterday, the maid's stinging hand, the gun's sharp refrain.

Quite a change for a woman who had spent her life with satin bed sheets and chauffeured cars. But then, things had changed a lot in the last five years.

The first year she'd fled to the hills had been the hardest, she recalled as she tentatively made her way out of the bed. There were the endless blisters and backaches as she learned to haul her own water, hoe her own garden. But it had had its rewards as well: the first time the corn stalks had poked through the hardened ground; the first time she had fended off a squawking mother hen to gather the egg.

It had been the first time that she had ever really been on her own. The first time she'd taken on nature and really seen just what she could do. She wasn't so soft after all, she wasn't so spoiled. When the chips were down, she'd learned to survive. And somewhere along the way, she'd even convinced herself it was enough.

But Sam was right. For all her accomplishments, she'd still avoided the biggest challenges. Society. People. The monsters. For all her minor victories, deep in her heart, she still hadn't really conquered the fear.

Yet, last night, she'd gone into that house. Hell, in the last two days alone she had done things she'd never dreamed she could. She had learned how to dismantle car alarms, con bank tellers, even sneak her way into a house. Well, she certainly hadn't been able to beat the monsters on her terms. Perhaps she could on Sam's.

And yet she wondered where it would lead. Sam was right there, too. No matter what she did, no matter how many children they saved, Daniel wouldn't be coming back. So in the end, when all was said and done, she would still be alone.

Maybe she would go back to the hills, anyway. Life was simpler there. She missed the clean air, she missed rising in the mornings for no other reason than to catch the sunrise. She missed watching the hills go from their light green to dark, from pink to dusky mauve as the sun slowly sank each night. She missed the simple rhythm of her garden, the crisp taste of her lettuce. She even missed her chickens.

But maybe, just a little, she told herself, she missed the museums of Paris. And then there were the Italian operas. And Broadway plays. And skiing in the Alps, scuba diving in the Cayman Islands. Maybe she missed her other life, too.

She still couldn't see herself going back. She had nothing in common anymore with the people of the jet set. People who spent their time worrying about whether or not their plastic surgeon was the best. And she missed even less all those who asked her about her art because it was the sophisticated thing to do, yet cared not a whit for her answer.

With a long sigh, she pulled open the curtains, momentarily blinding herself with the brightness of the early morning sun. It was later than she'd thought.

But then she was sidetracked by a scene taking place down below. The sun was slowly washing into the narrow alleyway, creating an intriguing combination of light and shadows. And somewhere in between, the sun slanting sharply across her face, an gnarled old woman was painstakingly working her way through the knots of her granddaughter's hair. They were both clad in rags, the little girl's face smudged with dirt, but she was composed, even patient as her grandmother labored through the long black strands. The only thing that gave her true feelings away was the incessant swinging of her legs as she sat on the edge of the porch.

For a moment María felt the tingling in her fingertips. It would be such a perfect portrait, with the shadowed light and rich contrast of old and young. A perfect picture, just like the ones she had once been able to paint.

She turned away sharply. But what about now? What about that little log cabin filled with row after row after row of unfinished canvases? She'd tried and tried and tried to recapture the ability, tried to make the paintbrush sing across the canvas. But it just didn't work anymore. The technique was still there. If anything, she could probably continue to earn a reputable income as a landscape artist. But the magic, the magic was gone, the ability to capture not just the moment, but the emotion, had fled from her. That special something that had made a María Chenney Pegauchi painting a masterpiece had vanished with Daniel, leaving just one more empty spot in a woman who already had so many. Artist? Painter? Who was she trying to fool? The magic was gone. Daniel wasn't coming back, and the magic probably never would, either.

And that was why she didn't go back to Europe, she reminded herself harshly. Because, quite frankly, she wasn't María Chenney Pegauchi, world-famous painter, anymore. Now she was just plain María Chenney Pegauchi, an Indian woman with a small farm and long, lonely nights. A woman who was just now learning to fight, but who was still too late to save her son.

Dully, she sat back down on the bed. Yes, it was all too late to correct the mess her life had become. She'd failed her son, lost her art. That was the end of it.

At least, she told herself, she could farm. And she was strong, she thought, crossing the room to run the shower. She'd made it this far, after all, and she could make it farther. She had survived much, and she could survive more.

Like what? whispered the tiny voice insidiously. *Like Sam Mathers?*

Yes, she hurled back in a moment of defiance. But the thought wasn't comforting because she couldn't truly believe it.

It was nearly seven by the time she'd finished her shower. She was forced to go slowly, since her right arm was still unbelievably stiff and sore. The mirror revealed that her lower jaw was a now a brilliant mix of purples and blues and yellows. She grimaced, but there was nothing she could do about it.

She finished dressing and then crossed the hall to knock at Sam's room. After a long moment she heard the sound of locks being drawn back and the door opened.

There was a long, tense moment when they met eye-to-eye. Sam had only to look at her bruised jaw to feel the guilt rushing back. And María had only to look at his lips to remember how they'd felt on her breast.

Both looked away sharply. María's eyes settled on the pattern in the carpet.

"Breakfast?" she asked after a moment.

"There's some stuff in here," Sam replied, moving away from the door long enough to let her in. He was just wearing jeans, she realized with a start. His chest was bare. With effort, she kept her eyes away from the naked skin. When he pulled a dark green polo shirt over his head, she didn't know whether to be relieved or disappointed.

She sat down on the still-made bed while Sam pulled out some more fruit and cheese. He offered it to her, and then carefully sat down on the other bed, a few feet away.

They both ate in silence.

"I think we got our big break," Sam said at last.

"We did?" María asked, looking at him for the first time. "What break was that?"

"Well, I've been thinking," Sam began. "You see, we have a few problems. The first being we're only guessing at who the bad guys are. We have no evidence. The second being, that if these really are the right men, we still need to figure out where they have the kid, and when they plan on moving him. Now, you helped us out yesterday. We know that the move should be happening by the end of the week. But we still need to get something concrete. Therefore, I'm going to have to break into Santiago's house."

María looked startled. "But you can't just break into his house," she exclaimed. "He has security guards and everything. Sam, they've already shot at me. You can't risk that."

He brushed her protest off with a wave of his hand. "No, no. I'm not going to do something completely suicidal. I came up with a better idea last night. You see, I walked around the neighborhood a few times—"

"You went out last night?" María interrupted.

"Yes," he replied. "And I learned a few interesting things. For instance, all the houses are set in the hillside in layers. And they aren't uniform. The level of the house seems to be based on whatever the owner preferred when it was built. So, while Santiago's house appears to be surrounded by a tall fence, it's really only in the front. In the back, his next door neighbor's yard just happens to be nearly level with the top of his fence."

"I don't get it," María said flatly. For some reason she was angry at the thought of him going out alone. Somehow she'd come to think of them as partners. But, she reminded herself sternly, Sam had said from the very beginning that he liked to work alone. She had to accept the truth. She was just along for the ride. Wherever that would lead.

She continued crossly, "You'd still have to break into the neighbors' yard to take advantage of that."

"Break in or be invited," Sam said triumphantly.

"Invited? How are you going to manage that?"

Sam looked smug. "Well, I just so happened to run into the owner of the house. He's an American, you know. Works at the embassy. And it just so happens that his wife is an art buff."

María narrowed her eyes suspiciously. "Just what did you tell this Mr...."

"Richardson. Mr. Eric Richardson and his wife, Janice. Well, I 'dropped' your name."

"My name?"

"You are a famous painter."

"Was," she told him sharply, beginning to feel truly worried now.

"Well, Richardson recognized your name," Sam continued. "And he said how much it would please his wife if she could meet you in person. So, tonight, at nine o'clock, we have been cordially invited for cocktails and dinner at the Richardsons's. During which time you'll entertain them with your wonderful personality while I make my way into the backyard sometime after eleven and jump over the fence right into Mr. Santiago's house. Perfect."

She looked at him critically.

"I see," she said dryly. "And what am I supposed to tell them while you're jumping over fences, that you're in the bathroom for two hours?"

Sam gave a small shrug. "That's rather a sticky point to the plan right now. However, I'm sure once we're in the situation, some sort of opportunity will present itself. The detective business really is kind of a fly-by-the-seat-of-your-pants job."

María wasn't convinced.

"You're going to get yourself killed," she said flatly. "And that's all there is to it."

"María," he began softly. "We don't really have a choice anymore. We only have two or three days left. If we want to find the boy, we have to move, and we have to move fast. I didn't come all this way to fail now."

His words weren't exactly comforting, but then she didn't know of any words that might ease the feeling of impending doom. Ultimately, he was right. The child needed them. She took a deep breath.

"I know," she said at last. "Just . . . just be careful."

"I will," he assured her and briskly stood up. "Well then, let's get to work."

She nodded, grabbing her poncho as they headed for the door. "You know," María said as she closed it behind them, "with my black eye and wounded arm, they're probably going to think you beat me."

"We'll tell them we were in a car accident," Sam replied easily. He paused for a moment, then in one last breath he rushed out the other small detail he'd neglected to tell her. "By the way," he said as they climbed into the elevator, "we're . . . um, married."

Chapter 11

By the time nightfall had arrived, María's nerves had bunched themselves into tight little knots and her arm throbbed with a passion. She and Sam had already walked for a good four hours that day, going from graphic shops to identification shops, asking lots of questions and receiving few answers. Sam still wanted to know who was making the passports for the children exiting the country, but so far, they'd had no luck.

Finally, Sam had called the search to a halt. Instead, he'd redirected them to a very modern-looking mall and had started hunting for a suit. María still had her purple silk dress, but Sam thought it would be best if she also bought a new dress for the evening. Augustine Pero knew that a woman in a purple dress had posed as his wife at the bank and had walked away with two statements. He very well could have relayed this information to Santiago, and Sam didn't want to take any chances since they were going to the house next door.

As it was, he'd informed María there was little chance of anyone recognizing them. Santiago had seen her only as an old, filthy fruit vendor, not as a world-famous painter traveling with her husband. Still, María was nervous.

She wasn't completely convinced that she could pull off this charade for an entire evening. Really, what Sam was asking her to do should have been her easiest role yet; simply play herself. But it had been five years since she'd lived the life of an internationally known artist. And sooner or later, Mrs. Richardson was bound to ask what María was working on now. María didn't know the answer to that one herself.

Not to mention that she was supposed to be Sam's wife. She still wasn't sure just what that entailed. Was she supposed to call him "dear" or "honey"? Hold his hand? What about kissing? Hopefully the Richardsons were a very conservative couple, María thought desperately as she began to get ready for the evening. She wasn't sure how much playacting she could take.

After a quick shower, María dried off and picked up her new dress. It was a simple cocktail affair, an elegant black velvet that clung tightly to her skin, ending just an inch above her knees. A wide band of material circled around to cover her wounded shoulder, but her arms and neck were still bare. When she turned around, except for the encircling band, her back was completely bare, as well.

Face it, María told herself as her stomach fluttered again, the dress was just plain sexy.

And that made her nervous, too. Sexy dresses were what other women with long legs and slinky figures wore. Sexy dresses weren't for ex-wives who couldn't even hold their husband's attention. But somehow the saleswoman had looked so impressed when María had tried it on that she'd given in to the urge and taken it. Now, back in the sanity of her room, she was beginning to wonder why.

But she did know why, that voice spoke up firmly. *Because she wanted to see if Sam would notice. Because she wanted to see if his eyes would darken when he looked at her. Because she wanted to see if she could make him burn.*

She wanted him to touch her.

With a small cry, she let the dress fall from her fingertips back onto the bed. She didn't want this, she thought frantically as she fled back to the bathroom to do her hair. She didn't want to want Sam. She didn't want to want anyone.

She was a woman with no emotions. Wasn't she?

Still, she remembered clearly the night of the storm, Sam's body laboring above hers. And she could recall last night, the burning feel of his lips upon her breast. Even now, she shivered at the memory.

Oh, she did want it. She wanted Sam Mathers.

After all these years, all these miles, the isolation was gone. This man had come and destroyed all the barriers she'd so carefully built in her life.

She wasn't a woman without emotion anymore, she realized suddenly.

No, she was a woman in love.

What in the world was she going to do?

He didn't want her, she reminded herself brutally. In the beginning he hadn't even liked her. Now, at least, he had grown kinder. Perhaps he even felt a small measure of respect for her after yesterday's events. But for him, it was still just a matter of business. He was a detective doing his job, and his only association with her was because of the case. It would end, and he would leave. Why in the world would he stay? What could she offer a man like Sam Mathers?

Nothing.

She was the woman who had failed her little boy. She was the woman who hadn't been able to keep her own husband's attention. She was the artist who couldn't paint anymore. Why, how, would he possibly want someone like her? Besides, they had nothing in common; he still saw her as a princess. So that was the end of it. The case would end, and Sam would go.

Just a few more days and it would all be over with. And what then? What then, María?

She had no answers. With a small sigh, she shook the last of the thoughts free. She might have fallen in love, but she'd be better off just letting it go. A woman could only stand so much pain in one lifetime.

It took her a good hour to do her face and her hair. The bruise on her jaw was still too fresh to cover with makeup, so instead she attempted to use her hair. First she swept it into a French twist in the back, then she very carefully loosened some of the shorter hairs that began at her right temple, curving them around her face to her chin. It created a slightly more exotic look that managed to partially conceal the ugly bruise.

Luckily, applying makeup was a lot like riding a bike. Though it had been nearly five years since her last attempt, she did a fairly nice job. She was almost happy when she was done.

But then she slid on the silky black hose, shimmied into the velvety dress, slipped into the high heels and realized she was ready. The woman in the mirror didn't even look like her, she thought dimly. The woman in the mirror looked sophisticated and young and . . . sexy. Yes, even sexy.

Her nerves came back in full force, and for one frantic moment she was sure she couldn't do it. The whole "her" in the mirror was a facade. The real María Chenney Pegauchi didn't look like this, didn't wear things like this. The real María Chenney Pegauchi was a wallflower, a quiet woman who had never enjoyed sex and had been considered inadequate by her own husband.

But she didn't pull the dress off. She didn't scrub the makeup from her face. Instead she simply stared at the woman in the mirror. The woman that probably wasn't her, but was the woman she had always wished she could be.

The reflection, she thought suddenly with a pang, was a woman who could be Sam's wife. The reflection was a woman who could paint masterpieces and hold the attention of the man she loved. The reflection was the woman María was supposed to be. Just for this one night.

And why not? she thought defiantly. Why not give it a try for one night? Next week there would be plenty of time to go back to peasant blouses and cotton skirts. Next week she could hoe her garden and fight with her canvases. Next week she could be the real María Chenney Pegauchi.

Tonight, she would be Sam Mathers's wife.

With another deep breath, she checked her image one more time, gave her hair one last self-conscious pat and stepped into the hallway.

It was worth it all just to see the look on Sam's face. He didn't say anything as he stood in the open doorway. He didn't even move. Instead his eyes roamed slowly over her figure, drinking it in. And then for a fraction of an instant, his eyes met hers, and they *burned*.

"I'm ready," María managed to say, the words coming out soft and husky.

Sam still didn't speak. He could only nod.

But he was an impressive sight himself, María thought as he offered her his arm. He'd chosen a deep charcoal gray suit that was perfectly tailored to define the wide breadth of his shoulders and the narrow mold of his hips.

It wasn't until they started walking that María could see his slight discomfort in the unfamiliar garb. He walked slightly self-consciously, his fingers coming up periodically to touch the knot of the tie before falling back to his side. Perhaps she should have thought less of him for it. After all, she had seen far more expensive suits and far more elegant men in her lifetime. But she didn't. She liked the way he moved, she liked the way his fingers worried his collar.

She liked the way that, even under the protection of the suit, he was still the Sam Mathers she'd come to know.

He was safe, she thought suddenly. Safe in a way all the other men she'd met never would be. He wasn't slick or smooth. He wasn't concerned with trying to maintain some image. He wasn't hung up on looks, and he wasn't hung up on being in the right place with the right person at the right time.

He was simply a man. An honest, straightforward, down-to-earth man. A man she'd fallen in love with.

Don't, she told herself suddenly. Don't care. Don't forget the pain. Don't forget your own limitations. Don't forget how hard it is to let them go.

Her silence matched his own. Finally he hailed a cab. It wasn't until they were almost to the house that the silence was broken, and even then it was Sam who spoke.

"Are you nervous?" he asked.

"A little," she admitted.

"Don't be. Tonight actually shouldn't be that rough. After all, for a change you're posing as yourself. The only difference is that Eric seemed to assume that we were a couple, and I never bothered to correct him. It's not uncommon for one couple to invite another over for dinner, and I figured it would be more of a solid cover, just in case something happened."

If he'd meant it as a simple explanation to calm her nerves, he'd failed. Instead, it seemed to her to be a pointed rebuff. It wasn't like he would want her for a wife, was it? It was simply easier that way. Part of the job.

"I'll be okay," María said tightly. "Don't worry about me. You, after all, are the one that gets to play James Bond."

The edge in her voice must have caught him slightly off guard, for he looked at her sharply for a moment, then shrugged his massive shoulders under the confines of the jacket.

"I'll be all right," he told her. "After all, this is what I do for a living."

That only made her madder, and with a closed look on her face, María abruptly turned away from him to stare out the window. It was only then that she realized they'd turned down the final street.

Santiago's house loomed large and dark in the falling dusk. It looked too gloomy, María thought apprehensively as they approached it. Perhaps she was getting carried away, perhaps the trauma of being shot by a man in front of that house was playing tricks on her mind. Because, for all intents and purposes, perched up on the hillside and circled by a tall spiked fence, the house looked like a dungeon to her now.

She shivered in the seat. "Don't go," she said softly, unthinkingly.

But Sam merely reached out and attempted a reassuring squeeze of her hand. "Don't worry about it," he told her. "I can handle myself."

"No. Just don't go. Don't." She could feel hysteria building as they moved just past the house, pulling up against the curb, Santiago's guard's box keeping its menacing vigil just four feet away. *"I don't want you to go."*

"María," Sam said calmly as he heard the panic in her voice. "María, it's the only way. And we've got to find that child. You know that."

Dimly she heard him, dimly the words penetrated. Yes, that was right, wasn't it? This was all for the missing child. It had nothing to do with her, did it?

The cab driver was looking at them both, waiting for his money. Abruptly María opened the door, stepping out into the cool night air as Sam reached for his wallet. The goose bumps rippled down her bare arms, shivering up her back. But she didn't wrap her arms around herself. Instead she forced herself to turn and look at the man sitting in the guard box in front of Santiago's house. It was just a few feet away.

"Good evening," she spoke to the guard and watched him nod politely in return. It was a different man, she thought suddenly. Of course. They probably all had shifts. So this was the man with the evening shift. This was the man whose comrade had shot her just the day before. She forced herself to smile, though chilling fear had her in its grip once more.

"Let's go," Sam said in her ear. "There's no reason to flaunt our presence."

"I wasn't," she whispered tightly, and simultaneously gave one last nod at the guard as Sam pulled her to the entrance. "This guard is different."

"Well, his job is the same."

"Maybe I can take care of myself, too," she said defiantly as Sam pushed the buzzer. Her earlier anger returned. So he didn't care about her, so he was just doing his job—already he'd reminded her of this several times tonight. Well, she'd been on her own for years now. She could take care of herself. Her chin came up, her eyes cooled and she found herself saying out loud, "Maybe I don't need you, either, Sam Mathers."

The words struck him as odd, and once again, he looked at her sharply. "Are you mad at me for something?" he asked her.

"As you like to say," she replied coolly, "don't worry about it."

Sam felt his own temper rise. "I won't," he said grimly. "Just as long as you remember that, for tonight, you're supposed to be my wife. And we wouldn't want to have a domestic spat in front of the Richardsons, now, would we?"

"Of course not, *darling.*"

He was saved from replying by the maid suddenly opening the gate in front of them. Sam calmly introduced them as Mr. and Mrs. Mathers and with a small nod, the maid led them to the house.

The Richardsons seemed a nice-enough couple. Janice Richardson had a gushing sort of sophistication that María was accustomed to. She fawned over her guests—the famous painter in *her* house, imagine!—fawned over her husband, and pretty much fawned over dinner, as well. Eric Richardson also seemed nice enough. A bit more down-to-earth than his wife, he involved Sam in a long conversation about football and just who was going to win the Super Bowl this year. Sam's answers seemed short, if not constrained, and María received the distinct impression that despite his build, football was not his strong suit. When Eric switched to baseball, Sam relaxed visibly and even María was impressed by his extensive knowledge.

"So what do you do for a living?" Janice cooed at Sam during a brief pause in conversation.

"I run a business in New York," Sam said easily.

"Ooh." There was a small moment as Janice seemed to digest this, then perked back up. "Is that where you and María met?"

Sam looked at María, but she simply looked back. The Richardsons looked at both of them.

"Actually, no," Sam said after a bit. "We met here in Ecuador, as a matter of fact. Isn't that right, María?"

She simply nodded. Then, suddenly seeing an opportunity to get back at Sam and all his indifference, she found herself saying, "It was wonderfully romantic. There I was in Otavalo, looking at some pottery, you know. And suddenly I looked up into the most riveting blue eyes I'd ever seen. Why, Sam was looking at me so intensely, I thought maybe he knew me. So I asked, 'Is there something I can do for you?' And he said, 'Yes, you can run away with me and be my love forever.' Now how can a woman resist such an offer? Isn't that so, sweetheart?" She ended with a devastating smile, glancing over at Sam in time to see his face.

Momentarily shocked, he recovered all too quickly. He turned to the Richardsons with a careless shrug. "What can I say? It's not every day a man travels to another country and encounters the most beautiful woman on earth. I think it was her hair, cascading down her back. Or maybe it was her hands. She has such delicate yet strong artist's hand. They feel like silk, yet can mold the toughest clay. Yes, I believe it was her hands."

The look he gave her was so heated, María felt her cheeks turn a fiery red. Eric Richardson struggled for a polite cough, but the discretion was lost on his wife.

"Ooh, that is just so sweet," Janice gushed. "Simply marvelous. So how long are you going to remain in Ecuador?"

"Oh, we don't have definite plans yet," Sam answered first this time. "Do we, *sweetheart?* But we'll probably be returning to the States shortly."

María could only nod while Janice Richardson seemed to sigh deeply. Across from her, María could see Mr. Richardson roll his eyes.

"Well, you know," Janice began, and María already knew what was coming next, "I just couldn't help wondering that, as long as you're in Ecuador, well, if maybe you couldn't paint a portrait of Eric and me. You know, it really would just be so wonderful if you could."

"I . . . I don't know," María said, glancing over at Sam for guidance.

"Oh," said Janice, leaning forward confidentially. "Are you working on something really spectacular now? You know, it's been years since we've seen any new works of yours. Why, I was just telling Eric the other day, I bet she's working on some grand masterpiece. Isn't that right, Eric?''

Eric nodded, but his gaze was much more speculative and sharply observant as he looked at María.

"Well," María said carefully. "as a matter of fact, I *am* working on something right now. But I'll think about it.''

It seemed to be the right answer, for Janice immediately clapped her hands together like some overanxious cheerleader and beamed at her husband. "Didn't I just tell you, Eric? Didn't I just tell you that she'd do our portraits?''

María didn't intend to do any such thing, but she didn't bother to correct Janice. She couldn't afford to anger the gushing woman at this point. Not when she and Sam needed to be able to stay long enough for Sam to figure out a way to sneak in next door.

She shivered.

"Are you cold?'' Eric asked suddenly. "Janice dear, why don't you close those windows over there. The night *is* a bit chilly.''

But for some reason that only caused María's fears to blossom all the more. Because the night was cold. Cold and lonely and filled with unknown terrors that were just waiting out there. What if Sam did make it over the wall? What if he did break in? What if someone saw him? What if they killed him?

What if . . .

Dimly she realized that both Eric and Janice were looking at her with concerned eyes, then she felt the warm strength of Sam's hand on her shoulders.

"You will have to excuse my wife," he was saying to the Richardsons quietly, standing behind her. "These last few days have been a little traumatic for her. The automobile accident has shaken her up a little.''

"Of course, of course," soothed Janice. "Why don't we move into the living room, where everyone can be a bit more comfortable." Sam nodded, letting the Richardsons go ahead. As soon as they were out of immediate hearing, he pulled back María's chair and looked at her intensely.

"Are you all right?''

"Sure," she said weakly. "I do this kind of thing all the time, you know.''

"You don't have to be sarcastic," he told her sharply, his hand falling back to his side. "Look, I know this is difficult for you. But just hang in there. It's already almost eleven. The maids at Santiago's must have gone to bed by now. I saw the last light go off about fifteen minutes ago. Now, I'm going to sit in the living room where I can still see the house through the windows. If everything remains quiet over there, I'll probably take off in the next half hour or so. Actually, María, I think we have a great opportunity here. The Richardsons already seem concerned about how pale you look. Why don't you faint or something? From what I can tell of Janice, she'll probably immediately suggest you lie down somewhere. I, being the concerned husband, will accompany you, of course. From there, maybe I can get next door for an hour or so without anyone noticing. They'll just assume we're resting. It's worth a shot.''

Wordlessly, she nodded. Faint? She'd never fainted before in her life, but at this point in time, it didn't quite seem so far-fetched. She really wasn't feeling that great.

With another nod, she followed Sam into the living room. There they sat side by side on the couch, talking with the Richardsons about a variety of subjects. María was having trouble following any of it, her mind too caught up in the feel of Sam's arm, strong and warm across her shoulders. She could even feel the heat radiating from his chest, and every now and then when he shifted, she would catch the faint scent of spicy soap. Once, she felt his thumb flick idly up and brush against her ear. She almost jumped off the couch at the contact.

As if sensing her nervousness, he leaned down low and whispered in her ear, "You're doing fine, María." Then to cover the words, he lightly kissed her lips.

She was too dazed after that to pay attention to anything. But her combination of nervousness and fear worked well. After another fifteen minutes of idle chitchat, the Richardsons exchanged glances and a decision seemed to have been made.

"María, dear," Eric began. "You really do look beat, and it would be a shame to make the two of you grab a cab at this time of night. Really, we have plenty of room here. Why don't you and Sam do us the honor of staying the night?"

Sam spoke up with some polite, trivial objections, but the end was never in doubt. A half hour later María found herself in a very nicely decorated bedroom with Sam. It had only one bed. Sam, however, didn't seem to notice. Instead, he was taking off his suit jacket even as he was closing the door.

While María watched, he pulled off his tie and unbuttoned his shirt in smooth, rapid motions. Within minutes he'd stripped down to the black T-shirt he'd donned under his suit and pulled a pair of black gloves out of his pocket. Then he fumbled with his jacket, producing a black cap, a length of rope and a miniature camera.

María suddenly felt as if she was in the middle of some old movie. God knows, in her normal life men didn't wear black T-shirts under their suits and keep rope, gloves and spy cameras in their pockets. This was too much, too real for her relatively limited life.

"You really are going," she said softly. "You're really going to break into his house."

"Of course," Sam said and finished pulling the dark hat over his lighter hair.

"What if there are dogs?"

"There *are* dogs," he said calmly. "Two Dobermans, not exactly my favorite type." He pulled four white capsules from his pocket. "And once they swallow these, they'll be sleeping peacefully until morning. Could you sneak into the kitchen and find some leftover meat to plant the capsules in?"

She nodded but didn't move.

"And if there's an alarm?"

"I checked that out last night. I couldn't see any signs of a sophisticated setup, no hidden cameras or lasers. He may have the doors wired, but I can take care of that."

She nodded again. She'd known this was going to happen. The whole night had been planned for the express purpose of Sam going next door. Yet now that the moment had arrived, she couldn't shake the feeling of dread in her stomach. It must have shown in her eyes, for just as he was about to walk out the door, he abruptly turned around.

He couldn't stand to see so much concern on her face. God knows he'd already caused her enough pain. Leaning down, wanting it to be casual, he lightly touched her cheek.

"It'll be all right," he said quietly. "I've done this a time or two before. I'll be back before you know it."

But her eyes remained worried. They pulled at him, and before he knew it, he was bending down and capturing her lips with his own. He'd meant it to be simple, gentle, fleeting. But the minute his lips touched hers, he was lost.

All night he'd been looking at her. All night he'd been watching the way the black velvet of her dress seemed to shift with her, caressing her skin the way his hands longed to. The bare, golden skin of her arms and back had been beckoning to him, until he'd wanted nothing more than to reach out and trace one finger up the silky trail. And then follow it with his tongue.

All night, he'd wanted her.

Now, he took.

It started slow. It had been so long since the last kiss. Too many nights, too many moments of wanting, of aching. But now his lips were on hers, warm, coaxing, seductive. And her lips were responding, parting, wanting more though she was uncertain of how to ask.

In the end the emotion took over where the doubts held her back. In the end all her fear and desperation rushed suddenly to the surface, until it was she who pushed against him, pulling him closer. With a groan, Sam gave in to the demands, letting himself drown in the exquisite sensations even as he told himself he should hold back.

But he couldn't. Suddenly his hands were burying themselves in her neatly twisted hair, arching her head back until he could slant his mouth hungrily across hers. And it felt good. So good, so wonderful, so right.

Until neither of them wanted to stop, until both were drowning in this wonderful sea of sensation they'd been waiting too long to feel again. Until both were starving for more.

Her lips were as soft as he'd remembered, warm and moist and welcoming. He traced them with his tongue and felt her moaning response. Teasingly, his tongue dipped in, exploring, licking, tasting. Her nails dug into his back, begging for more. He found her tongue with his own, and drew it into his own mouth, sucking gently.

The desire exploded in them both, enveloping them in the white-hot heat of passion.

Somewhere in another part of the house, a floorboard creaked, jerking Sam back to the grimness of reality. Swearing softly, he pulled away.

María sighed, a small sigh of protest. But then her eyes opened and reality intruded upon her as well. All at once her cheeks flushed a fiery crimson and she turned away, unable to meet his eyes.

"I have to go now," Sam said.

She simply nodded.

"Can you sneak into the kitchen and grab the meat for me now? In this outfit, I'd probably get mistaken for a burglar and shot."

"So then you'd be killed here instead of there," María quipped softly, the feeling of uneasiness still strong within her.

"María," Sam said with a sigh, and took a step closer, raising his hands to put them on her shoulders. But the tops of her shoulders were bare, the skin too smooth, the curves too enticing. Just a little to the right, he could see the beginnings of the puffy bruise where the bullet had grazed her. He stepped back, letting his hands fall, feeling the hopelessness ripple through him. "I have to go," he said finally. "It's the only way. I'll try to play it safe. And you can either help me with that now, or you can keep your back to me. But either way, I have to go. Either way, I'm still taking the risk."

"I know. I know. It's just..." She didn't know what to say. Just that she cared? That she wanted him to be safe? But she wasn't a woman who cared, was she? She wasn't a woman of emotion, and she wouldn't start now. "I just don't like the house," she finished at last. "It makes me nervous. That's all."

Sam could understand that, but nonetheless he felt a small twinge of disappointment. Of course she didn't like the house, not after her experience there. But... But what? He'd hoped just a little that maybe she would worry about him. He shook his head. It didn't matter. All he cared about was his job. She was just a means to that end. That was all.

"I'll be back in a minute," María said abruptly. "Just wait here."

He nodded and she slipped out the door, looking even more nervous and pale than ever. Hell, she probably couldn't wait until he finally got out of her life, he thought heavily. Probably couldn't wait to get back to the peace and quiet of the hills, where she could live her life and attempt to escape the nightmares that he'd reawakened. She could get on with her life, perhaps even set aside the past once and for all. Whereas it seemed he was constantly dredging it up for her. Constantly making her think of her dead son. And really, it was none of his business. He'd never even had a son to lose. He probably never would.

And so it goes, he thought bitterly. He earned his living solving other people's problems, saving other people's lives. So much so that he never really had time for one of his own. In all honesty, though, he knew that was the way it had to be. Love and marriage existed for other people, other fools. He himself knew better than to get caught up in passion and poetry. He believed in lust. He was much too smart for love.

The door creaked open, and María slid in.

"Here," she whispered nervously and handed him a plastic sack. "There were two pieces of steak left, so I grabbed them. I hope the Richardsons don't mind."

"Thank you," said Sam, and suddenly, for the first time in a long time, he felt a little nervous himself. It was María's fault, he told himself. She stood there, looking so damn beautiful, so damn fragile. And all he could think of was, what if something *did* go wrong? What would she do then? Santiago and Pero had both seen her. What if they tracked her down some day when he wasn't around to protect her? What if—

He felt suddenly grim. He would just have to make sure nothing went wrong. He would have to make sure he *didn't* get caught.

María was still looking at him, her hair rumpled from his hands, her cheeks still flushed from his kiss. Her eyes were wide, dark with fear, and her hands unconsciously folded and unfolded in front of her.

He wanted to kiss her again. To hold her close just for one last moment, but he knew better by now. If he touched her, it would be impossible to leave again. Because the next time he touched her, he wasn't going to stop.

"It's time to go," he said abruptly, but still didn't move.

"You have everything?"

"I think so. You said the study was at the top of the stairs, right?"

"Yes. What if it's locked?"

"I can take care of that."

"Do you have a flashlight?"

"I have a penlight. It's very small, but that's all I need."

"Be careful."

"I will."

"If you're not back by a certain time, is there something I should do? What about the Richardsons?"

"If anything goes wrong, María, I want you to tell them you didn't know anything. You already said we had a whirlwind romance, that we met and married in only a few days. Use that. For all intents and purposes, I'll look like a thief who was trying to break in. Go along with it. Tell them you had no idea. With your reputation, they'll believe you. Then leave the country, just get the hell out."

"You think Santiago will come after me next?"

There was a slight pause. "I don't know, María. I don't know for sure. But he might. He might."

"I have no place to go," she said softly. "All my family is dead. I haven't spoken to my friends in years."

"Go to your godfather," Sam said suddenly. "Russell O'Conner will help you."

"Russell O'Conner?" she repeated, looking surprised at hearing the name. "It's been years since I've seen him." Then suddenly her eyes narrowed. "How do you know about Russ?"

Sam hesitated for a moment, then went with his instinct. O'Conner seemed to care about his goddaughter. Certainly given the circumstances, he would want Sam to finally give out his name.

"O'Conner is who hired me," Sam admitted. "Your godfather is a true philanthropist. Look, it's getting late, I've got to go." Sam said urgently. "Do you understand what to do? Just remember, if I'm not back by morning, forget about me. Take care of yourself first."

She nodded, though the starkness of the words pounded within her. And once again, desperately, she didn't want him to go. But she didn't have the power to make him stay. Somewhere out in the darkness, the monsters waited. There was no way of knowing where.

She didn't say anything more, afraid of the frantic words that might tumble out if she even attempted to speak. Sam didn't speak, either. Instead, with a brisk nod, he brushed past her and crept down the hall.

She watched until he was out of sight, turning into the living room where the sliding glass doors led to the backyard. Once there he could jump down to the yard next door. And then?

There was no way of knowing.

María curled up in the guest room's armchair, her arms wrapped tightly around her knees. It was 1:00 a.m., and now, much as it had five years ago on another night, the waiting began. She could only hope that this time the person she loved would come back safe.

Chapter 12

Deep into the night she sat curled in the chair. Deep into the night frightening thoughts swarmed and gathered in her mind, burying her in the darkness.

What demons lurked in the house for him to find? What cold-eyed monster waited at the top of the stairs, armed with a gun, ready for Sam's ascent? One pull of the trigger, one small muscular spasm, and he would be dead.

The possibility filled her with a terror she couldn't quite comprehend, an overwhelming sense of dread that simply built and built and built. She shouldn't care so much. She should put it out of her mind. She should forget.

But she couldn't.

Because deep in her heart, she knew she *did* care. Except maybe caring was too weak a word for the powerful emotion she felt tightening her chest.

Maybe...

Don't, she told herself, blocking the forbidden word from her mind, don't think it, don't say it, don't feel it. Just don't care. Because she knew that if she did, surely some worse fate would befall him. Like her parents, who had simply been driving along one day and had been wiped out by a truck driver who had fallen asleep at the wheel. Like Daniel who had simply been playing with the local kids when the men had come and snatched him.

When she cared, she lost. How could she bear to lose again?

Don't care, María. Let him go. Because time never stands still for you. Because the minutes still tick, the hours still change, the days still pass, and all of it leaves you behind. Today you're with Sam Mathers, tomorrow he may well be gone. And what do you do then? How many times can one woman pick up the pieces? How many times can one woman convince herself she really can live after all? How many times can one woman care, lose, and still find the courage to care again?

She couldn't do it. She couldn't set herself up that badly for a fall.

But deep in her heart, she knew that it was hopeless. She couldn't stop the process. Somehow, some way, when she hadn't been looking, Sam had managed to squirm his way into her heart. And now she didn't know how to get him out.

So she sat in the darkness, terrified by her own fears as pictures of guns and monsters swarmed through her head.

God, she thought desperately, keep him safe. *Please just keep him safe.*

But it wouldn't be enough, she thought with foreboding, and watched the shadows dance across the wall. It would never be enough.

At two, she contemplated jumping the wall herself. Perhaps if she was there, seeing for herself what was happening, it wouldn't be so bad. Maybe she could even help him. But she doubted it as soon as she thought of it. He was the James Bond. She was simply an artist. She would probably alert every single person in the house and get them both killed.

At two-thirty, the thought resurfaced, gaining in intensity now. Maybe she could at least walk out to the backyard. From there she could see the house, see if any lights were on. And if there were... If there were, at least the waiting would be over. At least then she'd know it had all gone wrong. If the lights were still off, well then, she could wait for him at the wall. Maybe he needed help or something. Maybe...

At three she couldn't take it anymore, and, pulling on Sam's discarded suit jacket for warmth, she crept into the hall. The house was silent, more silent than she'd realized. It seemed that each step she made creaked in the darkness, giving her away. But no lights came on, no voices questioned her. Then at last she was at the sliding glass door, carefully easing it open and wincing as it rasped along the gliders.

The night wind whipped in, making her shiver almost instantly at the chilling contact. But resolutely she stepped out into the cold air, sliding the door shut behind her. Now, huddled beneath the jacket, she could see the house next door, rising black and ominous in the night. But no lights were on, no sounds erupted. It looked like the house of the dead.

She walked over to the edge of the lawn. From there she could look down into the other yard, a good seven feet below. A short three-foot fence separated them, nothing that would be too difficult to jump over. Except that on the other side the distance would be a good ten-foot drop. She couldn't resist. Being careful not to touch the fence in case it was wired, she moved a step closer and peered down. No inert bodies lying down there. So Sam must have made it over okay. He must be in the house.

At the house with the monsters. What if Santiago woke up, what if Santiago—

A muscled arm swept tightly around her neck, a ready hand catching her scream against its callused palm. A small click, and she felt the heart-stopping feel of cold steel against her forehead.

"María," a familiar voice rasped in her ear. Then, abruptly, the arm was gone, and Sam was fairly pushing her away. Too shocked to compensate for the sudden motion, she fell to the ground.

"What are you doing here?" he demanded at once. His voice was too loud, but he couldn't completely help himself. Having just seen a person materialize in the night out of the corner of his eye, he had automatically assumed the worst. If he hadn't recognized her, God only knew what would have happened.

Still on the grass, she was half-propped on her elbows. Her face was much too pale in the moonlight, her eyes dark pools of worry and fear. Immediately he felt a sharp pang of remorse. Squatting down, he looked at her intently.

"Are you all right?" he asked with concern.

She nodded slowly, her eyes absorbing his huge frame. His face was slightly smeared with dirt or dust. His black T-shirt now had a small tear. But there were no bruises, no new cuts. Everything seemed to be in place. He was safe.

Safe . . . and he'd come back to her.

The emotion that welled up was too strong to allow her to speak. She could only nod helplessly, her eyes a river of drowning intensity she knew she couldn't explain.

All that fear, all that terror that something bad would happen to him, too. And now he was here, safe, strong. The undefeatable Sam Mathers.

And she loved him. She couldn't admit it until now, when she could have lost him. Loved him helplessly, hopelessly, endlessly.

The depths of her eyes pulled Sam in, swamping him with a tidal wave of emotion he didn't completely understand. She was beautiful in the moonlight, her face so delicate and perfect, her eyes so intense. She looked small and vulnerable in his huge mass of a jacket, and a sudden fierce need to pull her into his arms, to protect her, struck him, for surely someone so delicate needed protection. He wanted to hold her, to keep all the terrors away from the dark pools of her eyes.

The urge was so strong, he almost reached out. He almost touched her.

Abruptly, he rose, unsettled by the fierce need. He focused his eyes on the horizon, struggling to gain his bearings.

"We should go in," he said tensely, and then, not waiting for a reply, he turned and untied the rope he'd used to scale the wall between the Richardsons's and Santiago's. He gestured at her to follow him back into the house, moving in careful silence.

When they finally reached the door of their room, Sam eased it open, motioned her inside, and then closed the door securely behind them both.

"How did it go?" she asked at last, searching for at least some kind of contact.

Sam shrugged, pulling off his hat and gloves as he sat down on the edge of the bed. "It went okay, I guess."

"Did you find out anything more?"

"Won't know until tomorrow. I took pictures of all the important-looking files. We can develop them in the morning, and then between the two of us, we can plow through them."

"How many are there?"

"A lot." He reached into his pants pocket and pulled out four small rolls of films. "How fast do you read?"

She smiled wryly in the dim light of the room. "Not that fast."

"Well, hopefully we can eliminate a lot of it just by looking at the headings. Hopefully."

"All right."

There was a long pause as each looked at the other, then back down at the floor. For the first time, Sam became aware of the fact that there was only one bed.

"I'll—uh—I'll take the floor," he offered softly, still not quite looking at her. María simply nodded.

"We really should be going to bed," Sam said again. "Tomorrow's going to be a long day."

María nodded again, but still didn't move. Her nerves wrapped themselves a little tighter and her hands began to shake. But this time it wasn't from fear.

He looked so good, sitting just a few feet away, his blond hair burnished under the light, the black T-shirt stretched tight across the broad expanse of his chest. It would be so simple. Just reach out and touch the granite outline of his jaw. Just reach out and run her finger down the rippling muscles. Just reach out. Just touch. One touch, that was all she promised herself. Just one touch to feel so alive again. To feel so wanted, needed, desired and...

She still didn't move. But her eyes had grown wide again, her face soft with vulnerable yearning, her lips parting in longing. Sam took one look and felt it slam deep into his gut. God, she was so close. He could still feel the wonderful ripeness of their earlier kiss, still remember the satin glory of her hair under his hands.

"Go to bed," he ordered gruffly, a hint of desperation in his voice. But María didn't move.

"For God's sake, María," he tried again, feeling decidedly desperate now. He wanted to keep his distance, he wanted to do the right thing and protect her, even from himself. But tonight, the way she was looking at him with those dark eyes...

"If you keep looking at me like that," he managed to get out, "I can't be held responsible for the consequences."

But she didn't look away. And the significance of it hit him squarely. She wanted *him*. She really wanted him. He should be the strong one, he knew, he should be the one to pull away. They were tormenting themselves with desire that could never lead anywhere. He'd already barged into her life and taken enough from her. She would be grateful when he was gone, when they could at last go their separate ways.

He should leave her alone, give her the distance that maybe right now, in the heat of the moment, she didn't realize she needed. He should . . .

None of it mattered. She looked at him again with those beautiful eyes, and the rest flew out of his head. There was no more room for logic on this night. Just this beautiful woman and the fires that burned between them.

With a groan, he succumbed. One arm came out, catching her by the wrist and dragging her against him. And she came, followed the pull willingly, allowed herself to be thrown against him. And when his lips found hers, bruising them both with their demands, she didn't protest. Instead she arched her head, instinctively giving him greater access.

There was no roar of thunder this time, no flashing lightning to hide her fears. But she forgot them soon enough, losing herself in the onslaught of the touch she'd been waiting so long to feel. Now her hands did find the expanse of his chest. Now her fingers did run across the rippling muscles, outlining each one. She pushed herself against him, wanting more. And when it still wasn't enough, her hands crept lower, finding the edge of his shirt and fairly tearing it from him.

She wanted his bare skin against hers. Wanted to feel the blazing heat, the slick sweat—and he was only too happy to oblige. Desperate with urgency, his hand found the zipper at the back of her dress and pulled it down, her dress quickly following suit. Her nylons were rolled down her shapely legs and discarded into a heap on the floor. That left her with just a pair of black satin panties, and he took care of them, too. Until she was naked before him, soft and silky beneath his roaming hands.

She sighed as his hands cupped her breasts. She arched back farther at the first touch of his lips, giving herself up to the wonders of the sensations he created with such ease. Her hands found the back of his neck, kneading the corded muscles, weaving into the thickness of his hair, pulling him closer.

His lips drifted upward, discovering the hollow of her neck, the curve of her ear. Then he moved to the side, finding the bruised area of her upper shoulder. He kissed that, too, gently now, as if to soothe away the pain he'd been too late to prevent.

But María's blood was raging with the forces he'd unleashed. Her hips moved and twisted with yearnings that were still too new for her to completely understand but she knew only Sam could fulfill. It was she who finished pulling them onto the bed, she who rubbed the entire length of her body against his, reveling in the feel of his muscled hardness against her own soft curves.

"Easy," Sam muttered, wanting to prolong the moment even as she drove his passion out of control.

With a low groan he finished stripping off his pants. Then he rolled onto his back, carrying her with him until she was on top of him. And it felt good. Everything he'd imagined it could be all those long nights when he had lain in bed and driven himself mad with the need to touch her.

Hungrily he kissed her again. Hungrily his hands roamed down the smooth satin of her skin. Hungrily he pulled her against him.

And her own hands roamed, as well—exploring the feel of his skin, the crispy contact of the hair on his legs as they rubbed against her own. Then they drifted a little lower, less certain now, slightly hesitant. Yet it was the very uncertainty of the touch, its light, almost tickling caress, that drove him half-crazy. Until he could take it no more and with a low groan he guided her to where they both longed for her to touch. Under his light coaxing, her fingers grew bolder, exploring, learning, mastering all on their own.

He would have taken her then, driven fiercely into her body in an explosion of desire. But bold now in her own passion, she pulled away from his guiding hands, pushing them above his head. Freed, she could roam his body at leisure, touching all the places she'd longed to touch. Feeling, caressing, licking.

She rubbed her breasts against his chest, discovering the rough texture of chest hair, reveling in the heady sounds of his groans. Lightly she bent down, her tongue finding his nipple and flickering across it with lightning touches. It seemed to drive him mad, and she reveled in that, too.

Enraptured by the raging heat, she drifted lower, her fingers once more finding him, rubbing the length of his velvety shaft. Her head drifted down momentarily, and for one heart-stopping instant she drew him into her mouth and tasted him. He almost exploded off the bed.

"Now," he said fiercely. "María, now!"

She didn't need any more encouragement. Her own blood was thundering, her own eyes burning with the hunger. She moved up, positioned herself carefully, and then, very slowly, she sank down onto his hard length.

They gasped in unison, the sweet stretching of the first penetration rocking them both. And then his hands found her hips, guiding her, urging her on until she rode him with all the fire in her blood, all the passion in her soul, all the longing in her heart. Faster. Higher. Fiercer. Brighter. Now!

For a long while both of them simply lay there, savoring the soft ripples of the aftermath. Unconsciously his hands continued to stroke the long length of her back. Unconsciously, she settled deeper against the wonderful heat of his muscled frame.

Neither of them spoke, for there were no words for the moment. At least, no words that either knew of to express the incredible experience they had just shared. So they both simply lay there, quiet and content. Gradually, wrapped up together, satisfied in the way only deep human contact can bring, they both drifted off to sleep.

María came awake slowly, stretching and turning slightly as the part of her that was really comfortable tried to persuade her to fall back asleep. But then she became aware of an unaccustomed weight across her stomach, and the light tickling of hairs against her legs.

Abruptly, her eyes snapped open and the memories came rushing back. Simultaneously, her cheeks flushed a brilliant crimson.

Oh, God. What was she going to do now?

It was the essential dilemma. She'd realized it last time. What did you say the morning after? Was it as good for you as it was for me? Thanks for the evening, now feel free to leave? She certainly couldn't ask the questions she wanted to ask. Like, had he really enjoyed it? Had she been that bad? And where did it leave them now?

How is it one man could make her feel so alive, and so thoroughly confused, all at once? Maybe she could sneak off to the bathroom again. Maybe she could just creep out of bed, and he'd never notice—and then she'd never have to mention it.

It wasn't as if they truly had a relationship or anything. It wasn't even as if they were dating. He was simply the stranger who had arrived in her life one day, and would be leaving again very shortly. So if that was all, then why was she having such a hard time with it?

Because for a stranger he'd taught her more than any person she had ever met. She trusted him in a way she'd never trusted anyone. And he made her feel more than she'd ever thought she would feel.

She would creep off to the bathroom, after all. It was the only way. Otherwise, the first time she opened her mouth she would give herself away. It was bad enough she had come to care. Bad enough she would lose him, anyway. The least she could do was keep her pride.

Having made up her mind, she stretched slowly, turning toward the side of the bed. The arm abruptly clamped tighter around her stomach. She froze.

"Good morning," Sam said. His voice sounded easy enough, but she could have sworn there was an undercurrent there somewhere.

"Good morning," she managed to repeat, though she didn't dare roll over and face him. He took care of that easily enough, for the next thing she knew she was flat on her back with his face looming above hers.

"Anxious to go someplace?" he asked.

"No," she returned slowly. "Just rolling over."

"You don't lie well."

"How do you know I'm lying?" she countered bravely, but already she could feel the blush creeping up her cheeks. He looked at it pointedly.

"María," he asked suddenly. "Just how long were you and your husband married?"

The question was out of the blue, and she looked at him suspiciously. "Do you always sleep with women and then ask them about their ex-husbands in the morning?"

"Only when they blush as much as you do."

"What does that have to do with anything?"

"Oh, perhaps nothing. But don't you think it's a little odd that a woman who was married, even had a child, should get so embarrassed about these things? That this said woman doesn't even like to remove her shirt in the company of a man when she definitely needs medical care? That this said woman not only blushes a lot, but seems to be decidedly...hesitant...when with this same man?"

"Was I that bad?" she asked softly, lowering her eyes.

The very softness of the words hit Sam hard. It had only been an hour before—when he had awakened and the events of the evening had run through his mind—that all the discrepancies had occurred to him. And while he had told himself that it was none of his business, the moment he had watched her come awake and seen that she intended to run from him once more, he'd decided that he had to ask. But he'd never imagined, in all the theories that had run through his mind, that she truly thought she was no good in bed.

"Is that what your husband told you?" he asked gently. "Is that really what he said?"

She didn't answer. She didn't think she could. Never in her life had she felt so mortified. She never should have slept with Sam. She should have known it would show, should have known that she couldn't possibly fool a man like him who had probably known so many sexy and attractive women. She wanted to curl up and slowly die.

"María," Sam prodded, trying to get her to look at him. But her eyes still wouldn't come back up. "María, how many lovers have you had?"

"That's none of your business," she managed to whisper this time, though the words came out faint and prim.

"I want to know, anyway."

"Why?"

"Because I don't understand where you got this impression that you're so lousy in bed," he shot back gruffly.

"Well, aren't I?"

"No," he said, quieter this time. "I actually thought it was pretty terrific."

Her ears pricked up a little, trying to interpret this new line. He thought she was pretty terrific in bed. But then another horrible thought overrode it. He probably felt bad now at her obvious mortification. He was taking pity on her.

"Can I go now?" she barely choked out, her throat becoming much too thick, her eyes burning. "Please, just let me go now."

He looked down at her trembling form in indecision. Maybe he should just drop the subject for now. It had probably been a bad idea to bring it up, anyway. All he'd managed to do was upset her, and it wasn't any of his business. In a few days he would be thousands of miles from here, sitting in his office in New York. And she would be back in her cabin, back to sleeping in her little room, and . . . And what? Back to crying in her sleep, back to waking up alone with the tears streaming down her cheeks?

Abruptly he closed his own eyes, but the image was too vivid in his mind. Damn it, it wasn't right that someone like her should have to live like that. So alone. She was so brave in her own way, and she'd suffered more than any one person deserved. And she really did have so much to give. If someone just took the time to get to know her, to open her up, there was so much there—

If someone? Like who? Like himself? Himself, who had lived his entire life as a bachelor and probably always would? Himself, who was just passing through?

But he couldn't leave her like this, looking so hurt, looking so destroyed.

"I'm sorry," he found himself saying, and it occurred to him that he seemed to say those words to her a lot. "I didn't mean to upset you," he said sincerely. "But María, I honestly think you're a wonderful woman and a wonderful lover. I don't know what your husband or anyone else might have told you, but whoever they were, whatever they said, they must have really had some problems of their own."

She still didn't say anything. She still didn't move.

"María, are you listening to me?"

She was listening, she'd heard it all and it was running around in her mind like one big mess. She wanted to believe him. She wanted to believe that last night had been pleasing for him. But mostly, she wanted to believe it had been special. She didn't want to be just some wonderful woman, as he had said. She wanted . . . She wanted to be his woman. She wanted him to care. She wanted him to stay. And with cold abruptness, she knew that it would never happen. He was basically a good man, and he said all the right things. But in a matter of days, he would still walk away.

She had nothing to offer a man like him. No way of making him stay. And yet, she'd already given him her heart.

When she finally spoke, she tried to keep her voice cool, though a small tremor did escape. "It's okay," she told him quietly. "You don't owe me anything. Last night was last night. There were never any commitments. There were never any obligations that you had to fulfill. I think we both got what we wanted. So if you don't mind, I really would like to get up now."

The words half stunned him. Once more she was simply shutting him out, turning away. But abruptly, he clamped down on the emotion. Instead of saying anything, he simply rolled over, freeing her to leave. In a matter of moments she had scrambled off the bed and disappeared into the bathroom. But long after she left he still lay there, listening to the sound of the running water as she showered, replaying the words in his mind.

No, he didn't think he agreed with her. In fact, he was dead certain he didn't. They hadn't gotten what they wanted at all.

When María came back out of the bathroom, one towel was wrapped tightly under her arms while she used another to dry her hair. She found that not only had Sam left, but Janice Richardson was now sitting in the middle of the rumpled bed.

"Oh, Sam just went down to eat with Eric," Janice said at María's questioning glance. "Really," she whispered confidentially, "Sam is such a hunk. I can see why you snagged him so quickly."

María just nodded, not trusting herself to talk. The image of this woman drooling after Sam was making her angry, and she had no grounds for possessiveness.

"Well," Janice was rushing on, "since your staying over was so unexpected," she giggled a little here, which made María wonder just how unexpected it had been, "I brought up some things for you to use."

She gestured to her right, and for the first time María noticed the small stack of clothes.

"Now," Janice continued, "we're not exactly the same size, as you really are the skinniest thing, but I did my best. There's a pair of slacks and a belt, just some old blouse I picked up in Miami, and I even brought some toiletries. Let's see. Here's a comb, and a toothbrush and toothpaste." Janice managed to giggle again. "There's nothing like being prepared."

María simply nodded again. Really, the woman was too much. No wonder her husband was prone to rolling his eyes so often.

"Thank you," María managed to say finally. She even smiled at the other woman. "Your hospitality has been more than kind."

"Oh, really," Janice gushed, "it was the *least* we could do. Why, do you know what my friends will say when I tell them *the* María Chenney Pegauchi—oh, and Sam now as well—stayed the night in *this* room? They will all simply die. Why, they will probably all ask to stay over just so they can use this room. Isn't that just wild?"

"I suppose." There was a faint pause while Janice beamed, and María looked back at the pile of clothes on the bed. "Janice," María said after a bit. "I really don't want to push, but if you don't mind, I'd like to change now. How about I meet you downstairs for breakfast in about ten minutes or so?"

"Oh, that would be just super. And then I can show you my collection and everything. How wonderful!" Janice hopped off the bed and headed for the door. "Ciao!" she exclaimed, and with a small click, she was gone.

María sighed in relief. Women like Janice were another reason she'd retreated to the hills. She'd never been good at all the chitchat and little social games one was supposed to play with women like that. And she didn't feel like relearning them now.

Stretching, María let the towels fall to the floor, then found her underwear and nylons. Somewhat suspiciously she eyed the pile brought by Janice. The clothes seemed simple enough. Cream-colored slacks, an olive-colored blouse that just happened to be silk. The belt was a dark brown braided leather that had probably cost well over one hundred dollars itself. María would have to make certain the clothes got back to the Richardsons, that was for sure. She was probably about to wear a good three hundred dollars' worth of clothing. Whatever job Eric had at the embassy, it certainly paid well.

It took her only a few minutes to slide into the articles and considerably more time to work out the knots in her hair. She combed it straight out, tucking one side back behind her ear, leaving the other hanging forward to cover her bruised jaw. It was a simple enough style, and one that actually suited her. Looking in the mirror now, it was almost like going back in time. In another lifetime, with other people, she'd worn clothes like this. Designer clothes from all the right houses. But where had it really gotten her in the end? Nowhere. All that money, and she still hadn't been able to protect her little boy. All that money, and she'd still been so lonely.

She'd had to come to Ecuador, going back to the basics, living like a virtual peasant, to find a night like last night. And a man like Sam.

She smiled somewhat wryly at the quirks of fate, walking over to fix the bed before going down. There were probably maids to do it, but after two years of making her own bed each morning, some habits were hard to break.

And then suddenly, thinking of Sam and nights like last night, she sat down hard on the edge of the bed. They hadn't used any birth control. She hadn't given it any thought. Living alone as she had, there wasn't a need for such things.

What if she was pregnant? What *if*, right now, a tiny life was beginning to grow inside her? Her hand came to rest on her midriff and she was filled with a small sense of wonder.

What would it be like to be pregnant again? To be a mommy again?

All at once she was filled with terror. And if she failed again? If she failed this child, too?

She couldn't bear it. She couldn't go through it all again.

But if she was pregnant, she would have no choice.

The thought came out of nowhere, and abruptly it calmed her. Yes, she could be pregnant. The chances were slim, but even now, she could be carrying Sam Mathers's baby. And if she was, she would bring that child into the world and love it with all the love buried so deeply in her heart.

Because while once she'd been a woman without emotion, she was now a woman learning to feel, to care again. And this time, she would be strong enough.

If she could love Sam Mathers, and still watch him walk away in three days, then she could love their child as well.

She was not some pampered, untried princess anymore.

She was a woman of strength.

Chapter 13

They worked for five long hours after developing the film Sam had shot during his midnight escapade. They pored over blown-up photos of Santiago's files, sifting through personal documents, financial records and receipts. They worked until María's eyes burned and Sam's jaw became rigid with impatience. And still they found no hint of the child they were so desperately trying to find.

At a little after five, María sat back from the photo she was scanning and rubbed her eyes in frustration. They'd been doing this far too long—the information blurred and swam before her. At one point, she'd felt that she almost knew what to look for. Now, she was lost.

Sighing, she picked up a pencil and absently began to doodle. Sam had said to look for discrepancies—expenses that couldn't be accounted for, extra bank accounts or homes. Revenue that was inexplicable, purchases that would be unusual for a bachelor. Anything at all.

The job, unfortunately, was made more difficult by Santiago's large business holdings. He held interests in some mining companies, as well as in textiles. Both industries involved a lot of importing and exporting, making it very easy for him to hide any revenue or expenses he might incur with his other "activity." By all accounts, Santiago was a cunningly successful man.

María frowned and sighed again.

"That's very good," Sam said softly over her shoulder.

She started and for the first time became conscious of the picture that had been forming under her pencil. For a moment she could only look at in shock, and then faint color began to flood her cheeks. She'd been drawing Sam.

She'd captured him from the waist up, leaning over a photo. The lines were clean and straight, much like the man himself. Her fingers had taken special care with the rippling muscularity of his physique under his snug-fitting polo shirt, using shadows to illustrate his almost overwhelming physical presence. But it was his face that was most gripping. The hard angles, the uncompromising starkness. The eyes were startling, piercingly sharp. And faint lines surrounded them with a steely determination, as well as an unrelenting tension. He looked a strong man, an intimidating man, a man carrying the burden of children's lives upon his shoulders.

"I thought you no longer did this kind of thing," Sam said. His voice was carefully neutral, giving nothing away. It was disconcerting, though, to see himself through her eyes. He'd never quite thought of himself as appearing so grim, so hard. Then again, in his life, there had been little room for softness.

María could only shrug. "I haven't," she said honestly. "Would you believe this is the first sketch I've completed in nearly five years?"

He looked at her sharply. "Five years?"

She smiled, a faint, sad smile. "Yes, since Daniel died."

For the first time then, he understood why no new work of hers had appeared on the market. She hadn't been able to paint. The loss made him angry. He had seen some of her work before, and it had been incredible, even to a small-town boy like himself. Her ability to capture people, to capture moments... Like himself, leaning over a photo. Like now.

He looked at her for a long time with eyes too dark to read. All at once too many things were racing through his head. He wanted to hold her, to protect her from the tragedy that had stolen not only her son, but her talent. He wanted to kiss her passionately, and tell her how strong she truly was. And how inspirational. He was the dark, stern man of the sketch. But she, the delicate woman with shadowed eyes, was far stronger.

Finally, he turned away, troubled by the intensity of his own emotions. He was supposed to be keeping his distance. But he certainly didn't feel distant anymore. Desperately, he searched for indifference.

"Perhaps then you'll paint again," he tried to say casually.

María looked back at the sketch. It was stark, simple and powerful. Much like her earlier works. "Yes," she said finally. "Maybe I will."

There was another long silence, and she could feel the tension radiating from him. He moved from behind her until he was directly in front. Still with no expression on his face, he picked up the sketch to examine it closer.

"Do I really look like that?" he asked finally.

"Like what?"

"So grim."

She looked at the sketch, and then she looked back at him. "Yes," she told him honestly. "You aren't a soft man, Sam. Only rarely have I seen you smile." But it's okay, she thought softly in her mind. Because having come to know seriousness, I think I may have fallen in love with it.

He didn't answer right away, but then, abruptly, he turned and pinned her with his riveting blue eyes. "I'm glad you completed this sketch," he told her fiercely. "And I think you should paint again. You have amazing talent, María Chenney Pegauchi. I'm honored you chose me."

She was too flustered to speak, too caught up in the depths of his eyes. And then all at once, as quickly as the intensity had come, it was gone again. His eyes cleared, he straightened and once more he was the poker-faced Sam Mathers she'd come to know.

"Have you come up with anything new?" he asked and began to peruse another photo.

Seeing no choice but to go along, she let him change the subject. Looking at the photos spread out in front of her, she shook her head. "I'm beginning to think this is hopeless."

"Nothing is hopeless," he informed her. "Some things just take more work than others."

"Is this traditional detective work?" she asked curiously, halfheartedly picking up yet another photo.

"Yes," he replied. "This is the real glamour side."

They both lapsed into a small silence after that.

"Sam?" María asked after a bit, bringing her eyes away from the information she was scanning to meet his. "What are you going to do when this is all over?"

He paused momentarily. "Go back to work," he said finally, looking a little puzzled at the question. "There's always plenty to do."

"Solve more cases. Rescue more children. Do you ever do anything else?"

He looked at her suspiciously. "I think that's enough to do," he said. "Don't you?"

"What about your own life?" she prodded. "Have you ever wanted to have your own children? What about a family, a wife? Have you ever been in love?"

The confusion left his face to be replaced by an impenetrable wall. "Love is for fools," he informed her flatly.

María looked shocked for one instant, then quickly recovered. She went back to looking at the photo. She wasn't really looking at it, though. She'd already seen what she needed to know.

"Who was she?" she asked finally, unable to help herself. She wanted to know. She *needed* to know.

"Who?"

"This woman who convinced you love is only for fools."

"Maybe I figured it out on my own."

María shook her head. "People aren't born with bitterness. We learn it. Was it a girlfriend? A wife, even? Your first love?"

"None of the above," he informed her curtly, but she wouldn't be put off. Despite her best intentions, she'd come to care for this man, only to learn he didn't believe in love.

"Then who?" she persisted. "Who actually managed to wiggle under that thick skin of yours?"

"No one. I simply became smart at a young age."

"I don't believe you."

"Why does it matter?"

"Because you know everything about me," she told him softly. "You know my greatest fears, you know my biggest failures."

"You know enough to be able to draw me," Sam said. Almost against his will, he picked the sketch back up and held it before her. "Look at this sketch, María. Your fingers know me. This is what they saw, this is what I am. Hard, strong, grim, relentless. That's all you ever need to know."

She shook her head. "It's not enough. It's the surface, the shell. It's what you've become, what you've trained yourself to be. But it isn't necessarily *who* you are. When you're alone, what do you think about, Sam Mathers? When you were a child, what did you dream? In the middle of the night, what do you fear?"

"I think of my work. I dreamed of leaving Alabama. And I fear nothing." He tossed out the words casually, still determined to remain removed, but she shook her head, easily dismissing the words.

"You're lying. I know you are. Everyone fears something." She paused, not sure if she should continue, but then the desire became too strong. She set aside the photograph she held to lean forward and hold the hard planes of his face between her own small hands. Her thumb caressed his cheek lightly, feeling the rasp of a day's worth of beard. Her eyes found and held his.

"I think you're afraid of poverty," she whispered softly. "I think you're afraid of going back to the hunger of your youth. I think you're afraid of failure, of another child dying like little Laura McCall because you weren't quite fast enough. I think you're afraid to care. Now I know why you have the first two fears, but who gave you the third? Who hurt you that much, Sam?"

He wanted to turn away, wanted to protect that last little secret that was safe from her. Because it was all going to end anyway, and he wanted to be able to walk away clean from this woman, as he had already walked away from so many others. But then, no other woman had ever touched him like she had. No other woman had ever garnered his respect, his admiration. And no other woman had ever held his face in her hands, and peered at him with such intensity in her eyes.

He wanted to fight it. But under the insistent pull of her eyes, the secrets came rushing forth, the bitterness still dark and deep even after all these years.

"No one," he told her harshly. "No one had to hurt me. Because I watched her hurt everyone else and that was enough to teach me. I watched her wound my father, I watched her tear the life right out of my brother. And I may be many things, sweetheart, but I'm not slow and I'm not stupid. I learned from their mistakes."

"Who?" she whispered, her eyes still probing the angry blue of his own. "Who?"

"Sarah Mathers," he growled. "My mother."

With a small jolt, María sat abruptly back. The bitterness of his words, the barely contained rage in his eyes, were stunning.

"Tell me," she asked softly. "Tell me what she did."

"She did nothing," he bit out. "Nothing at all, María. She simply waited until times got too rough, and then announced, all calm and coollike, that she was leaving. And then she went upstairs, packed her suitcase and walked out the door. Never looked back, not when my father asked her to, not when little Joshua wrapped himself around her leg and cried for her to stay. She was a coldhearted bitch who only cared for herself. She wanted money, she wanted the high life. My father couldn't get it for her, so she went off to find some other poor sucker who could. I pity the soul she found."

"And your father just let her? He didn't argue, he didn't fight?"

"Abe?" Sam questioned sardonically. "Abe wasn't a fighter. He was a quiet man, a man of the earth. His biggest flaw was a soft heart for all the wounded creatures of the world. My mother was wild, bitter, angry. I think he thought that in time his own gentleness would soothe her. And he loved her, in spite of all her flaws, her selfishness, her vanity. When she wanted to go, of course, he let her. But if you could have seen his eyes . . . It killed him that she wouldn't stay. It killed him, and he let her kill him. Sarah was a bitch, and Abe was a fool."

"And Joshua?"

"Joshua died, I told you that. He was too weak for poverty, too soft for that kind of existence. He might have been more of a fighter, but once Sarah left, that just took all the spark out of him. He'd always been sickly, and eventually he contracted a lingering fever he just couldn't beat. I tried to help him. I did everything I could think of. I went without food so he could eat. I shot deer on the neighbor's property to bring home solid nourishment. I worked extra hours to afford the medications. And then, one day, I took the pickax and buried him in the hard Alabama ground. That's the way things work in Sandy, Alabama. That's the way things work when you live in the dust."

The last words were aimed at her, she could tell. A clear hit on the huge differences between them—one raised in back-hills poverty, the other in the Swiss Alps. But the differences didn't matter to her. Instead, she was caught up by the visions he painted so vividly in her mind. The passionate, raging mother. The gentle, quiet father. And their eldest son, empowered by the fierceness of his mother, tempered by the soul of his father. With Sarah's leaving, it was his strength that had held them together. His strength that had helped take care of the gentle father and the sick brother. Of course he had the weight of the world on his shoulders, she thought abruptly. He had shouldered the burden at a young age and had been bearing it ever since.

And in that instant, she thought she might love him more than she'd ever loved anyone else in her life except for Daniel. The intensity of the feeling humbled her, forcing her to look away, because certainly it must show in her eyes. She'd fallen in love with one of the last great men on earth. He had made his life a mission to save the weak. And in but a day or so, he would leave her.

She looked back down at the photo next to her, the one she'd been turning in her hands such a short time ago.

"I know where the children are," she said softly.

Sam's gaze narrowed sharply. "What?" he demanded.

"Look here," she told him calmly, drawing upon the fountain of strength she'd always had but only recently discovered. She gestured at the photo. "This is a household budget sheet for Señora Rita Cielo Guapé. All expenses are covered, from food to household staff, rent. Everything—"

"His mistress," Sam interrupted.

She shook her head. "It might appear that way, yes. Except I know this name. It's his head housekeeper, the one that hit me. Sam, the woman is built like a tank, and at least fifty, if she's a day. I don't think Santiago is having an affair with her. She could, however, be in charge of caring for the kids in a safe house once they're stolen. How else can you explain him paying all these expenses?"

Sam thought about it. "The only other consideration might be blackmail, but Santiago doesn't seem the type to willfully pay off a blackmailer. She could be some sort of relation, say his half sister through an indiscretion of his father. But you're right. That's probably stretching it. I say it definitely bears looking into."

"Good," said María and her voice trembled only slightly. After all these miles it seemed almost incredulous to her that they might actually have found the child, or perhaps even the children. They were almost done. And then ... She couldn't think about the end yet. She forced her chin up, and kept her voice firm. "I'm glad you agree. Now when should we leave?"

"We?" Sam asked and looked at her pointedly.

"Yes," she repeated. "Do you think we should scout it out while there's still some daylight left, and then maybe come back after dark?"

"We," Sam enunciated sharply, "aren't doing anything. *I,* however, will be more than happy to scan the area."

"I think I should go with you," María said levelly. "That way," she hesitated before continuing, "well, that way if anything goes wrong, there will at least be two of us."

Inadvertently, Sam's eyes drifted to her right shoulder. Once more he could see her running toward him. Once more he could hear the sound of the gunshot, so clear in the evening air. What if, this time, the bullet didn't just hit her shoulder? What if ... His jaw tightened, and his eyes took on a steely determination. "No," he told her. "You're not coming with me."

She saw where his eyes went, and she instantly understood the thoughts going through his head. Things could go wrong. He'd told her from the beginning. *These men kill children for profit, I don't think one or two more murders will bother them any.* Suddenly she felt very cold. He did think it was going to be dangerous. That was why he wouldn't let her go. And it was all the more reason for her to do so.

"What about the child?" she said, trying a new tactic. "Or for that matter, what about the children? Chances are they have more than just the one we know of. What happens if you do find the kidnapped children? You'll be a white man, a *gringo,* holding a gun. That will hardly reassure them. I'm a woman and an Indian, my presence would help calm them."

Sam's face only became harsher at her words. "Look," he snapped back, growing angrier at the thought of her accompanying him into such danger. He had already interrupted her life enough. He'd barged in, insulting her, prodding her, forcing her along. She'd gotten shot because of him. It was enough. He wouldn't let it go any further. "You've done your part," he enunciated very clearly. "You helped in Otavalo, and you helped me here. But I don't need your help anymore, María.

Now we're getting into my area, what I know best. So thank you for what you've done, and I wish you the best in the future. But that's that. You're free to go back to your little cabin now."

"Oh. So it's that simple, is it? Just drag me along when you need me, then dump me the first moment you don't. Well, it's nice to know where I stand," María bit out, her eyes growing ominously dark as she rose to her feet. His words had stung her. She could still feel the dull roar of the pain, and she buried it in her rage. "You don't have a choice anymore," she stated haughtily. "I'm coming whether you like it or not."

"I don't think so." The words sounded calm, much too calm. That should have been her first warning, but in her own hurt, she didn't catch it.

"Just how do you plan on stopping me?" she goaded instead. "Just how do you plan on managing that?"

"I'll tie you down if I have to," he informed her quietly. "Hell, I'll even lock you in that closet if that's what it takes. But I am not going to that house tonight, where there could be trouble, with you tagging along. You've done your part, María. *Now go home.*"

Abruptly the clarity of the words cut through her rage, and she felt the color drain from her face. Her stomach seemed to drop out of her, and she heard a faint buzzing in her ears. That was it. *You've done your part. Now go home.* It was over. He would go, probably get himself killed, and she would return to the hills. End of story. He had rudely interrupted her life, and now she could get back to it.

Except...

Except that a week ago she'd never heard of Sam Mathers. A week ago she'd never seen the deep blueness of his eyes, the strong ripples of his muscles. A week ago she'd never felt the touch of his hands on her skin. A week ago, she'd never slept in his arms.

And now it was over? Just over? *You've done your part. Go home.*

Dimly she berated herself. Had she honestly thought he would stay? Had she honestly ever believed that she could hold him? She'd told herself in the beginning not to care, but she'd done far worse. She'd fallen in love. And hadn't everyone she'd ever loved left her in the end? She must have the world's flattest learning curve, she thought bitterly. No matter how many times she was burned, she still flew to the flame. Well, it was over now. She might as well take her singed wings and go back home. It wasn't as if he cared. He didn't even believe in love.

The emptiness came crashing back, the huge gaping emptiness that filled her soul. For one week, she had been alive. For one week, she had been a fighter. For one week, she had been in love.

And now, there was only the emptiness.

The memories will fade with time, she told herself. *Soon you won't remember what it was like to be held in arms so strong. Soon you won't remember the tenderness of waking up in his embrace. Soon you won't remember the taste of his skin, the smell of his soap, the feel of his caresses.*

Soon...

"All right," she said abruptly, and unconsciously her head bowed forward, her shoulders slumping down in defeat. The emptiness consumed her. "I'll go."

Sam nodded, waiting for the feeling of triumph to wash through him. She would be safe now, safe back in the mountains where she belonged, where he should have left her one week ago. But for the first time, Sam realized that it truly was over.

Funny, but had it really been just six days ago that he'd stumbled onto her place in the middle of the night? He hadn't thought so many things could happen in such a short span of time. Somehow, he'd gotten used to the fire of her eyes, the challenge of her words. He'd gotten used to her temper, he'd even come to enjoy it. And...

And he'd touched her. Touched her although they'd never planned it. He'd wiped the tears from her cheeks, seen the wet trails of her vulnerability. He'd seen her courage when she'd placed the oranges on her back and trudged down the street to Santiago's house. He'd even seen her determination when she'd come back, ready to fight now, wanting to win. And just last night he had held her in his arms, just last night he had felt the sweetness of her passion. Just last night...

But it was over now. All over now. She would go back to the mountains and she would probably start painting again. She would hoe her garden, collect the eggs from her chickens, finish playing out her life as a peasant. Hell, she would probably be back with the jet set in under a year or so. After all, there wasn't anything for her to run from anymore. She had finally fought back.

But he wondered still if she wouldn't wake up late at night, the tears streaming silently down her cheeks.

You never should have touched her, he told himself abruptly. You never should have kissed her. The intensity of his emotions startled him. He didn't want to feel this way. He didn't want to feel at all. It was just an assignment, and like all assignments, it had come to an end.

Right, Sam?

She needed to go back to her world, he reminded himself harshly. Back to the hills, back to her cabin, back to where she'd at least be safe. He owed that much to her.

"I'll bring all the photos back into my room," he said out loud. "It shouldn't take that long."

"I'll grab the map," María said.

Both bent down, grasping their appropriate loads, not quite meeting each other's eyes. The silence seemed different now. The room different, each other different. After an entire day of talking, María suddenly didn't have anything to say.

It only took ten minutes to finish moving everything. The map with the location of Santiago's businesses, banks and houses was pinned up on Sam's wall, the photos neatly stacked next to it. Everything was done.

"So you know where to go?" María asked at last.

Sam nodded.

"What about your rental back in Otavalo?"

"I'll arrange for someone to come and get it."

"It'll cost you a small fortune."

"That's okay."

There was another long pause, one that dragged longer this time as their eyes met, then quickly slipped away.

"I guess that's everything, then," María said.

"I think so, too."

More silence. "Thank you," Sam said suddenly. "Thank you for all your help. I know this was hard for you. And I . . . I really do appreciate it."

María shrugged. "It was good for me," she said simply. "Sooner or later I needed to learn how to fight back. I'll probably never become an ace detective like yourself, but I can manage."

There was another pause, and María felt the burn of tears welling up in her eyes. She forced herself to swallow and adopt an air of casualness. She'd lost enough to him already, she could at least preserve her pride.

"Well, then," she said with false bravado. "Good luck. If anything goes wrong, you know where to find me. And Sam . . . take care."

"Take care yourself," he told her.

And then it was over. There were no more words left to say, no more things to do. He had come, and now he would go. Things had a way of ending. And there was no going back. Even the memories would fade in time, until one late night in one faraway day she would think back to this week and wonder if it had really ever happened at all. So time passed, so the memories dimmed, so life progressed.

Alone again. But when had it ever been any different? She would survive now, just as she always had. Maybe there would even come a time when it wouldn't hurt quite so much.

Let him go, she told herself. *You knew this moment was coming. You knew a woman like you could never hold a man like him. So let him go.*

With a slight nod, María stepped back into her room. There was another slight pause, one last lingering moment, and she swallowed hard against the pain. Better to just do it.

She shut the door.

And so her one week with Sam Mathers ended.

As dusk descended upon the city, Sam was pulling on his black T-shirt, donning the dark cap and checking the spread of equipment before him. To the right lay a good fifty feet of nylon cable, next to it was his deluxe army knife, then his small lock-picking set, a pair of binoculars and, last but not least, the gleaming form of his gun.

He picked them up now, one by one, distributing them in his pockets. On second thought he grabbed his small camera, just in case, then he turned to the gun. He'd only been six when his father had taught him how to shoot a .22 rifle. Back in those days he'd shot at hay bales his father had outlined targets on. Then in later days, as the farm had deteriorated more, the money growing sparser, his father and he had gone out shooting deer, duck, pheasant, quail and squirrel. They'd dress the animal in the field, then bring it home. Often, that would be dinner for the whole week.

Abe Mathers had never pointed a gun at another man in his entire life. But sometime in the course of this evening, there was a good chance that his son would. And as sometimes occurred, the one who would walk away could very well be the one who was the quickest, the one who did not hesitate.

That was the way of it, Sam told himself as he tucked the gun into his belt. In the world the strong had a way of exploiting the weak, the rich often bought the poor. And if you wanted to change those odds, sometimes you just had to play the games by those very same rules. So he would go to that house tonight, knowing he was walking into danger, knowing it could cost his life, and knowing that perhaps he would even have to take someone else's.

He took another deep breath, then relaxed. Everything was in place, all his gear accessible. His mind was clear, the map firmly outlined in his head. It was 9:30 p.m. and he was ready.

There was one last niggling thought as he headed for the door, one last matter that tugged at his consciousness. Maybe he should say goodbye to María. The door was just there, only three feet away. His hand raised, paused, then almost reluctantly sank back down.

It's over, Sam, he told himself. And María was better off this way. She was safely tucked in her hotel room, perhaps already asleep after the strain of the last few days, dreaming of the mountains she loved so much. Yes, she was much better off without him. *Go,* he told himself. *There's work to be done. Just go.*

But his feet remained rooted to the spot, and he dimly realized somewhere deep down inside that he already missed her. Him, Sam Mathers, the perpetual bachelor, missed a woman he'd known for only one week. A woman who came from a totally different background than himself, a woman who was much better off without him.

He forced his feet to turn, walking quietly now down the hall. He would forget her soon enough, he told himself. Just as she would forget him. That was the way of it. On to another case, solving other people's problems, curing other people's pain. It wasn't such a bad life.

Tonight he would finally conclude the chase that had brought him to an entirely different country on an entirely different continent in an entirely different hemisphere. Tonight, or so he hoped, he would find the missing child at last.

By 10:30 p.m. Sam had finished scouting out the house. He had yet to see any sign of children, but the house certainly fit all the requirements. It was out in a remote area, and had extremely high fences surrounding a big yard. From his vantage point high up on a hillside, Sam could even make out the large round forms of four searchlights mounted on each corner, just waiting to beam upon any intruder or possible fugitive. There seemed to be an organized watch schedule, as every fifteen minutes a man would come out of the house and patrol the grounds. From this distance it was hard to see if it was always the same man, but three of them, so far, were clearly different. The question was, how many more men were inside the house?

He was getting that tingling feeling in the back of his neck, that whispering cross between anticipation and adrenaline. His sixth sense practically buzzed with the possibilities here. This just had to be the place. It had to be.

But how to get in?

At least three guards, an eight-foot-high fence, possible searchlights, and a moon in the sky as clear as a crystal ball. He was going to have the time of his life trying to make a surprise entrance.

On the other hand, the yard contained a fair number of small shrubs he could use for cover once he got there. And while there were a few men, they obviously knew very little about proper patrol training. All three of them followed the exact same watch pattern, leaving in exactly fifteen-minute intervals until Sam could practically set his watch by them. Their routes took only five minutes, leaving a ten-minute lapse before the next perusal. If he could just make it far enough in those ten minutes . . .

It would take at least seven minutes to scale the wall, assuming he encountered no difficulties at all. Using one of the bushes for cover, it wouldn't be too hard to take out an unsuspecting guard passing through. That brought the odds down to at least two other men. When the first didn't reenter after the usual five minutes, chances were the others would come out and check. Which brought Sam back to the first problem. What if they were smart enough to flip on the searchlights at the first sign of trouble? With those four mounted lights in the corners, the place would look like a prison camp come to life. And he would be the sitting duck in the middle.

So, he decided, first order of business would be to clip the wires running to the lights. Trace one back to the house, and he would know if there was an alarm. He rested his Swiss army knife in the palm of his hand. Simple, just a matter of keeping quiet, keeping down and keeping invisible. The navy had trained him in all three. He could do it.

All that was left, then, was what to do with the other men when they came looking for their companion. Well, he'd cross that bridge when he came to it. As long as they couldn't see him, he would have the advantage. The minute they separated, he could ambush them one by one.

At eleven-thirty, one of the shadowy guards reemerged, smoking his cigarette as he walked his rounds. Five minutes later he threw down the remains of the cigarette, ground it out with his heel and reentered the house. At 11:35, Sam made his move.

María woke up with a jerk, her heart beating rapidly in her chest, the sweat trailing down her cheek. Sharp images of the nightmare still flashed in random disorder in her mind. The photos of Santiago's accounts. A burly, evil-looking man holding a gun. The vivid flash of the barrel, and Sam, Sam down on the ground, red blood seeping into the soil around him.

She couldn't do it, she realized suddenly. She couldn't just walk away and go back to her old life. Damn it, he'd made her care! He'd touched her, held her. He'd made her feel, and he'd made her fight.

So what was she doing, simply letting him go? Hadn't she learned anything? Hadn't she learned yet that life was hard and you had to fight to win? Well, she'd already lost too many years of her life to running. She wasn't going to lose yet another five years waiting for another man like Sam Mathers to find her.

With determination, she threw back the covers on the bed. So he'd taught her to fight. Well, now he'd find out just how good she'd become. He said he didn't believe in love. But she'd show him. She'd prove him wrong.

She was still buttoning her blouse as she raced out of the room. Into the dead of night she went, charging toward the monster's den to help the man she loved.

Sam barely had time to take cover before the next guard came out. He crouched down low in the shadow of the fence, holding himself perfectly still as the guard went sauntering by. He only relaxed when the man disappeared back into the house. Then Sam darted around the perimeters, and with quick deft movements, found and clipped the wires to the lights.

At 12:14 a.m. he was crouched again, this time behind a bush in one of the darkened corners of the yard, waiting for the next guard to emerge. On cue, at 12:15, a shadowy man appeared in the doorway, lighting his traditional cigarette, inhaling deeply, and stepping down into the yard.

Sloppy, thought Sam. Very sloppy. The glowing butt of the man's cigarette stood out like a neon sign, advertising his slow progress across the yard, making him a clear target. Sam waited until the man was but twelve inches away.

The man was large, but Sam's muscular build outweighed him, and Sam also had the advantage of surprise on his side. In one fluid motion he had his hand covering the man's mouth even as the butt of his gun descended sharply on the unsuspecting head. The man folded quietly to the ground.

So far, so good. It took a few more minutes to tie the man securely with the lengths of nylon rope Sam had brought. Then he frisked the man briskly, pulling out not only a gun, but a knife. The gun he emptied and hurled into a bush. The knife he stuck in the waist of his jeans, then moving quickly now, he raced silently back into the darkness, just managing to disappear before another shadow appeared in the doorframe.

"Perry?" The shadow called out in distinct English. "Perry? What's up?"

Sam had already noticed that the first man, with his blond hair, was most likely from the States. Apparently, contestant number two was, as well. But then the shadow in the doorway did something that Sam hadn't counted on just yet. One arm reaching up, the man tried the light switch. When the lights didn't come on, he uttered a soft curse and disappeared from the doorway.

Damn, agreed Sam. He'd hoped to take out at least one more before having his presence discovered. Well, the party was just beginning. And he still had the advantage. He knew where they were, and they didn't know where he was, or how many of him there were.

His adrenaline flowing swiftly now, part of Sam was tempted to move in. But the rational part tempered him, making him wait. Sooner or later, one of them would step out, and then . . .

A shadow moved in one of the darkened windows, the glint of a gun barrel flashing under the moon's light before disappearing again. So one man was upstairs. And the other?

A small creak penetrated the silence and Sam instantly tensed. Back door, he told himself. Of course a house this size had a back door. Crouching down really low now, willing himself to be invisible, he crisscrossed toward the back of the house. Rounding the area, he took cover under another bush, just in time to make out the shadowy outline of a man not more than twenty feet away. Bending down, Sam felt for a good-size rock and hefted it in his hand. Just like baseball, he told himself. Slow and easy.

He tossed the rock to the left, and the man's head turned sharply at the landing thud. His head was just swiveling back around when the butt of Sam's gun came sharply down. There was a small cry as the man went down, and Sam swore softly. Less time now. Moving quickly, he pulled a long strand of nylon rope out of his pocket. Three minutes later and contestant number two was neatly hog-tied. Just like old times, thought Sam as he drifted back into the shadows. Just like old times.

There was no movement from the house now, and Sam didn't wait any longer. Time to move in before the guards he'd taken out regained consciousness and called for someone to untie them. There was definitely one other man, maybe two more in the worst case. After all, guarding a child or two couldn't require that much manpower and Santiago probably wouldn't want to involve any more people than necessary. The fewer who knew, the fewer who could squeal or attempt blackmail.

Sam darted forward, and a shot erupted from the upstairs window. The bullet zigged by his ear and, cursing silently, he ducked lower as he raced in. Another shot buried itself into the woodwork behind him, spraying his leg with slivers. Dimly he registered the pain of one driving deeply home, but the adrenline pumping within him was too sharp, his concentration too complete to notice much more.

Suddenly he stopped, ready, his knees bent, gun in hand. A split second later the blast came. But this time, as he threw himself to the side, he shot in the direction of the blast, hearing the sharp cry as his bullet found a target in the second before his own shoulder slammed hard against the earth.

He was just getting up when the distinctly cold steel of a gun barrel was pressed against his head.

"Good evening," came a voice in perfect English. "And just who the hell are you?"

Sam turned to find himself staring at a man who might as well have stepped out of a *GQ* magazine. Already after midnight and the man was impeccably dressed in a distinctly well-tailored suit. But the gun the man held ruined the picture, and it was the gun Sam paid attention to.

Wordlessly, he let his own gun drop from his fingers.

"Very good," the man told him, and smiled casually in the night. "Now I repeat, who are you?"

"Name's Sam Mathers," Sam replied, keeping his own voice casual even as his sharp eyes searched for weaknesses. But the other man seemed to know his intent, smiling once more in the darkness.

"I see, Mr. Mathers. You certainly aren't Ecuadoran, so just who are you working for?"

"I work for UNICEF," he told the man smoothly. "I was hired to investigate the disappearance of the missing children, to report back my findings each evening. They already know all about this place."

"I don't think so."

"Then don't. What you think won't help you when they come after you."

For the first time, the man looked a little less certain of himself. As if realizing that the small doubt showed, his eyes narrowed angrily.

"Where do you prefer to be shot, Mr. Mathers? The forehead or the chest? I'll let you choose."

The sweat beaded on Sam's brow, and once again his mind raced frantically. Now or never, he told himself. Either way, you'll probably be a dead man.

"Behind you," a voice suddenly rang out. The neatly suited man turned on instinct, raising and firing his gun at the sound

even as Sam saw his opportunity. He dove forward as the gu
exploded, catching the other man, driving him down in a br
tal tackle. Far off, he heard a sharp cry, and then his fist bu
ied itself in the face of the stranger. The man fell instantl
unconscious.

Rolling to the side, Sam came up in a low crouch, shakin
out his bruised knuckles while his eyes searched the darkne
for the source of the other voice.

And then he saw her.

María.

She was standing not five feet away, the white of her blous
like a beacon in the moonlight. She seemed to be swaying o
her feet, her left hand clutching her right shoulder.

"Sam?" she called out shakily. "Sam, are you all right?"

"What the hell?" he bit out angrily, storming forward. H
came to a stop just inches before her. "How the hell did you g
here?" he demanded harshly, the adrenaline still roaring in h
ears.

"I used your rope," she admitted weakly. "I'd seen it don
in the movies, but really, it looks much easier than it is." Sh
swayed slightly again, her eyelashes fluttering down. "Th
child?" she asked, trying to force herself to think even as sh
felt the blood flowing between her fingers, running down he
arm. The night seemed suddenly cold to her and she shivered
She felt that, in the last three minutes, she'd aged years, find
ing that man about to shoot Sam, hearing the gunshot, feelin
the bullet strike her, instead.

"María?" She heard Sam, but he seemed very far awa
"María, I want you to sit down." She felt his hands guide he
to the ground. She came down slightly hard, but he steadie
her. "Your shoulder again?" he asked, the anger completel
gone from his voice now.

She nodded.

"Didn't I tell you this was too dangerous?" he demanded
but there was no heat in his words. Now that the adrenaline wa
leaving him, he was left feeling floored. He'd sought to pro
tect her, and instead she'd come back to risk her life for his.

"And didn't I tell you I was no longer going to run?" Marí
managed to shoot back from the ground. Her chin came u
proudly for a minute, but she was too drained to leave it there

I'm okay, Sam," she said more calmly. "I'm becoming experienced about these things. Now go on, find the child. Find im."

He was torn for a minute about leaving her, but common nse took over. There could still be a sniper somewhere in the ouse. He should finish securing the area. As gently as possile, he bent down, picked her up and carried her to a dark cor-r against the fence.

"Stay here," he commanded softly. "I'll be back in just a w minutes."

"Don't worry," she managed tartly. "I'm hardly in any ndition to run."

He almost had to smile at that. But then his face turned grim nce more, and he crept quietly to the house.

He found no one on the first floor, and moving cautiously, e made his way to the second. In the first bedroom he found man staring at the ceiling with empty eyes. Dimly, as he hecked for the man's pulse, he registered that the man had old teeth. Not that it mattered anymore. The man who had een firing from the window was dead now. Perhaps Abe Mathers had taught his son too well.

He found them in the next room. Three huddled children on full-size bed, staring at him with huge eyes, covers pulled right p to their necks. A woman was there, too, hulking and cold in chair, with a gun on her lap. But she didn't pick it up. She imply looked at him.

"It's over now, isn't it?" she said bitterly in her thickly ac-ented English. "It's finally over."

"Yes."

"God has come to get us after all," she said heavily. "I knew e would."

Eyeing her carefully, Sam took the gun from her lap. It was hen he saw all the suitcases packed by the door.

"We were leaving in the morning," the maid said when she aw where he was looking. "Five hours later, and we would ave been gone."

"Let's go," he told her briskly. He turned to the children.

"Pedro?" he called out softly.

One of the boys looked up with scared black eyes. The child odded.

For the first time, Sam smiled, feeling the relief wash throu
him as he began soothing the children in Spanish.

He'd done it. The children were safe, the innocent
deemed.

And the case was truly over now.

Chapter 14

"I thought I'd told you to go home," Sam said tersely. He sounded angry, but in truth his blue eyes were dark with worry as he took in María's fragile form sunk deep into the stark whiteness of the hospital bed.

She tried to shrug, then winced instantly as the movement irritated her arm. The doctor had already removed the bullet and assured her that she would live, though she needed a good rest. Unfortunately, her arm throbbed too much to accomplish that. They had offered her drugs, but she had a deep suspicion of pills after seeing too many of her peers become hooked on them. No, she'd decided that she was tough enough to handle a small wound. Now if only she could survive Sam's temper.

"I had to go," she managed to reply.

Sam had seen her wince, and his jaw clenched.

"It was a foolish thing to do," he bit out, feeling the helplessness engulf him once more. Damn it, he'd never meant to put her in such danger. He'd been trying to protect her. And instead, she was the one that had saved him. Why? Didn't she realize she was supposed to be selfish and petty and all the other things he'd always believed about women? He was comfortable with his contempt. He understood bitterness. And now...

What in the world was he to do with a beautiful, caring, bra
and passionate woman who had taken a bullet meant for hin

"If you're here just to berate me, you can leave now," s
informed him. "I'm not exactly feeling up to it at the m
ment."

He was instantly contrite. "I'm sorry," he said, faltering f
the right words. Finding none, he lapsed once more into s
lence. María's eyes drifted shut, and after a moment she a
peared to be sleeping.

She looked so damn fragile, lying against the white pillow
Her face was ashen from the blood she'd lost and dark circl
rimmed her eyes with exhaustion. Even her thick black ha
seemed duller against the pillows, looking tangled and tired. I
was almost tempted to find a brush and start combing all tl
luster and life back into it. Except he didn't trust himse
enough to touch her right now.

Fierce emotions raged and stormed inside him. Emotions l
didn't understand and wasn't prepared to deal with. He wante
to hold her, he wanted to run. He wanted to soothe his han
tenderly down her cheek just to make sure she truly was sa
and alive. He wanted to walk right out that door and never loc
back.

He didn't know what to do, so he stayed where he wa
standing at the foot of the bed with his hands tightly fisted :
his sides.

Damn. Even now she was beautiful.

He didn't want to walk away, he realized suddenly. No, l
wanted to stay right here by her side. He wanted to be the o
to greet her when she woke up. He wanted to be the one to ho
her if the nightmares returned. He wanted to be the one t
gently rub the tears from her cheeks in the middle of the nigh

He loved her, he recognized that now. He, Sam Mathers, tl
world's staunchest bachelor, had fallen in love. And why no
He had met a woman so courageous that she had risked her li
for his. What could he do but fall in love with a woman s
brave she had confronted the evil that had beaten her once be
fore? How could he resist a woman so generous, so good, s
perfect?

Funny, he'd told himself from the beginning to keep his di
tance and had never thought it would be a problem. She was
woman, and a rich woman, at that. He'd figured she wa
nothing more than another Sarah Mathers—vain, selfish, m

nipulative. But this woman was none of the things he'd expected. She was extraordinary.

And he didn't know how to deal with extraordinary.

All his life, he'd used his past as his armor. It had shaped him, made him who he was: a tough, hard man who got things done. He had turned his back on softness, barred his soul from vulnerability, because he had no room for such weaknesses in his life. He didn't want to be another Abe Mathers. He wanted to be someone stronger. Someone invulnerable.

Now, looking at María, Sam realized that it was too late. Somehow, some way, she had managed to get under his skin. And he had only to look at her, lying so pale against the hospital bed, to feel the pain. He'd done this to this beautiful, courageous woman. He, the man who had pledged to protect all things weak, hadn't be able to protect her.

Instead, she had protected him.

Because she wasn't weak, he concluded fiercely. Because she was one of the strongest people he'd ever met, male or female. Because she was intelligent and compassionate and brave. Everything he admired in a human being.

She wasn't Sarah Mathers. Instead, this woman was the living, breathing antithesis to all the things he'd ever believed. Yet she was very real. He'd held her, he'd kissed her. He'd watched her eyes darken in passion, he'd plunged inside her and heard her gasp his name.

Oh, she was very real, and . . .

And he loved her.

He'd finally been struck by the same arrow that had broken Abe Mathers's heart.

And it scared him. The fierceness, the intensity, and yes, the vulnerability that came with that emotion frightened him as no bullet could have.

What if she walked all over him, like Sarah had done to Abe? What if, one day, she simply packed her bags and walked out the door without ever looking back?

None of it mattered, he thought abruptly. He couldn't possibly love her, surely he was mistaken. And even if he did, where could it go? She was still María Chenney Pegauchi, world-famous painter, wealthy heiress. She came from the limelight, the beautiful people. He, despite his success, was still closer to the boy who had grown up in the dust of Alabama. What could he offer her, anyway? Security? She'd already been

shot twice because of him. Tenderness? He'd try, but after
entire life of rigid isolation, he wasn't sure he could be good
those things. Besides, his job needed his one-hundred-perce
concentration and would take him away from her, anyway.

In short, he had nothing to offer her. Except, maybe t
force of emotion that kept tightening his chest, the intensity
all the feelings he wasn't supposed to have.

He would walk away. It was best for her. She could ret
once more to the serenity of her farm, the call of her art. Af
having confronted the evil once and for all, she would do b
ter now.

She would definitely be better off without him. It was rea
that simple.

The tightening in his chest became a little too much, a
abruptly, he looked away. Breathing deep, he sought to clear
mind with the rigid control that had always worked befor
Think of your job, Sam. The children are what matter.

Sam had called Eric Richardson from the house after t
shoot-out, and had told him in calm and cool words ever
thing that had happened. Then Sam had picked María up in
arms and driven her to the nearest hospital, leaving Eric to s
out the mess. As Eric held a high position in the American e
bassy, and there were Americans involved, he had assured Sa
that he had the contacts to take care of things. So, once Sa
had been assured that María was all right, he'd consented
answer questions. Basically, he'd stood in the lobby of t
hospital while being drilled by the local police. They were
tough bunch, and their faces had given nothing away as they
made him go over everything time and again. Eric had stood
the background, careful not to interrupt, but supporting Sa
with a nod here, a gesture there. Eventually, after they'd d
termined there were no inconsistencies in Sam's story, they'd
him go. Eric had then informed him that his story had actual
just confirmed most of the things the children had related.

The children had been taken away. They had been given f
medical exams, and then, at long last, reunited with their pa
ents. Sam had been allowed to meet the three sets of paren
involved and had been greatly touched by their fierce apprec
ation.

Given the government's attitude toward such things, Sa
tiago and his maid would be dealt with harshly, not to me
tion Augustine Pero. The American embassy had also agree

to cooperate by exploring the Miami connection. As the trafficking of children's organs was also illegal under American law, any American perpetrators would be dealt with under the American legal system. It wasn't quite what the Ecuadoran government had hoped for, but Eric felt confident they could prove the Americans involved had been punished with equal vigor. And hopefully, Santiago would help supply some of the names in order to save his own scrawny neck.

And now it was over, all the loose ends slowly being wrapped up. Except for the woman on the bed.

"Sam?" María whispered suddenly, capturing his full attention as her eyelids fluttered open, "Are you going back to the States now?"

He nodded.

"I see," she said, and her eyelids drifted back down.

"Don't worry," he said gruffly. "I'll wait until you're okay first. Get you settled back down in the mountains."

"Don't worry," she told him and smiled faintly as her eyes opened once more to meet his. "Janice has told me I can stay with her and Eric for as long as I need. I could do their portraits, you know."

"Don't be ridiculous. I got you into this, I'll take care of everything."

"There you go again," she said softly. "Trying to take responsibility for the whole world. You didn't get me into this, Sam. *I* did. I chose to follow you. I'm the one who decided to go over the fence. It's not your fault."

He shifted at the foot of the bed. So she said, but looking at her pale form, it was hard to believe. God, when he'd seen that she'd been shot again... It seemed that all he ever did was hurt her. She'd probably be eternally grateful when he got out of her life once and for all.

"I'm sorry," he whispered.

"Stop it!" she told him sharply, and in anger she managed to summon enough energy to prop herself up on one arm. "I already told you, it's not your fault. And, furthermore, I'm sick and tired of you taking responsibility for everything. You saved the children, you beat the bad guys. You're the hero. Now give yourself a break. Set down that chip on your shoulder. I don't want your apology. I want..." She faltered and sank back down against the pillows. He immediately took a step forward, but she waved him away with her hand.

I want you to love me. I want you to look in my eyes and see your future, not your shame. I want you to hold me, touch me. Make me feel alive again. Make me feel whole.

But she voiced none of her thoughts, and the silence dragged on as her eyes closed wearily. He didn't believe in love. And even if he did, he was too busy trying to save the world to take time out for it.

At the foot of the bed, he shifted once more.

"Sam," she said finally. "Have a safe flight back to the States. And good luck."

He opened his mouth, wanting to say something, wanting to ease the unbearable tightness in his chest. "María," he began. But then he faltered, the words drying up. He couldn't say it, he couldn't say anything. She deserved so much more than him.

Abruptly, he looked down, feeling the weight of the silence on his shoulders.

"I think I'm going to sleep now, Sam," she whispered quietly, eyes already shut. "I could use the rest."

He nodded, but still lingered. He watched her eyelids drift down, the sooty lashes coming to rest against the pale hue of her cheeks. Once again the urge to touch her was almost overwhelming. Once again, he held back.

All his life he'd known what to do, and he'd done it regardless of the personal cost to himself. He'd been firm in his convictions, and if that had made him a hard, unyielding man, well it had also made him strong.

But looking at María now, he wasn't thinking of the need to be stronger, better, faster. He wasn't thinking of the newest child to save, or the latest wrong to right.

He was thinking of how good it had felt to hold her. He was thinking of the wonder of making love to her. How she made him feel good, how she made him feel like a man. And not a superhuman man, but an elemental, primal, simple man.

He wanted to touch her, hold her, kiss her.

Never let her go.

Still he didn't move. And deep in his mind, he summoned up the sound of Joshua's cries as he'd begged for his mother's return. Sam remembered the dry taste of dust as he'd picked the hardened ground to dig his brother's grave. He remembered the sad gray eyes of his worn-down father.

He remembered the treachery of his mother, and used it to harden his heart and steel his soul. He wasn't going to make the mistakes of his father and brother. He wasn't going to leave himself vulnerable, weak. He was a man on a mission, and that mission was the most important thing.

Yes, this woman was extraordinary, but what did he have to offer her? He shook his head wearily. He'd been a fool to let her affect him. He should have kept his distance, as he'd always managed in the past. They were still two different people from two different worlds, and nothing had changed any of that. He'd been a fool to even contemplate otherwise.

He looked at her one last time. And one last time, the need to reach out and just touch her was so strong it threatened to bring him to his knees. But he remained standing, for that was the kind of man he was. The hard kind, the strong kind.

The kind that, even now, could hear his brother's cries and taste the bitter tears of dust. There was a whole world out there of children who needed him. He should get going now, before he lost his resolve completely.

But somehow, as he turned and finally headed for the door, Joshua's cries were harder to bear, and the burning sting of tears in his eyes wasn't from a memory.

"Pedro and two other children have been found and reunited with their parents," Sam said into the phone. Through the crackling of the long-distance connection, he could hear the grunt of Russell O'Conner's satisfaction. He'd already called and given the news to his assistants, ending their respective assignments. Now he just had to clear up the details with O'Conner.

"Good, good," the old man was saying. "Everything wrapped up, then? Accounted for?"

"Yes. Between the maid's testimony, the children and myself, there's plenty of evidence against Santiago. He's a powerful man, though, with lots of influence. What the final result will be, I don't know. But I have no power over the legal system, so that's not my concern. The children are back at their homes, and that's what's important."

"So..." O'Conner dragged out speculatively. "What are your plans now?"

Sam shrugged. "I should be back in the States within the next two days."

"I see," O'Conner stated after a moment. Then abruptly he said, "How is my goddaughter doing?"

"Her injury isn't serious," Sam recited dully. "She should be released from the hospital tomorrow."

Once more there was a pause at the other end of the line.

"It was her shoulder, you said?" O'Conner questioned.

"Yes."

"Seems like it might take a while to heal," the older man seemed to muse. "Might be a little difficult, you know, trying to work a farm when you can't move one arm. Then again, if I remember María, she's one tough little girl. She can probably manage."

Sam's blood had turned to ice on the other end of the line. He hadn't thought about that. In fact, he'd been trying not to think about her at all since leaving the hospital. But what O'Conner had just said made sense. It would probably be a good four weeks before she'd have full use of her arm. And yes, running a farm one-handed was not an easy task.

"I'll stay and help her," Sam said abruptly into the phone. "After all, I am responsible for her being injured."

"Yes," O'Conner said speculatively, "that responsibility thing again. And as we've already established, you always do the right thing. Tell me, Samuel, do you ever do anything for yourself?"

Sam instantly went rigid, his voice frosty as he replied, "I don't see where that's any of your concern."

At the other end, O'Conner waved a thinly veined hand. "Now, now, my dear boy, no need to get so riled up. I'm not attacking you, not at all. I was just wondering out loud. María always was extraordinarily beautiful, even as a child. I remember she had the biggest black eyes, the kind you'd do anything to see light up. I don't suppose that kind of beauty is something a woman loses over time? And you two *have* been together day and night for nearly a week now. I'm old, but I'm not daft. Seems to me that maybe you might have noticed each other by now."

Still rigid, Sam replied, "That isn't an issue."

O'Conner sighed into the phone. "Well, then it isn't. But take it from an old man, Samuel. Life is too damn short to let the beautiful things get away. People these days, they let everything get too complicated. Timing has to be right, responsibility means more, the details are too difficult to work out. It's a bunch of blarney. In our lives, we only meet a few people who will ever really touch us. To let even one get away is a waste you'll regret forever. Ah, so much for the prattlings of an old man. I'm glad to hear the children are all right. Give my goddaughter my regards, and when you get to the States, by all means, come and see me.''

Then there was a click, and the line went dead. Sam felt the phone slide absently from his fingers. He wanted to block out the images that O'Conner's words had evoked, but they swam around in his mind, anyway.

María alone. Working alone, eating alone, sleeping alone. What if she woke up in the middle of the night, her mind swamped with nightmares, her cheeks stained with tears? Who would hold her? Who would ease her back to the gentleness of sleep?

Maybe she would meet someone. She was beautiful, she was smart, she was kind. But the minute he thought of another man holding her, his mind rebelled at the image. No. Absolutely not.

He wanted it to be him. He wanted to be the one to hold her at night. He wanted to rub her shoulder when it ached on rainy nights and remember how she'd taken the bullet meant for him. He wanted to kiss away her tears, and he wanted to bathe in the soft glow of her smile. He wanted to feel her nails raking down his back in passion, he wanted to hear her soft moans of satisfaction.

His jaw clenched, his stomach tightened.

He wanted her.

And what was it O'Conner had said? *In our lives, we only meet a few people who will ever really touch us. To let even one get away is a waste you'll regret forever.*

In that instant, Sam felt the conviction flood his veins. This was right, this was meant to be.

This had nothing to do with Sarah Mathers or Joshua or Abe. This was the present now, his own life. And he had found the one woman who was different from all other women. He had thought all women would be like Sarah, and so he had kept himself distant, firm in his conviction.

But Sarah was Sarah, and she was gone now. She'd walked out on them all more than twenty years ago. It was time he finally left her as well.

Because now he knew what a woman could be. He had met María, a woman whose courage and compassion surpassed even his own. She was his match, his soul mate.

And he wasn't going to let her go.

She was still sleeping when he quietly opened the door of the hospital room. But she stirred when the door clicked shut behind him, her eyelids fluttering open.

"Sam?" she whispered. He nodded, and she rubbed her eyes groggily with her left hand to clear them.

"What time is it?" she asked.

He looked at his watch. "Almost five," he said and stepped closer to the bed. She looked better already, the sleep having cleared some of the shadows from around her eyes. Her skin was still pale, looking translucent against the sheets. Once more he was struck by how fragile she looked in the large bed. Once more he was overwhelmed by the need to touch her.

Very carefully, he reached out his hand and gently touched her cheek.

"How are you feeling?" he asked softly.

Her eyes came up to meet his, and immediately she frowned. He looked different. His face was more relaxed, the lines around his eyes had eased. He looked younger, she thought. Still strong, still determined, but as if his burden had eased.

Of course, she thought abruptly. He'd saved the children and now he was going back to the States. Of course he was more relaxed. She took a deep breath. Sometime in the course of her sleep-soaked afternoon, she'd made her decision. She'd told herself she was a fighter now. She'd told herself she could do it.

So carefully now, before she could lose her courage, she brought her own hand up to cover his. Once more her solemn eyes searched his, seeking some sort of encouragement. She saw him relax a bit more at her touch, and that was enough for her.

"Sam," she said clearly. "Sam, I've fallen in love with you. But it's okay," she rushed on. "I know you don't believe in love and I know you think all women are as evil as your mother. I'm not demanding anything of you. I'm not expecting anything. It's just that I do believe in love. And I think love can be caring and beautiful and unselfish. That's why I went after you last night. Because I wanted to be there if you needed me, even if it did endanger me. That's what love's about, Sam. You had a bad experience, but don't condemn the rest of us for your mother's actions. Now, I don't expect you to accept this all at once. Just tell me you'll think about it. Because regardless of what you may want, I do love you. And someday, I'd like to be able to share all that love with you.''

Her eyes were solemn when she finished, her gaze never wavered. And with just as much dignity, Sam bent down and slowly, thoroughly, kissed her. He could feel her start, but then her lips parted, letting him in, showing him the love she'd already told him of.

Reluctantly, he pulled back. And for the first time, he smiled softly at her.

"I've hurt you, María," he said softly. "I want you to know I realize that. When I first came here, I really thought you would be like Sarah, selfish and spoiled. I treated you harshly. You were right that first night, when you told me I had no right to simply barge into your life and demand things from you. And over this past week, I've watched how hard it's been for you, and trust me, at times I've felt like dirt for putting you through this. I've also thought that you're the bravest woman I've ever known.

"The last few hours have been hell for me, María, seeing you here in the hospital, knowing I'd contributed to you being hurt once again. All my life I've fought against the innocent being hurt. All my life I've tried to be the strong one, the protector. All my life, I've remembered the cries of my brother, I've remembered watching Joshua die. I guess you're not the only one who has problems letting go.

"But, María, you made me feel things I never thought to feel. You touched me, and now I just can't seem to walk away anymore. I don't think of Joshua anymore, I think of you, always you. Maybe it's time for me to let Joshua go, and time for you to let Daniel go. It's time for us to be ourselves. And speaking for just Sam Mathers, I love you, too, María, and I don't ever want to walk away again."

Her eyes rounded in shock and he felt a small moment of fear. But then she threw her one good arm around his neck, pulling him down in a tight hug.

"Oh, Sam," she whispered fiercely. "Sam, I love you so much. I've been lying here in terror, thinking that you would turn away again. That I'd have to return to the hills all alone again. In the past five years, I've tried to bury myself, tried to feel nothing. But then you came and you made me feel everything. You made me angry, you challenged me. You held me, you touched me. You made me feel alive after the coldness of all those years. And now I don't want it to end anymore. I want to stay with you, hold you, touch you forever. I'll go anywhere with you. I don't need my farm anymore, you know. Because it wasn't the isolation I needed, it was you.''

He hugged her tight, this small woman who had taught him real strength, and the love in his heart was overwhelming. He buried his face in her neck and kissed the silkiness of her hair, whispering his love in her ear.

''Together,'' he whispered, ''we can do anything.''

She nodded against his throat, feeling the wonderful burn of tears down her cheeks.

''María,'' he stated fiercely, ''I will love you forever.''

And he meant it. He was a man of conviction, and having finally found this one extraordinary woman, he would never let her go. Never.

* * * * *

Dark secrets, dangerous desire...

Lovers DARK AND DANGEROUS

Three spine-tingling tales from the dark side of love.

This October, enter the world of shadowy romance as Silhouette presents the third in their annual tradition of thrilling love stories and chilling story lines. Written by three of Silhouette's top names:

LINDSAY McKENNA
LEE KARR
RACHEL LEE

Haunting a store near you this October.

Only from ▼ *Silhouette*®

™   ...where passion lives.

Take 4 bestselling love stories FREE

Plus get a FREE surprise gift!

Fifty red-blooded, white-hot, true-blue hunks
from every State in the Union!

Look for MEN MADE IN AMERICA! Written by some of
our most popular authors, these stories feature fifty of
the strongest, sexiest men, each from a different state in
the union!

Two titles available every month at your favorite retail
outlet.

In August, look for:

PROS AND CONS by Bethany Campbell
(Massachusetts)
TO TAME A WOLF by Anne McAllister (Michigan)

In September, look for:

WINTER LADY by Janet Joyce (Minnesota)
AFTER THE STORM by Rebecca Flanders (Mississippi)

You won't be able to resist MEN MADE IN AMERICA!

Is the future what it's cracked up to be?

This August, find out how C. J. Clarke copes with being on her own in

GETTING IT TOGETHER: CJ
by Wendy Corsi Staub

Her diet was a flop. Her "beautiful" apartment was cramped. Her "glamour" job consisted of fetching coffee. And her love life was less than zero. But what C.J. didn't know was that things were about to get better....

The ups and downs of modern life continue with

GETTING IT RIGHT: JESSICA
by Carla Cassidy in September

GETTING REAL: CHRISTOPHER
by Kathryn Jensen in October

Get smart. Get into "The Loop!"

Only from *Silhouette*®

where passion lives.

MONTANA
Mavericks

Stories that capture living and loving beneath the Big Sky, where legends live on...and the mystery is just beginning.

This September, look for

THE WIDOW AND THE RODEO MAN
by Jackie Merritt

And don't miss a minute of the loving as the mystery continues with:

SLEEPING WITH THE ENEMY
by Myrna Temte (October)
THE ONCE AND FUTURE WIFE
by Laurie Paige (November)
THE RANCHER TAKES A WIFE
by Jackie Merritt (December),
and many more!

Wait, there's more! Win a trip to a Montana mountain resort. For details, look for this month's MONTANA MAVERICKS title at your favorite retail outlet.

Only from ▼ *Silhouette*® where passion lives.

**And now Silhouette offers you
something completely different....**

SPELLBOUND
R O M A N C E

**In September, look for
SOMEWHERE IN TIME (IM #593)
by Merline Lovelace**

Commander Lucius Antonius was intrigued
by his newest prisoner. Although spirited
Aurora Durant didn't behave like any woman
he knew, he found her captivating. But why did
she wear such strange clothing, speak Rome's
language so haltingly and claim to fly in a silver
chariot? Lucius needed to uncover *all* Aurora's
secrets—including what "an air force pilot lost
in time" meant—before he succumbed to her
tempting lures and lost his head, as well as
his heart....

SILHOUETTE® Desire®

They're sexy, they're determined, they're trouble with a capital *T!*

Meet six of the steamiest, most stubborn heroes you'd ever want to know, and learn *everything* about them....

August's *Man of the Month,* Quinn Donovan, in
FUSION by Cait London

Mr. Bad Timing, Dan Kingman, in
DREAMS AND SCHEMES by Merline Lovelace

Mr. Marriage-phobic, Connor Devlin, in
WHAT ARE FRIENDS FOR? by Naomi Horton

Mr. Sensible, Lucas McCall, in **HOT PROPERTY**
by Rita Rainville

Mr. Know-it-all, Thomas Kane, in **NIGHTFIRE**
by Barbara McCauley

Mr. Macho, Jake Powers, in **LOVE POWER**
by Susan Carroll

Look for them on the covers so you can see just how handsome and irresistible they are!

Coming in August only from Silhouette Desire!   CENTER

Don't miss the newest miniseries from
Silhouette Intimate Moments

Southern
Knights

by Marilyn Pappano

A police detective. An FBI agent. A government
prosecutor. Three men for whom friendship and
the law mean everything. Three men for whom
true love has remained elusive—until now. Join
award-winning author Marilyn Pappano as she
brings her **Southern Knights** series to you, starting
in August 1994 with MICHAEL'S GIFT, IM #583.

The visions were back. And detective
Michael Bennett knew well the danger they
prophesied. Yet he couldn't refuse to help
beautiful fugitive Valery Navarre, not after her
image had been branded on his mind—and
his heart.

Then look for Remy's story in December, as
Southern Knights continues, only in...

INTIMATE MOMENTS®
™ **Silhouette**®